Gilbert L. Harney, Edwin C. Pierce

The Lives Of Benjamin Harrison And Levi P. Morton

Gilbert L. Harney, Edwin C. Pierce

The Lives Of Benjamin Harrison And Levi P. Morton

ISBN/EAN: 9783337112523

Printed in Europe, USA, Canada, Australia, Japan

Cover: Foto ©Raphael Reischuk / pixelio.de

BENJAMIN HARRISON.

THE LIVES

OF

BENJAMIN HARRISON

AND

LEVI P. MORTON,

BY

REV. GILBERT L. HARNEY.

WITH A HISTORY OF THE REPUBLICAN PARTY, AND A STATEMENT OF ITS POSITION ON THE GREAT ISSUES OF THE PRESENT DAY—THE PLATFORM OF THE PARTY—THE LETTER OF ACCEPTANCE OF BENJAMIN HARRISON—STATISTICS OF ELECTIONS, ETC.

BY EDWIN C. PIERCE.

ILLUSTRATED.

PROVIDENCE, R. I.: J. A. & R. A. REID, PUBLISHERS.
1888.

ENGRAVERS.

KILBURN & CROSS, ... BOSTON, MASS.

J. P. MURPHY & CO., ... BOSTON, MASS.

ARTISTS.

SCHELL & HOGAN, NEW YORK.

FRANK MYRICK, BOSTON, MASS.

PREFACE.

THERE is no more instructive reading than faithful biographies of great men. Every period of the world's history is represented by a few lives; and every important event of that period bears some relation to one or more of those lives; and the spirit of the period is the spirit of those lives. Religion, philosophy, science, government, politics, have very little attraction for the common reader, or even the majority of students, when treated abstractly; they are dull, dry morsels, not easily assimilated by minds not abnormally disposed toward them. But when the sympathy of the reader, or student, is awakened in a person who bears, in study or daily life, a close relation to the religion, philosophy, science, government, or politics, and the life is traced with interest, he rises from the reading of the story instructed and benefited.

In writing the stories of the lives of Benjamin Harrison and Levi P. Morton, constant care has been given to accuracy, to harmony and relationship of details with the absorbing themes of public interest with which the people associate them, and to the story-like features of their lives that will make the book interesting to the general reader.

1st. If accuracy be wanting, the book could be of no value. The desire and purpose has been to make no statement as of fact that would not bear the criticism even of the men themselves, and in that respect receive their indorsement.

2d. Choice has fallen upon them for high offices because it was believed they were eminently qualified for them. If they are, they have come to their present qualifications, partly by inheritance and circumstance, but mostly by their course of life from birth to manhood. It required long years to make them what they are — fitting representatives of mighty issues and principles. It is no straining of facts, therefore, but a pleasing adherence to truth, to observe that harmony and relationship of the details of their lives with these great themes.

3d. If a character is consistent, the line of life will carry its central principles from first to last, and a faithful record of it will read like a story-book. This is its charm to all readers; and this is the special charm of the lives of these men. Particular care has been taken to discover these lines of principles and trace them, not in a philosophical manner, as if writing a treatise on those principles, but in a simple, straight-forward narrative.

Sources of information have been various, but not always reliable. It has been, therefore, no easy task to separate the true from the fictitious and sensational. Thanks are due to those friends who have kindly assisted in this task, as well as supplied further points for record.

If this book shall succeed in honoring these men as they deserve to be honored, and in showing them forth as representatives of those principles they are selected to champion, and in stirring the ambition of young men to like noble lives, its object shall have been accomplished.

G. L. H.

CONTENTS.

PART FIRST.

LIFE OF GENERAL BENJAMIN HARRISON.

CHAPTER III.

The Young Student.

CHAPTER IV.

The Law Student.

CHAPTER V.

The Young Lawyer.

CHAPTER VI.

The Young Politician.

CHAPTER VII.

The Patriot Soldier.

CHAPTER VIII.

A Lawyer of Experience.

CHAPTER XII.

CITIZEN AND CANDIDATE.

CHAPTER XIII.

A CHARACTERISTIC SPEECH.

CHAPTER XIV.

Record in Speeches.

PART SECOND.

THE LIFE OF LEVI PARSONS MORTON.

CHAPTER I.

Ancestry.

CHAPTER II.

The Boyhood of Morton.

CHAPTER III.

Business and Financial Record.

CHAPTER IV.

Congressional Experience.

CHAPTER V.

Minister to France.

CHAPTER VI.

Brilliant Closing of Ministry to France.

CHAPTER IV.

The Labor Question.

CHAPTER V.

Free and Fair Elections.

CHAPTER VI.

Pensions.

CHAPTER VII.

Civil Service Reform.

CHAPTER VIII.

The Fisheries Question.

CHAPTER IX.

The Temperance Question.

CHAPTER X.

CHAPTER XI.

ILLUSTRATIONS.

PORTRAITS.

WILLIAM HENRY HARRISON,

NINTH PRESIDENT OF THE UNITED STATES.

PART FIRST.

THE LIFE OF BENJAMIN HARRISON.

CHAPTER I.

ANCESTRAL LINE.

BIRTH OF HARRISON — A VALUABLE ANCESTRAL LINE — A MEMORABLE EVENT IN ENGLISH HISTORY — THOMAS HARRISON'S PRINCIPLES SUCCESSFUL — HARRISONS IDENTIFIED WITH VIRGINIA HISTORY — A BRIEF BUT SUGGESTIVE RECORD — A FAMOUS HOMESTEAD — A FAMOUS SON — RECORD OF TIPPECANOE — A NOTABLE BIRTH IN VINCENNES — A MORE NOTABLE ONE IN NORTH BEND.

BENJAMIN HARRISON was born August 20, 1833, at North Bend, Ohio.

A truly great man does not depend for honor upon prestige or ancestry. He wins his own fame, and the record of his personal life is his glory among his fellows. This is true of this man. If honor and praise were all that is to be sought for him, the simple recital of the story of his life from the cradle to the prime of his manhood would be sufficient. No ambition can be purer in quality and more honorable in itself, than that of the man who, possessing all the requirements for fame without merit or noble effort, seeks to rise on personal merit, or not to rise at all.

This ambition has marked the life of Benjamin Harrison. While not despising those ancestors of renown, and pleased that blood so noble flows in his own veins, he has sought, with something of anxiety, to win what laurels he might win, solely by his own merits. If good blood is of any value, let it be manifested in the deeds of the man, not in the heralding of the circumstance.

But a record of lineage is sometimes valuable. First, it is a revelation, in some degree, of the man's inherited possibilities; and while this is an inquiry the public, with proper motive, has a right to make, it allows the man the additional triumph of exhibiting in his life the prophesy of blood fulfilled. Second, it allows the tracing of those influences — family traits and inclinations and ways of thinking — that helped to make the boy what he was, and the man what he is. No biography can be complete, therefore, without some such record.

One of the first Harrisons of whom there is any authorized public account, and from whom General Harrison descended, was a martyr to the cause of human liberty. Major-General Thomas Harrison was one of Cromwell's generals. He conveyed the king, Charles I., from Hurst to Windsor Castle; from Windsor Castle to Whitehall for trial; sat as one of his judges, and signed his death-warrant.

It is of some interest to note the character of that Harrison, as it was manifested in his manner of performing those tragic duties. Charles had been warned that his escort's instructions were to assassinate him on the way; but when he saw the soldierly bearing of the latter, he frankly confessed his fear, aroused by the warning, and that it had now been somewhat quieted. Harrison informed his majesty that "he needed not to entertain any such imagination or apprehension; that the parliament had too much honor and justice to cherish so foul an intention; and whatever it resolved to do would be public, and in a way of justice to which the world should be witness, and would never endure a thought of secret violence."

When Charles II. was restored to the throne, of course those most active in the revolution fell under his wrath. The inimitable Samuel Pepys made the following statements in his diary of October 13, 1660:

"I went out to Charing Cross to see Major-General Harrison hanged, drawn and quartered; which was done there, he looking as cheerful as any man could do in that condition. . . . It is said that he said that he was sure to come shortly at the right hand of Christ, to judge them that now had judged him; and that his wife do expect his coming again."

Had the cause of Cromwell been successful, even English writers would not have considered General Harrison's offense a crime, nor even an offense at all. But that cause, though unsuccessful as to its immediate aims, was not a failure. The principles for which Thomas Harrison fought and died flourish to-day both there and here, while with the death of Charles I. died from the hearts of Englishmen his doctrines; for though the son of Charles, as well as subsequent sovereigns of England, may have presumptuously recognized those doctrines in petty ways, yet in policy they have recognized the changed feeling of the English Nation. By that revolution was our revolution made possible.

Men of the spirit of the Harrisons are intolerant of intolerance. For this reason, even before the bloody times of the English revolution, some of them emigrated to the freer American Colonies. They came to Virginia; and from that day to this the Harrisons have been identified with the soil and blood of that great State. And there they fostered the principles of human freedom.

In the northwest of England, through the county of Lancaster into the Irish Sea, flows the River Ribble. Here, along the banks of this stream, according to private records, was the English home of the Harrisons. From this region Benjamin Harrison, cousin to the martyr, emigrated to the shores of America, in 1635 — twenty-five years before the execution of his illustrious relative.

That Benjamin Harrison — first of the name and family in this country — settled in Surry County, Virginia, on Wamiskioke Creek, just across the James from Jamestown, and only twenty-eight years after the settlement of that colony. Either here, or in England just before the emigration, a son was born to him, who was also named Benjamin.

This son grew up on his father's farm in Surry; and when he was of age he married Hannah Churchill, of the renowned family of Churchills in England, to which belonged the Duke of Marlborough. The happy couple lived at Huntingdon, Surry County, and there died; and in the churchyard which he himself gave to Southwark Parish, near Huntingdon, the tombstone of this Benjamin Harrison may be seen to-day.

To Benjamin and Hannah Churchill Harrison was born a son, whom they also named Benjamin — the third of the name in America. This son married a daughter of Lewis Burwell, of Gloucester County, Virginia. He settled at Berkeley, on the north bank of the James River, in Charles City County, at a point about twenty-five miles above the site of Jamestown, and twenty-five miles below Richmond. Here he built a typical mansion of those times, which became known from that day as the homestead of the Harrisons.

The fourth Benjamin Harrison was a son of this gentleman. He married a daughter of Robert Carter, of Carotoman, in the northern neck of Virginia. From this time on the name of Harrison is included in the Carter family list — the list of one of the most noted families of the Old Dominion, and one that has added much to her honor.

This gentleman lived at the old homestead built by his father, at Berkeley. One day, during a heavy thunder-storm, he was standing with two of his daughters in the hall of the old mansion, when a stroke of lightning ended all their lives. He left, besides his widow, several sons, two of whom preserved the honor of the old family name in public capacity. His son Charles was a general of artillery during the Revolutionary War, and did efficient service in the cause of independence. Benjamin, the brother of Charles, achieved greater fame, however, and became the historic Harrison of the Revolution.

Thus, Benjamin Harrison, of the American Revolution, was descended in a direct line from Benjamin Harrison, cousin of Major-General Thomas Harrison, of the English

Revolution. The simplest record that can be made of his life is enough to give him high rank among America's most famous heroes. He was a member of the Virginia House of Burgesses, and one of its renowned leaders; a member of the first Colonial Congress; the reporter of the Resolution of Independence; a signer of the Declaration of Independence; president of the Virginia House of Burgesses from 1777 to 1781; thrice elected governor of Virginia; a member of the convention that ratified the Constitution of the United States; and father of William Henry Harrison.

This Benjamin Harrison married a Miss Bassett, who was a sister of the wife of Peyton Randolph. Before he was twenty-one, he was sent to the House of Burgesses. Here he was so outspoken, and withal so sternly true in his patriotism, and so talented, that, spite of his youth, he was made speaker of the House. Afterwards he was sent to the "rebel Congress," and there he so distinguished himself that he barely escaped the honor of being made president of the Congress. The following story is told of the circumstance:

When his brother-in-law, Peyton Randolph, who was president of the Congress, died, Ben Harrison was immediately thought of as his successor: and would have been elected, had he not withdrawn in favor of John Hancock, of Massachusetts, in the interest of harmony between the Northern and Southern colonies. He himself secured the unanimous election of Hancock, who, on account of British proscription for his faithfulness to the colonial cause, rather feared to assume so lofty and dangerous a post. But Ben Harrison — almost a giant in physical proportions and strength — lifted the hesitating president-elect from the floor, carried him to the official chair, and placed him in it, giving utterance to these characteristic words, which showed both the temper of the Congress and the rugged and unfaltering nature of Harrison's devotion to his country:

"We will show Mother Britain how little we care for her by making a Massachusetts man our president, whom she has excluded from pardon by public proclamation."

Harrison was chairman of the Committee of the Whole that considered the Declaration of Independence, and on the 10th of June, 1776, he reported the resolution for Independence to the Congress. On the 4th of July he voted for it; and one month afterwards it received his signature, between those of Thomas Jefferson and Lewis Morris. While that noble host of patriots was engaged in that act which meant liberty or death to them, and perhaps to all who were dear to them, not the least confident of the success of the liberty side was "Bluff Ben Harrison." He turned to Elbridge Gerry, and in a jovial taunt, that expressed his utter fearlessness of any chance of defeat, he said: "Gerry, when we shall be hung for high treason, I shall die quicker, because I am heavier."

When he resigned his seat in Congress, in 1777, he was again elected to the House of Burgesses in Virginia, and served there as speaker until near 1782. His subsequent career is already given; but in 1791, after he had been elected governor of Virginia the third time, he died before the inauguration took place.

William Henry Harrison was born at Berkeley, Charles City County, Virginia, February 9, 1773, just one year before the first meeting of the Continental Congress. He was therefore three years and a half old when his father signed the Declaration of Independence. He grew up on the plantation at Berkeley. He had the best instruction a good mother and competent tutors could give him until he entered college. But meanwhile he was receiving a training in a different sort of school. The War of the Revolution raged all around him, if it did not at first come within range of his vision. In 1775 Norfolk was burned, and from that time the patriots who lived at Berkeley and in the vicinity, had only the themes of patriotism on their tongues. In January, 1781, the traitor, Benedict Arnold, landed with his marauding forces at Westover, but a short distance from Berkeley. Then British and Hessians continued to arrive, a fleet was in the James, and the forces of Cornwallis began to march from Carolina up toward Yorktown, to the northeast of Berkeley. But it was not long until the danger to the plantations was over, and Cornwallis had surrendered to Washington. Then, in 1783, the war was declared at an end.

The father of William Henry Harrison, while not rich, yet possessed enough means by which to manifest great liberality. But the Berkeley homestead could not, in money, be valued at half what it is to-day—for it yet stands on the bank of the James, a typical old Virginia home. When William Henry had been sometime in his "teens," he was permitted to enter Hampton-Sidney College, for which, by application under his tutors, he was thoroughly prepared.

From the time of the peace of 1783, hostilities were carried on by the Indians in the Northwest Territory, who were urged on by British agents and traders. There were yet British posts within the United States, and these exercised great influence upon the red men. Matters grew worse as the years went on. It is said that from 1783 to 1791 fifteen hundred men, women, and children were killed or captured by the Indians.

Washington, from the first of his administration, strove to put an end to these hostilities, and to protect the frontier. It was the influence of these depredations, and of the spirit of Washington, his father's friend, in endeavoring to marshall forces for the defense of the frontier, and of the hostility still manifested by British power through the Indians, that led William Henry Harrison to give up his studies for the medical profession, which he had been pursuing, and determine to enter the army. It was, in the minds of most of his friends, a most extraordinary and hazardous decision. He had always been a "book-worm." His appearance was effeminate. He was mild in manner, and unobtrusive. The resolution was taken about the time of his father's death, and the great banker, Robert Morris, was his guardian — for he was but eighteen. Mr. Morris was so opposed to the plan that he consulted Washington about it. But Washington approved, and the result was that, in April, 1791, William Henry Harrison received a commission as ensign in the First Regiment of the United States Artillery, which was then stationed at Fort Washington, near the present site of Cincinnati.

The event proved Washington's estimate of the lad to be correct. His garrison life was a good military discipline for young Harrison, and he soon so won the confidence of his superior officers, that he was intrusted with dangerous and important duties. Then came the disastrous defeat of the army of St. Clair, the commander-in-chief. More than five hundred officers and privates perished, and the rest fled to Fort Washington, arriving one by one at the fort.

"Mad Anthony" Wayne superseded St. Clair in command, and being a man of great shrewdness, and having the young ensign under his vigilant eye, it was not long until he demanded his promotion. So, in 1792, Harrison became a lieutenant. He had been present at the council with the chiefs of the Six Nations, which Wayne held at Fort Washington, in March, of that year; he had escorted a train of pack horses to Fort Hamilton, thirty miles up the Miami, through a most dangerous wilderness; he had closely studied the training and instruction under which General Wayne had been placing the troops since he had assumed command: he had been a close observer of the whole method of Indian warfare, and of the Indian questions which then agitated the country — the relation of the British to them, and so on — and of all this General Wayne was aware; and hence the promotion of the youth.

Young Harrison went, on December 23, 1794, with the detachment sent to occupy the ground of St. Clair's defeat; and assisted in burying the bones of the slain, in recovering the cannon, and in building Fort Recovery. In the thanks officially given for that important work he was mentioned by name.

He took part in the great battle of the Miami, fought August 20, 1794, in which the Indians were routed and the

British influence over them for awhile broken. He was at this time both lieutenant and aide-de-camp. One of the results of this victory was the Treaty of Greenville, January 1, 1795, by which the Indians released much of the Northwest Territory forever. Another result was that young Lieutenant Harrison was promoted to a captaincy, and placed in command of Fort Washington. With this trust were also given others of great importance.

During the year 1795, while in command at the fort, Captain Harrison met and married Miss Anna Tuthill Symmes, daughter of John Cleves Symmes. Her father had been one of the prominent patriots of the Revolution. He had moved from his birthplace, Riverhead, Long Island, to Flat Brook, New Jersey, in 1770, was made a colonel of a regiment in 1775, and did good service until the close of the war. He had been lieutenant-governor of New Jersey; six years a member of the council; associate judge of the Supreme Court of New Jersey; a member of Congress, and one of the supreme judges of the "territory northwest of the Ohio." In 1787 he bought of Congress 1,000,000 acres of land between the two Miamis, which became known on the maps as "Symmes' Purchase." He founded the town of North Bend, Ohio; and it was while on a visit to that place, fifteen miles from Fort Washington, that William Henry Harrison first met the judge's daughter. Mr. Symmes gave his consent to the marriage, but withdrew it on hearing slanderous reports against young Captain Harrison. But he managed to be from home on the day for which the wedding was set — November 29th — as if in ignorance of the event, and on returning home was not hard to pacify.

In 1798 the young captain resigned his place in the army, and accepted the position of secretary of the Northwest Territory, under Governor St. Clair. In 1799, the territorial legislature elected him a delegate to Congress. In May, 1800, the Territory of Indiana was created by act of Congress, and Mr. Harrison was appointed its first governor.

He had been in Congress when the separation of what is now the State of Ohio had been made from the Northwest Territory, and all that remained had been christened the Territory of Indiana. It included all the land west of the western boundary of Ohio, south of Lake Superior, north of the Ohio River, and east of the farthest western limits of Louisiana. Mr. Harrison's commission was autocratic. "He was Indian commissioner, land commissioner, sole legislator, and law-giver." He was commander of the militia. He appointed all civil officers. He was to divide the lands into counties and townships. He sat in judgment upon land grant titles, and his decision was final. He was general Indian agent, made all treaties and negotiated all payments in connections therewith. If there had been any doubt as to his integrity, he would not have been appointed. If he had in any wise ever failed to conscientiously fill his trusts, he would not have been kept in the position. He was strictly honorable in all his transactions.

He held this post until 1812, being reappointed by Jefferson and Madison. He sought to improve the condition of the Indians by preventing traffic in intoxicants, introducing inoculation for small-pox, and by other means. He held many councils with them, frequently at the risk of his life. On the 30th of September, 1809, he concluded a treaty with several tribes, by which 3,000,000 acres of land were sold to the United States.

This treaty was opposed by Tecumseh, a powerful chief, and his brother Ellskwatawa, the "prophet." These two brothers were Shawnees, ambitious, the uncompromising enemies of all white men, and noted, even when young, for savage and bloody exploits among other tribes, or among the settlements of the white people. They were no doubt flattered by British agents, and urged on by promises of help. They fancied they could form a confederation that would drive the pale faces from the country. The union was to include all the tribes of the North, and the Cherokees, Choctaws, Red Stick Creeks, and Seminoles, of the South. The treaty of September was their pretext. They claimed that it was unlawful, on the ground that the consent of all the tribes was necessary to a sale.

The governor pursued a conciliatory course. He invited the two to a council at Vincennes, the seat of his territorial government, requesting them to bring not more than thirty others with them. They came August 12, 1810, with 400 armed warriors. Two days were spent with no result—they wanted back the land. On the 14th Harrison visited the Indian camp with only an interpreter, but with no success. The next spring, on his threatening to punish them for depredations, they professed friendship and granted a council, to which they brought 300 followers. The presence of 750 militia prevented any outbreak, and secured renewed pledges.

The general government had no faith in Tecumseh's promises, and advised that he be seized. Harrison had no faith in him, but proposed a military station at Tippecanoe, the "prophet's town," on the river by that name, where, it was reported, the Indians were collecting in great numbers. Harrison's counsel prevailed, and over one thousand regulars and volunteers set out with him from Vincennes on September 26, 1811. They rendezvoused sixty miles north, established Fort Harrison near where Terre Haute now stands, and leaving a garrison there, proceeded on their way October 28th. They arrived within a mile and a half of the village November 6th. Here they were met by messengers from the "prophet," demanding a parley. It was granted for the next day, and Harrison, having first led his men to an eminence commanding a view of the town a mile away on a hill, went into camp for the night.

The camp was arranged with special caution. Harrison knew the treachery of his foes too well to depend upon their professions of desire for treaty. Every soldier was commanded to keep his accoutrements on him and his arms near by. Sentries were posted with most vigilant orders — orders hardly necessary, for they knew their lives depended on their watchfulness. And all night the soldiers slept lightly and were ready for a moment's warning.

Shortly before 4 o'clock on the morning of the 7th, Harrison was sitting by his camp fire. The sentries were on duty, careful for their own lives and those of their comrades. Suddenly, one of them saw the form of a red man in the darkness near him in the grass, and fired. The report rang over the camp. Harrison sprang from his tent, the soldiers were on

BIRTHPLACE OF GENERAL HARRISON, NORTH BEND, OHIO.

their feet, their commander was in the lead. and the fight was now going on. The roar of musketry, the yells of savages, the groans of wounded and dying, and the voice of the commander were all mingled together.

It was difficult, however, to fight a foe who fought in irregular ranks, in the dark. Many of the brave men fell, but those who remained fought on until daylight. Then a cavalry charge drove the Indians from the field, completely routed. Thus ended the famous battle of Tippecanoe, which gained for Mr. Harrison that stirring sobriquet. It virtually ended the Indian hostility until the breaking out of the war with England. Harrison was thanked in the President's message, and by the legislatures of Kentucky and Indiana.

At the beginning of the War of 1812, Mr. Harrison was appointed brigadier-general, and assigned to the command of the Northwest frontier. The letter from the Secretary of War appointing him, said: "You will exercise your own discretion, and act in all cases according to your own judgment." On March 2, 1813, he was commissioned major-general. October 5th, he fought and won the famous battle of the Thames against Colonel Proctor, in Canada, in which Tecumseh, who had led his warriors as British allies, was killed, the warriors scattered to their tribes, and the Indian power and presumptuous claims broken and silenced forever, and in which the British army was completely routed.

Not long after this, the Secretary of War, Armstrong, who through jealously had hindered Harrison's movements in every way possible, issued an order to one of the inferior officers of the western army, ignoring the commander entirely. Mr. Harrison could do nothing but resign, and Armstrong, in the absence of President Madison, accepted the resignation. Harrison then went back to his home at North Bend, Ohio.

In 1816 he was elected to Congress from the Cincinnati district, and was in Congress three years. In 1819, he was elected to the Ohio State Senate, and remained there two years. He was United States Senator from 1824 to 1828. Then he was appointed minister plenipotentiary to Colombia, under John Quincy Adams, where he remained until recalled by Jackson, and he then returned to his old home at North Bend. He soon after became clerk of the court of common pleas of his county, and filled that position twelve years. In 1836, he was candidate for President of the United States, receiving seventy-three electoral votes. In 1840, he was again the Whig candidate, and received 234 electoral votes against sixty for Martin Van Buren.

But long before that wonderful campaign, whose memory stirs the old Whig blood to enthusiasm yet, the birth of a son, and then of a grandson, made possible the carrying forward of the stern and true Harrison principles and patriotism into the midst of another generation, to stir it up to enthusiastic and patriotic achievements, such as characterized the campaign of 1840. While William Henry Harrison lived at Vincennes, as governor of the Indiana Territory, his son, John Scott Harrison, was born. The house where he was born still stands, at Vincennes: and near it stand the trees under which the governor held the famous conference with the Indian chief, Tecumseh. In the same house was planned the civil government of Indiana; and many of her laws and customs to-day reflect those first influences.

John Scott Harrison grew up no less patriotic than his father, but with somewhat less inclination toward public life. Nevertheless, the records place him in the list of those who have served their country in a public way. But a more important record than that comes before it; and others, also, full as interesting.

John Scott Harrison was first married to Miss Johnson, of Kentucky. By this union, there were two daughters and one son, William Henry Harrison. The son died; one daughter lives at Ottumwa, Iowa, and the other lives yet at North Bend, on the site where stood the home of her grandfather. Soon the mother followed her son to her last resting place.

The next marriage was with Miss Elizabeth Irwin, daughter of Captain Archibald Irwin, of Pennsylvania. Her father was also a farmer, and owned a large farm near Mercersburg, Franklin County, Pennsylvania. Of this marriage were ten children, four of whom are now living: A son, Carter Bassett Harrison, lives in Murfreesboro', Tennessee; another son, John Scott Harrison, lives in Kansas City, Missouri; a daughter, Mrs. Anna Morris, lives in Indianapolis; and the remaining child living is Benjamin Harrison.

While William Henry Harrison was at Colombia, his son, John Scott, was left in charge of the estate at North Bend. The house was then but a log cabin, for though quite a large tract of land belonged to the estate, it was not as valuable then as land farther from the cities and towns in Indiana and Ohio is now; besides, the elder Harrison was so simple in his tastes, and such a man of the people, that he would not dream of making an effort to place himself socially above them; nor was he, in any sense, rich, though he had had ample opportunities for becoming so, had not his great liberality, and sensitive conscientiousness in the matter of taking pay for services, prevented. Here lived the family of John Scott Harrison for several years, and thus it came about that Benjamin Harrison was born in his grandfather's house, at North Bend, Ohio.

CHAPTER II.

BOYHOOD OF HARRISON.

A TYPICAL AMERICAN BOY — TYPICAL AMERICAN PEOPLE — THE BOY AT HOME — CHARACTERISTICS — HIS SURROUNDINGS — THE FAMILY — HIS TUTORS — HIS MANNER OF STUDY AND APPLICATION — THE LOG CABIN UNDERGOES CHANGES — THE CAMPAIGN OF 1840 — FIRST WHIG VICTORY — HISTORY OF A MOVEMENT — A PEOPLE'S CAMPAIGN — SONGS, BANNERS, AND BADGES — A GREAT DAY AT THE HARRISONS' — DEATH OF THE PRESIDENT — IMPRESSIONS ON THE BOY.

BENJAMIN HARRISON was a typical American boy, and destined to be a typical American man. This was true, not only in respect to his education. but in respect to his inheritance; not only in respect to his inherited way of thinking, but in respect to the blood that flowed in his veins.

He was born and brought up in a region where those of such blood were found. The North Ohio Valley was settled, to a large extent, by those who came from Kentucky, Virginia, and other Southern and Southeastern States. Many of these settlers were of the best blood which those regions afforded. Many of them were young men, unmarried. and having yet to make choice of life companions. Others brought wives and children from the South; but these children grew up to look out for helps meet for themselves. Thus was formed the substrata of North Ohio Valley society.

These people brought the conservative customs and ways of

thinking that had belonged to established society. They were American in their ideas, and many of them Whigs. Many of them who afterwards became inveterate Democrats were influenced, not by the fundamental principles of the two parties, but by the immediate issues between the new Republican party and the Democrats; for, in the days when they had lived in the South, slavery was not a party issue. Its right to exist had not, in that manner, been called in question. Then they had come from cleared lands and hospitable homes and friends and loved ones in the South, to the inhospitable forests of the North, to toil in loneliness often, to suffer inconvenience and hardship, and live in rough log cabins. They were human, and remembered fondly all that they had left behind. When the new issue was sprung, it seemed as if their old homes and dear ones, and institutions dear by association, were menaced. They might have trusted the dear old Whig party, had it lived, and had it, in its wisdom, concluded to lay its hand, in the name of the government, upon that institution; but this *new* party — what did tired toilers know about its principles, in the confusion of the time? They only knew it had attacked what they had never thought was wrong, and what was dear to them. They only knew the issue. Had they known it, the issue, on the Republican side, was based on principles they ardently believed in — Whig principles: liberty, the kingship of every American; protection to Americans in home, society, and labor. They saw not the inevitable logic of these principles which was working out, else they would have followed it — would have been willing to sacrifice the dear idol of the South for them. In principle they were Whigs; in issue they were

Democrats. Nevertheless, there were many others who saw the point, and entered the Republican party, where the Whig principles were safely conserved. The general manner of thinking among all these people was the same.

But there was an immigration from the East: people true as steel, but of a different type of mind from the first-comers, not coming as they had from the shadow of a great curse, nor holding it in sacred remembrance, but with an independence and enterprise impossible under conditions of slavery. They spread over the valley and plains. Then there were marriages; and many a young man from the South found a wife from the North and East, as did William Henry Harrison.

The subsequent generations are typical Americans. With the blood of the South, they mingle the independent manhood of the North; with the fine, serious temper of the South, they join the irrepressible spirit of the North that will scarcely pause in the pursuit to resent even an insult; with the conservative and thoughtful habit of the South, they unite the enterprising and habit-breaking manners of the North. The Northern disposition drives them over the face of the land, bends everything to their service, gives them the best the earth affords, in goods and knowledge: the Southern compels a conscientious pause before every undertaking, a serious and sacred consideration of every issue involved. And Benjamin Harrison was a boy with such blood in him — a typical American boy.

The first year or two of this American boy was spent at his grandfather's house; for they still lived there after his grandfather had returned from South America. But his father had been so faithful in caring for the estate, and his grandfather was so well pleased, that the latter gave the former a warranty deed for quite a large farm about five miles from North Bend; and thither little Benjamin was taken, and there he was brought up.

The house was a square brick house, of the style of the best houses of those days. It was somewhat of the style of a Kentucky or Virginia mansion. Its ample rooms and cheerful portico, and spacious porch, gave a delightful, home-like echo to the tread of childish feet.

The boy was not sent to school. In the first place, the common schools were not then the progressive educational systems of to-day. In the second place, the Southern custom of having governors and governesses in the plantation home was not only held in reverence for its association, but for its wisdom. So tutors were employed at the new homestead near North Bend.

The first of these was Miss Harriet Root, a niece of the Rev. Horace Bushnell, of Cincinnati. She was employed as governess in the family of John Scott Harrison, perhaps even before the removal to their own new home in the country. She was very young for the position, but was earnest, competent, and thorough. The children learned to love her, and her interest and devotion to them was not without its effects on their after lives.

Thus the little boy, Benjamin, was fortunate in his first teacher — a most important fact to record. He was a chubby little fellow, square-shouldered even then, and he had a head of almost white hair. He was studious and thoughtful, but fond of play. He was always bright, and advanced rapidly from the day he began his A B C's.

The next teacher was a Mr. Joseph Porter, from Massachusetts, and a graduate of an Eastern college. This gentleman also won the hearts of the children, and he remained in the family for a long time. After Mr. Porter came Mr. Skinner, a graduate of Marshall College, Pennsylvania.

But the home-school was not wholly unlike the early common schools of the West, as to its methods and appointments. Nephews and nieces of Mr. and Mrs. Harrison also came to receive instruction; and it was necessary to have a school-room apart from the residence. This was a cabin, with rough floor and benches. At playtime the children were full of sport, and Ben was often the leader. Then, and at other times, he delighted in hunting and fishing.

This, however, did not make up the boy's life. In those days farmers, for many reasons, could not let their children be idle, and some of them were compelled to require of them more hard toil than their paternal hearts would have led them to require had it not been for "stern necessity." Ben had his share of carrying water and wood, of feeding the horses, cattle, hogs, and sheep, and not infrequently, when night came, his limbs were tired and sore. But he was always ready, when morning came, for whatever duties awaited him. He never complained of his lot, nor filled his mind with dreams that made his life and its duties distasteful to him.

So the boy Ben never, in earliest years, had demoralizing influences such as are sometimes thrown around children on the school-house play-grounds. He had constantly the influences of a pure home, a devoted father and mother, and the association of brothers and sisters. His mother was a faithful and devoted Christian woman, and always kept alive the influence of religious devotion in the home. Nor was she uninterested in general themes, nor unacquainted with the progress her children were making in their daily studies. She sought to provide good books, and she loved to hear her children read and talk about their studies, as she sat with them before the wide fire-place of an evening. From his mother young Harrison learned his reverence for the Christian religion.

Meanwhile, as the years went on, the log cabin at North Bend underwent a change. The logs were hid by planed and painted boards, and two wings were added, so that a stranger would never have known that it was a log cabin. It stood not far from the river, and the yard reached down to the water's edge. But it stood on ground too high to be in danger from the disastrous floods that sometimes, even yet, sweep down the valley, carrying low-ground houses with them. The cabin was rude in its construction — half-hewn logs, rough floor, an outside wooden chimney, doors swung on wooden hinges, loose boards laid across rough joists for a loft (it could not be called an "up-stairs," for the "stairway" was a common ladder), and all the accompaniments of such an humble log hut. But at the change, the roughness disappeared, and the cabin became a house with two stories and more pretentious appearance.

Nevertheless, this change did not prevent the glorification of the cabin in the approaching great campaign, nor the enthusiasm it raised that spread over all the country. And the centre of this enthusiasm was at North Bend; and those in the log cabin, and those who had lived in it, were in the midst of perhaps the greatest political excitement that ever shook the country during a campaign; and while men, women, and children came about with songs of Harrison—of Tippecanoe—and with flags and banners and badges, the boy received impressions and a turn of thought that can never be effaced or changed.

It was the first great Whig victory, and it was won purely on Whig principles. It was the culmination of the movement begun as far back as the close of the war of 1812—the deflection, as far as political opinion was concerned, from the ranks of the so-called united "one party" of its best elements, when the fundamental principles of our government were endangered. True, that growing "movement" had been unfortunate in carrying with it through the years, discontented factions, having local interests to serve, and clinging to the slender but growing stem solely for the policy of defeating the party in power, with which, but for local schemes, they were in greater sympathy.

But that early deflection was of an element that had always been true to American principles, and ready to rally for their defense. It had now grown to gigantic proportions, in spite of incumbrances. It had been christened "National Republican" in 1828, and "Whig" in 1834. Whatever the political schemes of certain political leeches, called "leaders," in 1840, it was the people that elected William Henry Harrison, and elected him as their ideal leader and representative in protection to American liberties.

There is no parallel to the campaign of 1840. It was preeminently a people's campaign. It was the beginning of those great mass-meetings that have, in a less degree, characterized all campaigns since. There never was as much singing; and all the watch-words of the songs and shouts were freighted with patriotic meaning. The old log cabin in which the little hero, who stood with wondering eyes and breast heaving with early patriotic pride and feeling, and looked on the grand commotion around him, was born, was made the war-cry. The Democrats, strong in their old organization, feeling aristocratic security, had been foolish enough to ridicule the candidate who lived in a log cabin, and who, instead of having fine, aristocratic wines on his board, had cider.

The campaign was the yell of rage at the insult, and the people resolved to hurl a party that had no more sympathy with them from power. So it became known throughout the Union that the candidate for President on the Whig ticket had lived in a log cabin; and the people, by the campaign and by their votes, showed that in American eyes, that was nothing against him — that the humblest might, in America, rise by effort and merit even to be President of the United States. The campaign became known in history as the "Log Cabin and Hard Cider Campaign." The banners, badges, and medals had always on them a log cabin, and by it a keg of cider. Something like "William H. Harrison, the People's Choice," or, "We Hold the Constitution and Laws Sacred," or, "Union of the Whigs for the Sake of the Union," or, "We will Take Him from the Plough," was printed on every one of them, and these mottoes indicate sufficiently what the people had in mind.

One of the characteristic songs of the time was entitled "When My Old Hat Was New," and the two stanzas here given show the real feeling of the people on some points:

"When my old hat was new, Van Buren was a Fed,
An enemy to every man who labored for his bread;
And if the people of New York have kept their records true,
He voted 'gainst the poor man's rights, when my old hat was new.

"When my old hat was new, the friends of liberty
Knew well the merits of old Tip while fighting at Maumee:
Come now, huzza for Harrison, just as we used to do
When first we heard of Proctor's fall, when my old hat was new."

The following is the first verse of another song, and it is not difficult, as one reads it, to catch something of the honest, patriotic thrill of that great campaign:

"The people are coming from plain and from mountain
To join the brave band of the honest and free.
Like the stream which flows down from the leaf-sheltered fountain,
Grows broad and more broad till it reaches the sea,
No force can restrain it; no strength can detain it,
Whate'er may resist, it breaks gallantly through,
And born by its motion, like a ship on the ocean,
So speeds in his glory old Tippecanoe!
The iron-hearted soldier, the brave-hearted soldier,
The gallant old soldier of Tippecanoe."

The following breathes the same spirit:

"Down in the West, the fair river beside,
That waters North Bend in its beauty and pride,
And shows in its mirror the summer sky blue,
O, there dwells the hero of Tippecanoe.

The honest old farmer of Tippecanoe!
The gallant old soldier of Tippecanoe!
With an arm that is strong and a heart that is true,
O, there dwells the hero of Tippecanoe."

It was no mere enthusiasm for a favorite that was manifested in these songs. It was not hard to see that the favorite was to the people the representative of principles dear to them; that they considered those principles their salvation; that, therefore, they felt themselves threatened with some disaster, or under some heavy yoke which they determined to shake off. It was this that gave the sting to the insult of the sneer at the log cabin and hard cider. Bourbonism, proud, aristocratic, caring nothing for the people if only it could make them its servants, had shown the real meaning of state-sovereignty to be the lifting up of states into so many petty aristocracies, and the virtual recognition of the clan-system — the class-system — in the government of the Nation. When it had destroyed the United States Bank because it suggested a national idea, and caused the establishment of "wild-cat" state banks, that were so many unsecured and unlimited independent inflation-banks; when it reduced the tariff by a method recognizing the same petty sovereign desires — as if it were only a "local issue"; when it left internal improvements, as well as protection, to the states; and when this Bourbonism would not abate this policy of holding up its system of state-supremacy at the expense of the welfare of the people in these matters, then the people resolved that Bourbonism should rule no longer. This was the key-note of the enthusiasm of 1840.

From that day to this, Ben Harrison has never ceased to be

the friend of the people. It is impossible to overestimate the influence of such times upon the mind of the boy.

It was a great day for the Harrison households when the news of the victory came to them. It was a greater day when the inauguration came; but that day was marred by one sad feature — Grandmother Harrison could not go to Washington with her husband, but remained in the cabin, sick. The position of mistress of the Presidential mansion was filled by her son's wife, the aunt of the boy Ben, and sister of his mother. John Scott and William Harrison had married sisters.

The new President gathered around him such counsellors as Daniel Webster and Henry Clay, and began a policy that would have wrought out great things for our government had he not been cut off in one month from the beginning of his administration. The news was brought to North Bend that he was sick with a fever; and then the sad news came that he was dead. His body was placed in a vault at Washington, but was subsequently removed to North Bend and placed in a tomb overlooking the Ohio River.

Carrying with him the ineffaceable impressions of the past year, the boy went on with his learning; and when he had reached the age of fourteen, he was far in advance of most boys of his age, and ready to try new experiences for the sake of higher attainments.

RESIDENCE OF BENJAMIN HARRISON, INDIANAPOLIS, IND.

[*From a Photograph by Rose, Indianapolis.*]

CHAPTER III.

THE YOUNG STUDENT.

THE BOY GOES FROM HOME — THE HOME HE LEFT — FARMER'S COLLEGE — KEEPS UP HIS REPUTATION — HIS TEACHERS — RETURNS HOME — DEATH OF HIS MOTHER — GOES TO MIAMI UNIVERSITY — TWO YOUNG FRIENDS — JOINS THE PRESBYTERIAN CHURCH — PROFESSORS AND CLASSMATES — A SUCCESSFUL TWO YEARS — INCLINES TOWARD THE LAW — ANOTHER COLLEGE IN THE TOWN — A ROMANTIC EPISODE — HE GRADUATES WITH HONORS.

WHEN it was decided that young Harrison must go away to school, it was also decided that he must go to a school as near home as it was possible to find a good one; and Farmer's College, at College Hill, Cincinnati, was the school chosen.

He was perhaps the youngest and the smallest of his class, and had it not been for his quiet, grave demeanor, would have looked younger than he was. He had a tow head, but a large one, on small and frail, but square shoulders. He spent his vacations at home, and as far as his habits were concerned, they were but little like vacations. He was seldom satisfied unless he had a book in his hand. His delight was to lay his head in a favorite sister's lap, and while, at his demand, she kept rubbing his temples, he would be absorbed in a book.

He loved to come back to his home. The brick walls, the echoing rooms, the porch and portico, the spacious yard with its trees, were all sacred to him, as were also the horses, cattle, sheep, and hogs, and the farm. He liked to go barefooted as when a child, and to assist his father on the farm in feeding the stock at night, or in hauling hay with a chain in the day-time. He was domestic in his tastes then, and his love for home and its environment has ever continued.

Farmer's College was not all its name might imply at that time, but it was a good school, and the young student found himself under excellent instructors. It had been founded by Dr. Freeman Carey, brother of Samuel Carey, the well-known temperance orator, and had been called Carey's Academy. But just before the advent of young Benjamin Harrison to College Hill, the institution was changed to the more dignified grade and title of a college. One of the professors was the celebrated Scotch educator, Dr. R. H. Bishop, and another was Dr. John Witherspoon Scott, who had been a professor in Miami University and other institutions of learning, and was an educator of refinement and rare experience.

Ben Harrison was a studious boy, and kept up with the classes. Among his classmates were several who have since risen to prominence as lawyers, physicians, journalists, or ministers; and the names of Murat Halstead and O. W. Nixon do not detract from the dignity of the list. He kept up his reputation, which he had won under his tutors at home, of a boy of thorough application and determination to master every subject that came before his mind, and to accomplish every duty. He studied hard and long at his tasks, if he could not perform them easily, not because he considered them as tasks, but because of his real interest in them.

In two years he returned from the college with a better education than the majority of people obtain during their whole lives. He was now sixteen and ambitious for knowledge and success in life. He began at once to make preparation for college in the fall; but a sad event meanwhile filled him with sorrow and beclouded his prospects for awhile and his immediate interests for them. This was the death of his mother. He felt that he had lost his dearest friend. He went about sorrowfully for weeks, and when he entered college in the fall, the cloud had not left his heart.

His mother had been a faithful and devoted member of the Presbyterian Church, and by her piety had exercised no small influence on the minds of all her children; and his mind, through his love for her and his love for her kind of life, was not the least susceptible to her influence. She had prayed regularly, and this habit, even when Ben was a child, had caught his wondering attention. Her presence was now missed by no one of the household more than by himself. Her death seemed for awhile to take from him a support on which his life depended.

In the fall he went to Miami University, in Oxford, Ohio. In that day it was a long distance from home, but now it would be but comparatively a short ride on the train. Oxford was a beautiful town in the Miami Valley, and was the seat of two institutions of learning, Miami University and Oxford Female College. The Rev. W. C. Anderson was then president of the former, and the Rev. John W. Scott, the young student's former friend and professor in Farmer's College, was president of the latter.

Doctor Scott had just entered on his duties at Oxford. Although the boy was but sixteen when he left College Hill, it may be that the fact that Doctor Scott had taken his family to Oxford had something to do with turning his steps thither, for the doctor had a daughter, Carrie, who was not far from young Harrison's age; and during the days at College Hill, a warm and earnest friendship had sprung up between the two young people.

In the fall of 1850, the first year of his life at the university, he was converted and joined the Presbyterian Church. He was as sincere in the step as was possible for his sincere nature to be. All his early life had had a tendency to give him a strong, uncompromising conscientiousness. Besides, the death of his mother increased in him his strong desire to live a Christian life, and to meet her again. He became an earnest and faithful worker in the church, though with his retiring disposition, inherited largely from his mother, he was not presumptuous in his Christian service.

Here is a trait that is well to be remembered in estimating his after life — his Christian conscientiousness, coupled with his natural disposition, and all his training. A young man of more impulsive temperament might, under extraordinary excitement, enter just as earnestly into the Christian life, but there would then be a chance of his falling away under great temptation. But a nature as steady, serious, and conscientious as Harrison's, when once it counts the cost and takes such a step, cannot be imagined to turn back. The meaning of this is, that he was conscious of the connection of honor, integrity, and every noble virtue with the profession of religion and could not make the mistake of joining unmindful of them, and that he deliberately accepted their obligation for life. This influence and continuation of purpose may be safely counted on in pointing out what course he has taken in his subsequent career, even if the facts were not known.

Among his college-mates at Miami were Oliver P. Morton, afterwards the renowned war governor of Indiana, W. P. Fishback, a subsequent law partner, the Rev. James Brooks, and Professor David Swing. All these bear testimony to his application and proficiency in college. Professor Swing says that he was a studious scholar, and early manifested that he would succeed in whatever he might undertake. "He there acquired the habits of study and mental discipline which have characterized him through life, enabling him to grapple any subject on short notice, to concentrate his intellectual forces, and give his mental energies that sort of direct and effective operation that indicates the trained and disciplined mind." But his mind seemed to take naturally to this discipline. The truth is, that his past habits of study, his ambition and his zeal, prepared him for it.

As a student Harrison kept abreast of his class. Like all students he excelled in some studies, while his average in others was not so good. He liked history, and he took a special interest in any study whenever it led him into the consideration of questions of social life or of government. He liked political economy, and was one of the best students in that class. He was interested in languages and English literature, and, next to the studies before mentioned, he liked them best. But he was not a mathematician nor a scientist; though in both these studies he did well. His mind was the mind of a lawyer; and he had already made choice of that profession, not for its popularity, nor through the fancy that struck him when he came to "choose a profession," but because it suited the character of his mind.

He had also the qualities of oratory: that is, he was such a master of his thoughts that it was not hard to express them, and he had such interest in his themes that, even in college, he could sometimes rise above his embarrassment and modesty and control himself before an audience. This ability manifested itself in a greater degree in after years. But he was not bombastic; he spoke calmly, thoughtfully, and generally without demonstration, though appropriate and even forcible gestures were not wanting, if in demand for emphasis. He chose his words well, and, even in the college literary society seldom made a speech that did not excel in diction, though his adjectives, as a student, were more numerous than perhaps was necessary — a fault in which he did not excel other students. His efforts were generally extemporaneous. He had also other occasions for using his gift while in college. He was reserved and modest to a degree that interfered with the development of his gift, but there were occasions on which he could not keep still. It is said that once, when a free-trade advocate had delivered an address in town, and had grossly misrepresented some facts, Student Harrison was not hard to persuade to reply to him. He was a protectionist and a Whig; and from his fund of knowledge of the issues he met the arguments of the man and overthrew them.

As has been said, there was another college in the town, over which, as president, was Carrie Scott's father, his own former professor. In attendance at that college were bright and intelligent young ladies, and it can be imagined that the social features of Oxford were not neglected in those days. The modesty of young Harrison did not prevent his full enjoyment of the social occasions, nor his participation in them.

One of the brightest and most intelligent of the young lady students was Carrie Scott, and it has already been related that her friendship with Ben Harrison began while the latter was at Farmer's College. Thus the closer attachment and ultimate engagement came about by the most natural train of circumstances. Novelists could find little in the facts for the "basis" of a sensational romance, and yet it was romantic. But the story writers who make interesting the realities of life because they are interesting, could find much in the beautiful town, the natural coincidences and circumstances to make a charming story and teach beautiful lessons.

She was every way worthy of him, though her talents were not just the same. He cared more for forms and laws; she for art and literature. She was cultivated, having passed her young life among the educated and students. Her features, of the brunette shade, were firm but pleasing, winning, and beautiful. She had dark brown hair and dark brown eyes. She had the faculty of making every one easy in her presence, and glad to be near her; and so the pathway of the rather modest young student was not a rough one. And so they were engaged.

Another two years were spent, and the graduating day in 1852 came around. There was a great concourse of friends, and there were speeches from the graduates, and bouquets without number falling in showers around them. Young Harrison's speech was on the subject, "The Poor in England." What is unusual with students who choose such subjects for graduation display, but what was usual for him in any speeches he ever made, he showed that he thoroughly understood his subject. He showed also an acquaintance with the subject of protection, when he pointed out the remedy for poverty in England. He was one of the best in standing and merit in an unusually good class, and with the blessings of professors and friends resting upon him, he returned home.

CHAPTER IV.

THE LAW STUDENT.

A CHARACTERISTIC RESOLUTION — A NOTED LAW FIRM — FIRST CONTACT WITH PUBLIC MEN — A REVIEW OF THE POLITICAL SITUATION — HIS HOME WHILE READING LAW — HEART TURNS TOWARD OXFORD — THE ROMANCE ENDS PROPITIOUSLY — A HAPPY EVENT — LIVING WITH THE OLD FOLKS — AN UNEXPECTED INHERITANCE — ANOTHER CHARACTERISTIC RESOLUTION.

WHEN the young man returned home, it was not to indulge the boyish sense of security in his home that had characterized him up to the time of his leaving at the age of fourteen. His old reverence for the place and the scenes had, indeed, never left him, and never would. But the shadow of the future was now upon him. He was nearly nineteen, and was a graduate, apparently ready for life. He had, moreover, completed a contract that is always full of serious meaning, and lets down an invisible barrier between the past and present, and turns the thoughts with a feeling of inexorable responsibility to the future.

His mother was not there. His sisters were grown older. His grandmother, always dear, had come to live with the family; but still it was a change. The old place did not seem as it had in his earlier boyhood. His father had not made much headway against financial currents, and the young man felt that the time was at hand when he ought to depend no longer upon his father. True, he was aware that he had been a help on the farm, even when a small boy, and that he had also the right of inheritance and blood relationship to the care, and even anxiety, of those at home. But he did not believe in inherited honors; and he felt that to claim, or to accept, his legal or family rights, under the circumstances, would be unmanly; and he felt that honor must come upon merit. Perhaps he had caught the spirit of 1840, which rated every man a king who sought to rise by the merit of labor and character, and every man a slave who depended upon family and favoritism for position and honor.

In obedience to these feelings, so characteristic of his subsequent life, and no doubt to that other feeling described, that looked toward a new home, he determined to go right on and make his success in life sure. He had the foundation in a college education; he needed some training and study in the art of rearing a special structure. To this end he began at once the study of law in the office of Storer & Gwynne; and his preceptor was the head of the firm, the Honorable Belamy Storer. This was one of the best law firms in Cincinnati, and here, for the first time, young Harrison had the advantage of contact, in a business and professional way, with public men. He had sat under the teachings of excellent masters, who possessed trained and powerful intellects, but he had never dealt with them nor counselled with them as in the same profession, as in some degree he was called on to do now. A law student in a law office is more of an apprentice than a literary student in college.

This was a great help to him. It gave him a practical view of his profession, and a practical grasp of his subjects. It gave him that confidence in his own ability to master and present a subject that has characterized him, and to which his success has largely been due. Many a young man has started in life with good talents and attainments, but with no courage nor tact before men. In practice they lose command of self and talents, and their abilities are never known and never called for. There is perhaps no profession that enables a man to become so thoroughly acquainted with society as it is, and with the business and professional methods of controlling it, as that of the law.

Ben Harrison was, physically and mentally, vigorous and independent. In school and at home he had shown a tact in solving knotty problems, a skill in diving to the depths of his subjects. On taking hold of a problem, he had the confidence that he could master it. In the law office he learned not only to master for himself, but in the presence of others. He could not only present the slate with the "sum" worked out, or the essay or oration studied and written in his room, but he could work among thinkers and as one of them, and bring out the result while he talked with them.

While in this association, it was very natural that his interest should be awakened in politics: for of all men, lawyers are most apt to aspire to become political leaders; and he could not be in the office long without hearing these subjects discussed. It is a tribute to his power of mind, his independence of judgment, and to his patriotism, that he kept his head and heart in the midst of the political confusion and wrangling of that day.

It was now twelve years since the first campaign he could

remember — that of his grandfather. Affairs had not gone well with the Whigs as a party; but their original principles were taking more and more a firm hold upon the popular mind. The first formal declaration of their principles in convention was in 1844; but this was only the echo of the preaching and teaching, and popular demand of 1840. It is not necessary, in order for a party to be a party based on clearly defined principles, for a few men to come together and announce what they believe. When these few men have means of knowing what the people want, having taught them from their own honest convictions, or having heard them in some definite demand and found themselves in honest sympathy with them, then they may construct a platform of the *party of the people* formally in convention. The campaign of 1840 had been definite enough, and the platform of 1844 was its echo.

"A well-regulated currency; a tariff for revenue to defray the necessary expenses of the government, and *discriminating with special reference to the protection of the domestic labor of the country;* the distribution of proceeds from the sale of public lands; a single term for the presidency; a reform of executive usurpations; and generally such an administration of the affairs of the country as shall impart to every branch of public service the greatest practical efficiency, controlled by well-regulated and wise economy." These were the issues of 1844, expressed in convention at Baltimore on May 1st, of that year; and underneath them is the recognition of a *people's government*, protection of the people's interests, people's financial safety: in short, American principles.

But the result was not the same as in 1840. An abolition

candidate, voted for in New York and Michigan, took the electoral votes of those States from Clay and gave them to Polk. These alone added to Clay's 105, and taken from Polk's 170, would have elected Clay. But that movement was honest; and, compared with others, but for which Clay might have been elected anyhow, it was wise. The Democrats in some states advocated free trade, and in some protection —a characteristic policy, as the present generation knows. Again, there were 1,000 fraudulent votes cast in one parish in Louisiana, which gave Polk a majority in that State of only 699. Again, in New York, there was a large amount of fraudulent naturalizing for voting purposes on the part of the Democrats. And again, even while Calhoun had formerly been professing to be a Whig, he had been working to sometime spring the question of slavery by the question of the annexation of Texas. It was this that caused the abolition movement in the North: it was this that appealed to Southern prejudice rather than to Southern principle, and lost Clay the majority of the Southern votes.

The majority of the people, North and South, had really Whig convictions; but the Machiavelian policy of springing an issue *wholly on sectional prejudice*, drew them away. Had the slave question come up in its own good time, by way of the natural growth of Americanism away from the class-ideas of the old world, allowing a chance for its discussion while the fires of patriotism burned, there might have been a different termination of that question, so far as the enormity of the struggle was concerned.

The people of the South, and many of like opinions in the

North, were more sincere on the slavery question than Calhoun and his associates, who seemed to raise the question for political effect. The Mexican War had as its real incentive among the leaders at first, the extension of slavery and the overshadowing by the slave power of free state influence by the addition of new territory. But among the people who enlisted, the declaration of Congress, secured by Democrats, that the war was already begun "by the act of the Republic of Mexico," had stirred a deeper patriotism. It was this patriotism among Southern Whigs, and the prejudice on the slavery question among them and many Northerners, stirred up by Calhoun and others, that put the Northern Whigs in Congress between two fires.

The Mexican battles were fought and won, and new glory was added to the American arms. The bill in Congress, in 1846, to make an appropriation to negotiate a peace with Mexico, had called out the famous amendment by David Wilmot, "that there shall be neither slavery nor involuntary servitude in any territory on the Continent of America, which shall hereafter be acquired by, or annexed to, the United States by virtue of this appropriation, or in any other manner whatever except for crime." The amendment had failed, but had produced its wonderful effect, and had gone into history as the "Wilmot Proviso." The slavery question had been dividing both parties; the note of secession had been sounded in the South, the note of hasty resistance in the North. Divisions were made on the issues, not on the principles of the parties. Whigs at heart had rallied to Democratic ranks; and Whigs at heart, impatient of delay, had formed the Free Soil party. Seceders also from the Democratic ranks had joined the Free Soil movement, and the Buffalo Convention of 1848 had been held by the new party. Notwithstanding the disruptions, Taylor had led the hosts in 1848, and had been made President of the United States. He had died in office, and Fillmore, the milder Whig, had guided the administration through a period of apparent calm.

But the mutterings of the storm were in the South and in Kansas. Another campaign was on. The Free Soilers had nominated Hale and Julian; the Whigs, General Scott and William A. Graham; and the Democrats, Pierce and King. Such was the political situation when Ben Harrison began to study law. He could not help being interested in the outcome of the canvass. He was a Whig, believing the time not yet for the settling of the slave question; believing that the *extension* of slavery should indeed be prohibited (as, not believing in slavery at all as a moral institution, he with others believed it to be constitutional to prevent its extension, but that its overthrow where it did exist would be violence uncalled for while opinions of great and good men on the constitutional right differed); and believing that strict American principles should be always at the front as issues, while other important issues should rise in their natural order and be discussed from the stand-point of those principles.

He had had his convictions from his boyhood. His natural indignation in 1844, when *unlawful* naturalization in New York had carried that State to the Democrats, was expressed emphatically then and afterwards, although he was at that time but eleven years old; but he never opposed, even then, *lawful* naturalization. More than other boys, he had the spirit of 1840, that allowed every citizen a right to express his opinion in a vote, whether natural or foreign born. And this belief characterized him all his youth and manhood. Up to 1852, he was a Whig in every sense of the word. And now, naturally, being in the midst of politicians in the office, he was more interested than ever — and more of a Whig.

The result of the campaign of 1852, as might have been foreseen, was that Pierce was elected by a large majority, and "fire eaters" and other foes to the country came again to the front.

While he studied law, he walked back and forth between his sister's house, in North Bend, and the office. This was to save the expense of board, for meanwhile the family purse grew no heavier.

The heart of the young law student had never for a moment ceased its loyalty to its queen at Oxford, and in October, 1853, he went to fulfil the marriage contract. This, to the young couple was far more than a legal transaction. It was the leaving parents for each other, and becoming, in heart and mind and life, as well as in legal relation, "one flesh"; it was the founding on a holy and sanctified and divine basis, a home, a family. Both of them believed implicitly in the sacredness of the marriage tie.

Both of them, as soon as the engagement had been made, had felt a change of attitude, as it were, of their affections. They loved the old homes and dear ones no less, but they loved each other more, and felt they were soon to enter a society established and hallowed by Jehovah — a society with bonds irrevocable.

Miss Carrie L. Scott was just the woman to glorify a relationship like that, and to make ready her heart, and purpose, and life, beforehand. to carry out sacredly the solemn pledge. Reared in a family of rich cultivation and of conscience, she was ready with such instincts to make such a home. Her father had long been a professor, and had made his house the the welcome place for the refined and educated. In his own life he always, at home and abroad, manifested the traits of a well-educated gentleman. His cultivation was not mere cultivation, but was the development of rare natural powers and their training by a long experience. He was as gentle as a child, and as graceful. And Carrie's mother was no less of the noble and refined type.

Carrie's was a religious home, full of the graces and sweet influences that religion can bring around the hearthstone. Her sparkling and half-roguish and captivating brown eyes were not those of the careless-hearted maiden, and betrayed no feeling or instinct of the coquette, but spoke rather the deeper and more earnest joy of a deeper nature. She was every way charming: her shapely form, her shapely hands with neat, tapering fingers, her regular features, all making her a beauty; and above all, the intelligent and captivating expressions of her countenance were winning qualities. She was the charm of her circle, and her grace and manner made her the idol of her lady acquaintances. Withal, she was serious and intensely religious.

During the winter of 1853–4, the happy couple lived at the home near North Bend, preparing meanwhile to begin life's battle alone in the spring. When spring came, it was all arranged that the young lawyer should take his bride and settle in Indianapolis. He was also the better enabled to run this risk by receiving a bequest about that time of $800. An aunt, Mrs. Findly, died and left him that amount. Nevertheless, it required no small courage to face the uncertainties of an entirely strange locality with but eight hundred dollars and an untried profession, and a wife depending upon him. But the resolution was characteristic of him: he wanted to be independent, to go where he would be compelled to work; above all, he wanted to rise by his own merits, and not by the name of his grandfather.

MRS. BENJAMIN HARRISON,

WIFE OF GENERAL HARRISON.

CHAPTER V.

THE YOUNG LAWYER.

JOURNEY TO LAWRENCEBURG — THENCE TO INDIANAPOLIS — THE CITY AT THAT TIME — A HUMBLE COTTAGE — HE PUTS OUT HIS "SHINGLE" — POOR PROMISE OF SUCCESS — DAYS SPENT IN ABSTRACT OFFICE — OFFICE OF JOHN H. REA, CLERK OF DISTRICT COURT OF UNITED STATES — A PROVIDENTIAL OPPORTUNITY — POINT LOOKOUT BURGLARY CASE — PARTNERSHIP WITH WILLIAM WALLACE — ANOTHER CASE BRINGS HONOR — PARTNERSHIP WITH W. P. FISHBACK.

THE journey of the young couple to Lawrenceburg must be made in wagons. It was about fourteen miles distant, and there was no railroad to that point. They carried with them boxes of provisions, some bedding, and a few other necessities of home life. From Lawrenceburg they sent the wagon back, and took the train to Indianapolis. They had no express trains and steel rails on the road then. The road was rough, the seats were uncomfortable — at least modern travelers would consider them so. But at last they arrived in the capital of Indiana.

Indianapolis gave no promise then of its present magnificence, though it was a growing little town. Most of the houses were near the east bank of the White River; but that quarter was not destined to become the centre of the city, for business soon left it, and it is to-day comparatively a deserted quarter.

The first thing necessary, on arriving at the new capital, was to find a place to stay. So the young husband secured board for himself and wife, at what was known as the Roll House, until they could find a home. Meanwhile he "kept a look-out" for a house with rent within his probable ability to pay. This was the usual way of expressing it; but, in truth, Benjamin Harrison never had a doubt as to his success, although he really under-rated his own abilities when he sat in judgment on them. He knew that he should not fail, because he knew he was going to work, and he had confidence in perseverance; while he knew that, however few talents he might have, others who had fewer had succeeded.

At last a small house was found, on the corner of North and Alabama streets — in the eastern suburbs of the city as it was then, but in the heart of the present city of Indianapolis. The house had a gable front in which was a window and a door. It was a low, one-story building; but it had an air of cosiness and home-likeness, in spite of its humbleness. A large shade-tree stood just by the walk before the door, adding its attractiveness to the scene. On entering, they found that the house contained but three rooms; but that was quite sufficient for their wants and comfort, and it was hired at $6.00 a month: and this was their first Indianapolis home.

Here was the first realization of home — the dream of their young lives. So happy were they in it that it mattered not to them that the cottage was humble, and that there were but three rooms. Here gathered the associations of early married life. The house stands yet, as it used to stand; and the present General Benjamin Harrison and his estimable wife cannot look upon it without a throng of delicious memories rising before them. Here they began life in humblest manner; but somehow there is even a halo about that as it is recalled by them. The sickness, the trial, and the suffering are either forgotten, or hallowed by association with the good that arose out of them. Here the first child was born; and the wife was no longer so lonely while her husband was absent about the task of finding paying cases.

He was fair-haired and boyish — appearing younger than he was. There was not that maturity in his looks and expression that won, at a glance, the confidence of those seeking lawyers to befriend them in court. He had not that self-assertion that is a positive necessity in getting along with some classes. His slender form, and stature below the average, were not apt to impress one.

Hence, his first year at Indianapolis was not one of brilliant success. He spent, during that time, many hours in abstract offices, hunting up titles, and getting small pay for his pains — his highest fee being five dollars. He secured, through John L. Robinson, the position of court-crier, at $3.50 a day, but court was not in session long enough in the year to add much to his slender purse.

Before he had received a fee in this or any other manner, he was standing one day on the sidewalk just before his door, and under the tree. It was the first Sunday after they had gone to house-keeping. He was looking up at the cottage and thinking with some pride of it, as his home; there is no purer or more comforting pride a man has in life than in the contemplation of his first home after marriage. While he was thus contentedly engaged, a horseman came dashing up the street, and stopped before the door. Mr. Harrison turned to know the errand of this breaker of his reverie.

The man had come from Clermont, a small village eight miles west of there, to find a lawyer to prosecute, before a justice of the peace, a man who had been arrested on a charge of obtaining money under false pretenses. Would Mr. Harrison go down and prosecute? Mr. Harrison agreed that he would go. Then the man dropped a five-dollar gold-piece into the young lawyer's hand, gave directions about reaching Clermont and the hour for trial, and left.

Five dollars! That was a god-send, indeed! But part of that must be paid for some means of going, for he could not walk. It would not do to hire a horse and buggy—that would take too much from the welcome fee. So the next morning, he hired a pony at a stable, and when the hour for starting came, set off to win his first laurels in legal contest. And he won them.

He demonstrated, in that successful suit, as he subsequently did in every case with which he had to do, that, in spite of disadvantages of poverty and youth, he was cut out for a lawyer. However, as it generally requires a lawyer of some greatness and established fame to recognize the abilities of the rising young lawyer, and as men of that class were not apt to be pleading cases before a country justice, Benjamin Harrison must wait for recognition until some future day. He entered the office of John H. Rea, Clerk of the District Court of the United States. He had little success until a rather fortunate incident occurred.

The famous "Point Lookout" burglary case was before the court, with Governor David Wallace on one side, and Major Jonathan W. Gordon, the prosecuting attorney, on the other. Major Gordon was a man of great ability, and had formed a high estimate of the real abilities of young Harrison. Governor Wallace was assisted in the defense by Sims Colley.

The closing appeal to the jury, it was found, would not come until the evening of the closing day, and Major Gordon found himself confronted by duties in two places at the same hour. He desired to attend a lecture by Horace Mann in the evening, and it was necessary to find some one to fill his place before the jury. The choice fell on Mr. Harrison, whom he knew was careful, earnest, capable, and would spare no pains to make his speech a success.

Governor Wallace, for the defense, was one of the leading Indiana lawyers. He was an old and experienced lawyer, skilled in making all out of the testimony possible in its presentation to the jury. He was, moreover, an old friend of Mr. Harrison's grandfather. The records of 1840 show that John Scott Harrison desired to be appointed by his father to a West Point cadetship, and that the father preferred the son of his friend, Governor Wallace, for the place, rather than his own son; and so Wallace was appointed.

It is perhaps worthy of remembrance that it is not an easy thing for a young man, with that degree of modesty that had always characterized Benjamin Harrison, to enter the lists with a man whom he had always been wont to look up to with some reverence as his grandfather's friend. Those associated with our fathers when we are very young we learn to reverence almost as much as we do our fathers themselves. To face duty in such a case is worthy of more honor, because it is the manifestation of real courage, than to egotistically and with brazen effrontery seek to contend with great men.

The evening session met at "candle lighting," and the candles cast very shadowy light over the old low, dingy court-room, crowded with people. The room was full of smoke, from candles and stove, and the fumes of tobacco made the air nauseating. The prospect was not encouraging.

At the time for his speech, Mr. Harrison took from his pocket his notes that he had written during the day, and began to scan them. To his disgust he could see nothing in the dim light but very uncertain tracings with a hard pencil — not a word could he make out in that light. He began his speech, but soon found, from the almost breathless audience, that he was winning more sympathy for his youth, or his misfortune, than for the wisdom of his utterances. His voice was heard at the farthest corner. He tried again to scan the apparently almost blank leaves. He could tell nothing, and after discovering that he must fail if he depended on those notes, he threw them aside, and boldly launched forth into the argument without them. He remembered the essential parts of the testimony, and was not hindered by details; so perhaps it was best. At any rate he canvassed the ground so thoroughly and so clearly that he called down the praises of audience and old lawyers on his head.

When Governor Wallace rose to reply he took occasion first to gracefully and earnestly compliment the young lawyer on his speech. And this, Mr. Harrison's first jury case, was the beginning of a warm friendship that rose between himself and Governor Wallace, which was not hindered in the least by the young lawyer's triumph in that case. This circumstance had also, no doubt, something to do with linking the fortunes of Mr. Harrison and of Governor Wallace's son, William Wallace, together for a time.

This was the same son who had obtained the West Point cadetship when it was desired by Mr. Harrison's father. The partnership came about in this way: Young Wallace, who had already won some success in his practice, received, in 1855, the nomination for county clerk. As the canvass required a good deal of time, he desired some one to assist him in his practice. He met his young friend, Ben Harrison, on the street one day, and told him that he had some clients, and that if he would go into the office and take them, he would share the profits with him. This is all the contract that was ever made, and the young firm began its existence with little experience, but with the energy of young blood and brains to carry to success.

Mr. Wallace, since that time, has borne testimony in favor of the admirable qualities of young Benjamin Harrison, as he then knew him. He has ascribed to the young lawyer from North Bend, quickness of apprehension, clearness, method and logic in analysis and statement of cases, natural ability to draw truth from witnesses, successfulness in winning from courts and juries their closest attention. Said Mr. Wallace: "He was poor. The truth is, it was a struggle for bread and meat with both of us. He had a noble young wife, who cheerfully shared with him the plainest and simplest style of living. He did the work about his home for a long time himself, and thus made his professional income, not large, keep him independent and free from debt."

Among those of the Indianapolis bar, with whom Mr. Harrison came in contact in those days, were Oliver H. Smith, John L. Ketchum, Simon Yandes, Hugh O'Neal, and David Wallace. These were all men of note as lawyers, and they all, then and afterwards, bore testimony to the rare abilities of the young lawyer. This, to him was a larger school than that of the office of Storer & Gwynne at Cincinnati, for here he was not an apprentice; yet he always made use of his surroundings, of whatever nature, to draw from them information and experience.

Not long after the burglary trial, another case gave Ben Harrison a chance of manifesting the metal that was in him. A negro cook at the Ray House, Indianapolis, was accused of putting poison into the coffee of some of the boarders with a view to murder. The case was attracting wide attention. Harrison was called to the prosecution, and had but one night to prepare. He went to the office of young Dr. T. Parvin, who afterwards became noted as one of the professors of Jefferson Medical College, of Philadelphia, and the two spent the whole night experimenting, Harrison studying thoroughly the effect of poisons, and thus gaining a knowledge of the subject superior to that of his opponents in the case. The next day the defense met more than its match in the thoroughly prepared young lawyer. He applied himself so vigorously that he won the case, and secured conviction for the prisoner.

He won also additional praise for himself from noted lawyers and from all who were acquainted with the case.

The two young men, William Wallace and Benjamin Harrison, continued as partners in law for some years. In the West, especially among the older class of citizens, there is a prejudice against young men in profession, as to their ability. A young lawyer, however brilliantly he may have succeeded in a few cases, will not be employed half so readily as an old lawyer who fails to win more than half his cases. In spite of the lack of prestige the Harrison & Wallace firm grew in favor and success.

In 1860 Wallace had retired from the partnership, and Harrison formed another with W. P. Fishback. But in that same year another chance offered itself, and he was not slow to seize the opportunity.

CHAPTER VI.

THE YOUNG POLITICIAN.

THE CAMPAIGN OF 1856 — THE NEW PARTY AND ITS PRINCIPLES — A SUCCESSFUL CANDIDACY — A MEMORABLE DEBATE AT ROCKVILLE — THE LINCOLN CAMPAIGN — A RETROSPECTIVE VIEW OF THE POLITICAL PARTIES — THE SITUATION IN 1860 — WHIG PRINCIPLES AND FREE SOIL ISSUES — THE SUCCESSFUL CAMPAIGN — THE REPORTER IN OFFICE — THE GUNS OF SUMTER — BOUND AT HOME — A PATRIOT.

THE enthusiasm awakened in the breast of the boy of 1840 was still in the breast of the young man of 1856. But he was not a demonstrative young man; and was never found on the street corners, in groceries, in offices, or in bar-rooms, counting off arguments on his fingers. He was rather chary of his opinions; not through any haughtiness, nor yet because he had no confidence in them, but because rather of a native diffidence, and no doubt also of a sense of the "fitness of things" — rather the unfitness of the assumption of a mere youth.

Nevertheless, he could express his opinions clearly and tersely when pressed, or at a time when in doing so he could accomplish any good object. His political views were not unknown in Indianapolis, and when the campaign of 1856 came on, he was positively pressed into the service of speech-making.

Many remember that campaign. It had not, perhaps, the

enthusiasm of 1840; but it had, at least on one side, that enthusiasm born of deep conviction, fervent patriotism, and indomitable purpose. As the Whigs, in the memorable Harrison campaign, had for the first time crystallized into a party with definite principles and aims, so far as the people were concerned, so in the Fremont campaign, the Republican party was standing at the threshold of its active life. The party had not sprung into existence on a mere issue, however important, which being successful, would leave no reason for the party's longer existence. It came into being for the conservation of principles born with the Republic and that will last while the Republic lasts. So long as these principles are opposed by men or parties there will be a necessity of organized society for their defense. When the Republican party shall prove untrue to this trust, on the springing of issues that involve the principles, that element in the Nation which has rallied around and defended them from the days before the Revolution, will combine for their defense under more favorable conditions for success, and more patriotic leadership. "The Union must and shall be preserved."

It is a significant fact that men who, as boys, caught the spirit of 1840, are chosen and trusted, as men, as standard bearers to-day. Hope need not "close her bright eyes, nor curb her high career," so far as the party is concerned, while men like Benjamin Harrison are leaders.

The nominations had just been made. "Fremont and Dayton" was a signal of safety in the approaching storm. Though they might not hope for success at the polls that year, they knew that the elements of patriotism predominated in the

Nation, and as time would make known their intentions, a mighty majority would come up in the future. Of this prescient confidence, young Benjamin Harrison had his full share; and this fact was known.

A ratification meeting was called in Indianapolis. Somebody must speak; and a good many thought of Mr. Harrison. He was at work in his office, which was in Temperance Hall, a building that stood on Washington Street, between Illinois and Meridian streets. He heard a stamping of many feet up the stairway, and he heard many loud voices. Then he saw an excited crowd of men rush in, and the leader seize him by the arm. He must go and make the ratification speech; the crowd had gathered and was waiting, and there was no speaker.

He protested. He was interested, of course — they knew that; but he was a lawyer, not a politician. Besides, he was not prepared. Let older men speak; they could do more good; they had experience and study which he did not have. But no excuse would be taken — he must speak. When he protested again, the men lifted him up onto their shoulders and carried him to the assembled throng, made him stand upon a goods box, and required of him a speech.

He was introduced as the grandson of William Henry Harrison. "I want it understood," said he, on facing the people, "that I am the grandson of nobody. I believe every man should stand on his own merits." He was not without pride, of course, that he was the grandson of an illustrious man; and that relationship — that blood — he knew helped to make him the man that needed not to be ashamed; and the consciousness of it was fuel to the fire of courage within him. But it was a cardinal doctrine with him that honor and success should follow the honest effort of personal and inherent virtues, as effect follows cause; that they should not be hindered by any arbitrary rules or favoritism in society; and that honor, and even prestige, claimed or assumed on account of blood, or anything acquired by nature or accident, defrauds merit of its rightful and lawfully acquired possession.

But under the circumstances it became his duty to speak; and speak he did. And the effect followed the cause — he was honored for his worth and ability. He was in demand from that time for the stump, and right loyally he did his part. In Franklin County, not long after, he was called on again, and some enthusiastic friend, to capture the crowd for him before he had shown whether he was worthy of it, introduced him again as the grandson of the renowned President. Again he protested against that method of introduction, saying that he preferred to speak for himself, not for his grandfather. These incidents taught his friends that they had in him a thorough American; and he has done nothing since to shake that confidence. He took part, not only in the campaign to its close, but in every state or local campaign from that time until 1860.

Meanwhile, whatever was good in the old Whig party had adjusted itself to a new setting in the Republican party; and the old settings — organization, name, watch-words and tokens of successful issues, and successful issues themselves — were cast aside. It may not be uninteresting to record, that even the old log cabin, of the campaign of 1840, was totally destroyed by fire, on the 25th of February, 1858 — the malicious work of a discharged servant. This may serve as a token, or an illustration of the fact that the malicious servants of the old Whig party, whom it had refused to glorify in office and spoils, were really the destroyers of the party. And as the sacred influences of the old cabin at North Bend had now centered in the newer brick house on the farm,— for even Grandmother Harrison, on whose birthday the cabin was burned, was living with her son, and knew not of the burning for several years,— so all the sacred principles and memorials of the Whigs had been safely conserved in the new and safe Republican structure before the Whig organization was swept away.

In 1860 Ben Harrison's circumstances and his growing confidence in his own ability made him feel justified in having his name presented for the suffrages of his fellow-citizens, and he became the candidate for the office of reporter of the Supreme Court of Indiana. Throughout the memorable campaign of that year his voice was heard, almost from one end of the State to the other, pleading for the principles of the American Union.

An incident illustrating his grasp of those principles, his power in debate, and the thorough mastery he always had of his subjects before he undertook to speak, occurred during this campaign. He had an appointment to speak in the Court House at Rockville, in Park County. When he arrived, he learned that Thomas A. Hendricks, one of the most noted Democratic leaders of the State, and in that campaign candidate for governor of Indiana, and already near to the conspicuous position he afterwards held in national fame, was also to speak in the town. Park was a strong Democratic county, but the Republicans were anxious to gain further ground, and to counteract the influence of Hendricks on that day. In a forlorn hope they asked Harrison if he would undertake a joint discussion with Hendricks. The Democrats also, fearing nothing from the boyish-looking Harrison, were anxious for the debate; but Hendricks would not condescend to enter into a formal debate with so youthful an opponent. He would speak two hours, he said, and the young man might talk two hours longer, if he wanted to, and Hendricks would listen.

The issues were local, as well as national. The Democrats were in power in the State, and under their administration of affairs huge swindles had been carried on, notably what was known as the swamp-land frauds. Mr. Harrison had made himself thoroughly acquainted with this subject, as well as with the general questions. While Mr. Hendricks was speaking, it seemed to Democrats and Republicans that the victory was already his. The crowded Court House rang with cheer after cheer, as the speech proceeded. On the platform sat Daniel Voorhees, who was already rising to fame, and other local Democratic leaders; while the youthful Harrison, not having either the courtesy of a chair, or a condescending notice of his presence by Mr. Hendricks or his colleagues, sat on a desk and let his feet hang *toward* the floor. And thus Mr. Hendricks' speech went on until it was twice two hours in length — at least young Harrison felt it so. At last the "great speech" ended, and Mr. Hendricks, suddenly remembering a forgotten duty, quietly and politely let the people know that they ought to remain.

When Mr. Harrison rose before the tired audience, there was not a cheer, nor a motion of any kind that gave him to understand that his friends were with him. He felt that his friends were wishing for some greater man to answer that speech. When he began, his voice was heard throughout the large room, and for a moment one might have been reminded of his first utterances when he appeared the first time before a jury. But only for a moment. His first statement was a proposition which he then said the Democrats had once believed.

Here Mr. Voorhees arose with great dignity and denied that the Democrats had ever believed the proposition.

"Fellow-citizens," rang out the clear voice of the young candidate, before Mr. Voorhees had time to regain his seat, "the denial of the gentleman induces me to amend my statement. I now assert that every Democrat believed the proposition, except Mr. Voorhees — he was then a Whig."

The applause that followed showed the appreciation of the retort by the audience; while the sharpness of the thrust made Mr. Voorhees conclude to keep his seat thereafter. So the young speaker went on, and before he had filled out half his time, the tide had turned in his favor, as the cheering and applause and eager attention of the audience plainly indicated. His sarcasm went to the heart of the arguments that had been set up in the belief that he knew nothing of the matters. When he closed, cheers rose up as if to rend the roof of the large auditorium. Mr. Hendricks told him, when the meeting had adjourned, that he would never again consent to give him a two-hours closing speech. In speaking of the affair afterwards, the chairman of the meeting said: "I have heard a good many political debates in my day, but I never heard a man skin an opponent as quickly as Ben Harrison did Hendricks that day."

In that year there was a much larger rallying of forces to the Republican standard. Time was doing its work. When the election was over, it was apparent that Lincoln had received 180 electoral votes against 123 for all the other candidates; and then were fairly begun the trying times of the Republic — the times foreshadowed in 1854, and even earlier.

Great men are seldom in haste. It is hard for good men to believe that bad men are so bad. It was hard for men like Webster and Clay to believe that the South could not be conciliated, earlier than 1854, when the mutterings of discontent and threats of disunion were heard throughout her borders. These men had labored all their lives to build up the Union, and it was hard for them to realize the idea of rebellion. They were not ready for Free Soil issues. They believed that the discontented portion of our country might be conciliated.

But in 1854, the startling news ran over the country that Congress was about to repeal the Missouri Compromise Bill of 1820. By that bill it had been provided "that in all the territory ceded by France to the United States, under the name of Louisiana, which lies north of latitude 36°, 30′ N., except only such part thereof as is included within the limit of the State (Missouri) contemplated by this act, slavery and involuntary servitude, otherwise than in the punishment of crime, whereof the party shall have been duly convicted, shall be and is hereby forever prohibited." To repeal this would be a proclamation of irreconciliation, and a greater insult to those who had urged conciliation than to those who had not. It would be a plain profession, on the part of the South, that they did not intend to be conciliated with anything less than unqualified submission to their demands in all things. It would be slavery in all the territories, a designedly taking advantage of a majority in Congress to force an overbalancing of slave power, that slavery might go wherever the South commanded it (and that was not uncertain, for the expressed declaration of incautious leaders had already pointed to states not territories), and it would be bad faith.

Genuine old Whigs declared that, while slavery might stay where it was, it should advance no further: the manner of these southern threats, and the proposed repeal, were anything but echoes of Union and liberty-loving hearts. Men who, while issues had been conflicting had been uncertain in their party moorings, began to rally to the standard of the grand old defenders of American faith. But these defenders — tired of intrigue, and grown at last impatient of the dallying of mere politicians with questions now grown so serious — had bound themselves together in a new party. It was the very best Whig element — the element that, first of all, could be touched and warned by any threatened danger to human liberties. For the bill had now been repealed —" declared inoperative and void "— and that was warning enough.

The Whigs brought into the new organization the elements of body and blood. From the beginning of its existence the

Whig party had championed those principles which recognize the equal rights of all American citizens. "Protection to home industries"— that means equal rights in living and getting a living. "Internal improvements"— that means equal facilities for trade to all sections, equal enjoyment of great advantages, and the example of employment at wages of Americans. "A just and dignified foreign policy"— that means that a government "by the people, for the people," should command the respect of all nations; for "foreign policy" in a monarchy means the welfare of the king, and "foreign policy" in a republic means the welfare and honor of the people. "The Union, one and inseparable" — that means the husbanding of the powers that sustain these principles, the balancing of equal elements, the possibility of the success of our government principles, which "states' rights," especially as then held by Democrats, made impossible.

When an issue is made, involving the continued existence of equal rights as fundamental in our government, those believing in it, and seeing its danger in the issue, rally together, and the party is formed. At such a trumpet call the Republican party was organized. The "Anti-Nebraska" movement in Ohio and other States heralded the gathering of the clans. Other movements came quickly. Then the first National Convention of the Republican party, in 1856, nominated Fremont and Dayton for President and Vice-President, with the result already named. In Indiana, alone, Fremont received 94,375 votes against 22,386 for Fillmore, and 118,670 for Buchanan — no small showing for the first campaign of a party.

The consolidation was not complete, however, even as late

as 1860, for there were four tickets in the field that year. This, indeed, apparently, did not seriously affect the Republican party, and not at all as to the result. But one of the divisions, at least, shows that there were loyal men who still refused to believe the South capable of the high-handed wickedness of rebellion. These were, for the most part, men who had affiliated with the Democrats, who loved the name, and who, though they could not believe their brethren meditated crime so dire, would not go with them even to the declaration of principles so adverse to American government. These, wherever they might formerly have wandered when party lines were falsely pointed out along local and personal issues, and however the unnatural affiliation may have become sacred, were really Whigs in principle, for they would not go where Democratic opinions logically led them, and when the war came on, their declarations on behalf of union were as clear sounding as those of the old Whigs. Witness the speech of Mr. Douglas, in Chicago, at the outset of the Rebellion.

It need not be said that Benjamin Harrison kept close watch of the march of events, as the years went on, and that he was always in full sympathy with the new Republican party. The fires of indignation grew hotter in his breast from the days of the discussion of the repeal of the Missouri Compromise Bill, and of the Dred Scott Decision. It was the zeal of patriotism that gave power to his words in 1860.

As one of the results of this campaign, he was elected and soon entered upon the duties of his office of reporter of the Supreme Court. It will, perhaps, never be a matter of history just how much, or how little, he contributed to the success of the State ticket — to the election of Henry S. Lane as governor of Indiana — and of the National ticket in that State. But it is certain that, young as he was, his services were highly appreciated by his Republican colleagues, and that he won not a few votes to the Republican candidates.

This office, coming to him at that time, was of great financial benefit. He had just negotiated for a house, for which he was to pay $2,900 — a large sum for the young lawyer. He had been fortunate enough to get the house "at a bargain," from the Honorable A. G. Porter, afterwards governor of Indiana. He was to pay for it by installments, and it was understood that Mr. Porter would not be "hard on him" in case of failure in promptness in some payments. But this did not lessen Mr. Harrison's sense of obligation, and he felt that the contract was just as binding as if his creditor had been unmerciful. He hoped to be able, in not many months, to pay the full amount, by the help of the income of his office added to that of his profession. He had only made one small payment, so far, and he realized the struggle before him, in spite of the aid of his office. The house stood on North New Jersey Street, near the corner of Vermont. It was larger and more commodious than the cottage in which they had made their home since coming to Indianapolis. In this house, which, so far as the terms were concerned, they could now call their own, their daughter was born, just a year before he became a candidate for the office of reporter — that is, in 1859.

Thus, with a fair income from his office and profession combined, and in a fair way to pay for his home, with a loving wife and two beautiful and dear children, this husband and father could have been no happier.

But he had scarcely "settled himself" in his office, when

the guns of Sumter startled the country. The Southern leaders had dashed down the fond hopes of their Northern friends—they would not be conciliated. Calm judgment had decided this before, while the States were "formally" seceding, if not even earlier: but now all could know the situation. Then came the call for 75,000 three-months volunteers. That meant, on the other hand, a hope, even in the hearts of the most patriotic and those of the coolest judgment in the North, that the rebellion was not so formidable but that it could soon be put down.

Benjamin Harrison wanted to go to the battle-field. He felt the spirit of patriotism rising in him, and the almost irrepressible desire to be in the nation's vanguard that characterized so many of the time. But it was only for three months; the rebellion would be ended by that time, and the welfare of the country assured, and business not retarded; and he was under a solemn contract which he would return in three months to find practically violated and impossible to meet, as agreed. Moreover, his office claimed him; and his canvass had been made with the understanding of fidelity on his part. And then his wife and children lived by what he earned, and the source of supplies for their sustenance would be cut off by his going. He felt that his duty was at home, at least until there was a more urgent demand for soldiers.

But he was none the less interested in the success of those who went, and his voice continued to be heard in favor of the Union. There was no part of Benjamin Harrison's history—education, training, early influences, reading, natural disposition, inheritance—that did not tend to make him every inch a patriot.

Chapter VII.

THE PATRIOT SOLDIER.

"THREE HUNDRED THOUSAND MORE" — THE EFFECT ON THE YOUNG PATRIOT — A VOLUNTEER RECRUITING AND ENLISTING SERVICE — COLONEL OF THE SEVENTIETH INDIANA — KENTUCKY AND TENNESSEE — FIRST BRIGADE OF THE THIRD DIVISION OF THE TWENTIETH ARMY CORPS — THE ATLANTA CAMPAIGN — THE BATTLE OF RESACA — "COME ON, BOYS!" — THE BATTLE OF PEACH TREE CREEK — A LETTER FROM GENERAL HOOKER TO THE SECRETARY OF WAR — ITS RESULT A PROMOTION — A PARTISAN INSULT AT HOME — THIRTY DAYS LEAVE OF ABSENCE — REËLECTION — SHERMAN AT SAVANNAH — AN OLD-FASHIONED BATTLE AT NARROWSBURG — VICTORY — JOINS SHERMAN — THE GENERAL RETURNS HOME.

Mr. Harrison always possessed the qualities of leadership, namely, the warmth of good-fellowship, and the spirit of discipline. As to the first, no boy or man who was ever with him long would fail to find it, and feel its glow and influence. But there was one quality he possessed, as grand and noble as any other, which, however, prevented the display of his warm-heartedness and friendship when there was no apparent occasion for them. This quality he inherited largely from his mother. It was what may be called "singleness of mind in study." From both ancestral branches he inherited the power to think. From his mother came not only a quiet, thoughtful disposition.

but the power of concentration — of forgetting all else but his subject, and giving the whole force of his mind to that. A natural and persistent student, this quality manifested itself more than any other. Hence to the more communicative he sometimes seemed cold, until he woke from his meditations. Then the more communicative always made a discovery — of a warm heart, communicative power, a good nature, a genial spirit, an enthusiasm and a power that won the lasting friendship of the man or boy.

As to the spirit of discipline, it was first manifested in his own yielding to it. He who loves discipline, loves it in his own life and affairs. To apply himself, to be regular in his habits, to submit himself to rules, were all natural to him. Order was a law of his mind. Add to this the study and the practical discipline of years, and we have all the conditions but one of the thorough soldier; for even courage is a natural concomitant of these qualities.

That one condition is the occasion; and when the occasion came, the soldier, Benjamin Harrison, chafed until he was free to use his abilities for his country. His patriotism was unbounded. Indignation for the insults that had been heaped on his country was burning within him; and the fact that he did not burst away from all restraint, and leave his wife and infant children to suffer alone, and involve himself in the complications of a broken contract, when he did not believe the government was in such serious danger but that the rebellion could be shortly put down by those who had gone, and were going, whose circumstances made it less of a sacrifice, shows the control he had over himself.

So the call of May 3d went by; then those of July 22d and 25th. Hope had risen as battles one after another had been fought, though now and then the Confederates were successful. But such battles as those of Philippi and Carrick's seemed to indicate what the Union arms might do in a decisive engagement. The defeat in the battle of Carthage, in Missouri, seemed small in comparison with the indications that the Union soldiers were about to be victorious. So great was this confidence everywhere that the call for the "decisive battle" went over the land in the cry, "On to Richmond!"

Mr. Harrison shared this confidence, and was impatient; but he knew enough to understand that decisive battles cannot be called at once. Still, as the armies took up the march from Washington and Alexandria, as premature as the movement was, even such men as Harrison were yet hopeful. Then came that dreadful disaster at Bull Run, which threw the country into gloom, and stopped the clamor of over-enthusiasts and complainers in the North. Mr. Harrison had not been among the over-enthusiasts nor the complainers, but he felt the keen sorrow that came to every loyal heart, and the bitter disappointment at the result; yet it did not shake his faith in what the Northern arms could do.

When the call for 500,000 came, there was such a generous response that instead of 500,000 there were nearly 700,000 soldiers enlisted. The rebellion had grown to enormous proportions, but few could realize that it was so well organized. Surely 700,000 faithful soldiers would be sufficient, even if three years were consumed in planning and executing.

So the summer and autumn went on, with varying success.

The engagements were generally between insignificant forces, as to numbers, and not comparatively important, though there were a few exceptions, notably the victory of Forts Hatteras and Clark, the defeat at Lexington, Missouri, and others. The winter and spring witnessed several more important battles. But the vastness of the rebel preparations began to be manifest, and also the measures necessary to overcome the rebel forces. The meaning of the intrigues of the preceding years began to be seen. A sense of the depth of the Southern purpose began to be felt. The embarrassments thrown in the way of the government previous to the attack on Fort Sumter began to reflect the shadow of the planning that had had its origin years before, while the Southern leaders were professing love for the Union.

The condition of affairs before Richmond was not flattering to the North. The Union was apparently in as much danger as ever. The desperation of the South would allow no yielding until their last hope was gone. But the indignation of the North, raised as the disclosures went on, had lulled for a time. A sort of apathy seemed to succeed its early outcry — the natural reaction from the intense excitement of the first months of the war.

Then came the call of the 2d of July, 1862, for "300,000 more." In many quarters there was awakening; but in Indiana there was apparently but little response. Governor Morton had by no means given up hope of raising the share allotted to the State, but he was half discouraged — at least sad at the apathy. While he was one day in his office, at this time, he was called on by Benjamin Harrison and William Wallace. A cousin of the latter desired a position of second lieutenant in one of the new regiments. The governor called them into a back room, and closed the door.

"Gentlemen," said he, "there is absolutely no response to Mr. Lincoln's last call for troops. The people do not appear to realize the necessities of the situation. Something must be done to break the spirit of apathy and indifference which now prevails. See here! Look at those workmen across the street, toiling to put up a new building, as if such things could be possible when the country itself is in danger of destruction."

Mr. Harrison was a man whose patriotism had never flagged. The interest of such a man does not depend upon popular excitement, and is not subject to the law of reaction. The strain upon his good reasons for staying at home had been heavy and constant. He now saw the real situation, and he knew that his duty to his country, in this extremity, outweighed his duty to his loved ones and his home. Before, this had not been the case, so far as the views commonly held were concerned. But when it came to the point that his country needed him at a special post for a special emergency, he could not feel that others ought to bear his burden. Besides, he could not now say that "the war will soon end, and there are more than enough to end it propitiously." That hope had fled. There was a call for troops, and the call was now for any who were willing to sacrifice; and he was willing. He said to the governor that he would help to raise the quota for the State, and he was certain he could raise a regiment.

"I feel certain you can," said Morton; "but I would not ask you to do more than that. I know your situation, and would not think of asking you to go yourself."

This was the feeling of a heart as loyal as any in the North as to Mr. Harrison's situation and his duty with reference to going.

"No," said Mr. Harrison. "If I make a recruiting speech, and ask any man to enlist, I propose to go with him, and stay with him as long as he stays, if I live so long."

"Well," said Mr. Morton, "you can command the regiment."

"I don't know that I shall want to," replied Mr. Harrison. "I have no military experience. We can see about that."

He went out with Mr. Wallace, and the two proceeded along the street. He went into a store and bought a military cap. He advertised a meeting at Masonic Hall. He hired a drummer and fifer, and stationed them before his law office. He hung out the American flag from his window. He converted his office into a recruiting station.

The city woke from its lethargy. Military caps appeared here and there, as if by magic. Very soon Company A, of the Seventieth Indiana, was made up. The meeting at the Masonic Hall was successful, and so were all Mr. Harrison's efforts. In an exceedingly short time the whole Seventieth Regiment was made up, and Mr. Harrison was placed at the head as its colonel. Within a month after he received his recruiting commission, on the 14th of July, he was with his regiment in Kentucky, ready for action.

Thus it was that the man who, because he had not been of the demonstrative temperament at the first, and had felt it his duty to remain at home, was the first man who could be depended on when the gloomiest hour came. Upon him fell the task of bringing back the enthusiasm of the people. He did not hesitate a moment when his duty lay clear before him. He did not, at that time, even consult with his wife. He went straight from the governor's office to find his military cap, the fife and drum, the hand-bills for the meeting and to swing out the stars and stripes.

His wife knew nothing of all this, until he went home at the regular hour, and told her. But she had never hindered him in any duty of his life; she would not hinder him now. She gave him her blessing. And when he left her for the field the tears and words at parting showed what a sacrifice she had made. He left his business affairs in good hands, and in as good shape as was possible. And when he was ordered to the front, he obeyed with as clear a conscience as he ever had in his life.

The Seventieth Indiana was composed of men without training or knowledge in military affairs. Colonel Harrison at once set about the task of drilling them. Every possible opportunity he put them under drill, and all his spare time was spent in studying military tactics.

When they arrived in Louisville, whither they had been hastened, they were scarcely able to load their Springfield and Enfield muzzle-loaders. It is said that Colonel Harrison ordered them to load in the depot before boarding the train for Bowling Green. They began to show to the rebel sympathizers standing about how awkward they were, and so received the sneers of the throng. Some of them attempting to drive down too much paper with their balls, found the balls wedged half-way down the barrels of their guns. They had recourse to the walls of the depot, against which they hammered the ends of the steel ramrods to drive down the balls. But at last they were on the train; and it was not many hours before they were in Bowling Green.

Colonel Harrison's regiment was at once assigned to the First (Ward's) Brigade of the Third Division of the Twentieth Army Corps. He began drilling his men again, and getting them ready for whatever service might be required of them. And this practice he kept up at every opportunity during his entire service, so that no troops were better in discipline than his. He also sought to advance himself in the science and art of war, for he felt in this, as well as in everything else he was ever called to do, that his duty was not done if energy at the supreme moment was not accompanied with all the knowledge and skill it had been possible for him to acquire. He sat up late at night, when possible, studying tactics, and during the day, when he could, kept his men under constant drill, perfecting them for more dangerous work. This was also particularly fortunate, as it was all needed for their hard and brilliant service afterwards.

It fell to the lot of the Seventieth Indiana — the first in the field in response to the July call — to be sent for some months' skirmishing through Kentucky and Tennessee, as a part of the Army of the Cumberland. Why this was done may not be known. It has been attributed to lack of sagacity on the part of the brave general under whom Harrison and his men were placed. In any case, these marches and skirmishes were not unimportant, and the service was not light. It was also a school for the regiment.

At last the Union armies of the West began to gather at Chattanooga. General Grant had been appointed lieutenant-general of all the armies, and had gone to the Potomac. General Sherman had taken command of the consolidated Western armies. For a time Nashville, Tennessee, was his headquarters and the base of operations, but it was not to remain so long. The rebel stronghold had been at Chattanooga, but the terrible battles of Chickamauga and Chattanooga had succeeded in dislodging them from it, and cooping up the Union forces there instead. Afterwards had come Sherman's reinforcements, and the brilliant storming and capturing of Lookout Mountain and Missionary Ridge; and thus Chattanooga had been made secure for occupancy by the Union troops, and important as the starting-point for a great campaign. Thence Sherman had gone down into Mississippi, capturing artillery and ammunition, destroying arsenals and railroads, and other things that had strengthened the rebel hands.

But before that memorable march began, the sad news was carried to the soldier in the field that Grandmother Harrison was dead. On the 25th of February, at the residence of her son, John Scott Harrison, near North Bend, Ohio, she had quietly laid down the burdens of a long and useful earthly life, and found the rest that remains for the faithful. Thus passed away the consort of William Henry Harrison, the sharer of his labors, his studies, his faith, and his successes and joys of life.

She was the last personal representative, in that family, of the early history of Indiana and Ohio, of the principles and issues based upon them that stirred the western heart and established the earnest and honest patriotism that has since characterized that part of our country. To her influence had been due the conservation of the principles of 1840 in the Harrison home. To her influence had been due, not a little, the instilling into the heart of the boy Ben the American principles that had now given to our army the manly and brave soldier and colonel, Benjamin Harrison. She could now lie down to rest with the sweet consciousness that the grand American qualities of her husband flourished yet in the life of her grandson.

The 7th of May, 1864, came. The armies moved out 100,000 strong. The divisions were commanded by Generals Thomas, McPherson, and Schofield. The boys began "Marching through Georgia." General Thomas' division, to which the Twentieth Army Corps belonged, had been massed at Ringgold, but was now before the rocky cliffs of Rocky Face, upon which Johnston had strongly fortified himself to dispute the passage of our armies through Buzzard Roost Gap below. On the 8th of May occurred the assault upon Rocky Face Ridge, and the terrible carnage that followed.

Then Johnston suddenly discovered that the wily general of the Union forces had been sending a division through Snake Creek Gap, some distance south, to the rear, and was threatening the railroad and Resaca. General Johnston withdrew from his works on Rocky Face, and quickly intrenched himself at Resaca.

Around Resaca, which was a small town on the Oostanula River, were hills, swamps, ravines, and the densest of thickets. All this ground was familiar to the enemy, while it was a strange land to the Union men. On the 15th of May the attack was made.

Perched on the crest of a hill that commanded the approach to the town, were rebel batteries that poured incessant fire into the Union ranks. It became positively necessary to silence them, but it would require brave men and a desperate struggle to do it. The order came to General Ward, of the First Brigade, and was repeated to Colonel Harrison.

Between the brigade and the batteries was a dense pine thicket and then a quarter of a mile of open field, so that Colonel Harrison knew nothing of the position of the enemy he was to charge. But he commanded his officers to dismount, and did so himself, as he knew it would be impossible to charge through that thicket on horseback. Then he said to the aide-de-camp who brought the order:

"You are familiar with the ground outside. I am not. Will you go ahead with me alone and show me this battery? For if I were to charge out now, I would be as apt to charge flank on to it as any other way."

The two had not proceeded far when a puff of smoke from the hill-crest, and the report which followed, indicated the position of the battery, and the ball screaming by, emphasized the importance of the order. Colonel Harrison instantly waved his sword to his men, and called in a voice that caught the ear and heart of every man within its reach:

"*Come on, boys!*"

Instantly four regiments came pouring after him. They crashed into the thicket and tore along, shouting meanwhile, and crying "forward!" to each other, all in the wildest disorder — for it was impossible to preserve the lines in that tangled underwood. All were full of the spirit of their leader. They soon emerged from the wood, and followed him on double-quick toward the hill, shouting in a way that meant death to the Confederates. It is seldom a command produces such effect so instantaneously as did that call "Come on, boys!" attended as it was by the flash of the sword and the ready attitude of the man. The Confederates saw it and felt it. and in desperation poured a murderous fire into the advancing columns. Shot and shell flew thick about the brave leader, and his men were falling fast. Still he went on, and had it not been for the spirit that seemed to go from him to his followers, one might have thought he was courting death. or shielding his brave men from it.

They rushed on under the savage fire; and only the roar of cannons and muskets. the cries of wounded and dying, the shouts of brave, determined men, and the dense smoke that hovered over and amidst them in clouds and hid the sight from heaven, might indicate that the battle was going on, until the outer Confederate lines were reached: then they leaped over the breastworks, and, hand-to-hand, they grappled with the desperate defenders. The cold steel bayonets shone no longer in sunlight. Muskets were clubbed — only pistol reports were heard above the din. Then all the enemy that were left in the outer works were taken prisoners.

But the work was apparently not half done, and that commander never left any work of his in that condition. The battery was still at the crest, and there was an impassable line of brushwood and stakes below it. Night fell, and the men were still busy. They were digging into the hill-side, and up toward the enemy's guns. If the enemy were feeling secure for a time, behind the barrier, and at all satisfied at the havoc made in the Union ranks — for fully a third of those brave soldiers lay wounded, dying, and dead on the field — evidently, also, a counter feeling of uneasiness rested upon them, for the spirit with which the assault had been made, and the contest kept up, and the carrying of their outer lines, meant that the Union colonel and his soldiers did not intend to be thwarted.

The tunnels broke through the hill behind the works. The guns were lowered into them. And when the morning came, and General Sherman looked to see the battle for the hill-top to be renewed, lo! the work was done — the enemy had withdrawn.

Thus did Colonel Harrison perform his duty at Resaca. He illustrated in his strict obedience how a man can be a free and independent man, untrammeled in his thoughts and resources, and still obey. His enthusiasm, his making the cause his own, his fertility of method in carrying out, all showed him the grand man that he was.

Johnston withdrew his forces across the Oostanula, and the victorious Union soldiers marched into Resaca, with their prisoners and captured guns. In a few days Johnston was followed by our armies, which began to concentrate about Adairsville and Cassville, while he took his stand down on the Etow River. After some skirmishing, however, he crossed that river and went on to Allatoona Pass and Pumpkinvine Creek. At both those points, and also at Dallas, his men were the greater sufferers.

Thus the advance toward Atlanta went on until Sherman came to the mountains that sheltered Marietta. He soon had Pine and Lost Mountains for his trophies, and on the 27th of June made a vigorous assault on Kenesaw Mountain, where Johnston was now intrenched behind brushwood, fallen trees, natural barriers, and works that had taken six months to make almost impregnable. This was the "citadel" of Marietta. On July 2d, another assault was made and then Sherman began moving his forces south toward the Chattahoochie, when Johnston hastened from his now useless fortress to intercept the way to Atlanta. So our troops marched into Marietta.

After some days, during which the two armies were camped, one on each side of the Chattahoochie, while, for a time, it was dangerous for a soldier to venture from behind the works on either side, our forces succeeded in crossing. But bloody days awaited them before the few miles to Atlanta could be compassed.

In the hard fighting of the previous days, Colonel Harrison and his regiment had been conspicuous. He was in the corps commanded by General Joe Hooker, which led the "march to the sea," and was therefore the first in the assaults. He was in the Third Division, commanded by General Thomas, and that division became famous for its bravery and successes, as it was always at the front. He was in the First Brigade, under Ward, which consisted of the One Hundred and Twenty-ninth Illinois, One Hundred and Fifth Illinois, Seventy-ninth Ohio, and the Seventieth Indiana, and which did most valiant service in the van of our victorious Western armies in those days.

His character, in those trying times, stood every test. On the field he was the same as at home, around his fireside, or in his church. No better testimony can be given to the character of any soldier or commander than this, given by one of those who followed him in those dark days:

"One scene has always lived in my memory. Our old chaplain, Allen, a man who was beloved by all the boys, and for whom almost every man in the regiment would have given his life, conducted service on Sunday with Colonel Harrison, as he was then, and Lieutenant-Colonel Sam Merrill assisting. I have often heard General Harrison offer up the prayer for the boys' welfare and protection down there on those Southern fields, so far away from home, and many times have heard him address the boys in place of the chaplain. Never, to my knowledge, in all the trying times of war, did I ever see one thing from him unbecoming a Christian. I think the battle-field and the camp bring out what there is in a man about as well as anything can, and I have seen General Harrison tested in every way. As a soldier, courageous, sympathetic, and enduring, the army had no better."

His care and sympathy for the boys won all their hearts. He never took authority over them that did not belong to him. Many instances could be related of his generous and sympathetic help which he rendered to the sick, or wounded, or dying. One or two must suffice at this point.

In the battle of Chickamauga, a captain in the Seventy-ninth Indiana Volunteers was seriously wounded. Colonel Harrison informed the captain's brother, a sergeant, of it, and ordered him to report at headquarters. The colonel had his own horse saddled, and telling the sergeant to mount, he bade him hasten to his brother. In a short time Colonel Harrison followed, and going up to the wounded man, he greeted him sympathetically, and said:

"Captain, you are badly wounded, and must get home. You have been at the front, and of course have no money. Here is a hundred dollars; take it, and get home."

At another time Colonel Harrison found a soldier — a total stranger — on the field, seriously wounded. He told him to go to the hospital, and then added: "You will need money — here is twenty dollars."

A time was now coming when these rare qualities of the colonel were to be manifested again; but before that time there was to be another terrible struggle.

General Johnston had been removed from the command of the Southern army at Atlanta, and General Hood had been appointed in his place. The rebels now made every possible effort to save the city. They sallied out at unexpected moments; they harassed our troops in almost every quarter; they brought on many and serious skirmishes. From the time Sherman's men stepped upon the southern bank of the Chattahoochie until the fall of Atlanta, blood scarcely ceased to flow.

On July 20th, during the hard-fought battle at Peach Tree Creek, the same signal courage, valor, and judgment that had shown themselves in Colonel Harrison at Resaca, were again displayed. While he was holding his forces in reserve, not thinking that immediate service would be demanded of them, and yet ready for any warning, he ordered them to stack their arms. A skirmish line was sent out, and the brigade was busy at dinner; suddenly they heard firing, and looking up they saw upon a hill, some distance away, the men of the skirmish line waving their caps, and heard their shouts for assistance. A large detachment of Hood's forces was over beyond the hill. It would not do to let them come over and attack him at the foot of the hill. Not an instant was to be lost. The battle might depend upon him. General Hooker was already sorely pressed. Colonel Harrison did not wait for orders. He swung himself into line before his men, and cried:

"Come on, boys! We've never been licked yet, and we won't begin now. We haven't much ammunition, but if necessary we can give them the cold steel, and before we get licked we will club them down; so come on."

They charged up the hill after "Little Ben," getting ready as they ran. They were joined by the skirmish line, eager for the fray. Just over the hill, among the trees, and behind a rail fence, they saw the Confederates crouching like tigers. They charged on them, and for half an hour there was hot and terrible fighting. Finally the Confederate force was repulsed. But the gallant brigade lost 250 men in that short thirty minutes. This was the decisive stroke; and the day was soon won.

The next day the fiery General Hooker rode the lines, and

seeing Harrison, he called out with an oath that he would have him made a brigadier-general for yesterday's work.

Later General Hooker was as good as his word. Before many months he sent the following letter to Washington:

HEADQUARTERS NORTHERN DEPARTMENT,
CINCINNATI, O., Oct. 31, 1864.

HON. E. M. STANTON, *Secretary of War:*

I desire to call the attention of the Department to the claims of Col. Benjamin Harrison, of the Seventieth Indiana Volunteers, for promotion to the rank of brigadier-general volunteers.

Colonel Harrison first joined me in command of a brigade of Ward's division in Lookout Valley, preparatory to entering upon what is called the Campaign of Atlanta. My attention was first attracted to this young officer by the superior excellence of his brigade in discipline and instruction, the result of his labor, skill, and devotion. With more foresight than I have witnessed in any officer of his experience, he seemed to act upon the principle that success depended upon the thorough preparation in discipline and *esprit* of his command for conflict more than on any influence that could be exerted in the field itself, and when collision came his command vindicated his wisdom as much as his valor. In all the achievements of the Twentieth Corps in that campaign, Colonel Harrison bore a conspicuous part. At Resaca and Peach Tree Creek, the conduct of himself and command were especially distinguished. Colonel Harrison is an officer of superior abilities and of great professional and personal worth. It gives me great favor to commend him favorably to the Honorable Secretary, with the assurance that his preferment will be a just recognition of his services and martial accomplishments.

Very respectfully, your obedient servant,

JOSEPH HOOKER,
Major-General Commanding.

The justness of this high praise was fully appreciated by

the troops under Mr. Harrison, and by all his associate and superior officers.

But it was not alone in the courageous charge at Peach Tree Creek that Colonel Harrison won glory there. He discovered, when the fight was over that day that his surgeon and assistants had by some means become entangled with another brigade, and could not get back ; and his field hospital was full of men — wounded and dying. He could not wait to find surgeons. He took off his coat, gathered his tent, tore the latter into strips, and began bandaging wounds. He had words of cheer for every despondent wounded soldier, sympathy for his pain, and tenderness for his wounds. He received dying messages, and, in short, administered comfort wherever it was possible. It is said that when the surgeons arrived, they found him, his bare arms covered with blood, still going about attending to these duties.

This record is but in accordance with his record during his entire army service.

He continued with the army until the fall of Atlanta, September 1st. His services were conspicuous for their bravery and valor. He never dishonored the record made at Resaca and Peach Tree Creek. Moreover, he was popular with officers and privates. He knew "the boys," and never, except in the performance of official duty, assumed to be in any way above them.

Up to the fall of Atlanta, Colonel Harrison had asked no leave of absence, but had remained at his post, ready for any orders. But about this time he heard from his friends in Indiana, that he had been nominated again for reporter of the

Supreme Court. Ordinarily perhaps, he might not have considered this a good reason for returning home. But during his absence, he had received a wanton insult from the Democratic Supreme Court in Indiana, in their declaring the office of reporter vacant, and electing another to the position, solely because the rightful official was fighting the battles of his country. It was natural that he should want to give a proper rebuke to that spirit, and assert himself by securing an election again.

So he obtained leave for thirty days' absence, and receiving orders from the War Department to report to Governor Morton, he returned to Indianapolis. Glad indeed was he to see his wife and children, and they were rejoiced to see him again. After a short rest at home with them, he began a vigorous canvass for the reporter's office. Nor did he forget the issue of the general campaign as he made his speeches. He forgot, rather, his special purpose in coming home.

But that purpose was accomplished, nevertheless, he receiving a handsome majority over his opponent. To his influence, also, was due, in no small degree, the large majority which Indiana gave to Lincoln in the succeeding November.

After his election, he returned to the seat of war. Soon after the November election came the fall of Savannah. The expedition of Sherman was terminating gloriously. Hardee and his rebel troops evacuated the city on the night of the 20th of November. Sherman brought with him into the city 1,000 prisoners, 150 cannons, 190 railroad cars, twelve locomotives, much ammunition, three steamers, 32,000 bales of cotton, and 15,000 slaves. These things had been gathered along the route from Chattanooga, and especially from Atlanta. But the hardest fighting and the most difficult marching had been done between these two places: and Colonel Harrison, now General Harrison, had borne no small part, therefore, in making the expedition successful.

Simultaneous with the fall of Savannah, General Hood, with his Confederate forces, turned backward and marched toward Pulaski, Tennessee. Here Generals Schofield and Smith were concentrating their Union forces in order to oppose him. Ten days after the evacuation of Savannah, the battle of Franklin was fought, in which the Confederates were defeated with a loss, in killed, wounded, and prisoners, of more than five thousand. Then came the sharp conflict near Murfreesboro', Tennessee, early in December; and soon after the decisive battle of Nashville, on December 15th and 16th. In this battle General Harrison and his brigades bore a most conspicuous and important part. He led in the bloody conflicts, and Hood was driven from Tennessee. This put an end to the war in that State, and practically in the West. Henceforth the field was the Southern Atlantic States.

About this time, General Harrison heard of the sickness of his two children with scarlet fever. He hastened home, and soon had the satisfaction of witnessing their recovery. He then received orders to join Sherman, who was yet in Savannah. He started, this time with his wife and children, to go by way of New York. On the way he himself was stricken down with the scarlet fever. He left the train at Narrowsburg, and there during the coldest of the New York winter, he fought the disease in the old-fashioned manner.

It was a small way station, and the conveniences were few. His physician was seventeen miles away, and could not be in constant attendance. His nurse was an orderly who had attended him, and who was experienced also in nursing. But soon the orderly was taken down with the disease, and nursing devolved upon Mrs. Harrison. No wife was ever more faithful, and soon by her care he was able to be up. By spring he was able to travel; and was soon on the way towards North Carolina.

Meanwhile, Sherman had marched triumphantly from Savannah to Wilmington, North Carolina; Columbia had surrendered; Charleston had been evacuated by the rebel forces, and the American flag waved over the ruins of Sumter. Sherman's army was coming up from the South: part from the southeast, part from the victories of Nashville. Grant's army was pushing the enemy from the North. It was evident that the end was not far off.

General Harrison was in time to take part in the closing and triumphant movements of Sherman's army, and the war. On the 9th of April occurred the surrender of General Lee's army to Grant at Appomattox. Then came the darkest—at least the saddest—day of the Rebellion—the 15th of April. The evening before was heard the shot at Washington that rang louder than the cannons of all the battles, and on the 15th Abraham Lincoln, to whom, more than to any other, was due the prosecution of the war to its glorious assurance of success, breathed out his life.

On the 26th of April, 1865, at Durham's Station, North Carolina, General Johnston surrendered to General Sherman.

General Harrison was present on that occasion, having taken a part in bringing about that welcome result. Thus finally triumphed the Northern armies.

It was a grand review that was held in Washington soon after. Four of the darkest pages in the history of the world had been written since the review there at the beginning of the war. Now the banners were riddled and torn, the swords were broken and stained, the guns were battered and the uniforms were old, and torn, and tattered. But every thread of the old flags was more sacred than the brightest flag that had ever floated from the dome of the Capitol. The soldiers stepped more proudly than four years before; and altogether, Washington never saw a grander sight. Nor was there a prouder heart there that day than that of Benjamin Harrison. And no man stepped more gladly, for there was not a more patriotic soldier, nor one who had performed a more conscientious and faithful service, than he. So the soldiers went home.

ABRAHAM LINCOLN,

THE FIRST REPUBLICAN PRESIDENT OF THE UNITED STATES.

CHAPTER VIII.

A LAWYER OF EXPERIENCE.

TAKES UP ROUTINE OF OFFICE OF REPORTER — A VIEW OF THE SITUATION — GENERAL HARRISON RESUMES PRACTICE OF LAW — SOME NOTED CASES — THE CHARACTER OF THE MAN — THE CITIZEN AND CHRISTIAN — CONFIDENCE OF ASSOCIATES — FAMILY — MR. FISHBACK LEAVES THE FIRM — "PORTER, HARRISON & HINES" — "HARRISON & HINES" — "HARRISON, HINES & MILLER" — THE "CLEM" CASE.

IMMEDIATELY on returning home, General Harrison took up the routine of his office. He felt that his long absence made diligence more incumbent upon him — but it was only his keen sense of duty, and the remembrance of the situation in which he had left his affairs for the army. His sensitive conscience was thoroughly satisfied with the course he had taken.

In 1861 and 1862, he had kept pace with his work in the office. He had prepared volumes XV. and XVI. of reports, and had almost finished volume XVII. It was now like taking up the office for the first time, so far as the work on hand was concerned; but his previous experience made it easier than before.

Notwithstanding the stormy period of the reconstruction, which now began, the difficult questions of finance, and grumbling speeches of the Democratic party — always warning of failures that never came—people of all parties now felt more secure in their homes and business than they had felt for years. The shadow of the vanishing war-cloud did not depress. When that cloud had been looming up before the awful storm, no one knew what it portended. Doubt and fear were in every heart. Though the Northern Democrats sympathized with the Southern people, so far as the mere questions of the right of states to secede and the slavery extension were concerned, they dreaded the war and its results. Though they all blamed the Republican party for the war, and many of them sympathized outright with rebel feelings and threw the weight of their influence against the Northern arms, they did not want the war in the North, and dreaded the frequent menacing attitude of the Southern armies toward the Northern States. In spite of their ungrateful professions, they now rejoiced in the security of a country saved by the Union soldiers: and in their hearts they felt a gratitude their prejudice and partyism prevented their expressing. General Harrison's reputation, therefore, had not really suffered with the Democrats, and was greater than ever with the Republicans. The gratitude of the latter was openly and honestly shown. The soldiers of Indiana all received the most cordial ovation the grateful people could give them. There were also other brave Indiana officers — captains, colonels, generals — but none of them were more honored than General Harrison.

Immediately on his return he took up again the profession of law. A partnership was again formed with Mr. Fishback, this time including the Honorable A. G. Porter, and the name of the firm became Porter, Harrison & Fishback. There was not a better combination of talent in the state. Mr. Harrison bore his full share of responsibility, and did his full portion of the work, notwithstanding his official duties. He slighted neither the one nor the other. It would be impossible to suppose, from the habits long formed, that he could bring himself to face an uncompleted task at the hour for its completion. He sat up many a night until near morning; he lost not a moment during the day in studying his work, and he never failed to be ready at the appointed time.

Some of the most noted cases before the courts of Indiana during the years from 1865 to 1870 had, on one side or the other, these lawyers; and the best talent of the country was often arrayed against them. But Mr. Harrison and colleagues, if for the plaintiff, in most cases secured conviction; if for the defendant, in most cases succeeded in clearing. There were clients that deserved conviction. and yet deserved a full chance, and the best talent on their side. In such cases all was done for them that honest lawyers could do — frequently the lightening of the penalty. This firm did much in allaying the prejudice against lawyers as a class, that existed so generally in Indiana. The feeling prevailed, especially among the poorer class of people, that all lawyers were dishonest. Such firms as that of Porter, Harrison & Fishback proved that the honest law of demand and supply was as steady in the lawyer's trade as in any other. There are more men with honest cases than get justice. When a lawyer becomes noted for his faithfulness and honesty, he may refuse all dishonest clients, and still have more than he can attend to.

This explains why Mr. Harrison did not become a brilliant meteor at the start of his profession in 1854. He chose the old-fashioned rough path of honesty, that led indeed more surely to success, but to success at a greater distance. He seemed to think this method the only one he could tolerate. As he avoided the path to fame that led through the heralding of his ancestry, so he avoided that which led through anything but effort and genuine merit. He had, indeed, a different and more conscientious reason for avoiding the littleness and dishonesty of pettifoggery, but it was repulsive to his sense of independence, nevertheless.

The lawyer in the office now was not the same that was in the office before the war. Then the uncertain term "rising young lawyer" might fitly be applied to him. Now he was older; his army service had given him a rugged, but valuable experience with men; he had broader views of law, of politics, of life; he had his past experience as a lawyer firmly set in memory and character. He could now, with fitness, be called an experienced lawyer; and that term conveys an impression that he was more than a mere lawyer: he was a citizen, a man among men, a master of his profession. His character as a citizen was of the highest type. He loved his home, his wife, and children. He instilled into his children's hearts those principles of honor and integrity, without which no youth can grow up a benefit to others, a noble citizen. His home was a little republic; and if he and his wife held the ruling power in their hands, they deemed that they held also the education, the training, and the welfare of their subjects in their hands. Thus educating, instilling, their commands became mere guides to the children's desires; and in the highest sense they, in this way, represented them. There was none of that stern, rigid inforcement of rule, before the child was taught the meaning of the rule, or the faith and confidence that saw in their superior wisdom the highest reason why the rule should be followed. So, in his home, its organization, its government, its teachings, Mr. Harrison proved himself a true citizen of his country.

But he did this, also, in the carrying out of his own immediate public duties. He was a faithful, trusty lawyer. He was faithful in his business affairs. He was a faithful friend to the poor. He was faithful to the needs of his town, of his county, of his State, ot his country. He considered himself a part of the city, and held himself ready to bear even more than his share in its service. In a like attitude he stood toward his country. In all his conduct toward others, he manifested no selfishness. But he was no fawning servant of men. He conformed to no unreasonable whims or demands of any class. He stood on his own plane, and reached down, or up, or out, toward others. He was himself, Benjamin Harrison, or nobody. He was never guilty of wearing old clothes, covered with dirt, having the legs of his trousers in his muddy boots, and hayseeds in his whiskers, on purpose to win the affections and votes of farmers. If, for any reason, he had little money, and could not afford any but old clothes, and if tramping through mud had made it necessary to wear his trouser legs in his boots, and if by working, or otherwise, hayseeds had been scattered over him, he would not have been ashamed before any man, or if compelled to face it, any audience—for that would have been a predicament for which he was not to blame, and in which there was no dishonor, and he would have been himself. But if he must violate his own tastes for cleanliness, and change his own customs, and be what he was not, in order to win the farmers, or any other class, then he did not want their affections nor their votes. His soul revolted from that species of hypocrisy, as well as from all other species.

He was not ashamed to be himself. Whatever his tastes, or opinions, or faith, he was not ashamed to own them. He and his family were members of the First Presbyterian Church, of Indianapolis, and he was always to be found at his post. He was one of the most faithful leaders in the church. He belonged to the regular officers of the church, and taught the large Bible class in the Sunday School. His manner of teaching showed his great interest in that work: he sought to interest every member of the class, by asking the questions personally, and by personal talk, and the class in general by illustration, and being constantly at work; and he brought such thorough knowledge of the Scriptures, and especially of the subject of the day to his class, as showed that his interest extended beyond the class-room and the recitation hour. He was a Christian at home. He taught it to his children; he practiced it in his conduct toward them, toward his wife, toward all guests, and in his personal life; he never failed to give thanks at table, and kept up family prayers. He was a Christian abroad. He practiced it in his profession, and in all his relations to others. In other words, he was thoroughly unselfish in his conduct toward his God and his fellow-men — that was his Christianity.

No man ever had the confidence of his associates in profession and business, more than did Mr. Harrison. He had been tried in all his opinions, and in his integrity at every point, and had not failed. His magnetism was the magnetism of character; men were drawn to him always through the consciousness of his thorough reliability. It was like a safe shelter from a storm to be in his presence and feel that here was a man that could be depended on. Though one might not agree with his opinions, yet one felt that whatever his opinions were, they would be carried out, and that all his conduct would be consistent with them.

What has been written of him may also be written of his family, as to character. His faithful wife was a companion indeed in his thoughts, his opinions, his methods, his religion, his life. As a consequence of parental influence, and partly, also as an inheritance, the son and daughter were of the same convictions, and sincerity, and character. It was one of those families in which the guest has impressions of the beauty and sacredness of the family and the home. His son was now approaching the age of sixteen, when boys begin to consider themselves young men, and feel the restraints of home. But in Russell Harrison there was little of such chafing. He loved his home, his father, mother, and sister, and the sacred place. The daughter was yet scarce fourteen, but was already somewhat educated and accomplished, though in manner and character she was far from the premature dreams of "society."

In 1870 Mr. Fishback left the firm to take charge of the Indianapolis *Journal*. He afterwards resigned control of that paper to become editor of the St. Louis *Globe-Democrat*. He left his testimony in Indiana as to the ability and honesty of

General Harrison as a lawyer; and has since, in a direct manner, testified to his high qualities. On his retirement, Judge Hines, a lawyer of no mean ability and reputation, entered the firm, which then became "Porter, Harrison & Hines." Subsequently Mr. Porter retired from the firm, which continued until 1874 as "Harrison & Hines." In that year Mr. Miller joined the firm, and it was "Harrison, Hines & Miller." Mr. Porter also bore testimony to the high character and worth, and to the great abilities as a lawyer, of his partner, General Harrison. The following words of Mr. Porter refer both to his early and his subsequent career as a lawyer: "Amplitude of preparation, large views of questions, the widest knowledge of his profession that could be acquired in such a time, distinguished him, and he rose rapidly in his profession." The following testimony of Mr. Porter, applies to Mr. Harrison's ability as an orator in politics, as well as at the bar: "With all his eloquence as an orator, he never spoke for oratorical effect; his words always went like a bullet to the mark. He reminds one of the saying of the great Irish orator and patriot, O'Connell, that a good speech is a good thing, but the verdict is *the* thing. He therefore always pierced the core of every question that he discussed, and in every contest in which he was engaged he fought to win." Again, said Mr. Porter of him: "He is in every respect a complete lawyer."

Further testimony may be given. A gentleman of large legal attainments, and years of practical observation, once said of Mr. Harrison: "His power to go through a case beats any man's I ever saw. He will take the testimony of a case stretching over days, or weeks, and will sift every particle of evidence pertaining to the various heads to which it belongs, according to the points or plans of battle he has laid out. Everything *pro* and *con*, by every witness, is thus grouped, and the whole marshaled in order — as one might say, by division, brigade, regiment, company, and all bearing down on the assault." Said another lawyer of ability and experience, concerning him: "I have not often seen Harrison equaled as a cross-examiner, and I have never seen but one instance in which I thought him surpassed." Another witness testifies: "He is regarded by his fellow-members of the Indiana bar, irrespective of party, as a judicious counsellor, an able advocate, a keen cross-examiner, and a man of indefatigable industry. He is full of resource. He never says anything imprudent himself, but he is quick as lightning to catch at the imprudence of an opponent. Yet, with all his skill, he has never been accused of unfairness." The testimony of his partner, Mr. Miller, will be sufficient to complete the list: "General Harrison is always cool and level-headed. He never loses his balance. He is always, under the most trying circumstances, self-possessed and of unshaken poise. He is most thorough in his preparation, always making himself complete master of a case. He is a most searching and efficient cross-examiner, and yet he is always quiet and pleasant, as if in ordinary conversation. He never bull-dozes, and I have never heard of a witness who called him discourteous."

His reputation as a cross-examiner is merited. It is said that on once being asked by a student to define the theory of cross-examination, he replied. "It is the application of logic to an illogical mind." His success in that line, therefore, was due, not to the entanglement of witnesses, but to his marking out the logical lines, and so hedging them about that witnesses would be compelled to follow them.

Instances may be given, showing how others not lawyers regarded his ability. In a certain case, near the beginning of his practice, he was opposed by a number of old and able lawyers. An Irishman, who was keenly observing the trial, said: "I loike that little Harrison. He has so many ways. When they bate 'im wan way, he bates them anoother way; and they can't cahner 'im at all, at all!" And the qualities he had when a young lawyer, he now manifested in a greater degree.

A poor German laborer once brought a case to Mr. Harrison, who undertook it for him, carried it through several trials, and on the appeal of the opposition to the Supreme Court, won it there; all at great expense of time and money. The German paid the fee as agreed; and Mr. Harrison was satisfied. But the client, who was a cabinet-maker, built a very costly book-case and presented it to his lawyer, in testimony of his appreciation of his ability and his gratefulness for what had been done for him.

One of the most prominent cases of the period now under considerattion, was what was known as the "Mulligan Case." The plaintiff had been charged with treason, brought before a military commission, tried and acquitted. They then brought suit for damages in the United States Court. But they found opposed to them, conducting the defense for the State, General Harrison, who, by his manner of conducting it, and especially his great speech on May 22, 1871, cut down their "damages" to one cent and costs.

But perhaps a more noted case was that of Nancy E. Clem, which began the same year. This woman had deliberately plotted and carried out the murder of a man named Young, under circumstances of the most horrifying barbarity, but also of some mystery. She had accomplished this murder in 1868, at a lonely place called Cold Spring, not far from Indianapolis. On the second indictment, on which Mr. Harrison was called for the prosecution, the defense pleaded acquittal on the former indictment, but the State demurred, the demurrer was sustained, and the defendant pleaded not guilty, and filed an exception. As a result of this, and several subsequent trials, through the efforts of General Harrison, she was sentenced for life to the State prison.

By a change of venue, the case was taken from Marion to Boone County, and tried at Lebanon before Judge Davidson. This circumstance, with others attending it, and the peculiar circumstances of the murder, and the plea of former acquittal, made this, perhaps, the most celebrated murder case Indiana ever had.

An incident of the first trial shows what complete mastery Mr. Harrison always had of his subjects, how he took his cases thoroughly in hand, how he knew confidently from the first the winning course, and how, in this case, he manifested a tact and shrewdness far beyond those of one lawyer of much larger experience, and at that time of greater reputation — Daniel W. Voorhees. In stating the case, Lawyer Harrison boldly outlined the whole theory of the prosecution. In this he manifested such apparent lack of policy, and so apparently put the case in the hands of the defense, that Mr. Voorhees was highly elated.

"Harrison is a very able lawyer," said Mr. Voorhees, "but he is over-rated. He has laid himself open here — given his case away in the start."

"Don't be too sure," was the reply of a friend. "He knows what he is about."

"You will see," said Mr. Voorhees.

But the case went on, and Mr. Harrison listened carefully to the masterly speech of Mr. Voorhees, and took notes. When he arose for the closing argument, he took these points, one by one, and exposed them in the light of the theory of the prosecution which he had been so careful to state. This was another time in his life when Mr. Harrison taught Mr. Voorhees, to that gentleman's cost, that Mr. Voorhees had far *under-rated* Mr. Harrison.

There was at one time a noted and very important case before the United States Court at Chicago. Associated with Mr. Harrison in the case was George Hoadly, recently the governor of Ohio. On account of being compelled to leave, Mr. Harrison had the privilege of the first speech, which he delivered, and immediately after which he retired from the court-room. Mr. Hoadly then withdrew from the argument, signifying that Mr. Harrison had so thoroughly done the work that nothing more in that line was necessary.

CHAPTER IX.

VICTORY IN DEFEAT.

THE CAMPAIGN OF 1876 — THE NATIONAL CANDIDATES — BEFORE AND AFTER THE CRISIS OF 1873 — THE CAMPAIGN IN INDIANA — THE CORRUPTION FUND — THE STATE TICKET — A CHANGE — A POPULAR DEMAND — TASK NO OTHER COULD FILL — AN ENERGETIC CANVASS — INCIDENTS — "COME ON, BOYS!" — THE RESULT A VICTORY IN DEFEAT — ACQUAINTANCE IN THE STATE — IN DEMAND FOR THE GENERAL CAMPAIGN.

IN 1875, the friends of General Harrison began to urge him to make the race for governor of Indiana the following year. In answer to a letter from the Honorable L. M. Campbell, insisting that the State had claims upon him, and asking that he permit his name to be used, he wrote the following reply, which shows not only the lack of office-seeking qualities in him, but his patriotism :

HONORABLE L. M. CAMPBELL, DANVILLE, IND.

My Dear Sir: Your letter of the 25th ultimo has remained unanswered until now for want of earlier leisure. After a careful consideration of the matter in every view in which it has presented itself, I have arrived at this conclusion, viz.: To decline to allow my name to go before the convention in connection with the nomination for governor. In announcing this conclusion, I have only one regret, and that is the temporary disappointment of some very warm personal friends, among the oldest and most partial of whom I reckon yourself. To these, and to the somewhat wider circle of political friends who have with great kindness urged me to be a candidate, I feel under a very real obligation. Some of the reasons which have led me to this conclusion are already known to you. I need only say here that my personal affairs are not in a situation to make it wise for me to abandon the pursuit of my profession to engage in such a canvass. You will not think that I am without a proper sense of public obligation, or devoid of interest in the success of the Republican party. If any should so think, the time I have given to the public service, and the humble part I have taken in every political campaign since 1860, must witness for me. In every important campaign which our State convention will inaugurate, I hope to have some part; but you must allow me to follow, not to lead.

It could hardly be possible that the party who has rejected the greatest idea of our immortal declaration — the equality of all men before the law — and has denied the right to preserve by force the national unity, will, in this year of great memories, be called to administer our national affairs.

Please accept for yourself, and for all those who have united in your request, my thanks and good wishes.

Very sincerely yours,

BENJAMIN HARRISON.

INDIANAPOLIS, December 1, 1875.

The year of 1876 was, in many respects, a most remarkable political year. The candidates for the national offices were, on the Republican side, Rutherford B. Hayes and William A. Wheeler; and on the Democratic side, Samuel J. Tilden and Thomas A. Hendricks. In addition, there was a Greenback ticket with General J. B. Weaver for President, and Samuel Carey for Vice-President.

The Greenback movement in the West was very strong that year; and it was drawing most of its voters from the Republican ranks. There was great fear that the proposed resumption of specie payment would bring disaster upon the country. It was at a time of great financial depression — one of the closing years of gloom following the financial crash of 1873. The excitement in Indiana was especially great. It was also the year preceding the great strikes and the riots, that threatened destruction to railroad and other property, and even to the lives of peaceful citizens; and already, the designing mob-leaders were fanning the flames of discontent, while unfortunate hot-headed men, more innocent than the leaders, were suffering themselves to be drawn into the vortex of lawlessness.

Some special facts in connection with this state of things, deserve to be mentioned here, in order that certain influences of the campaign may be accounted for. The years immediately preceding the great panic were years of enormous speculation in Indiana. Hundreds, and even thousands, of men who had never before considered it a moral business, were drawn into the whirl of excitement, and began to speculate on a larger or smaller scale. Fortunes were made and lost in a day. Thousands and millions of dollars changed hands with great rapidity. Poor men entered the list "for homes," and being caught by excitement in the first blush of success, were carried into the life they had always condemned.

Indianapolis was the centre of the craze — for a craze it was. Property rose to unheard-of values in an hour. Suburbs sprang up, as if in a night; and one looked out in the morning, and where there had been desolate soil, or fine pastures where quiet farmers grazed their cattle, there were now fine mansions and fine villages, in successful imitation of the noted suburbs of the oldest cities in the land. The population of Indianapolis ran up from 48,000 to more than a hundred thousand. Workmen came in on every train, from every part of the State, and there was always a demand for more of them, and all at high wages. Workmen of the city and elsewhere became independent, ceased to work, and began to speculate and imitate the social grandeeism of those who, from below, they had always condemned. All prices of real estate were fictitious, but few engaged in the speculations believed it, and those few promised warning friends that they would cease the business when this one more trade was consummated, for it was about to bring them into independence—then the crash might come; they would be secure. But though the independence came, the fever for ventures would not allay, and they plunged in again. So it continued until 1873, and even later. In that year the crisis came.

One case will illustrate the situation then: A man with good sense and moral and Christian principles, and, withal, a good business man, having some money, invested in real estate, and sold and found himself rich. He then purchased a beautiful tract in a fine suburb. The tract consisted of several acres, in which were fruit trees, a grove of maples, and a large house of just the home-like style to suit him. It was all most beautiful, indeed. He paid for it $16,000, and determined to keep it always for a homestead, while he used other money for speculation. So he moved his family, and felt at home. Then he took the sum he had remaining, and invested in other real estate; and being a shrewd man, he increased his wealth at every turn. At last, in one venture, he invested all he had, except his homestead; and the investment was a large one, for the man was now independent. But then the crash came.

He saw his danger and tried to avert it. With three thousand dollars he could make his "turn," and save his money, and "come out ahead." But the panic had struck everywhere, and he could not borrow anything. He had but one resource — to mortgage his homestead. This he did — for three thousand dollars — and he sank that. He came out with nothing, and worse, for he was in debt. He finally succeeded in borrowing seven hundred dollars from a friend, with which to set up in his old trade. And so he began life anew, when nearly fifty years of age.

This was only one case in a thousand. This man became a Greenbacker; for most of those who suffered at that time, either laid the blame at the door of the government, or felt that "fiat" money, to take the place of that which, being withdrawn from them by the shrewder capitalists, lay in Eastern vaults, would relieve them. Those who had property could not sell it. Huge mansions were occupied rent free, for the taking care of them. Others that had cost many thousand dollars in building were rented at a few dollars a month. The great mass of workingmen who had moved into Indianapolis, were out of work. Many of them, having sold their farms and bought homes in the city, now found themselves with nothing to bring an income, and unable to get back what they had paid for city "homes."

The discontent that followed may be imagined. Bread! bread! bread! became the cry everywhere. Everything was in confusion. Men who had been respectable men in their homes in other parts of the State, were now so excited and exasperated that they talked about burning and revenge; and when the strike of 1877 came on, they declared they did not blame the rioters, and would not if they burnt the city. It was easy for men in that condition of mind to say and do and believe what they would not in calmer moods.

The crisis of 1873 spread its baneful influence everywhere. Not only speculators, but honest business men and honest farmers, suffered. Hence, the Democrats who had been complainers and fault-finders since 1860, found a good field in Indiana for sowing pernicious slander and accusation. They charged the condition of things upon Republican blundering, intriguing, and what not; and they found many disposed to believe them. Through influences like this they carried the State by a large majority in 1874; and, notwithstanding they had accomplished nothing in two years, they still used the cry of corruption against the general government, and their prospects were as good as before.

No great party ever started into a campaign with so few assurances of success as did the Republican party into the campaign of 1876. To add to their great embarrassment, they had alienated a large element by their passing a local option law in 1873—a measure they did not regret, by any means, but one for which they suffered. It was natural for them to turn, now, to a strong man, on desiring a candidate for governor of the State; and as they knew Mr. Harrison's record and opinions and strength, and trusted him implicitly, they asked him to take the helm. But when he wrote the disappointing letter, already given, they turned to another.

The choice now fell on Godlove S. Orth, who was very popular in the State, especially among the alienated Germans, —as he was himself a German. Mr. Orth had served several terms in Congress, and was at that time minister to Austria. His nomination was, therefore, well received, and the Republicans started out with enthusiasm, in spite of the odds against them. Yet, for a time, it looked as if they might gain back what they had lost. Their candidate for lieutenant-governor was the Honorable Robert Robertson.

Mr. Harrison bore his share of the work, but, as he had told the committee, "his personal affairs were not in a situation to make it wise for him to abandon the pursuit of his profession," and he was much of the time in the court-room. He had always been a hard worker, and free from doubtful methods of earning his living. He was yet comparatively poor, and it became him still to work.

The campaign went on, and on the part of the Republicans everything was energy and enthusiasm. The Democrats, also, were exerting every power to hold their ground of two years before; and, so far as human eye could see, they had everything on their side. In Thomas A. Hendricks, they had a far-seeing, shrewd, and able leader. They had unlimited supplies of money. Their candidate for governor was James D. Williams, a farmer, nominated with a shrewd political calculation that the farmers must play the most important part in that campaign. They were not slow in making the fight a personal one, and engaging in personal abuse.

In this connection, the Democrats revived an old scandal against Mr. Orth, connecting him dishonorably with the

Venezuela claims. They knew that the charges against him were false, and that a Democratic committee of Congress had so pronounced them. Nevertheless, they knew the power of the cry of "fraud" in Indiana, especially at that time. Soon every Democratic paper was teeming with the accusation, and the Democratic stump speakers repeated it again and again before the people. It would before long have produced the effect of surfeiting, as such scandals urged always do, had not the Republican managers done a very unfortunate thing—caused Mr. Orth to withdraw from the contest, thus at once producing that uncertain feeling that such an implied ackowledgment always does, showing injustice to Mr. Orth, and alienating the large German vote of the State as well as all the rest of Mr. Orth's friends.

Mr. Harrison was at that time out of the State, and knew nothing of what was going on at the Republican headquarters in Indiana. While he was on his way home shortly afterwards, he saw an account of the affair in a Chicago paper, and with it the astounding statement that his own name had been placed at the head of the ticket in place of that of Mr. Orth. He returned home, and severely criticised the committee for its action, not only on account of the lack of good policy in them, but also on account of the injustice to Mr. Orth and his friends. He predicted thorough defeat. He at first refused to accept the place at the head of the ticket; but at last, at the earnest solicitation of his friends, and considering that his withdrawal would make the defeat of the party still surer, by precipitating confusion, and perhaps division, he consented to lead in the already crippled campaign. But it was a most

RUSSELL B. HARRISON, OF MONTANA,

SON OF GENERAL HARRISON.

[*From a Photograph by Sarony, N. Y.*]

thankless task, under the circumstances. It was only six weeks until the election; the population of Indiana was largely agricultural; farmers were busy on their farms; the State was large; there were ninety-two counties to thoroughly canvass; and there was as much to undo as there was to do.

The evidence of a corruption fund in the campaign of 1876 on the part of the Democrats, is well-known. The chairman of their National Committee was W. H. Barnum. Their methods that year were what they have been since. But "corruption funds" may be used in various ways, and often honest people are beguiled by promises and glittering hopes whose origin is under cover.

There never was a greater field for this kind of work than Indiana was in 1876. Let "high living," "extravagance," "misuse of public funds," and such absurdities be charged upon the Republican administration, while the people feel the terrible depression of the times; let it be stated that these things brought on the hard times; let the Democratic stump speakers reiterate these statements at every cross-roads in the State: let papers with these falsehoods in them be circulated everywhere; —then let promises be held out of reform, of replenished pocket-books through better administration, and the Democrats will have formidable weapons to fight with at such a time. All this requires money— money spent to circulate falsehoods — and that is corruption in itself. But that is by far the least unrighteous of methods of using "corruption funds"; and Indiana was a ripe field for worse ones. The seed was well sown.

Against Mr. Harrison and Mr. Robertson were pitted James D. Williams and Isaac P. Gray. The former was a "farmers' candidate," put up for appealing to the very class who, throughout the State, felt the depression most, and were the most suspicious on account of it. He prided himself on his "farmer-like" appearance, which meant more to the Indiana farmer in those times, perhaps, than in any time since, or even before, subsequent to pioneer days. He wore a suit of blue jeans, even on public occasions; and this fact was boasted of over the State. He became to the Democratic farmers, and perhaps, to some discontented ones not Democrats, a sort of personal token of easier times; for the Republicans were believed to be spendthrifts, and the authors of the hard times. On account of this suit, and the use that could be made of it, Mr. Williams became known in the campaign as "Blue Jeans," and this became the Democratic watchword. It was unwisely given by Republicans, in disgust, at first, but it became a power to the Democrats, through the peculiar circumstances of the times.

On the other hand, though Mr. Harrison pursued the more honest course of wearing clothes such as he had always worn in public, with no reference whatever to an influence in the campaign, and never thought to be anybody but Benjamin Harrison, the Democrats saw fit, in order to give "Blue Jeans" the weight of the full meaning they desired it to have before the people, to forge a contrast wholly misleading, by speaking of the Republican candidate as arrayed on the side of spendthrifts, clothed in costly garb, a representative of "kid glove aristocracy." A falser accusation was never couched in two words than was implied and emphasized in the words "Kid Gloves," applied by the Democrats to Mr. Harrison. Wherever he went, the delusion was thoroughly dispelled from the minds of the thousands who came out to hear him speak, and to see him. A plainer man they seldom found, and yet he impressed every one as a thorough gentleman — not by birth, or wealth, or favoritism, but by cultivation and true character.

Against all these odds he entered the contest; but as in former campaigns when his interests were at stake, he forgot his personal interests for those of his State and his country. He made no personal allusions, in his speeches or elsewhere, to his opponent that would be in the least derogatory, or that would show that he felt him to be a rival for honors. He set up no personal pleas. He discussed the issues of the campaign from the stand-point of Republican principles. His mind was wholly taken up with these. He seemed to feel the necessity of their defense in the emergency — the danger threatening his country in the event of Democratic success. The spirit of the days of the great crisis was upon him. He felt that Indiana was his division, and that he must lead the Resaca assault in October. He identified himself with "the boys" wherever he went — at Fort Wayne, Richmond, Greensburg, Lafayette, Lebanon, Danville, Greencastle, Terre Haute, everywhere — as in the days of 1862, '3, '4, and '5. In these places he met many of the old soldiers who had fought under him, and shared his glory at Resaca, Peach Tree Creek, Atlanta, and Nashville.

At Lebanon, where he spoke, he had already friends who had heard him during the Clem trial; but there was little said afterwards about "Kid Gloves" by those who listened to him for the first time on that day. The outline of his speech at Danville, August 18, was given by the Indianapolis *Journal* as follows: "Personal Matters — Democratic Party Should Die — Democracy and Rebellion — 'The Bloody Shirt' — Tilden a Secessionist — Mr. Tilden Predicts the Rebellion — Tilden in an Unenviable Light —No Influence for the Union Cause — Tilden Responsible for the Credit Mobilier." At Greensburg, his patriotic and martial feelings seemed to take possession of him, and he cried," *Come on, boys!*" And the old soldiers felt like following him again to the rescue of their country.

The result of this energetic canvass was a victory — such as Washington sometimes gained out of his defeats. Mr. Harrison was not elected, but he gained what led to other victories. The enemy were crippled, and their ranks depleted; their majority of 1874 reduced more than half. But his own county gave him a large majority, and that showed that from henceforth he was their recognized leader. The Republican ticket was beaten by an average plurality of more than seven thousand votes; but General Harrison was beaten by a plurality of only 5,084. The total vote of the State was 434,457; and there was a Greenback vote of 13,000. The following shows how he compared with his associate candidates, in the estimation of the people:

Harrison, for Governor, ...	208,080
Robertson, for Lieutenant-Governor, ...	206,641
Watts, for Secretary of State, ...	206,774
Herriott, for Treasurer, ...	206,197
Hess, for Auditor, ...	207,774
Smith, for Superintendent of Public Instruction, . . .	205,332

Mr. Harrison's vote, therefore, was 1,536 above the average vote of the other five. But when we consider that the combined vote of the thirteen congressmen voted for by Republicans was only 204,419, we find his lead of his ticket to be more than eighteen hundred, and that his vote was 3,664 ahead of that of the congressmen.

But this personal popularity was the least of his victories. By his organization and energetic work the whole Republican vote was made larger. No one can look at the situation as it was in Indiana that year, without wondering why the Republican defeat was not greater than it was, unless Mr. Harrison's work be taken into account. The Greenback vote must certainly have been larger than it was, had it not been for him. The Greenback candidate for governor withdrew, however, in favor of Mr. Harrison, which operated more against the Republicans than for them, for the cry of "bargain and sale" was raised by the Democrats, and thus Mr. Harrison's hard task was apparently increased. Nevertheless, the vote did not all go to the Democrats; and more of it would have been against him had it not been for his diligence. But Mr. Harrison's canvass also set the Republican party again on the upward grade toward success. It turned the sinking fortunes of the party. It restored it again — right in the midst of troublous times — to the confidence of the people.

For Mr. Harrison himself, the State canvass brought increased popularity. It made Indiana aware that a giant was leading Republican hosts. It made him friends throughout the State — not among the old soldiers, for they were his friends before, but among farmers, who, in spite of the false impressions "Blue Jeans" and "Kid Gloves" had given them, knew an honest man when they saw and heard him. He also became acquainted with the people, their ways of thinking, their feelings, and their wants. He was now in greater demand for the general campaign, in spite of his apparent October defeat; and right royally did he lend his services until November.

CHAPTER X.

LAWYER AND POLITICIAN.

A LEADER OF THE INDIANA BAR — THE STRIKE OF 1877 — ON THE SIDE OF SYMPATHY — THE CAMPAIGN OF 1878 — CONTEST WITH GREENBACKERS — MEMBER OF THE MISSISSIPPI RIVER COMMISSION — AN INDUSTRIAL PARADE — THE CAMPAIGN OF 1880 — THE UNITED STATES SENATE — A VIEW OF THE LAWYER, THE POLITICIAN, THE MAN.

AFTER the campaign, Mr. Harrison quietly resumed the practice of his profession, just as if he had not won for himself additional fame during his absence.

By this time he was one of the recognized leaders of the Indiana bar. Had he been as well known by the people in his law practice as he now was in his political life, he would have been considered by them the ablest lawyer in the State. Those, however, who came in contact with him knew his ability, and were not slow to pronounce judgment as to his superiority as a lawyer.

The year of 1877 was scarcely ushered in, when the people in many of the states began to be uneasy on account of the mutterings of a threatening storm, the exact nature of which no one could tell. The feeling had existed a long time that things could not remain many months as they then were. For men must live, though manufacturers and other employers might give them nothing to do.

There were many who were now suffering that had brought their troubles upon their own heads in the manner already described. But there were thousands of others who, during all the "flush times," had wrought for wages, and joined not in the speculative excitement of the times. They were responsible neither for gilded, fictitious prices, nor for the result that came. The wealthy were responsible for it all, and the poor were the greatest sufferers when the crash came. Their complaints were now well-founded, whether the methods that many of them proposed for obtaining justice were right or not.

A simple, but terrible problem was before the workingmen, and before the capitalists as well. The former had no bread in their houses, and no means of getting any; they were willing to work, but no man hired them; they must live, but how? Employers might have apparent cause for reduction of wages, and for turning workmen away, in the financial depression. They certainly could not make large profits while demand was low and wages to workingmen were high. Some of them might lose. But living was high — strangely — and what could the workingmen do? To employers — individuals or corporations — who had no interests but their own, who made money by "salting down" the profits, who dealt in margins manipulated by themselves, but trusted nothing to human nature in society, casting no "bread upon the waters," the problem was impossible of solution, and perhaps without interest. But there were others who invested in the charity of letting their workmen live, even though they themselves apparently suffered, and the returns came in after the panic was over. There were others, such as General Harrison, who, though they were not rich, and not employers, saw the real situation, and advised for the suffering classes.

But with threats of violence Mr. Harrison had no sympathy, although he appreciated the complaints. In the first place, the leaders in such outbreaks were seldom the honest workmen. The real sufferers were generally the last to engage in them, if they ever did. In the next place, there could be no relief by it. Again, it was morally and socially wrong. Every consideration decreed that men should suffer rather than resort to violence.

The disturbance began, as usual, with the railroads. It broke out on the Baltimore and Ohio railroad in Maryland. It was not long until nearly all the roads in Pennsylvania were involved. Soon the trains on most of the roads in Ohio and Indiana were stopped. On the 22d of July, which was Sunday, a riot broke out in Pittsburg, and over $4,000,000 worth of property was destroyed. On the 23d, the employés of the Vandalia, and the Indianapolis, Terre Haute, and St. Louis railroads ceased running trains. On the 24th, no trains of any kind were permitted to leave Indianapolis, except mail trains. The strikers took possession of the Union Depot. The people of the city were trembling lest the scenes of Pittsburg should be repeated. The peculiar situation, already described, made such an outbreak especially to be dreaded. There were too many unemployed workingmen of all classes. In the extremity the following proclamation was issued by the mayor:

INDIANAPOLIS, July 24, 1877.

TO THE LAW-ABIDING CITIZENS OF INDIANAPOLIS:

You are requested to meet *en masse* in front of the new court house, on Washington Street, this evening at 7.30 P. M., to counsel as to measures for the public safety. Let your numbers be so large, and the addresses of such a character, that it will be demonstrated that the people of this city are on the side of law and order. Measures for organization for the protection of life and property will also be adopted.

MAYOR CAVIN.

The meeting was largely attended by all parties. Addresses were made by prominent Democrats and Republicans. A Committee of Public Safety was appointed. One of the leaders of this movement was Senator Joseph E. McDonald, and he was on the committee with many other Democrats and many Republicans. Political lines were forgotten in the common peril.

Another committee was appointed, consisting of "ten of the most prudent that could be selected, to confer with the committee of strikers in a friendly spirit, and ascertain just what their demands are, and what they propose to do, also to consult with officials of the various roads and see what their determination is." It was the purpose of this committee to see if concessions could not be made on both sides, and if measures could not be adopted to which both could agree, and the troubles be ended. To this committee belonged such men as Governor James D. Williams, Franklin Landers (afterwards Democratic candidate for governor), Benjamin Harrison, Albert G. Porter, Mayor Cavin, and others. They met the following afternoon at the council chamber. The committee sent by the strikers was W. H. Sayre, Grand Secretary of the Brotherhood of Locomotive Engineers. One of the leading dailies, the Indianapolis *Journal*, made, in reporting the meeting, the following statements:

"General Harrison made an eloquent and logical speech of some length, replete with legal lore and sound good sense. He counselled obedience to the law, but at the same time strongly expressed the opinion that the wages as stated were too low, and desired very much that they should be raised. He was willing to use his influence with those in authority, in favor of this desired increase."

On account of the disasters to travel and business that were following in the wake of the strike, as well as the danger to property and life, the continued anxiety and suspense, it was hard for such sentiments as these to find much favor at first with the citizens. Violence was already committed about the depots. On the 26th, another meeting of citizens was called. General John Coburn was made chairman. On taking the chair, he said that they must provide measures to protect themselves, their neighbors, and their rights. There was danger to property, peace, and personal safety. They could not wait longer for the settlement of the troubles by those who began them. They must prevent riots. Peace, good order, and life, must not, and should not be endangered there. Such was the temper of that meeting. The sentiments were echoed by such men as Major Gordon, Judge Newton, and Judge Gresham. Hence it was, that General Harrison's counsel of the day before could not prevail. Nevertheless, he was willing to do anything that was lawful and right to put a stop to the difficulties and dangers that existed. He could be depended on for this, in any case.

Judge Gresham made a motion that a committee be appointed to confer with the committee appointed at the meeting at the court house. That conference met, and the result was the reorganization of the Committee of Public Safety, as follows: General Walter Q. Gresham, Joseph E. McDonald, General Benjamin Harrison, Honorable Conrad Baker, General John Love, General T. A. Morris, and General Daniel McCauley. This committee was to act with the mayor, and many citizens enrolled their names for service under the committee.

This reorganization of the Committee of Safety was due to the proclamation of Governor Williams, who, though during the campaign could make speeches against "moneyed classes," "capital," "manufacturers," and talk about the oppressed wage-worker, was now thoroughly alarmed, and spoke out in no conciliating nor flattering terms. The following is the proclamation:

THE STATE OF INDIANA,
EXECUTIVE DEPARTMENT.

A Proclamation by the Governor Relative to Certain Disturbances of the Peace by Striking Employés of the Railroad Companies.

TO THE PEOPLE OF INDIANA:

Many disaffected employés of railroad companies doing business in this State have renounced their employment because of alleged grievances, and have conspired to enforce their demands by detaining trains of their late employers, seizing and controlling their property, intimidating their managers, prohibiting by violence their attempts to conduct their business, and driving away passengers and freight offered for transportation. The peace of all the community is seriously disturbed by those lawless acts. Every class of society is made to suffer. The comfort and happiness of many families, not parties to the grievance, are sacrificed. A controversy which belongs to our courts, or to the province of peaceful arbitration or negotiation, is made the excuse for an obstruction of trade and travel over the chartered commercial highways of our State. The commerce of the entire country is interfered with, and the reputation of our community is threatened with dishonor among our neighbors. This disregard of law and the rights and privileges of our citizens, and those of sister States, cannot be tolerated. The machinery provided by law for the adjustment of private grievances must be used as the only resort against debtors, individual or corporate. The process of civil remedies, as well as the penalties of the criminal code must be executed equally in each case. To the end that the existing combination be dissolved and destroyed in its lawless form, I invoke the aid of all the law-abiding citizens of our State. I ask that they denounce and condemn this infraction of public order, and endeavor to dissuade these offenders against the peace and dignity of our State from further acts of lawlessness.

To the judiciary I appeal for the prompt and rigid administration of justice in proceedings of this nature.

To the sheriffs of the several counties I commend a careful study of the duties imposed upon them by statute, which they have sworn to discharge. I admonish each to use the full power of his county in the preservation of order and the suppression of breaches of the peace, assuring them of my hearty coöperation, with the power of the State at my command when satisfied that occasion requires its exercise.

To those who have arrayed themselves against the Government and are subverting law and order and the best interests of society by the waste and destruction of property, the derangement of trains, and the ruin of all classes of labor, I appeal for an immediate abandonment of their unwise and unlawful confederation. I convey to them the voice of the law, which they cannot afford to disregard. I trust that its admonition may be so promptly heeded that a resort to extreme measures will be unnecessary, and that the authority of the law and the dignity of the State, against which they have so grievously offended, may be restored and duly respected hereafter.

Given at Indianapolis, this twenty-sixth day of July, 1877.

Witness the seal of the State, and the signature of the Governor.

JAMES D. WILLIAMS.

The citizen volunteer forces were organized under various leaders, not the least of whom were Generals Gresham and Harrison. General Gresham had his barracks at the district court room. General Harrison's company was detailed to the protection of the United States Armory, in which were 300,000 Springfield rifles, with ammunition. Here was one effectual method of preventing much blood-shed — to prevent the rioters from securing arms. General Harrison put the place in a condition of defense.

Governor Williams had decided to appoint General Harrison commander of the whole volunteer forces. This was at the instance of the committee. But General Harrison declined to accept, saying that he was already captain of one company. Some hot-headed friends wished him to march out against the rioters and give them a lesson of powder and ball. He answered: "I don't propose to go out and shoot down my neighbors, unless it is positively necessary to do so in order to uphold the law." He used his utmost endeavors to bring about a reconciliation, and a peaceful settling of the dispute. His whole course during those terrible days showed both the qualities of the accomplished general and the faithful citizen. It would not have been hard to have shot down hundreds of rioters, but there would have been no bravery in it. General Harrison had taken not a step, performed not an act, during the Rebellion that was not for the preservation of the Union; he now chose to do nothing that was not necessary to defend his State and home.

At last the strike was ended; and apprehension as to danger ceased. Then came the trial of 200 of the unfortunate men, who, though having committed a great wrong, yet had struck for bread. These 200 had been arrested for hindering the operation of the Ohio and Mississippi railroad. Sentence was passed upon them of ninety days' imprisonment.

But General Harrison went to the judge and begged for their release. He showed that the object of prosecuting them had now been accomplished, that they had learned that it would not do to violate law and order. He thus succeeded in procuring their release, and thus he won the warm gratitude and friendship of those strikers.

After that time, Mr. Harrison had frequent cases before the courts, wherein the railroads were defendants and his clients plaintiffs. He was seldom counsel for any road in such a case. About ten years before this, he had become the attorney for the Vandalia Railroad Company, and when that company became defendant in suit for damages, he made it his rule to inquire into the case and bring about an amicable settlement; and in all such cases his advice was found to be just and satisfactory to both parties.

There was no man in Indiana, or in the country, who sympathized more with the masses in their prosperity or their adversity than General Harrison. This fact is plainly seen in his attitude during the great strike, and in his being sought for the defense of those who had grievances against monopolies.

There is a reason for this. He was thoroughly American in his principles. He had no sympathy with that sentiment in the South which declared that a certain class had no rights which a certain other class was bound to respect. He had no sympathy with the idea that any class conditions should hinder individuals in the free race for developed merit and for success, and that anything but real merit, possessed or developed in the race, ought to entitle to prestige or any sort of honor. He sought to take away every shackle that bound the poor man, and to place around him every favorable circumstance that any other man enjoyed.

In 1878 there was another Indiana State campaign for counties and districts. Again Mr. Harrison's voice was heard in almost every part of the State. This, also, was almost a hopeless campaign, so far as the Republicans were concerned. The Greenback movement was even growing, and in that year the Greenbackers were making a vigorous canvass. They had had an advantage ever since the crisis began, and a greater advantage since it was announced that specie payment would be resumed January 1, 1879. The fear of resumption had been one of the powerful influences against the Republicans in the campaign of 1876, and was a more powerful influence now. In the existing state of affairs, this can be readily understood, and needs no further explanation: but it must be constantly borne in mind, in making an estimate of all the influences against which the Republican

ULYSSES S. GRANT,

THE SECOND REPUBLICAN PRESIDENT OF THE UNITED STATES.

party had to contend, and of any one man's influence in the contest, until the triumph of the policy on the appointed day.

Among other important speeches delivered by Mr. Harrison during that campaign, was one at Richmond, Indiana, on the 9th of August. The following outline of the speech was made by one of the Indianapolis papers, and gives an idea of the questions discussed there and throughout the State: "Mr. Voorhees on the Presidential Title — Why the Army was Attacked — Democratic Governors Call for Help — South Carolina Again in Revolt — Fiat Dollars *vs.* Greenbacks — Labor Wants a Par Dollar — The Labor Question — Class Dissensions — Voorhees' Bloody Shirt — The Brighter Side." The Democratic and inflation organs endeavored to make a good deal of capital out of his use of the terms "fiat dollars" and "fiat money," as if in them he had sneered at the thousands of good people who then held that mistaken idea. But Mr. Harrison was a man who never made apologies for his positions, nor sought to win favor by conciliating explanations. He condemned the "fiat" principle without fear or favor, and when January came, successful resumption sustained him.

For a number of years the wants of the people along the banks of the Mississippi River had been presented to Congress in vain. That is, thousands of acres of alluvial lands needed to be reclaimed from the almost yearly overflow. Much money had indeed been spent in clearing the mouth of the river, as well as other ways. But in 1879, Congress at last took the matter in hand in earnest. The President was authorized to appoint a "Mississippi River Commission," consisting of seven able men, some of whom were to be surveying engineers, to take charge of the matter of the improvement of the river, and the reclaiming of the alluvial lands. President Hayes appointed Benjamin Harrison one of that commission, with Captain James B. Eads — who had just made himself famous in the constructing of the jetties at the Gulf end of the South Pass — and others of like ability. As in everything he undertook, here Mr. Harrison did efficient service. He had his special "calling," but with his power of application and his mastering every subject that came before him for consideration, he might have made a success in any calling. He was ready for any work he might be called on to do.

By this time the political situation was completely changed. The crisis — or what many considered a crisis — of resumption had passed. The Republican party had brought the country safely through another one of the dark periods of her history. Confidence was again restored, and prosperity began to rise like a bright sun over the land. The party stood forth with a clear record, in having not only accomplished everything it had undertaken to do for the country, but with the confession forced from its enemies that everything it had done was a good thing. The issue of resumption, like that of slavery, was settled forever. There was now absolutely no immediate issue. The Democrats had nothing to warn the country about; they had only one complaint to make, and that was a false one, so far as law and electoral votes were concerned. During the crisis, while men were in doubt as to the party policy, the electoral votes of several states were lost, but there were other gains; yet, the popular vote showed the real state of feeling in the country. But the triumph came now, and every man saw that if the policy of other parties had succeeded, the prosperity would not have come.

Indiana shared the general good feeling. She had given her electoral vote to the Republican candidates at every election since 1856, except that of 1876, and in both those years men feared her policy, which had afterwards proved so successful and right.

In 1879, President Hayes made a tour through the Western States, with his hero-Secretary of the Treasury, John Sherman. They came to Indianapolis. It was the year of agricultural rebound, as well as political triumph. There was a great industrial parade, the like of which Indiana — a State, perhaps, unequaled for mighty gatherings and displays — had never seen before. Washington Street, Market Street, Pennsylvania, Meridian, and Illinois streets, were thickly crowded with human beings; and it was almost impossible to find a path through the crowds for the parade, which itself was very long, and headed by the President, Mr. Sherman, Mr. Williams, and others. Indiana was happy. Mr. Harrison, also, was in the van; and he also shared the honor of entertaining the distinguished guests. He was their firm personal friend, and they could not have left — aside from considerations of honor — without enjoying the hospitality of his home.

Mr. Harrison was chairman of the Indiana delegation to the National Republican Convention that met in Chicago, June 7, 1880. When the question was there raised by some of his friends, as to putting his name before the convention as candidate for the nomination for President, he promptly checked the movement. He at length cast the solid Indiana vote for Garfield. When he went home, he entered into the canvass with great zeal. As usual, the State election was to be held in October, and he wrought faithfully to make the Republican success most brilliant in both contests. The Republican candidate for governor was his former law-partner, the Honorable Albert G. Porter, and together they made a most vigorous canvass.

Among the speeches which Mr. Harrison made that year was one at Terre Haute, on the 20th of August. Here he discussed the question of honest elections, which had been an open question — referring especially to the South — ever since the war: the efforts that had been made at election reform, which had been resisted by Democrats everywhere; the frauds in Indiana: the double position of ex-Governor Hendricks — the evidences of his insincerity in matters of reform: the interference of the Democratic Supreme Court: the general Democratic opposition to United States election laws: the Democratic frauds in Jennings County, Indiana, in Maine, and in New York: the South already counted for Hancock: Hancock and English, and Garfield and Arthur, and Albert G. Porter. It was a most masterful arraigning of the Democratic party for its unblushing frauds. Another notable speech was delivered September 11th, at Indianapolis, in reply to some slanderous charges that had been put forth by Mr. Hendricks against Mr. Garfield. Mr. Harrison never did better than when defending friends, or his country, or his party, from unjust accusations. He had so strong a sense of honor that dishonor done to any one else, and especially to those he loved.

stirred in him the deepest indignation. His eloquence at such times was like a flood sweeping everything before it.

Mr. Porter was elected governer by a handsome majority. Also, when the votes were counted, it was found that there was to be a respectable Republican majority in the next legislature. From this time until the close of the general campaign, Indiana was not considered a doubtful state, and the heat of the battle was in other quarters. Nevertheless, Mr. Harrison did not cease his activity until the grand and successful issue of the campaign was announced.

As soon as it was known that the legislature was Republican, it was plainly foreshadowed who was to be the next United States Senator from Indiana. There were many able men among the Indiana Republicans who were suitable for the high office. But there was one man who had stood by the party in every struggle since 1856. He had led in its hopeless, as well as its hopeful, battles. He had accepted certain defeat to save the party from complete disaster. He had suffered for his party; he had done more for it than any other one man now living in the State — and all this, not as a mere partisan, but as a patriotic citizen and a statesman. There were others thought of by a few, and at first there were movements made in their favor. But in the Republican caucus but one name was considered — that of Benjamin Harrison. So when the new legislature met, his name was presented before the joint convention as the unanimous choice of the Republicans, and he was elected to serve in the United States Senate six years — from March, 1881, until March, 1887.

To be eminently suitable for that high office the highest

qualities of statesmanship are necessary. One must be, if a lawyer, a lawyer and politician of the best types. A lawyer of the best type must be a man of education, breadth of thought, ability, and a man of principles rather than technical learning. Such a lawyer was Mr. Harrison. A politician of the best type must be first of all a patriot. Next, he must be thoroughly acquainted with the history, general and political, of his own country. Next, he must understand every kind of government, and be acquainted with the history of law and government in the world, and the special histories of nations. Then he must be a man of broad principles, broad culture, and broad learning. Such a politician was Benjamin Harrison, and being both a lawyer and a politician of the highest types, he was a statesman in the full meaning of the word, and was eminently fitted to be one of the law-makers and directors of the greatest nation on earth.

All this implies what he was as a citizen and a man. A Senator of the United States ought to be, intellectually and morally, a man of the highest type. And such was Benjamin Harrison.

CHAPTER XI.

SENATOR AND CITIZEN.

REMOVAL TO WASHINGTON — THE OLD HOME AT INDIANAPOLIS — A TYPICAL AMERICAN WOMAN — DAUGHTER AND SON — THE NEW HOME AND SOCIETY — SIX YEARS OF SOCIAL VICTORIES — TWO MARRIAGES — HARRISON IN THE SENATE — THE BURLINGAME TREATY — THE HISTORY OF CHINESE LEGISLATION — THE DAKOTA REPORT AND SPEECHES — MEMBER OF THE COMMITTEE ON FOREIGN RELATIONS — THE CONTRACT LABOR BILL — ALIEN OWNERSHIP OF AMERICAN SOIL — A REVIEW OF RECORD — HISTORY OF THE SECOND CONTEST FOR SENATORSHIP — HOME AGAIN.

THE time now came for the breaking-up of the Indianapolis home, for one in Washington. But this caused no great fluttering of hearts in the household.

Mrs. Harrison was too sensible to have her head turned by the event, or to manifest any trepidation when about to assume new social responsibilities. Even if she had never before graced such circles as she was now about to enter, she was too self-possessed and too well-equipped for the new duties to manifest anxiety as to the coming social change.

Her education was excellent. She had been reared, from infancy to marriage, in a home of refinement and culture, and all her surroundings until that day were those of the college and of learning and religion. At her marriage, she had become associated in life with one who not only had graduated with honors, but was a lover of books and of learning, cultivated and disciplined in heart and mind, and having the highest culture for his ideal. She had advanced with him since marriage, until he had attained to his first ideal life, and passed far beyond it.

The home at Indianapolis was a home in every sense of the word. There was no gaudiness, no outward display, about the plain and modest brick house that stood on one of the most beautiful streets in the city, and just far enough up town to be convenient to the Market Street law office, and at the same time be away from the hum of business. Thousands of such mansions are seen in the cities, towns, and country, East and West. A red-brick, square-built edifice, with two stories and an attic; fronting the east: set back in the yard on the west side of the street; three front windows above, and two below with a door on the north corner under the north window above,—that is a familiar object to the traveler on the streets and highways of our cities.

Many of such houses look cold and cheerless and prison-like, but not so with this one. An air of comfort reigned: but it was not occasioned by the maples and the flowers and the lawn; though the spirit of comfort seemed to pervade them. It cannot be described: but every one knows that where there is a happy, contented family, cultivated and pure, the fact is manifested on the outside of the house, in touches here and there, and arrangement — but touches and arrangement apparent only by effect. An almost irrepressible desire to enter and enjoy the welcome and home-comfort possessed the beholder at the gate.

Inside, the effects were all the same as those outside — cheerful, inviting, pleasing, home-like. The reception-room, off the entrance-hall, impressed the caller or the visitor on the instant of entering, with the feeling that he was welcome. The light that came through the curtained windows, and reflected from the light-colored finish, was not bright enough to invite inspection, nor sombre enough to debar it. If the visitor were not given to admiring art, he would go away pleased with everything he saw, but could not recall the contents of the room: everything was so natural and cosy, to use the language of those not artists. But looking closely, he would find that the reception-room was full of beauty; and the artistic eye found nothing to offend it. The contrasts were not bold nor harsh. The furniture was selected apparently more for comfort than effect; but the "harmony" was perfect. On the walls, on the centre-table, on the stands, and on the marble mantel, there were pictures, statuary and bric-a-brac — some that were costly and somewhat rare, and some that were of little cost, but all selected and arranged with artistic taste and skill. There were paintings and etchings and steel engravings and photographs.

The other rooms were arranged with the same taste — giving an air of culture that could only belong to the home of the cultivated. The large library-room, up-stairs, was a paradise for those of literary inclination. There were fiction, travels, histories, essays, and heavy philosophical and scientific works: there were books on art, literature, science, government, and religion. It required education, thorough knowledge, and well-disciplined judgment to select those books. Here, also, were pictures on the wall. Here were etchings, drapery, and panels. Here was a large steel engraving of William Henry Harrison. Here was a picture of General Benjamin Harrison and his staff. Here was an old-fashioned rocking-chair. And here was the room that was sacred by reason of its linking with the past. Some of those books had been gathered while the boy was under tutors in his father's house: some had been gathered while at Farmer's College: some while at Miami University: some had been bought while in their first Indianapolis home: and every stage of the lives of parents and children was represented by books in the library, as well as other objects in the same room.

Mrs. Harrison, at this time, was as beautiful as when, in 1854, she had become a bride. There were the same charms, with the added ones that had come through years of experience and culture. She was hospitable, charitable, cheerful, and had always a pleasant word and smile ready for those in her presence. She had the happy faculty of making other women her friends, and she had many of them. She loved her children, and was loved by them. She loved her husband, and was his companion in his life in every sense, and in return she received from him the affection and devotion and care of a strong, manly heart. In manner and dress she manifested the same taste as in the appointments of her home. Her dresses fitted neatly and snugly, and she attracted only by her beauty, her loveliness and grace of manner. She had no affected airs: she was frank and straightforward in her kindliness, and was neither unpleasantly obtrusive in her friendships and attentions, nor unpleasant in her manner or conversation.

Her son, Russell, was at that time 27 years old, a ruddy, agreeable, and cultivated young man. He was alert and keen-eyed. He dressed neatly and becomingly. Like his father, he was always cool and sober of thought, evidently resolved never to let a storm of any kind turn him aside when once he had started on a train of thinking.

Mrs. Harrison's daughter, Mary Scott Harrison, about five years younger than her brother, was beautiful, and not unlike her mother in form, features, and manner. She was one of the most attractive young ladies in the best Indianapolis circles.

Her cultivation was what she would find in such a home, and with such school advantages as parents like hers would seek to afford their children. There was then already a whisper afloat among her friends; and a certain young man named James Robert McKee, of a respectable business firm in the city, was said to have that noble affection for her that would lead him on to Washington many times before the senatorial days should be ended.

This was the family that General Harrison took with him to Washington. He was not rich, and he could not afford a rich home for them, even as a Senator of the United States. Nor was he close and covetous, and likely to subject his family to embarrassment and inconvenience on that account. This is seen from the description just given of his Indianapolis home; and it is also seen, from that description, that his family was not likely to involve him in expenses he could not meet. However, their son was not destined to become a constant element in Washington society, on account of other callings, but was to make frequent and long visits to the new home.

They took a suite of rooms at the Riggs House, and lived for a time neither expensively nor closely, and here they began to manifest the social qualities that had always marked them, and drew around themselves such friends as the prestige of Senatorship would bring, and as would be attracted by such refinement and accomplishments. Yet they had not the prestige of established social standing: but nevertheless, without this advantage, considered so necessary to success in Washington society, they made an "impression," they won themselves hosts of friends, and became the centre of such a circle as the proudest might long to enter. Mrs. Harrison's triumph here was a tribute to her strong personality. She was always "at home" on Thursday. Inviting a half-dozen lady friends to receive her guests with her, she succeeded in making the occasion so full of good cheer and hospitality that Thursday became to all a day of happy remembrance and of eager anticipation.

Thus went on six years of social victories. Sometime after their arrival, they moved from the Riggs House to a boarding-house near McPherson Square, and afterwards to the Woodmont, an apartment house on Iowa Circle. But wherever they went, it was the same — their friends came to enjoy their hospitality.

Among the special friends found in society at the capital were the wife and daughter of Senator Saunders, of Nebraska. The daughter, Miss Mamie Saunders, was a beautiful blonde, accomplished, true-hearted, and a thoroughly American young lady. In the winter of 1881–82, she met Russell, Senator Harrison's son, for the first time, while he was on a visit to his parents at the Riggs House. The acquaintance ripened into friendship and the friendship into love. Three years afterwards they were married: and very soon they returned to the far West.

Not long after this wedding, occurred another; and the only remaining child of the household was taken. Whispered prophesies had been fulfilled. James Robert McKee had made his pilgrimages to Washington. The two had resolved to share each other's life, and enter the most sacred of companionships. Thus the two children were gone: and the season of depression and loneliness that follows the departure of the sunshine of a home, followed in this home.

Mr. Harrison began his senatorial career March 4th, 1881, at the first special session of the Senate of the Forty-seventh Congress. The object of this special session was to enable the Senate to act upon the new appointments of President Garfield, who was that day inaugurated. On that day also Vice-President Arthur took the oath of office and became President of the United States Senate. There were just thirty-seven Republicans and thirty-seven Democrats; but there seemed to be but one cloud that threatened the calm and peaceful sailing of that session. The nominations for Cabinet officers were sent in, and all were promptly confirmed. Soon afterwards the Senate adjourned to meet again in extra session in May.

It was during this second extra session that the serious troubles over the appointments for New York posts occurred. Mr. Harrison regretted all this; and while he held positive opinions, he took so little part in the matter, and conducted himself so prudently, that he could not be considered an antagonist by either faction.

From that time Senator Harrison was in his place during sessions, whenever it was possible. From the first he was not forward to speak or to take any conspicuous part, and for a time he might have been called a "silent member." This was due, no doubt, to the same feeling that had always kept him from thrusting himself forward. This feeling has been referred to in relating the incidents of his protesting against taking the stump in 1856. He thought there were those present who, by reason of age and experience, might do better. Nevertheless, he held himself ready to do his duty: and he was ready now to speak, as he had been then, if it should be demanded.

This apparent hesitancy was also a manifestation of another trait of his character — carefulness that looks cautiously around, studies all the situation, and gains full command of forces, before striking. Any new situation is in the nature of things apt to confuse, and detract from the full command of ourselves. But Mr. Harrison's ability was known, and it was not long before his talents were in demand.

Perhaps the first measure of great importance, in the discussion of which Senator Harrison took a prominent part was that relating to the suspension of Chinese immigration. To understand this thoroughly, it will be necessary to go back and look at the treaties that were then in existence with China, and the manner and spirit of their negotiation.

At the beginning of the year 1866, the hitherto half-unknown empires of China and Japan came into a closer relationship to the United States, by reason of a steamship line that was then established. A wide interest in those countries was almost immediately awakened. Moreover, the changed attitude of the two countries toward our own and other civilized nations was awakening sympathy, as well as interest. It was in that year that the new and more liberal-minded Tycoon came into power in Japan. It was at the beginning of the next year that the old Mikado died, and that the young Mikado, but sixteen years old, came into his place. In April following, the Tycoon issued an invitation to all the leading powers to a conference, to be held in Osaca, January 1, 1868. The result of that conference was that Japan soon came into commercial and diplomatic communication with Belgium, Denmark, England, France, Holland, Italy, Portugal, Prussia, Switzerland, and the United States, and the ports of Yedo, Osaca, and Hiogo, and a port on the west coast of the Empire Island, were opened to our trade and travel. Every steamer that arrived brought us report of some new liberal movement. The interest deepened. Missionaries flocked thither, and the sympathy of the whole American Nation was stirred in behalf of the Japanese.

This had much to do with increasing national interest in China, also; and while that nation was making, at that time some advancement, the un-informed began to anticipate vast strides there, and premature sympathy was thus awakened. But the Empire of Ki-Tsiang was not breaking its own shackles of ignorance and superstition, as was the case with its more eastern neighbor. Nor were the subjects of the Chinese Emperor so easily persuaded to seek enlightenment from other people. Yet the rulers, and many who belong to the upper castes, were willing to learn, and heartily wished the knowledge of the West would penetrate to the centre of the empire. This feeling among those classes had been manifesting itself for some years, and much of it, of late years, had been due to the influence of one American at Pekin. About the time of the extraordinary revolution in Japan, China began to make some further advance, largely through the influence of this same man, and hence, Americans were deceived, for it was not at all like the other nation.

That man was Anson Burlingame. He was born in New Berlin, New York, in 1822. He graduated at Harvard in 1849. He was sent as Representative to Congress by the National party in 1855, but he soon became a Republican, and he was kept in his seat until 1861. In that year he was appointed Minister to China, and there he remained until 1867.

Burlingame won the confidence of the Emperor and officials, and was thus enabled to do much toward keeping up friendly relations between the two nations. He was also instrumental in setting forward certain improvements looking toward the advancement of the people in the Empire itself, and such benefits resulted from them that his influence with the government became extraordinary. In 1867 he resigned, against the earnest protest of all the chief officials of the Empire, who, when they could not prevail upon him to remain, conceived the idea of honoring him in a way that no foreigner had ever been honored by them before. An imperial decree, of November 21, 1867, announced that Anson Burlingame had been selected as a special embassador of the Chinese Government to the Great Powers.

This was accepted by Burlingame, and he prepared to leave upon his extraordinary mission. He stopped at Shanghai for some weeks, and while there the officials of the Empire crowded around and showed him marked reverence and awe, some of them falling down before him. They had never seen one with so great honors bestowed upon him. On the 25th of February, 1868, he sailed by way of Europe for the United States, with those Chinese officials sent with him to learn the art of being consul to a foreign country.

It can now be seen how easy it would have been for Burlingame to win concessions from the Chinese Government favorable to our own, and that, being an American, he would do nothing detrimental to his native country. It can also be seen that, having been six years in China, and interested in that government and people, he would do nothing against them. It can be seen, too, from the state of the American public mind regarding the Eastern empires at that time, by reason of the "awakenings" already described, a treaty most favorable to China would be acceptable to the people and our rulers. It was under these influences and circumstances that the famous Burlingame Treaty was made, which consisted only of "additional articles" to the treaty of June 18, 1868. The Burlingame Treaty was signed at Washington, July 4, 1868, and ratified by the United States Senate on the 16th of that month.

That part of it which afterwards came up while considering the question of the restriction of Chinese immigration, it is only necessary here to explain. It stipulated that the Chinese laborers and other Chinese immigrants might have the full enjoyment of the rights of labor and travel in the United

States, and that citizens of the United States might have the same rights in China; also, prohibited the naturalization of the Chinese. There was not a line in this part of the treaty that was not thought to be an echo of the principles set forth in the Declaration of Independence and in the Constitution of the United States, regarding the rights of people of any nation coming to our shores. It would be hard for a genuine American not to indorse it with genuine heartiness, not knowing the results that were to follow; and even knowing these, to desire to prevent them by any means that would destroy the American principles echoed in the treaty.

But the Mongolians were not the people to come purely for enlightenment by our institutions, nor to adopt our methods of living and labor, as those are expected to do who move to a foreign country for any purpose that involves living among the people. The late Chinese advancement was very insignificant, compared with that of Japan. We were deceived as to that, but had less reason to be deceived as to the hordes that would come. In 1866, China had a population of 450,000,000, and counting her dependencies, there were 477,500,000. This incredible number of people was within an area of 4,412,000 square miles, or one thousand and eight persons to the square mile. It was to be expected that if an "emigration fever" set in toward the United States, as was likely to be the case under circumstances so new to the people of China as Burlingame brought about, those vast half-living hordes would precipitate themselves on our shores. And so it came about: —a degenerate race flooded our western coasts, overran them, and threatened to predominate.

Naturally the people of those coasts saw the evil first. It was a long time before the matter could be understood by others, and before any steps were taken that looked toward relief of the Americans of the Pacific Coast. American laborers there suffered for lack of a degenerate and filthy style of living: that is, they could not live crowded together in hovels and pens, and so could not compete with the Chinese, who could so live. Then, it was not long until other questions of the financial, moral, and social influence of the "heathen Chinee" arose. Louder and louder came the demand that the evil be abated. In 1880, the Burlingame Treaty was somewhat modified — evidently the proper direction in which to work — but not sufficiently to eradicate the evil, or prevent its constant growing by the constant immigration of Chinese.

Then came the long discussions in Congress upon the matter. A bill was introduced during the Forty-seventh Congress "to enforce treaty stipulation relating to the Chinese." A substitute was proposed, and considered, whose important point was to limit Chinese immigration. Section 1 was as follows: "That from and after the expiration of sixty days next after the passage of this act, and until the expiration of twenty years next after the passage of this act, the coming of Chinese laborers to the United States be, and the same is hereby, suspended." Subsequently it was amended so as to read ninety days, instead of sixty.

On this question, Senator Harrison held with Senator Hoar, of Massachusetts, that the bill was contrary to treaty obligations. He saw, perhaps more clearly than many other Senators, that there was, indeed, an unfortunate evil thrust upon our country by the treaty of 1868, but he considered that the deliberate abrogation of that treaty by Congress would be unfair, unjust, and contrary to the solemn obligation of our government toward China. Again, he agreed with Senator Hoar in the following sentiment expressed by that gentleman in reply to statements made by Senator Edmunds: "The American doctrine affirms, as the Declaration of Independence affirms, and as the New Testament affirms, as I read it (two authorities which lie at the very foundation of all law — domestic, international, individual — which governs mankind), that the human being has a right, conforming to law, conforming to proper regulations of the place to which he goes, to go and seek his fortune, and to earn his living, by honest labor."

It could not be expected that a man who was so thoroughly an American as was Senator Harrison, from birth, training, and principle, could take any other view than this. It is not surprising that his noble American heart had been stirred in sympathy with the waking of the eastern nations in 1866–7, and that it had fully indorsed the sentiment of the treaty. It is not to be wondered at that such a man should inquire now, what had become of the treaty and the honor of our Nation, and the principles on which it was founded.

That bill passed both Senate and House. Mr. Harrison did not vote, being absent, but would no doubt have voted against it had he been present. It was sent for the approval of President Arthur, who returned it in four days with a long statement of the reasons why he could not approve it. Thus it did not become a law.

But on April 17th, a bill "to execute certain treaty stipulations with the Chinese" was reported from the Committee on Education in the House. It was before the Senate April 27th. Mr. Harrison made two brief speeches on that bill. He said that while the treaty used the word "laborers" in one sense, Congress could not change the meaning it had there by legislation. He said that in any law Congress might pass (referring to the subject of the treaty) the word must be used in the same sense as in the treaty. This position was sustained by the Senate. It has since been held by every President and Secretary of State down to the present time. The Honorable Mr. Morrow, present Representative to Congress from California, has said: "Mr. Harrison's views on the question are entirely satisfactory to us in California."

That bill prohibited Chinese immigration for ten years, instead of twenty: and there were some other slight modifications. It passed both houses, Mr. Harrison opposing it on purely American principles, and on the principle of our treaty obligations. It was signed by President Arthur, and became a law.

It has been thought necessary to give a detailed account of the Chinese treaty and legislation, that Mr. Harrison's short speeches and his vote may be interpreted in the light of history. He saw the evil and felt it: but he was an American, and did not believe in the unqualified right of exclusion or retaining. Yet he knew that *something* ought to be done; but was not willing to do what he considered evil that good might come. After all, it will sooner or later be found that it is always better to adhere strictly to the fundamental principles of our government in all cases, and that the true defense against cheap foreign labor must be found in definite and effective social organization, and contract labor laws.

In subsequent Chinese legislation Mr. Harrison took active part. He was made a member of the Foreign Relations Committee; and when the restriction bill offered by Senator Fair, of Nevada, was referred to that committee, he assisted in amending it, and in reporting it to the Senate, which it passed without division. It was declared to be one of the best bills ever reported by any committee on that subject.

Senator Harrison took a prominent part in the discussion on the admission of Dakota into the Union. The following are extracts from some of his speeches on that subject:

Congress and New States.

"I always felt that if there was to be a fight there ought not to be a fence between the people who wanted to engage in it; and yet the Senator from Missouri, finding no advocate here of the doctrine that Dakota is a state, or can become a state until Congress has passed some law recognizing her as a state, has gone out of the Senate to find one.

"It is well enough to bear in mind in this connection that Congress cannot make a state. I should like to see the Senator from South Carolina or the Senator from Missouri set about making a state by a law. We can frame no state constitution. We can set up no state government. Congress may, either in advance or by an act of ratification, approve what the people have done, but Congress cannot make a state any more than I can unmake one. The authority of a state constitution and organization rests upon the sure foundation of the popular will. Mr. President, what is the use of all this vain discussion? Here are two concurrent things that must be done. First, the state constitution must be formed. Who can do it? The people who are to live under it; and no other hand can intermeddle in the work. Congress cannot do it. What is the other efficient act to constitute a state of the American Union? It is recognition by Congress of the existence of the state. These two things must occur before a state can exist, and the simple question here is, is the initiative in that movement necessarily with Congress? I say it is not. Two bodies are necessary to act, Congress and the people, and all I contend for here to-day is that it is competent for either to take the initiative, and that the act is not consummated until both have concurred. Who will controvert that?

"Is this limitation upon the power of the people to come from the Democratic party, the party that has boasted through its history that it lay upon the breast of the people and was responsive to their impulses? Is it from Senators on that side of the chamber that the argument is to come that the people may not originate a movement to set up a state government and bring to Congress for ratification? It will be turning back the whole history of the party on this question if we divide here upon this bill on that proposition."

The Prayer of the People of Dakota.

"Enough, then, for this part of the case. Here are a people asking for admission, against whose fitness no Senator has ventured in this debate to allege a word. They are here pursuing methods that have been recognized in nearly one-half of the cases of the admission of states since the original thirteen, at least nearly one-half of those that passed through a territorial organization to statehood. They are here, not asserting themselves to be a state, not resisting the authority of the government, but respectfully, and yet in a manly way, asking those rights guaranteed by treaty and ordinance, guaranteed by tradition and precedent, guaranteed by the very organization of the government under which we live, a government of the people, a government that treats it as an anomaly that anywhere under her flag there should be a people who do not choose their own rulers and regulate their own local and domestic affairs. Yet I am to expect here that Senators on the other side of the chamber who so strenuously in debate, and even in open war, asserted this right of local control, are to resist the appeal of nearly three hundred thousand American citizens who ask here to share with you the immunities and privileges of American citizenship. I do not know what the party stress may be: I have not been disposed to discuss that question: but if I were at all to take the part of adviser to my Democratic friends, I should ask them to consider for a moment whether they can thus safely turn back upon the traditions of their own party, whether a momentary advantage may not be more than lost in thus antagonizing the just rights of this people, for it cannot be made a local wrong. Wrong is never local; it is universal. The relationships of the people who dwell there stretch out into every neighborhood in all the states. Every manly man who values his own rights as a citizen will be regardful of the rights of others."

Partisanship and Statemanship.

"The movement for the admission of a new member into the sisterhood of States should originate with the people to be affected by it. Such movement should not have its initiative or its impetus outside of people of the state to be constituted. I do not need to say that this discussion, if it is kept up on the plane to which it belongs, cannot degenerate into a partisan discussion: that we cannot divide upon it on party lines, because to consider the application of this people for admission to the Union in its relations to the successes or reverses of a political party is to consider it from a level altogether below that of statesmanship."

On the Contract Labor bill, Senator Harrison spoke in opposition to the wholesale immigration of foreigners for cheap labor. He was in favor of opening wide the doors for voluntary immigration on the part of those desiring to become American citizens. He also spoke, at one time, against foreign ownership of American soil. He strongly condemned the practice of foreigners securing large bodies of land in the West, excluding actual settlers. He favored the Blair bill, which provided for aid to common schools on the basis of illiteracy. He proposed amendments to the bill which were adopted. He voted for the bill. He voted for the Civil Service Reform bill. He voted for the Tariff Commission. In short Mr. Harrison's record while in the United States Senate was that of an honest, able, laborious, faithful Republican Senator. He made no speech, cast no vote, offered no bills, amendments, or suggestions, in committee or Senate, that were not in strict harmony with the principles of American liberty, so rooted and grounded in him from a boy.

His term expired March 4, 1887. The legislature that was to choose his successor was elected in 1886. It was a close contest, during which the Republicans were more discouraged than hopeful. But Mr. Harrison was never discouraged in any fight. He was cheerful and hopeful, and led where others almost feared to follow. The result justified his efforts. The Republicans carried the state by an average majority of 4,530; while the legislative majority was 9,580. But the Democratic legislature of 1884–5 had so gerrymandered the state that the result of the election of 1886 was that the Democrats had a majority on joint ballot of two. This was obtained by the unseating of one Republican Senator. The following, taken from the *Political Hand-Book of Indiana for 1888*, indicates the balloting for United States Senator:

"1887, February 2.—Hon. David Turpie (Democrat) was declared by one of the two presiding officers of the Convention, chosen for six years from March 3, 1887, to succeed Hon. Benjamin Harrison as a Senator of the United States from Indiana. The other presiding officer declared that no one had received a majority of the legal votes cast and no person was elected on the sixteenth ballot. Governor Gray, however, gave Mr. Turpie a certificate of election.

"The first vote in each house, January 18, was: Senate—Benjamin Harrison, 18; Turpie, 32. House—Harrison, 53; Turpie, 43; Jason H. Allen (Labor), 4.

"The votes in joint convention were:

NAMES.	1st.	2d.	3d.	4th.	5th.	6th.	7th.	8th.	9th.	10th.	11th	12th.	13th	14th.	15th.	16th.
Benjamin Harrison...	71	71	71	71	71	70	70	71	71	70	70	68		10	70	
David Turpie.....	75	75	75	75	75	74	74	75	75	74	74	72	37	14	74	74
Jason H. Allen, ...	4	4	4	4	4	4	4	4	4	4	4	4	3	4	4	70
Total.........	150	150	150	150	150	148	148	150	150	148	148	144	40	28	148	150
Necessary to choice.	76	76	76	76	76	75	75	76	76	75	75	73			75	76

So the will of the majority of Indiana voters was lost.

Mr. Harrison and family returned to the old home at Indianapolis; and they found more friends to welcome them, than had bidden them adieu six years before. His fame had preceded him home, and every one in the city, who took pride in the city's honor, was glad to have back the illustrious citizen, though they were sorry to know that his honor, and theirs, had not been magnified by his return to the United States Senate.

CHAPTER XII.

CITIZEN AND CANDIDATE.

RESUMES THE PRACTICE OF LAW — CASES — A VIEW OF THE MAN AS A CITIZEN — WHOM THE INDIANIANS WANTED FOR PRESIDENT — WORK OF THE INDIANAPOLIS JOURNAL — OTHER CANDIDATES — HISTORY OF THE MOVEMENT — THE GREAT CONVENTION — ITS HISTORY — THE NOMINATION — GENERAL SATISFACTION AMONG DELEGATES — ENTHUSIASM THROUGHOUT THE COUNTRY — ENTHUSIASM AT HOME — "COME ON, BOYS!"

WHEN Mr. Harrison had made a canvass and been defeated, neither his judgment, temper, nor daily conduct was in the least affected by it. He went about his work as cheerful and happy, and apparently as on unconscious of what had occurred, as if he had never been in a canvass during his life. He had a pleasant word for all his friends, an open pocket-book for charity, a listening ear for stories of distress, a ready heart for every call for help, a hearty laugh for every innocent jest, an alert eye for every important item of political, governmental, or general news, a thorough and constant devotion to religious duties, a vigilant care for the welfare of his family, and a thorough enjoyment of their presence and company.

Not long after their return from Washington, the home was brightened again by the presence of the daughter, Mrs. McKee, who, with her husband, came to live with her parents. Only the absent son was now wanted to complete the old home-circle. But, besides her husband, the daughter brought with her another, who was like a flood of light to the home.

This was none other than Benjamin Harrison McKee, then only a few weeks old. A king never received a more royal welcome to any court or country, than did this young king of the household receive from his subjects there: for he began to rule the very day of his advent to the old home on Delaware Street. He had a grandfather, who, though an American, rendered him royal homage, as did also all the house. As he grew up he demanded this homage more than ever; and it was gladly given.

Mr. Harrison quietly resumed the practice of law. But such a man never ceases to improve the hours of his life: and the lawyer that returned from Washington, after six years of successful work in the Senate of the United States, was superior to the lawyer who had taken his seat there six years before. He had profited by his experience at every step. His ability and tact as a lawyer had been thoroughly tested in the Senate, and had come brighter from every trial. His knowledge of national and international law was greatly increased, as was also his knowledge of nations and men. But while he had sought for wisdom and not fame, it was given to him also to become more popular. He had won more and more the confidence of the people at home, as the six years went on: and when he returned, the hearty good-will and enthusiasm that were manifested were a constant ovation.

He had had no trouble in finding cases since his early experience in law; they had always come to him. He found them now in greater number than ever. But it must not be sup-

THE HOUSE IN WHICH GENERAL AND MRS. HARRISON COMMENCED HOUSE-KEEPING IN INDIANAPOLIS.

posed that he had been idle during the Congressional vacations of the six years. He was frequently, at those times, engaged in important suits.

His client in one of these cases, in 1886, was J. A. Whitehead, a marble-cutter of Indianapolis, who was plaintiff in a suit for damages, in which the Indiana, Bloomington and Western Railroad was defendant. In an accident in Hendricks County, which had occurred on account of a defective track, Mr. Whitehead had been terribly broken and shattered in body. His claims for damages were refused by the railroad, and suit was begun, Mr. Harrison appearing for the plaintiff. The best counsel possible to obtain was upon the other side, and a bitter and stubborn fight went on for three weeks. But Mr. Harrison won a verdict for $17,000 damages.

At another time, a poor woman, living in the suburbs of Indianapolis, was coming into the city to market, and while crossing the "Bee Line" tracks was run down by an engine. In that case, Mr. Harrison secured a verdict for $10,000, after a hotly-contested suit.

In another case, he won a verdict of $10.000 damages against the Belt Railroad Company for injuring a man, while running at a high rate of speed, and without signalling.

An engineer on the Cincinnati, Hamilton and Dayton road lost a leg in a wreck, and Mr. Harrison obtained for him $10,000. In the same wreck a brakeman was injured, but in a less degree, and Mr. Harrison won for him $3,000.

He often had clients with claims against railroads, or other corporations, and won their cases. But he took these clients because he believed them to be right, and not for the mere fee, nor for the fame of fighting corporations which some lawyers seem to seek after for political ends. If he believed a corporation was right, in any case, he did not hesitate to say so, and champion its cause.

Yet Mr. Harrison was opposed to the monopolizing tendencies of corporations from principle. He did not believe in any sort of monopoly. It was wholly opposed to the liberty taught by the Declaration of Independence and the Constitution of the United States. In November, 1887, he made a speech in Danville, Indiana, upon the tariff question, in which he uttered words that have no uncertain meaning, as to his position with regard to "trusts," "combines," and all monopolies. They may well be remembered in connection also with the tariff issue he was discussing. He said: "There are one or two things that, in some respects, are working against it, and one is this abominable and un-American system which is recently developed, called trusts. This thing is running too far. It is un-American; it is unpatriotic, in my judgment; and you will notice that those who are attacking our tariff system, take their position behind these facts, and use them as the ground of their assault. We must find some way to stop such combinations."

Such was this American man—always an American, never harboring a contrary principle. The following testimony, by a friend of General Harrison who had been constantly associated with him in his office, though written a year later than the time now referred to, sums up his character in just, if enthusiastic, words: "I have been with him (General Harrison) since October, 1867, and have been in his house often.

and enjoyed a very intimate acquaintance with him; and in all that time I never heard him utter an indecent word, an oath, or do, act, or suggest a thing that was not honorable. He is a perfect man of great intellectual powers — a religious man, and yet active in all business matters. He is the best host I ever saw. Indeed there is no defect in him anywhere."

That General Harrison committed faults is saying no more than may be said of any noble man: but that these faults or mistakes sprang from inherent defects of character cannot be believed by those who have known him, or who know the story of his life. He was conscientious in all his life; at home, in his manner of study, in his profession, in social life, on the stump, in the Senate — everywhere. No man ever felt a greater responsibility to any trust, than did he to his home, his wife and children, his religion, to his profession, to those for whom he wrought under any circumstances.

It is not strange that this man was thought of as a candidate for the Presidency of the United States, when, in 1888, the question came up of who could serve his country best. There were many others, grand and noble men, considered: for the Republican party has never lacked for efficient material for that great office. But those who were Mr. Harrison's friends, who knew he was every way qualified for the great office, joyfully recognized the fact that he was surrounded by a number of providential circumstances that filled up every condition of availability. They were not slow to announce that fact to the country. The Indianapolis *Journal* took up the work, and kept the State and country constantly aware of the circumstances. The admirable and efficient Republican organization in Indiana, represented by the *Journal*, scattered the intelligence broad-cast.

There were other men, older in their country's service because older in years, whose friends were urging for the candidacy, and whose statesmanship and personal worth were of the highest quality; of whose special fitness, also, everything could be truthfully urged. One of these was Mr. Sherman, of Ohio, whose political life could not be written without writing the history of the Republican party, giving an account of every important measure since its birth. There was not a part of the country that had not been affected and benefited by measures that John Sherman had originated, or had been mainly instrumental in making statute laws of our government. The simple knowledge concerning the man and his work that prevailed everywhere made him strong before the people; and there were many arguments of great weight favoring his nomination.

Another was the Honorable William B. Allison, of Iowa, a man of great ability and experience, who had proved himself a man fully capable of wielding the executive power of the greatest nation in the world. Another was Walter Q. Gresham, of Indiana. Others were Chauncey M. Depew, of New York, General Alger, of Michigan, Governor Rusk, of Wisconsin, and Senator Hawley, of Connecticut. Besides these, were many others, all men of ability sufficient for the position. And besides all these, was Mr. James G. Blaine, of Maine, whose influence in the country was apparently so strengthening every day, that, spite of his own protestations, he was likely to be nominated.

This was the situation when the great convention of 1888 met in Chicago, on the 19th of June. It was a day of great excitement, and great expectations among the Republicans throughout the Nation. Delegates began arriving the preceding week, and it was already evident that the contest among the friends of the candidates was to be close. Delegations of the different states established their headquarters at the great hotels, and advertised the same by placards and flags; and flags and bunting were seen everywhere in the city, and all gave evidence of some remarkable event to take place.

The 19th came, and, at the appointed hour, the vast hall was crowded with more than eight thousand people. It was several days before the real work of the convention began. Finally, the permanent organization was complete. The permanent chairman was Judge M. M. Estee, of California. About his table were his advisers and the secretaries. Grouped in an outer circle were distinguished men, one of the most noticeable of whom was John C. Fremont, the first candidate for President of the United States nominated by the Republican party, who was introduced to the convention, and made a brief address the first day. Arranged on either side, behind long tables, was the large corps of reporters with their paper and pencils. Behind this large platform, on which so many were seated, beginning two or three steps above it, and half-circling it, was a tier of seats the width of the hall, and running upward and backward, until a large number of seats were filled with people. Above that, and extending farther back and farther toward the front, was a gallery — larger than the one below. Before the chairman was the "parquet," where more than eight hundred delegates sat, the delegates of each State sitting together. Behind the parquet was a vast tier of seats, and all were full of people. There were three large galleries above that; there were three on each side of the hall. And all the seats were full. And so the great convention began its work.

On Thursday morning, Mr. McKinley, of Ohio, read the platform which had been prepared by the Committee on Resolutions. The platform was prepared by men whose hearts were full of Republican history and principles. Mr. McKinley himself was there as one of the champions of the claims of the Honorable John Sherman, who expected to win, if he won at all, by virtue of his embodiment of Republican principles, and not through any personal eulogies that might be passed upon him. His supporters, as well as those of Mr. Harrison, were charged more with the magnetism of patriotic feelings than that of blind devotion to their choice, but based on those feelings was that enthusiasm for their choice that rose to more sublime heights than the enthusiasm of mere hero-worshipers can attain. Such men prepared the platform, and as word by word it fell from the lips of Mr. McKinley, it was to all hearts like the echo of the days of '56 and '60; and to the older men, the stirring days of '40. Whenever reference was made to American liberty, and its defense; to American principles, and their defense; to American labor and homes, and their defense and protection, the mighty shout of all the people rose up "like the swelling sea," marking out the line along which the subsequent choice was to be made, and presaging defeat to all contemners of those principles.

One noticeable feature of the convention was the manner of its cheering. There were two spirits abroad in the large audience. One manifested itself by arrangement and method whenever favorite names were mentioned for the nomination. It was sincere and enthusiastic, but not spontaneous; it was loud, but not deep and magnetic. Its tendency was to division and bitterness, and had the Republicans of that convention been less patriotic than they were, a sadder ending might have been its fate. The other spirit manifested itself at unexpected moments, and always on patriotic calls. No word nor act could call it forth, until that word or act was American, in a distinctive sense, and then the slightest word or act was like a spark to powder. Once while the people were, impatiently or patiently, waiting for something to be done, the band played some lively airs, as if to entertain and keep the clamor down until business should begin, but not the slightest attention was paid to it, until the moment the notes of "America" were struck, then the people ceased their confusion and cheered heartily and enthusiastically. There was no arrangement, no method, in this spirit's manifestations. It seemed to lie dormant while the people were wholly absorbed in mere matters and movements of policy, that sometimes went on before their eyes.

At last it was announced that presentation of candidates was in order. The roll-call of states began, and those states having names to present, responded as called. Connecticut was called, and through Mr. Warner, of that delegation, presented the name of Joseph R. Hawley, as candidate for nomination for President of the United States. The next State that responded was Illinois, who through the Honorable Leonard Swett, presented the name of Walter Q. Gresham: for, though Judge Gresham then had his home nominally in his native state, his duties had compelled his residence for some time to be in Chicago. Mr. Swett was the same who presented the name of Abraham Lincoln in 1860, and many memories were stirred up by the incident. Next came Indiana.

When that State was called, Colonel Thompson rose and announced that ex-Governor Albert G. Porter would present the choice of Indiana. So Governor Porter, the former law-partner of Benjamin Harrison, went to the platform, and in the following eloquent words, presented the name of Benjamin Harrison for nomination:

"*Mr. Chairman and Gentlemen of the Convention:* When in 1880 Roscoe Conkling visited Indiana to take part in the memorable canvass of that year, he was asked on every hand, 'How will New York go at the Presidential election?' 'Tell me,' he replied, 'how Indiana will go in October, and I will tell you how New York will go in November.' In October, Indiana's majority of 7,000 for the Republican candidate for governor informed the country how she would go, and New York and the Nation echoed her October voice. As in 1880, Indiana held the key of the position, so, although not an October State now, she seems to hold the key of the position as before. Indiana is always called a doubtful state, but when the Republican party has thoroughly organized, when its preparatory work has been done well, and when the spirit of the Republican masses is kindled into a flame, she seldom fails to elect Republican candidates. There never was a time in the history of the Republican party in Indiana when it was more thoroughly organized. There never was a time when the preparatory work of the campaign had been better done. There never was a time when the Republican masses were more thoroughly alive and intent upon victory; and give us General Benjamin Harrison, give him your commission to be a candidate, and the Republicans will fall into line and move forward steadily to victory. The Democracy of Indiana have been disappointed by the failure of the St. Louis Convention to put in nomination an Indiana candidate on their National ticket. There is a tide in the affairs of parties as well as of men, that, taken at the flood, leads on to fortune. Indiana's present condition is the Republican party's opportunity, if we have an Indiana candidate, the choice of her delegated people. I speak the unanimous voice of the delegation from Indiana when I announce that he is Indiana's candidate.

"Benjamin Harrison came to Indiana in 1854, at the age of twenty-one. He came poor in purse, but rich in resolution. No one ever heard him make reference to the names of his ancestors. South of the line he mounted the back of prosperity without the aid of stirrup. The hospitality of his ancestors had given their property to those whom they had served, and the core had gone to the people, the rind to themselves and families. On his arrival in the State he immediately entered upon the practice of law, and at once achieved success. Amplitude of preparation, large views of questions, the widest knowledge of his profession that could be acquired in such a time, distinguished him, and he rose rapidly in his profession. He leaned upon no man's arm for aid. Modest and self-confident, he seemed to say, 'I am an honest tub that stands on its own bottom.' Everybody perceived that in web and woof he was of heroic stuff. While practicing his profession, the great rebellion raised its hand to strike down the Union. Relinquishing his profession, he took his sword, went into the army, and received his commission from Oliver P. Morton as the colonel of a regiment. He marched with Sherman to the sea; he was in the thick of the fight at Resaca and Atlanta. He was not unknown to the people of Indiana before he entered the army. Though so young, he had been chosen at a State election by the people as reporter of the decisions of the Supreme Court. While he was in the field as a soldier, his Democratic opponents took the office from him, but while he was still in the field the people of Indiana elected him; and at the disbandment of Sherman's forces, returning home, he received his commission.

"On account of his eloquence as a speaker and his power as a debater, he was called upon at an uncommonly early age to take part in the discussion of the mighty questions that then began to agitate the country, and was matched against some of the most eminent Democratic speakers. No man that ever felt the touch of his blade desired to be matched with him again. With all his eloquence as an orator, he never spoke for oratorical effect; his words always went like a bullet to the mark. He reminds one of the saying of the great Irish orator and patriot, O'Connell, that a good speech is a good thing, but the verdict is *the* thing. He therefore always pierced the core of every question that he discussed, and in every contest in which he was engaged he fought to win. In 1881, on account of his services in the ardent and prolonged struggles of the Republican party for the rights of man and the integrity and preservation of the Union, the Republican members of the legislature, by a unanimous vote, elected him as Senator of the United States. I need not enter into any detailed account of his services as Senator. It is sufficient to say that he always stood in the front rank. The delegates from Dakota can bear witness to the unremitting energy of his efforts to procure the admission of that Territory into the Union, when, on account of the fidelity of Dakota to Republican principles, the Democratic party resolved to keep it out. We all remember his exposure of the civil-service-reform sham of the present administration in Indiana. He possesses whatever you could desire in a President — soundness in Republican doctrine, comprehensiveness of mind, calm judgment, firm purpose, unquailing courage, and a pure character. The gentleman from Illinois has referred to another citizen of Indiana. A state's place in civilization is always determined by the manner in which she treats those who have served her faithfully. I honor old historic Massachusetts for the manner in which she cherishes the fame of those who, in whatever department of service, have reflected honor upon the Commonwealth. How she calls the rolls of their names with pride! How impatient she becomes if any one is unjustly aspersed or disparaged! If General Harrison were present to-day, he would bid me that I should say nothing against the honorable gentleman, the brave and just judge, and heroic soldier, who has been presented before him. In standing here, I should have said in reference to the soldier, that, if the roll of the soldiers of Indiana were to be called here to-day, she would bid me call them all. There is no need that I should endeavor to dwarf any other man, in order that Benjamin Harrison may appear conspicuous. He stands breast to breast with the foremost of Indiana's soldiers. Distinguished also in civic trusts, heroically faithful to every public duty, skillful in marshaling men,—to the sound of whose bugle they quickly rally and fall into ranks,—and who has never failed in Indiana's fiercest conflicts to come out of the charge crowned with victory.

"Standing here to-day on behalf of the man who, disdaining adventitious advantages, has risen merely by the force of his own merit, I would deem myself unchivalric did I not refer to some of the useful deeds of his ancestors. We stand here to-day in the imperial city of the great Northwest. The name of no family is more intimately associated with the Northwest than his. It is identified with the history of the Northwestern people. I shall give but a passing notice to the sturdy Ben Harrison from whom he is named, one of the signers of the Declaration of Indepedence. He was the first governor of Virginia, when the possessions of Virginia embraced the whole Northwest. When the Northwest was formed into a Territory by Congress, William Henry Harrison was appointed secretary of the Territory, and afterwards the delegate of the Territory in Congress. When the Indiana Territory was formed, embracing all of the Northwest but Ohio and a part of Michigan, William Henry Harrison was appointed its governor. He was a man of deeds. While he was a delegate in

Congress — the youngest, perhaps, on that floor — he procured the passage of a measure by which it was required that the public lands should be sold in smaller subdivisions than they had ever been before, and for the first time a man of humble means might purchase a home from the government. The historian, McMasters, in his admirable history of the people of the United States, has said of this measure that it was productive of far more good to the country than even his victory over the prophet at the battle of Tippecanoe, or his defeat of the British at the battle of the Thames. While he was governor of the Indiana Territory he obtained from the Indians the relinquishment of their title to 70,000,000 acres of land in a single treaty, and procured their relinquishment of lands that embraced one-third of Illinois and a large part of the southern portion of Wisconsin. He fought the battle of Tippecanoe, and by defeating the schemes of that great statesman and warrior, Tecumseh, he kept open the portals of the West to the entrance of the emigrant. The tongue of the farm was his native tongue. Benjamin Harrison's ancestors from the earliest generation had been farmers, and when old Tippecanoe parted from a regiment at Vincennes, he said to them: 'You will always find a plate and knife and fork on my table and the door will never be shut nor the latch-string be pulled in.' In 1813 he left the Indiana Territory to enter upon a larger field of activity, but the memory of his services was such, and the affection borne for him was such, that, twenty-seven years afterwards, when he was a candidate for President of the United States, the State of Indiana, although a Democratic State, gave him 14,000 majority. He died in one month after he had entered upon his great office. The people of Indiana had always associated his name with success and victory and they could not understand the providence which had cut him off at the beginning of what they thought would be a most useful career. And now, in the cabins and plain farm-houses of Indiana, the people who remember the old hero regard him as not yet dead. His spirit walks abroad among them, and they expect that, in the person of his heroic descendant, old Tippecanoe will yet fill out his term. And so to-day, the people of Indiana hold in high esteem the name of Benjamin Harrison, and holding in deep affection the memory of old Tippecanoe, have their latch-strings hospitably out to you, and their door ready to fly out at your touch to let in the grateful air that shall bear upon its wing the message that Benjamin Harrison, their soldier statesman, has been nominated for President of the United States."

It would not be surprising to discover that the applause that rang through the hall from time to time, during Governor Porter's speech, and that burst into a storm when he was done, was of that spirit, partly, which wrought by some arrangement; nor was it to the discredit of General Harrison's immediate friends that it was so. It was natural that their interest should be personal as well as national. Their anxiety was for their personal friend — that *he* should succeed. His patriotism, his Americanism, his great ability, his thorough qualification, they had settled long before in their minds. Their country honored, benefited, saved from un-American spirit, partyism and intrigue, by him, was a picture vivid to them months before, and it was to them but a long-settled matter, *if* he should but win the race in the convention. But the applause was not all of that spirit. He was to them an embodiment of their country's principles. Their personal devotion to him rested largely on their own patriotism. And, withal, the very name of Harrison had a significance in that convention. It stirred up old memories. And when it was known that in him dwelt the spirit of Tippecanoe, a confidence and enthusiasm was raised that increased steadily and flagged not until the consummation of his friends' hopes was reached.

Mr. Terrill, of Texas, seconded the nomination of Mr. Harrison. Among other things, he paid him this glowing, yet merited tribute:

"A full term in the United States Senate has given him a grasp of public issues and fitted him for the high duties of statesmanship. On the great political and economic questions now under discussion, his views are clear and comprehensive, and in full accord with the principles which have been enunciated by this convention. Strong in debate, forcible in expression, incisive in logic, fearless in his convictions, his voice has been heard in every political contest for thirty years. Time and again has he demonstrated the highest qualities of leadership; and the firm regard in which he is held by the people of Indiana, the great State that gave Garfield a plurality of 6,000, will cause that State to honor her own illustrious citizen with a majority twice as large. In the prime and vigor of manhood, free from the entanglements of faction, he voted for the interests and principles of his party. Of unquestioned ability, untiring industry, and inflexible moral courage, he stands the peer of any man mentioned for the high office of President. He will receive the enthusiastic support of his party in every state of the Union. Mr. President and gentlemen of the convention, General Benjamin Harrison is a man that any delegation in this hall may feel proud to support. Bearing a name that has been honorably identified with the civil and military history of the government from its very first, conspicuous in his own gallant record as a soldier, combining intellectual force with moral integrity, eminent at the bar, experienced in constructive statesmanship and accomplished in the art of government, harmonious in his relations with the elements of the party, and moreover possessing exceptional popular strength in the State whose support is absolutely essential to success, it seems to me, fellow Republicans, that the hand of destiny has pointed him out as the man to lead us on to victory."

The nomination was also seconded by Mr. Gallinger, of New Hampshire. The following extracts are given as indicating the spirit that led those outside of Indiana to adhere to Mr. Harrison, and finally led the whole convention to conclude that it made no compromise whatever of Republicanism, in giving him the standard to bear:

"Projecting myself into the future, I see in November next the battle of the ballots in this country. As silently as the snowflakes fall in New England on a winter's day, so silently will you find the ballots deposited for us in the ballot-box in a few months, if you give us that grand man that Indiana has presented; if you give to us that grand leader on the field of battle, that man who has done credit to himself and his State and his country, in the halls of the United States Senate, that man whose public and private life is unspotted and without blemish — General Benjamin Harrison, of Indiana.

"I say this is a contest unparalleled, in my judgment, in the history of this country. We are face to face with our ancient foe, the Democratic party. We have to fight corruption, we have to fight every possible species of bad politics at the ballot-box in November next, and I say to you that if we are true to the principles of our party, if we are true to the spirit that animated the Republican party when it nominated Fremont in 1856 and Lincoln in 1860, we will not fail to achieve a magnificent triumph in November next. Why, look at this grand party of ours. Look at its magnificent leaders. Look at the men who have carried it to victory in the past — the party of Fremont, of Lincoln, of Grant, of Sherman, of Sheridan; the party of Sumner, of Phillips, of Garfield, and of Blaine; the party of equality, of justice, of protection, of liberty, and of law; the party that rescued our government from bankruptcy in 1860; the party that beat back that gigantic rebellion; the party that lifted up its strong arms and placed them under 4,000,000 slaves, and lifted them up to the plane of manhood and citizenship. Tell me that that party can be defeated in the coming contest! I answer you 'No,' and when the verdict is rendered at the polls in November, it will be found that my prophecy has not been without truth. I say to you here to-day, give to us that grand man that Indiana presents; give to us General Benjamin Harrison as our standard-bearer, and the Republican hosts, who never have flinched in battle before, will go forward with a determination, with an energy, with a zeal, that will carry everything before them, restore to the rightful hands of the Republican party the sceptre of power, that

RUTHERFORD B. HAYES.

THE THIRD REPUBLICAN PRESIDENT OF THE UNITED STATES.

for four years has been usurped by the hypercritical and mock civil-service-reform Democratic party that has been masquerading before the people of this country under false pretenses."

Afterwards, Mr. Hepburn, of Iowa, placed in nomination the Honorable William B. Allison, of that State. Next, General Russell A. Alger was nominated by Mr. Robert E. Frazer. Then Senator Hiscock presented for nomination, as Republican candidate for President of the United States, Chauncey M. Depew. And then came the nomination of John Sherman by General Hastings, of Pennsylvania, and the second by Governor Foraker, of Ohio.

Here the chords of patriotism were swept by skillful hands. The response was quick and tremendous. It came like the bursting forth of a cataract in the hollows of a great cave. Thousands of voices rose up in the prolonged shouting. Thousands of men and women stood upon their feet, and waved their hands and hats and banners; and the great mass of human beings was like the sea in commotion. In spite of differing interests, the vast assemblage had found the sentiment of harmony. Hearts were in the shouts; and thus heart answered to heart, until the shouts rolled into cadences, and came and went like the healthful tones of many bells ringing the triumphs of a great cause. Then, as one listened, there were words in the harmonious and measured tones, and the song, "Marching through Georgia," swelled grandly up. And thus the enthusiasm went on, and many minutes passed, freighted with the burden of patriotic demonstration.

At last the tumult and singing died away, and left that

body of delegates, and that mighty concourse of men and women, fully awake to the facts that this was a Republican convention, and that their interests were all one. While it had been impossible to present the man, telling the truth about him, without sweeping those chords, and while the response came forth as in his honor, yet the character of the response demonstrated that no man could be nominated by that convention who did not, by his life and deeds, represent the principles of the Republican party and our Nation.

Afterwards, Mr. Fitler, of Philadelphia, and Governor Rusk, of Wisconsin, were placed before the convention as candidates for nomination, and at length the time for balloting came. But there was one man who had not been formally named, James G. Blaine, of Maine, who yet came in for a large share of delegate votes. And there were others, worthy men, and some of them of national reputation, loved for their loyalty to their country and great abilities, who also won some share of the homage of voting. But including Mr. Blaine, the confident prophesies were made on seven men, and as the balloting went on each of the seven men might have assured himself that the tide was really in his favor. Then that number fell to six, then to five, four, and three. Balloting continued Friday, Saturday, and Monday.

At the beginning, judging solely by the principle of favoritism, General Harrison's chances were small. But one knowing the real patriotic character of that convention would know that mere favoritism must ultimately succumb to the nobler principle, and, knowing the character and history of General Harrison, would know that he stood side by side with the strongest. On Saturday evening his cause, so far as the promise of politics was concerned, was waning. But on Monday, it required but three ballots to decide the contest.

The following are the ballots of the three days:

NAMES.	FRIDAY.		SATURDAY.			MONDAY.		
	1st.	2d.	3d.	4th.	5th.	6th.	7th.	8th.
Harrison	80	91	94	217	213	231	273	544
Sherman	229	249	244	235	224	244	231	118
Alger	84	116	122	135	142	137	120	100
Gresham	111	108	123	98	87	91	91	59
Allison	72	75	88	88	99	73	76	*
Depew	99	99	91	*				
Rusk	25	20	16				..	
Blaine	35	33	35	42	48	40	15	5
Ingalls	28	16	*					
Phelps	25	18	5					
Hawley	13	*						
Fitler	24	*						
McKinley	2	3	8	11	14	12	16	4
Lincoln	3	2	2	1			2	
Miller			2	..				
Foraker				1		1	1	
Douglas				1				
Grant						1		
Haymond							1	
Total	830	830	830	829	827	830	831	830
Necessary for choice	416	416	416	415	414	416	416	416

* Withdrawn.

The hearts of the Indiana delegation were somewhat lighter on Monday morning, when it was known that the tide had turned toward their friend. On the first ballot of the morning, a thrill of enthusiasm stirred their hearts, and a feeling crept over the assembly that the contest was nearly ended, and that it was ending well. On the announcing of the seventh ballot, a flutter went through the audience, cheers, but cheers that were soon checked, as if the indication was of something too good to be trusted; murmurs of approval, even by the friends of other candidates; murmurs of concession, and perhaps murmurs of disappointment on the part of some who had been too strict partisans in sustaining their favorites, and some shaking of the head with warnings, "Wait and see; it is not decided yet." The eighth ballot began. Almost every state now announced accessions to the Harrison vote. When Pennsylvania threw her large vote for Harrison, a cheer went up, but was checked, as if those who cheered could not trust their senses, or were determined to wait the vote that might decide beyond chance for doubt. Tennessee gave that vote; and even then it seemed too much to believe. Nevertheless, while some of Mr. Harrison's friends sat as if dazed, or rose and cheered mechanically, enough of them and of the people, delegates and others, realized the situation to make the great hall echo again and again with enthusiastic cheering. But order was required, and the balloting went on to the close, and it was ascertained that Mr. Harrison's vote was 544. Then for many minutes the great audience manifested that it had found its voice and tongue.

Since the balloting had begun, the contest had been between men all patriots, and the Republican issue or principle was not involved, except in the consideration of choosing a man who could and would lead the hosts to victory. When the balloting was ended, there was no rejoicing of friend over friend. But more and more as the day wore on, and a realization of the fact that Harrison was chosen asserted itself, there were heard words of satisfaction.

In the evening of that day, the great convention met for nominating the Vice-President, and to the entire satisfaction of all present, and of the Republican party, they chose the Honorable Levi P. Morton; and so the names Harrison and Morton were linked together as leaders in one of the most important campaigns for American principles that has been the lot of this generation to engage in. General Harrison was at home, and so was Mr. Morton, but their friends made the canvass for them — the organization for the nomination was not their own, except in so far as the regular Republican organization in their respective states, which they had borne their part in arranging, leading, or assisting, had contributed to that end.

General Harrison sat in his office on Market Street, in Indianapolis, surrounded by his friends. Now and then news from the convention was received and commented on — his friends showing more trepidation than himself. While they waited for news, they told stories or jested. At the report of the seventh ballot, the excitement rose in the office and on the street. At the beginning of the eighth ballot, a nervous eagerness was manifest in the office. "California votes for Harrison!" "Pennsylvania votes for Harrison!" The first on the seventh ballot brought cheers. The next, on the eighth, brought a tumult.

"What do you think?" asked a friend, of Mr. Harrison.

"I feel much more disturbed now than I did when I thought it would be defeat; there is too much seriousness about such a position," he answered.

His friends were crowding around him. A great crowd of people were on the street below, and flags and banners were flying, and bands were playing. When Tennessee was reached, the tumult broke into a roar. They crowded up stairs, and into the office. They took him by the hand. The streets were full of excited and rejoicing men and women. Indianapolis had started a many days' jubilee—the grandest and longest it had ever known.

Thousands took trains for the city from every part of the State, as soon as the news was known. When the delegations arrived next day, they were greeted with a demonstration that made them feel that the days of 1840 were here again, in such esteem was General Harrison held in Indiana.

He is leading the charge out of the tangles of the defeat of '84, across the valley and open field of an honest campaign, and the regiments follow him; and he calls them: "Come on, boys!"

Chapter XIII.

A CHARACTERISTIC SPEECH.

THE REPUBLICAN PARTY A YOUNG PARTY — A "BOOK OF MARTHYRS" — CONDITION OF THE COUNTRY IN 1861 — WAR, FINANCE, DIPLOMACY; GRANT, CHACE, SEWARD — ACHIEVEMENTS OF THE REPUBLICAN PARTY — WORK YET TO BE DONE — EQUALITY IN ALL THE STATES — PROTECTION TO AMERICAN INDUSTRIES AND AMERICAN LABOR.

On the 20th of March, 1888, the Marquette Club, of Chicago, held its second annual banquet at the Grand Pacific Hotel in that city. On that occasion, General Harrison, by invitation, delivered the following speech, in response to the toast, "The Republican Party":

"*Mr. President and Gentlemen of the Marquette Club:* I am under an obligation that I shall not soon forget, in having been permitted by your courtesy to sit at your table to-night, and to listen to the eloquent words which have fallen from the lips of those speakers who have preceded me. I count it a privilege to spend an evening with so many young Republicans. There seems to be a fitness in the association of young men with the Republican party. The Republican party is a young party. I have not yet begun to call myself an old man, and yet there is no older Republican in the United States than I am. My first presidential vote was given for the first presidential candidate of the Republican party, and I have supported with enthusiasm every successor of Fremont, including that matchless statesman who claimed our suffrages in 1884. We cannot match ages with the Democratic party, any more than that party can match achievements with us. It has lived longer, but to less purpose. 'Mossbacked' cannot be predicated of a Republican. Our Democratic friends have a monopoly of that distinction, and it is one of the few distinguished monopolies that they enjoy: and yet, when I hear a Democrat boasting himself of the age of his party, I feel like reminding him that there are other organized evils in the world older than the Democratic party. 'The Republican Party,' the toast which you have assigned to me to-night, seems to have a past, a present, and a future tense to it. It suggests history, and yet history so recent that it is to many here to-night, a story of current events in which they have been participants. The Republican party — the influences which called it together were eclectic in their character. The men who formed it, and organized it, were picked men. The first assembly call that sounded in its camp was a call to sacrifice, and not to spoils. It assembled about an altar to sacrifice, and in a temple beset with enemies. It is the only political party organized in America that has its 'Book of Martyrs.' On the bloody fields of Kansas Republicans died for their creed, and since then we have put in that book the sacred memory of our immortal leader, who has been mentioned here to-night — Abraham Lincoln — who died for his faith and devotion to the principles of human liberty and constitutional union. And there have followed it a great army of men, who have died by reason of the fact that they adhered to the political creed that we loved. It is the only party in this land which, in the past, has been proscribed and persecuted to death for its allegiance to the principles of human liberty. After Lincoln had triumphed in that great forum of debate, in his contest with Douglas, the Republican party carried that debate from the hustings to the battle-field, and forever established the doctrine that human liberty is of natural right, and universal. It clinched the matchless logic of Webster in his celebrated debate against the right of secession, by a demonstration of its inability.

"No party ever entered upon its administration of the affairs of this Nation under circumstances so beset with danger and difficulty, as those which surrounded the Republican party when it took up the reins of executive control. In all other political contests those who had resisted the victorious party yielded acquiescence at the polls, but the Republican party in its success was confronted by armed resistance to national authority. The first acts of Republican administration were to assemble armies to maintain the authority of the Nation throughout the rebellious states. It organized armies, it fed them, and it brought them through those years of war, with an undying and persistent faith that refused to be appalled by any dangers, or discouraged by any difficulties. In the darkest days of the rebellion, the Republican party by faith saw Appomattox through the smoke of Bull Run, and Raleigh through the mists of Chickamauga. And not only did it conduct this great civil war to a victorious end, not only did it restore the national authority, and set up the flag on all those places which had been overthrown and that flag torn down, but in doing these things, and as an incident in the restoration of national authority, it accomplished that act which, if no other had been recorded in its history, would have given it immortality. The emancipation of a race, brought about as an incident of war, under the proclamation of the first Republican President, has forever immortalized the party that accomplished it.

"But not only were there these dangers, and difficulties, and besetments, and discouragements of this long strife at home, but there was also a call for the highest statesmanship in dealing with the foreign affairs of the government during that period of war. England and France not only gave to the Confederacy belligerent rights, but threatened to extend recognition and even armed intervention. There was scarcely a higher achievement in the long history of brilliant statesmanship which stands to the credit of our party, than the matchless management of our diplomatic relations during the period of our war—dignified, yet reserved; masterful, yet patient. Those enemies of republican liberty were held at bay until we had accomplished perpetual peace at Appomattox. The grasping avarice which has attempted to coin commercial advantages out of the distress of other nations, which has so often characterized English diplomacy, naturally made the government of England the ally of the confederacy that had prohibited protective duties in its constitution; and yet Geneva followed Appomattox. A trinity of effort was necessary to that consummation—war, finance, and diplomacy; Grant, Chase, Seward, and Lincoln over all, and each a victor in his own sphere. When 500,000 veterans found themselves without any pressing engagement, and Phil Sheridan sauntered down towards the borders of Mexico. French evacuation was expedited; and when General Grant advised the English government that our claims for the depredations committed by those rebel cruisers that were sent out from British ports to prey upon our commerce must be paid, but that we were not in a hurry about it — we could wait, but in the meantime interest would accumulate — the Geneva arbitration was accepted and compensation made for these unfriendly invasions of our rights. It became fashionable again at the tables of the English nobility to speak of our common ancestry and our common tongue. Then, again, France began to remind us of Lafayette and De Grasse. Five hundred thousand veteran troops and an unemployed navy did more for us than a common tongue and ancient friendships would do in the time of our distress. And we must not forget that it is often easier to assemble armies than it is to assemble army revenues. Though no financial secretary ever had laid upon him a heavier burden than was placed upon Salmon P. Chase, to provide the enormous expenditures which the maintenance of our army required, this ceaseless, daily, gigantic drain upon the National Treasury called for the highest statesmanship. And it was found: and our credit was not only maintained through the war, but the debt that was accumulated, which our Democratic friends said never could be paid, we at once began to discharge when the army was disbanded.

"And so it is that in this timely effort — consisting first in this appeal to the courage and patriotism of the people of this country, who responded to the call of Lincoln and filled our armies with brave men that, under the leadership of Grant, and Sherman, and Thomas, suppressed the rebellion, and, under the wise, magnificent system of our revenue, enabled us to defray our expenses,— we, under the sagacious administration of our State Department, held Europe at bay while we were attending to the business at home. In these departments of administration the Republican party has shown itself conspicuously able to deal with the greatest questions that have ever been presented to American statesmanship for solution. We must not forget that in dealing with these questions we were met continually by the protest and opposition of the Democratic party: The war against the States was unconstitutional; there was no right to coerce sovereign states; the war was a failure, and a dishonorable peace was demanded; the legal tenders were illegal; the constitutional amendments were void. And so, through this whole brilliant history of achievement in this administration, we were followed by the Democratic statesmen protesting against every step and throwing every impediment in the way of national success, until it seemed to be true of many of their leaders that in their estimation nothing was lawful, nothing was lovely, that did not conduce to the success of the rebellion.

"Now, what conclusion shall we draw? Is there anything in the story, so briefly and imperfectly told, to suggest any conclusion as to the inadequacy or incompetency of the Republican party to deal with any question that is now presented for solution, or that we may meet in the progress of this people's history? Why, countrymen, these problems in government were new. We took the ship of State, when there was treachery at the helm, when there was mutiny on the deck, when the ship was among the rocks, and put loyalty at the helm; we brought the deck into order and subjection. We have brought the ship into the wide and open sea of prosperity, and is it to be suggested that the party that has accomplished these magnificent achievements cannot sail and manage the good ship in the frequented roadways of ordinary commerce?

"What is there now before us that presents itself for solution? What questions are we to grapple with? What unfinished work remains to be done? It seems to me that the work that is unfinished is to make that constitutional grant of citizenship — the franchise to the colored men of the South — a practical and living reality. The condition of things is such in this country — a government by constitutional majority — that whenever the people become convinced that an administration or a law does not represent the will of the majority of our qualified electors, then that administration ceases to challenge the respect of our people, and that law ceases to command their willing obedience. This is a Republican government, a government by majority, the majorities to be ascertained by a fair count, and each elector expressing his will at the ballot-box. I know of no reason why any law should bind my conscience that does not have this sanction behind it. I know of no reason why I should yield respect to any executive officer whose title is not based upon a majority vote of the qualified electors of this country. What is the condition of things in the Southern States to-day?

"The Republican vote is absolutely suppressed. Elections in many of those States have become a farce. In the last congressional election in the State of Alabama, there were several congressional districts where the entire vote for members of Congress did not reach two thousand; whereas, in most of the districts of the North, the vote cast at our congressional elections goes from thirty thousand to fifty thousand. I had occasion to say a day or two ago that, in a single congressional district in the State of Nebraska, there were more votes cast to elect one congressman than were cast in the State of Alabama at the same election to elect their whole delegation. Out of what does this come? The suppression of the Republican vote; the understanding among our Democratic friends that it is not necessary that they should vote, because their opponents are not allowed to vote.

"But some one will suggest, 'Is there a remedy for this?' I do not know, my fellow-citizens, how far there is a legal remedy under our Constitution, but it does not seem to me to be an adequate answer, it does not seem to me to be conclusive against the agitation of this question, even if we should be compelled to respond to the arrogant question that is asked us: 'What are you going to do about it?' even if we should be compelled to answer: 'We can do nothing but protest.' Is it not worth while here, and in relation to this American question, that we should at least lift up our protest; that we should at least denounce the wrong; that we should at least deprive the perpetrators of it of what we used to call the usufructs of the crime? If you cannot prevent a burglar from breaking into your house, you will do a good deal toward discouraging burglary if you prevent him from carrying off anything; and so it seems to me that if we can, upon this question, arouse the indignant protest of the North, and unite our efforts in a determination that those who perpetrate those wrongs against popular suffrage shall not, by means of these wrongs, seat a President at Washington, to secure the federal patronage in a state, we shall have done much to bring this wrong to an end. But at least, while we are protesting by representatives from our State Department at Washington, against wrongs perpetrated in Russia against the Jew, and in our popular assemblies here against the wrongs which England has inflicted upon Ireland, shall we not, in reference to this gigantic and intolerable wrong in our own country, as a party, lift up a stalwart and determined protest against it?

"But some of these independent journalists, about which our friend MacMillan talked, call this the 'bloody shirt.' They say we are trying to revive the strife of the war, to rake over the extinct embers, to kindle the fire again. I want it understood that, for one, I have no quarrel with the South for what took place between 1861 and 1865. I am willing to forget that they were rebels; at least, as soon as they are willing to forget it themselves, and that time does not seem to have come yet to them. But our complaint is against what was done in 1884, not against what was done during the war. Our complaint is against what will be done this year, not what was done between 1861 and 1865. No bloody shirt—though that cry never had any terrors for me. I believe we greatly underestimate the importance of bringing the issue to the front, and, with that oft-time Republican courage and outspoken fidelity to truth, denouncing it the land over. If we cannot do anything else, we can either make these people ashamed of this

THE WHITE HOUSE, OR EXECUTIVE MANSION, WASHINGTON, D. C.

[*Photographed by Hucker, Providence. Drawn by Myrick, Boston.*]

outrage against the ballot, or make the world ashamed of them.

"There is another question to which the Republican party has committed itself, and on the line of which it has accomplished, as I believe, much for the prosperity of this country. I believe the Republican party is pledged, and ought to be pledged, to the doctrine of the protection of American industries and American labor. I believe that in so far as our native inventive genius, which seems to have no limit in our productive forces, can supply the American market, we ought to keep it for ourselves. And yet this new captain on the bridge seems to congratulate himself on the fact that the voyage is still prosperous, notwithstanding the change of commanders: who seems to forget that the reason that the voyage is still prosperous is because the course of the ship was marked out and the rudder tied down before he went on the bridge. He has attempted to take a new direction since he has been in command, with a view of changing the sailing course of the old craft, but it has seemed to me that he has made the mistake of mistaking the flashlight of some British light-house for the light of day. I do not intend here to-night in this presence to discuss this tariff question in any detail. I only want to say that in the passage of what is now so flippantly called the war tariff, to raise revenue to carry on the war out of the protective duties which were then levied, there has come to this country a prosperity and development which would have been impossible without it, and that a reversal of this policy now, at the suggestion of Mr. Cleveland, according to the line of the blind statesman from Texas (Mr. Mills), would be to stay and interrupt this march of prosperity on which we have entered. I am one of those uninstructed political economists that have an impression that some things may be too cheap; that I cannot find myself in full sympathy with this demand for cheaper coats, which seems to me necessarily to involve a cheaper man, or woman, under the coat. I believe it is true to-day that we have many things in this country that are too cheap; because, whenever it is proved that the man, or woman, who produces any article cannot get a decent living out of it, then it is too cheap.

"But I have not intended to discuss in detail any of these questions with which we have grappled, upon which we have proclaimed a policy, or which we must meet in the near future. I am only here to-night briefly to sketch to you the magnificent career of this party to which we give allegiance—a union of the states, restored, cemented, regenerated: a Constitution cleansed of its compromises with slavery, and brought into harmony with the immortal Declaration; a race emancipated, given citizenship and the ballot; a national credit preserved and elevated, until it stands unequaled among the nations of the world; a currency more prized than the coin for which it may be exchanged; a story of prosperity more marvelous than was ever written by the historian before. This is, in brief, an outline of the magnificent way in which the Republican party has wrought. It stands to-day for a pure, equal, honest ballot the country over. It stands to-day, without prejudice or malice, the well-wisher of every state in this Union; disposed to fill all the streams of the South with prosperity, and demanding only that the terms of the surrender at Appomattox shall be complied with. When that magnificent act of clemency was witnessed, when those sublime and gracious words were uttered by General Grant at Appomattox, the country applauded. We said to these misguided men, 'Go home'—in the language of the parole—'and you shall be unmolested while you obey the laws in force at the place where you reside.' We ask nothing more; but we cannot quietly submit to the fact that, while it is true everywhere in the United States, that the man who fought four years against his country is allowed the full, free, unrestricted exercise of his new citizenship, it shall not also be true everywhere that every man who followed Lincoln in his political views, and every soldier who fought to uphold the flag, shall in the same full, ample manner be secure in his political rights.

"This disfranchisement question is hardly a Southern question, in all strictness. It has gone into Dakota, and the intelligent and loyal population of that Territory is deprived—was at the last election, and will be again—of any participation in the decision of national questions, solely because the prevailing sentiment of Dakota is Republican. Not only that, but this disregard of purity and honesty in our elections invaded Ohio in an attempt to seize the United States Senate, by cheating John Sherman, that gallant statesman, out of his seat in the Senate. And it came here to Illinois in an attempt also to defeat that man whom I loved so much, John A. Logan, out of his seat in the United States Senate. And it has come into our own State (Indiana) by tally-sheet frauds, committed by individuals, it is true, but justified and defended by the Democratic party of the State, in an attempt to cheat us all out of our fair election majorities. It was, and it is, a question that lies over every other question, for every other question must be submitted to this tribunal for decision; and if the tribunal is corrupt, why shall we debate questions at all? Who can doubt whether, in defeat or victory, in the future, as in the past, taking high ground upon all these questions, the same stirring cause that assembled our party in the beginning will yet be found drawing like a great magnet the young and intelligent moral elements of our country into the Republican organization? Defeated once, we are ready for this campaign which is impending, and I believe that the great party of 1860 is gathering together for the coming election, with a force and a zeal and a resolution that will inevitably carry it — under that standard bearer who may be chosen here, in June — to victory in November."

CHAPTER XIV.

RECORD IN SPEECHES.

THE PRINCIPLE OF CONTROL BY THE MAJORITY THE CORNER-STONE OF AMERICAN GOVERNMENT — DEMOCRATIC SLANDERS — TARIFF UTTERANCES — A CRUEL PAGE IN OUR HISTORY — PRINCIPLE OF THE DEPENDENT PENSION BILL — THE ADMISSION OF DAKOTA TO THE UNION — DISCOURAGED REPUBLICANS IN SOUTH CAROLINA — TENURE-OF-OFFICE ACT, AND THE DEMOCRATIC STAR CHAMBER — CIVIL SERVICE COMMISSION — SEA-COAST DEFENSE — PLACES FOR THE SURPLUS — A PLEA FOR THE UNION OF TEMPERANCE FORCES — HOME RULE IN IRELAND — WHY A CHANGE OF ADMINISTRATION IS DESIRABLE.

THE following is from a speech delivered at Detroit, February 22, 1888:

"The bottom principle — sometimes it is called the corner-stone, sometimes the foundation of our structure of government — is the principle of control by the majority. It is more than the corner-stone or foundation. The structure is a monolith, one from foundation to apex, and that monolith stands for and is this principle of government by majorities, legally ascertained by constitutional methods. Everything else about our government is appendage, is ornamentation. . . . .

"The equality of the ballot demands that our apportionments in the states for legislative and congressional purposes, shall be so adjusted that there shall be equality in the influence and the power of every elector, so that it will not be true anywhere that one man counts two or one-and-a-half, and some other man counts only one-half. . . . .

"The question of a free and equal ballot is the dominant question. It lies at the foundation of our government, embracing all others, because it involves the question of a free and fair tribunal, to which every question shall be submitted for arbitrament and final determination. . . . .

"Why is it to-day that we have legislation threatening the industries of this country? Why is it that the paralyzing shadow of free trade falls upon the manufacturers and upon the homes of our laboring classes? It is because the laboring vote in the Southern States is suppressed."

"But our Democratic friends, in 1884, supplemented their complaint that we had too much money in the Treasury, with the further suggestion, apparently a little paradoxical, that there was not enough — that some of it had been made away with. Slanderous and vague imputations upon the integrity of those who were disbursing public money, as a class, were freely indulged; they did not know who, but somebody — they did not know where, but somewhere. They professed their inability to give a bill of particulars until the books were turned over to them. Well, the books have been turned over, and the cash has been counted. The balances have been verified, and the result has been an unwilling but magnificent tribute to the integrity and intelligence with which the public affairs have been managed. The malicious charges against the integrity of Republican officials have been disproved. The instances of defalcations have been rare, and the per cent. of loss exceedingly small — smaller than under any Democratic administration. An attempt has been made, in a recent publication issued by the Democratic Congressional Committee, to support the slanders of the last campaign. It is only propping up one lie against another."

"It is not my purpose at this time to discuss the particular tariff measures proposed by Mr. Morrison and Mr. Randall, or, indeed, the general question of the tariff. I believe that the tariff duties should have regard, not only to revenue to be raised, but to the interest of our American producers, and especially of our American workmen. It is clear to my mind that free trade, or a tariff for revenue, or for revenue only — and these last are essentially the same thing — involves necessarily a sudden and severe cut in the wages of workingmen and women in this country. I know it is said that his diminished wages will have an enlarged purchasing power, that after he has submitted to a cut of from fifteen to thirty per cent. in his wages, what he has left will still buy as much as before. But all this is speculation; the workman has no indemnifying bond, only a philosopher's forecast. The question must be settled by the intelligent workingmen of this country. If they do not want protective duties, then they will go. If they think that it is good policy for them that an increased amount of work, necessary to supply the American markets, should be done by foreign shops, by foreign workingmen, then it will come to a pass."

The following is an extract from a letter written by Mr. Harrison in 1885:

"I have never believed that cheap money, in the sense of depreciated money, was desirable. I have always thought and said that the interest of the laboring and farming classes especially, was in the line of staple, par currency. The silver question may be presented in diverse forms. I am a bimetallist by my strong convictions. I think silver should be preserved as a coin metal, but it is very apparent that the present ratio between silver and gold is out of joint, and that something ought to be done to correct this inequality."

The following are extracts from a speech delivered at Danville, Indiana, November 26, 1887:

"There is not a man fit to transact the duties of the simplest vocation from day to day, that does not know that the Republican majorities in three or four of the Southern States are suppressed, are not allowed to find expression at the ballot-box. I do not accept the explanation recently given by a badly reconstructed Southern statesman in his speeches in Ohio. It has not been received with confidence by the people of the North. He tried to make the Ohio people believe that the reason the colored vote did not appear at their elections for members of Congress, and for President, was on account of the fact that the colored man did not take any interest in national elections, but, he said, whenever the 'fence question' comes up, then you have a full colored vote. The colored people are interested in the fence question and they turn out! My fellow-citizens, that was a very grim joke. If there is any class of voters in this country who do take an interest in national elections, who do take an interest in the question of who shall be President, it is the freedmen of the South and those colored men who have sought kindlier homes under more hopeful auspices here in our own and other Northern States. There has not been written in the history of any civilized nation a more abominable, cruel, bloody page than that which describes the treatment of the poor blacks in the South, since those states passed under Democratic control. Why are they not allowed to vote? Because they want to vote the Republican ticket. In the last presidential election, and this one to come, our Democratic opponents count with absolute certainty upon one hundred and fifty-three electoral votes from the South, when there is no man, not a fool, who does not know that if every qualified elector in those States was allowed to express himself, they would give their electoral vote for the Republican nominee."

"Up here in the Northwest is a fair territory, enormous in extent, the one-half of it applying for admission to the Union as a State more than twice as large as the State of Indiana, having a population of nearly a half million of souls at this time, kept out of the Union of States: was kept out in 1884, will be kept out and not allowed to cast an electoral vote in 1888. Why? Simply because a majority of the people in that territory are Republicans. That, and nothing more. For the whole period of my term in the Senate, as a member of the Committee on Territories, I fought with such ability as I could, I pleaded with such power as I could, with these Democratic Southern Senators and members to allow these free people of Dakota the common rights of American citizenship. In 1884, to placate, if I could, their opposition to the admission of that State, I put a clause in the bill that the constitutional convention should not assemble until after the presidential election of that year. But now, four years more have gone around; again a President is to be elected, and still that young State, peopled with the best blood of all the States, full of the veterans of the late war, loyal to the government and the Constitution, ready to share the perils and burdens of our national life, is being, will be, kept out of the Union, will be denied any right to cast any electoral vote for President by the Democratic House of Representatives at Washington, solely because a majority of her people hold the political sentiments which we hold.

. . . .

"Some national questions of interest turn upon the coming election. Soldiers, I believe that the question whether your fame and honor shall be exalted above the fame of those who fought against the flag, whether the rewards of your services shall be just and liberal and the care of your disabled comrades ungrudging and ample, depends upon the election of a Republican President in 1888. For the first time in the history of the American Nation, we have had a President, who, in dealing with the veto power, has used it not only to deny relief, but to impeach the reputations of the men who made it possible for him to be a President of the United States. The veto messages of Mr. Cleveland, sent in during the last Congress, were, many of them, tipped with poisonous arrows. He vetoed what is called the dependent pension bill. What is the principle of it? I believe that the first bill introduced in Congress embodying the principles of that bill was introduced by me. It was prepared in view of the fact that Congress was being overwhelmed with private pension bills for men now disabled and unable to maintain themselves, who could not, by proof, connect their disability with their army service. I said let us make the limitations of the pension law wider, and instead of taking in these men one at a time, let us take the whole class in at once — and hence this bill. Some men sneered at it: said I was simply trying a buncombe game with the soldiers. But, gentlemen, the general principles of that bill have come to stay. It has, with slight modifications, received now the vote, almost unanimous, of the Grand Army of the Republic. That will be laid before Congress at its approaching session. What is the principle of it? Why, it is something like the old rule we had in the army: as long as a man was able he marched and carried his own gun and knapsack, but when he got hurt or sick, and fell out, we had an ambulance to put him in: and that is the principle embodied in this bill — that we, the survivors of the late war, as long as God gives us strength and health, will march in this column of civil life, making our own living and carrying our own burden: but here is a comrade falling by the way: sickness, casualty — not his own fault — and he has to fall out; we want the great national ambulance to take him in. That was the idea of this bill. Is it not just? Is it not as much as the soldiers can now hope to secure? Why, my countrymen, somebody must care for these veterans who stood up amid shot and shell and sabre stroke, but cannot now trace their infirmities to the army by any satisfactory proof. They have fought the battle of life manfully since. They are dependent on their work for a living, and they cannot work. Somebody must take care of them: the expense cannot be avoided unless you kick the old veterans out and let them die on the roadside. Somebody must care for them, and the simple question is, shall they be cared for as paupers in the county poorhouse, or shall the great Nation they served and saved care for them as soldiers? I prefer the latter. I want the generations coming on to know that it is safe to abandon civil pursuits, throw wealth behind you and yourself into the bloody conflict for the Nation's life; that republics are grateful, and that its soldiers will be taken care of."

From speeches in the Senate on the question of the admission of Dakota:

"Mr. President, I have never anywhere, or at any time, here or on the hustings, had but one voice upon this subject, and that was, that the man who in the hour of his country's need had bravely gone to the rescue, had exposed himself to shot and shell and sabre stroke in defense of the flag, was entitled to choose his own politics, and, while I might object to his taste, I had no criticisms for him.

"Sir, who introduced all these personalities? Where has this tide of abuse, which has been heaped upon citizens of Dakota, had its strength? Not on this side of the chamber. But Senators on that side of the chamber, from the very beginning of this debate, have felt warranted in calling the men who had been conspicuous in this movement for the formation of a new state conspirators, ambitious and scheming politicians: and that course of vituperation has run through the whole debate, on the part of gentlemen on the other side of the chamber. What is the distinction between an ambitious politician and a statesman? Do all my friends on the other side of the chamber fall into the list of statesmen?

"Have they no ambition? I appeal to the Senators who have heard every word I have spoken in this debate, from first to last, whether I have not avoided, against strenuous temptation, the bringing into this debate of the private characters of men whose names have been drawn in here by the Senator from South Carolina, whose opposition to this bill has been so intense that I never regarded him as within the reach of reason or logic. It has seemed to me that nothing but Pasteur's new treatment would do in his case.

"But, I was saying, another objection we met with, was that the people of South Dakota did not want it; and my friend from Missouri (Mr. Vest)—whose absence to-day I much regret, not only because he is himself a sufferer, but because it puts some limitation upon what I should otherwise say—the Senator from Missouri at the last session had been so fortunate as to get two or three letters from people living in South Dakota—two, I think, was the limit—one from a gentleman by the name of Richmond, and another from a lady named Marietta Bones, and in order to satisfy the Senate that the people of South Dakota did not want to be admitted as a State he read those two formidable letters.

"He pursues the same policy in the debate this session: gathering up a few letters and pouring them in upon the Senate in order to give Senators a correct idea of the popular sentiment in the Territory. Every one of these people from whom the Senator reads letters has been counted once. I must suppose that when the vote was taken, they voted against the constitution; and if they did so, they are part of that number of 6,000 that is recorded against it. Do Senators think that it strengthened their case to parade these individual expressions again before the Senate?

"I once heard a celebrated theatrical manager say that there was one thing in the way of stage deception that the gallery gods would not stand, and that was to have an army of supes come around the second time. When they recognized the face of a fellow who had been on the stage once before, that business had to be stopped. And yet, just that stage deception these gentlemen are attempting to practice upon the Senate and the country. The persons in South Dakota who oppose this constitution have been counted once, and that is enough. We do not want this army of supes marched around again."

"So it is, Mr. President. The Senator from Alabama, who last season talked so blandly and kindly about the admission of Dakota that he absolutely persuaded me that I could count, if not upon his vote, at least upon his candid and kind consideration of this bill, goes about looking up some question of personal disqualification in some member of the convention, and that, as I think, upon insufficient information. Then the Senator does not like to adopt this constitution, because he says we have to take with it the Senators who have been elected by the legislature which was convened under it. 'We have to take,' Mr. President! What has the Senator, or any other Senator here, to do with the question as to who shall be the Senators from any state? We have to take the Senator and his colleague, and we do it agreeably and without protestation: we have to take the Senator from Missouri and his colleague, and why? Because they have been chosen by the legislatures of their respective states. I cannot understand why we should not deal in the same way with Dakota, when she shall be admitted. If these proceedings of Dakota have been such that we can approve them, then I submit it is for no Senator to say here that he objects to her demand because he has to take Senators whom her people have chosen."

"The Senator from South Carolina says that we did not encourage the Republicans down there to come out and vote; that they needed encouragement, and that the Senator from Illinois, and other leaders of the Republican party, failed to go down and encourage them. Well, Mr. President, they are a discouraged set, those Republicans in South Carolina. They have never had any encouragement since 1876, and the only efficient encouragement, according to their judgment, was the presence of some of the troops of the United States. We cannot do that any more, and perhaps it never ought to have been done. But this is aside from the question, altogether. The election in South Carolina may be fair: everybody who wants to vote may have a chance to vote; all the talk of intimidation may be absolutely false; all the stories of bloodshed and violence and red-shirted cavalry may all be imagination; all the stories of tissue ballots may be vain and fraudulent. For the purposes of this argument, I assume that they are, that there is nothing in them in the world; and yet I ask the Senator from South Carolina, if in a presidential election, if in the election of a legislature that is to choose Senators for this body, forty-four per cent. of the total vote in South Carolina is sufficiently expressive of the popular will there to choose these officers, may it not be that upon the mere question of voting on a constitution in Dakota, fifty-eight per cent. is enough?"

From a speech in the Senate:

Tenure-of-Office Act and the Democratic Star Chamber.

"In the President's recent message, speaking of the law of 1867, which required the President to transmit his reasons for a suspension, he says in substance: 'If that law were in force I would obey it,' showing that he submits himself to the provisions of the tenure-of-office law, and does not challenge its constitutionality. Under that law, I do not see how any man can doubt that, in the case of a suspended officer, nominated in place of another whose removal is proposed, the concurrence of the Senate is an essential, necessary, and effective part of the act of removal. The officer is not removed until the Senate acts in either case. He is an officer until, by the confirmation of his successor, we change the office and place it in other hands, and that quite as strictly in law, while he is suspended from the exercise of its functions, as while he is in their actual discharge. The question is clearly one with which we have to do. We are asked by the President to do an act which removes a man from office, and will any one insist that we are not entitled to all needful information: that we may not rightly consider that which is the constitutional and legal result of our act; that we must shut our eyes to the question whether there has been cause for suspicion, whether the office has been mismanaged, whether the man who previously held it has been recreant to official trust — that we must close our eyes to all these questions, when his removal from office is that which we are asked to consummate in the one case, the direct consequence of what we are asked to do? It has been said that the tenure-of-office act has been out of use. I shall not attempt to repeat the high-sounding terms in which the President conveyed to us this information. I have been in this body five years, and I affirm that the civil tenure-of-office law has never been out of use. I affirm, though my colleague (Mr. Voorhees) declared the contrary yesterday, that a Republican Senate under a Republican President put it to the very use to which we are putting it now. I affirm that not once, but many times, (and if he will spur his recollection, many of the instances will come to his own mind), has this same request for papers been made and complied with, and the Senate has considered upon the papers the question of whether there was cause for removal. I can call cases to mind when just such information, demanded by a Republican Senate of a Republican President, influenced my action and vote upon nominations that were proposed to us.

"It is not true, Mr. President. The fact is that the tenure-of-office law has been enforced; it has been continually in mind in the administration of that part of our duty connected with the confirmation of officers nominated by the President.

"Many of them, as the Senator from Connecticut suggests, were affidavits containing sworn charges that have been filed in the departments. Is there a Democratic Senator here who will get up and confess that he filed any? Is there one? Is it not true, my friends, that whenever this is suggested to you you are prompt to say: 'I never went into the business; I would not be guilty of filing such charges?' Is not that true?

"Is this the great issue upon which the Democracy is to be united? I affirm that there is not a Democrat who hears me — a member of this body — who will confess that he has become, or agree that he is willing to become, a party to this method of getting Democrats into office.

"It may be — though I would not impute such a motive to any Democratic Senator — I have thought sometimes that there might be gentlemen, connected with Congress possibly, or outside Democrats of influence, who had an interest in helping to hold down the lid of the box in which these secrets are buried, because if it were opened it would show that they had participated in this work.

"I think there must be in these files a great deal of matter of which the President is ignorant, a great many confidential papers which he withholds from us that he has never seen himself. I am bound to believe that is true, from the knowledge I have of the contents of some of them, or I am compelled to believe that he is utterly insincere in his public utterances as to his methods of administering the appointments to office.

"And now to turn from the grave to the gay. This non-partisan civil service administration has turned Republicans out because they were on committees, or published newspapers, or took some active part in campaigns. A friend of mine sent me the other day this post-office heading: it is a little post-office in Greene County, Indiana.

"Mr. Edmunds.— A Democratic post-office at the present time?

"Mr. Harrison.— I suppose so. He was appointed on July 20, 1885, and I believe no Republican has been appointed since that date. The printing is as follows:

"'JAMES H. QUINLAN, P. M.
"'Post-office at Lyons, Greene County, Indiana.'

"On this side (exhibiting) is a picture of Cleveland and Hendricks, with the words under it, 'Our benefactors.' I suppose the possessive pronoun refers to the postmasters, and not to the public generally. Some Republican postmasters were, I understand, convicted of offensive partisanship, and turned out because, during the last campaign, they had a picture of the late Honorable John A. Logan, our candidate for the Vice-Presidency, displayed in the office. That was thought to evince offensive partisanship, and without being allowed to prove whether it was a likeness or not, they were turned out. There were some of those campaign pictures of General Logan that I think a man might have raised an issue on. But here a Democratic postmaster is not guilty of offensive partisanship when he puts on a post-office letter-head the name of the Democratic President and Vice-President with the legend, 'Our benefactors.' The Postmaster-General's head ought to have been on there, because that is a fourth-class post-office."

CIVIL SERVICE COMMISSION.

"*Mr. President:* My colleague (Mr. Voorhees) mistakes the issue. The issue is not whether it is an appropriate thing that there should be Democrats in office or not. It is not whether, in the absence of law, it would be a just subject of criticism if the Secretery of the Interior, or any other head of a department here, appointed Democrats, or Democrats exclusively, if you please. The question here is one of the administration of the law, and a law that had a distinguished Democratic origin; though I am sorry to say it has never had much Democratic support, and the fact of originating it has been very creditable to its originator.

"The question here raised is as to the faithfulness of the administration of the law; and upon the facts I have before me, I do not intend to say that, on the part of the commissioners who are here appealing to Congress for some additional clerical force, there has been a maladministration or a corrupt administration of it. The investigation to which reference has been made is not yet concluded, and I am not one of those who rush into the discussion of a case until the evidence is closed. It does not appear, however, according to the facts as stated by the Senator from Kansas (Mr. Ingalls), that somehow or other, under the operations of this civil service law and the rules which have been made for its enforcement, which have in most cases required that only the three or four leading persons, the three or four highest upon the list, should be certified,—by some process or other, this has been accomplished in the Pension Office, namely, that seventy-two out of seventy-seven men, who have been selected under the law from lists furnished by the Civil Service Commission, have been Democrats, and that the other five are found without any politics at all.

"That is true. That may be consistent with an impartial, non-partisan administration of the Civil Service bureau. It may be so. We shall know more about it when we get through with the investigation which has been inaugurated on that subject. It is true, undoubtedly true, that prior to the passage of the civil service law, both on the part of the Republicans and the Democrats, when they were in power, the great bulk of the appointments were made of the political faith of the person having the appointing power.

"I know nothing about that. I did not rise to enter any complaint, and should not have said anything on such a subject, except for references that have been made by other Senators.

"If the Civil Service Commission need these clerks, as the chairman of the committee having that subject in charge assures us, I am willing to give them to them; and if it shall be found that the office is in some way administered so as to give a partisan turn, so that while things are put promiscuously and fairly into the mill, nothing but Democratic results come out — when we have ascertained that fact, then it will be time enough, so far as I am concerned, to arraign the commission, and to hold them to that just responsibility to which the country will hold them, if it is found to be the result of any maladministration or fraudulent administration of the law.

. . . .

"I desire simply to say that it seems to me this commission

should not be composed of men who are supposed to represent interests. The words which I move to strike out, would imply that there was to be a railroad man on the commission, perhaps a railroad president or officer, and that there was to be some one representing the agriculturists, some one representing the manufacturing interests, and so on. If this commission is to accomplish the good which is expected of it, it should not be made up of men who represent particular interests. We should not have there some one who understands that he is the representative of the railroad companies, and some one else that he is there as the representative of shippers who desire lower rates. We shall have no wise consideration of this question, and no useful recommendations, in my judgment, from such a commission. I believe the President should be left free to choose men who will represent the general interests of the whole country, rather than to choose men who will stand for special interests. Therefore I move to strike out these words."

Seacoast Defense.

"There is another thing we want done. We want our seacoast ports put in a position of defense, so that it will no longer be possible for some third-rate power of South America to run an ironclad in and put our cities under contribution. For the brutal treatment that was meted out to us by England, when our hands were full by reason of the great civil conflict, we have accepted a recompense in money; but no nation must repeat that experiment with our patience. We must also save enough revenue to put on the sea a navy worthy of this great

Nation, and capable of maintaining our old-time prestige on the ocean. We will no longer have our shame-faced naval officers creeping into foreign ports in wooden hulks, the laughing stock of all who see them. Republicans have been trying to do this for a good while, but while the Democrats had control of the House of Representatives they refused to make the necessary appropriations, because they said they could not trust a Republican secretary to spend them. Well, when they got a secretary of their own the Republicans were more magnanimous. We said he was not a whit better or a whit honester than our man was, but we are American citizens: and we walked grandly forward and gave them, to be expended in the construction of ships, all the money that a parsimonious Democratic House would let us give them."

Speech at Indianapolis, December 20, 1887.

"In connection with this surplus of about one hundred millions a year, there is danger; there are dangers of profligacy, of expenditure, and others that require us to address ourselves promptly and intelligently to the question of a reduction of our revenue. I have said before I would like to have that work done by the Republicans, because I would like to have it done with reference to some great questions connected with the use of the revenue, about which I cannot trust my Democratic friends. I would like to have our coast defenses made secure: I would like to have our navy made respectable, so that an American naval officer, as he trod the deck of the ship bearing the starry banner at its head in any port throughout the world, and looked about upon her equipment and armament, might eel that she wa s a match for the proudest ship that walked the sea under any other flag. I would like to feel that no third-rate power, aye, no first-rate power, could sail into our defenseless harbors and lay our great cities under tribute. I would like to feel that the just claims of the survivors of the Union Army of the war were made secure and safe. Therefore, I have a strong preference that this work of the reduction of our revenue, internal and external, shall be conducted by Republicans."

A plea for the union of Temperance forces:

"But to those more practical Temperance men who do not demand the unattainable, the Republican party appeals in this campaign. If some of us will not engage to accept the goal you have in view, need we part company till we reach the forks of the road? It would not have been good military tactics for Grant's army before Petersburg to have refused to unite in an assault until his soldiers could agree upon the precise terms of reconstruction. The first duty in hand was to whip Lee. The Liquor League is entrenched in this State behind the Democratic party and the legislative gerrymander. It has levied its assessments to create campaign funds for Democratic uses, and to corrupt legislatures. The Republican party has boldly declared that its repression must be shaken off, and its corrupt influence in politics destroyed. Is not that a work in which all men who favor temperance reform can unite? Can such afford to divide when that issue is presented?".

On the evening of October 5, 1887, a meeting was held in Indianapolis, in honor of Messrs. O'Connor and Osmond.

During the evening, Mr. Harrison was loudly called for, and spoke, in substance, as follows:

"The hour is already so late that I shall detain the audience but a moment. I am glad to have had the opportunity to hear the distinguished guests of the evening—men who in the British Parliament stand for Home Rule in Ireland. They have given me much fuller information than I had before of the oppressive character of the coercion acts. I was glad, also, to know that the Irish people have shown such a steady and self-contained adherence to their rights, and such steadfastness in the assertion of them by lawful methods. We know that Irishmen have many a time, in the struggle of their native land, and in our fight in America for free government, thrown themselves upon the bayonet of the enemies of liberty with reckless courage. It is gratifying to know that they can also make a quiet but unyielding resistance to oppression by Parliamentary methods. I would rather be William O'Brien in Tullamore jail, a martyr of free speech, than the Lord Lieutenant of Ireland, in Dublin Castle."

Why another change of administration is desirable:

"Our Democratic friends are now inclined to withdraw the suggestion that a change is a good thing, but I believe the people, in view of broken pledges and disappointed hopes, are willing to make one more. But if the hopes of individual benefit from the election of Mr. Cleveland have been disappointed, has any gain come to the Nation? Has its honor or its credit been lifted up? Have we any more reason to be proud that we are Americans? Has our diplomacy gained us increased respect? Has patriotism and loyalty been recrowned? No, my countrymen. The flag has dropped to half-mast in honor of a man who was not only disgracefully unfaithful to a civil trust before the war, and a rebel during the war, but who, from a safe haven in Canada, sought by his hired emissaries to give our peaceful cities to the flames. An unrestored rebel was named to represent this country at the court of St. Petersburg, unmindful of the fact that the Czar was on our side during the Rebellion. The courts of Europe were canvassed to find a place for a man who had declared the government he was to represent a "bloody usurpation." Our fishermen are badgered in Canadian waters, while the peaceful retaliatory powers confined by law to the President are unused. So general has been the condemnation of our diplomatic dealings with Mexico, that our distinguished Secretary of State is said to believe that the whole country has entered into a conspiracy against him, while the jockey club in Mexico has debauched his special envoy. The dying appeal of Mr. Tilden was not enough to arouse the patriotism of a Democratic majority in the House to make an appropriation for our coast defenses. The modest bill for new war ships — carrying $6,500,000 — was, by decree of the Democratic steering committee, reduced to $3,500,000, under a threat that it should not otherwise have consideration. Wounded and deserving soldiers have been expelled from public offices upon a secret charge, and their appeals to know the character of the charges have been treated by an arrogant head of department with contemptuous silence."

PART II.

LEVI PARSONS MORTON.

PART SECOND.

LIFE OF LEVI PARSONS MORTON.

CHAPTER I.

ANCESTRY.

A PASSENGER ON THE SHIP ANN — A SETTLER IN MIDDLEBORO', MASSACHUSETTS — LATER GENERATIONS — A BIRTH IN MAINE — REMOVAL TO VERMONT — SCHOOL AT MIDDLEBURY, VERMONT — STUDIES FOR THE MINISTRY — REMOVAL TO SHOREHAM — ANOTHER FAMILY OF MASSACHUSETTS — REMOVAL TO ADDISON COUNTY, VERMONT — THE FIRST AMERICAN MISSIONARY TO THE HOLY LAND — MARRIAGE — THE FOURTH CHILD — HIS NAME.

IN 1623 the good ship *Ann* cast anchor just off the Massachusetts shore Among her passengers was a young man of sterling piety, who sought the freedom to be found in the New World, and whose name was George Morton. This man settled at Plymouth.

But his son,. John Morton, became one of the famous "twenty-six men" who bought the lands at Nemasket, and settled the town of Middleboro'. He was the first deputy to the General Court of Plymouth, in 1670, and was chosen again in 1672.

According to accounts which seem accurate, the house he built before King Philip's War was saved from the conflagration, when the town was burned during that war, on account of friendly acts done to the Indians, and remained standing until but a few years ago. According to other accounts, that first house was burned in the war, and another was built immediately afterwards, which was not destroyed until about 1870.

This man's son, the second John Morton, bought extensive tracts of land, and enlarged the house which became famous as the "old Morton House."

A Mrs. Morton was living in the house about 1750. She was a member of the First Congregational Church, of Middleboro', and distinguished for her piety and social influence. She was a woman of great hospitality. Her home was the home of the clergymen who visited the church. On one occasion, when a couple of ministers called near the dinner-hour, she placed before them what she had, remarking that she had not time to prepare more. "But, gentlemen," said she, "if you are good Christians you will be thankful for this; if you are not, it is too good for you."

So the Mortons and their descendants lived for generations, —one of the noble, patriot families of the Commonwealth on whose shores "American liberty raised her first voice."

Two characteristics marked the people of Massachusetts, both in the earlier and later days: an intense piety and an intense patriotism. It has been said that they abused the former by linking it with the spirit of persecution. However that may be, the spirit of liberty was not wanting in any part of their natures, even in their religion. They only asked that the society which *they* had established enjoy its liberty without molestation by doctrines from *other* societies. The shores of the New World were long, and the fields were wide, and they had no objection to the presence of others near them, but in separate communities; they would even unite with others in the common defense of civil and religious liberty. This sort of persecution — which rose in self-defense, in the belief that doctrines were essential, and that foreign teachings would demoralize and ruin them and their children — was far different from that which had been carried on against them in England, to compel them to conform to other teaching.

This peculiarity was manifested in civil, as well as in religious affairs. The Puritans were aggressive in matters of human liberty; but not in matters of doctrine or philosophy, civil, social, or religious. In those things they merely desired liberty. English persecution, on the other hand, has always been the manifestation of the assumption of authority of class over the conscience and liberty of class. Daniel Webster, in later years, taught, with the Declaration of Independence, and according to the assumption of the Constitution of the United States, that men are already free and equal, and that government should be for the defense of this liberty, not to compel men to conform to anything civil or otherwise. And it may be noted, in the history of the Federalist, National Republican, Whig, and Republican parties, that their greatest rallyings of their forces, and their greatest uprisings, have been when the principles of liberty were in danger, and not when they sought to enforce conformity of any sort. The latter characteristic belongs strictly and solely to the Democratic party, and its greatest illustration is the War of the Rebellion. Every Whig sought conciliation until 1854, and many of them until Sumter was fired on. Then, the danger arising, they arose in defense of liberty.

Such was the spirit of the people, among whom George Morton and his descendants have not been insignificant.

One of the later Mortons moved to Maine, and there a son, Daniel O. Morton, was born to him. He removed, while this son was young, to Middlebury, Vermont, and there he brought him up strictly, and in the later Puritan faith. He gave him a good education, sending him until he graduated, to Middlebury College.

Daniel O. Morton thus became a strong, self-reliant, sturdy man, ready for any kind of life that Providence seemed to point out to him. He became a Congregational minister. When he had graduated, and was ready to enter on the life of a minister, he settled in Shoreham, Vermont, in 1812, and there he remained as pastor for many years. He afterwards became pastor of the church at Springfield, Vermont, and afterwards at Winchendon, Massachusetts. He became a powerful preacher, but noted more for his earnest, indefatigable pastoral work, and faithful and learned teachings, than for great eloquence. He seems to have gone quietly along, content to teach the humble in his parish, and utterly without that restless ambition that often characterizes those in public life, to acquire more notoriety. There is extant a pamphlet written by him, in which is described the great revival at Springfield about the year 1838, and it is, perhaps, his only published work.

There was another Massachusetts family — that of Rev.

Justyn Parsons. He moved from Western Massachusetts and settled in Addison County, Vermont, not far from Middlebury. He had a son named Levi, who also became a minister—educated, and a man of talent and culture and piety. Levi Parsons was associated with the Rev. Mr. Fisk, and the two were the first American missionaries to the Holy Land. Mr. Parsons died in 1824, and was buried in Alexandria, Egypt.

A daughter of the Rev. Justyn Parsons, sister to Levi, as pious and accomplished as her brother, was a light and comfort to the household when they moved to Vermont. But she there met the young student, Daniel O. Morton; they became engaged, and about the time he was to enter on his duties in Shoreham, they were married. The young minister took his bride to the rough and small village, and together they began the task of making out of it a typical New England village.

The New England villages have a characteristic quietness and steadiness and culture, due, more than to anything else, to the long pastorates of faithful ministers. A young man entered upon his pastorate when the village was young; he won the confidence of the quiet people; the young at last all came more or less under his influence; he officiated at all weddings, and all funerals; he patronized the public school; he encouraged every kind of knowledge; he set the example of beautifying his home by adornments of quiet art; and so ten, twenty, thirty, forty, and fifty years passed, and there was a quiet village nestled among the shade-trees, having a cleanly appearance, and somehow an air of culture; and the minister himself could scarcely tell how the touches of modern art and taste became mingled with the earlier adornments until he could not perceive where one ended and the other began, so imperceptibly and gradually had the changes come by the influence of the spirit he had given them years before. This is the typical New England village, with its cottages, and even with its mills.

Such, with the differences required by local circumstances, was Shoreham. The village was not in the centre of the stern Puritan society, but, with a few others in that region which were established by such influences, was isolated from it by the Green Mountains. It was situated on the shore of Lake Champlain, midway north and south between Ticonderoga and Crown Point, which were on the opposite side of the river. Here it was more accessible to the influences from the mouth of the Hudson, than to those from Massachusetts Bay. Nevertheless, the little village quietly grew under the care and vigilance of the village pastor and his faithful associates, and their influence was greater than any from other sources.

To the young couple were born, as many quiet years went by, six children — four daughters and two sons. Four of these are living to-day, and a daughter and a son are dead. This son, Daniel O. Morton, died at his home in Toledo, Ohio, December 5th, 1859, at the age of forty-four. He was a graduate of Middlebury College, and had achieved considerable fame in Ohio as an able lawyer. He was appointed by President Pierce United States District Attorney for Ohio. Some years before his death, he manifested that independence and patriotism that belonged to the people from whom he descended in a characteristic manner. He had been a member of the Democratic party, and one of its conscientious supporters. At the mutterings of rebellion and arrogance on the part of the South, and the disloyal apologies for it on the part of Democrats of the North, he deliberately separated himself from the party, and announced his purpose to stand by the government and the Union, at a time when the act involved the bitterest persecution from old friends.

Levi Parsons Morton, the fourth child, was born at Shoreham, May 16, 1824. Th's, it will be seen, was in the same year in which the missionary died at his lonely post and was buried in Alexandria, and it may be that that fact had something to do with naming the boy.

CHAPTER II.

THE BOYHOOD OF MORTON.

THE PREACHER'S SALARY — A FAMILY OF EIGHT — HOW TO EDUCATE THE CHILDREN — THE COMMON SCHOOL AT SHOREHAM — THE INFLUENCE OF HOME — COUNTRY STORE IN ENFIELD — A TWO YEARS' PRACTICAL SCHOOLING — APTITUDE FOR BUSINESS — HABITS — MIND — ANOTHER COUNTRY STORE — A MARK OF EMPLOYER'S CONFIDENCE — BRANCH STORE IN HANOVER — DARTMOUTH COLLEGE — FOUNDATION FOR FUTURE SUCCESS — FIRST VOTE AND POLITICAL VIEWS — ANOTHER ADVANCE IN 1849.

LEVI's father was poor; and he modestly chose a humble station, even for a minister. His salary was but six hundred dollars a year; a small amount, indeed, for the living of a family of eight, and the education of six children.

Levi was born at a time when his father's cares and expenses had increased, and were still increasing, by reason, not only of the added number to the household, but of the accumulating demands of living, benevolence, and enterprise as the village grew older. He was scarcely able to attend the country school when the sixth child was born; and the expenses of the education of his elder brother at Middlebury began to drain his father's purse. He was just nine years old when his brother graduated at the age of eighteen; but his father was not able to let Daniel's mantle of fortune fall upon Levi's shoulders, for he must not only pay the graduate's expenses in the office of Payne & Wilson, Cleveland, Ohio, where he pursued legal studies, until after his removal to Toledo, and the beginning of his practice in 1837, but must bear the increased burdens of a family of growing children, and of a larger parish.

With his small income, it was impossible for Mr. Morton to give his other children the advantages he had given the first. It became, indeed, a serious problem how to provide for them and educate them at all. True, he and his wife were educated and could teach; and in this home-school the children would always be under the best of influences. But the poor have little time or opportunity for giving their children direct courses of instruction; and the poor minister and his wife especially, are not spared such time and opportunity from the varied home and parish duties. Yet what training could be given in that way, was given, and at least the moral and religious influences should not be lacking.

It thus came about that the boy, Levi, did not receive a college education, and that he did receive good home-training instead. But he was also enabled to attend the common school in Shoreham, and this was all the school-training he ever received. That he made use of his talents, was a faithful pupil, and applied himself well, can easily be believed from his subsequent career. His teachers had no more promising pupil, and he justified their expectations.

Levi Morton furnishes in his life an illustration of the efficiency of the American home — the homes built by those ruled by conscience alone, and having broad, independent ideas and spirit to impart to their children.

Meanwhile, as the boy grew up, he had to assist in bearing

the common burdens. He could not attend school at Springfield, nor at Winchendon, for this reason. Soon after arriving at the latter village, it became necessary that he should earn wages; and to this end, he resolved to pursue a course that would lead him, by way of study, discipline, and experience, to those heights of culture that had been denied him through the schools. He was not of that cool and calculating business temper that has no ends in view but wealth, at any cost. His youthful eye looked longingly upon that culture, and no doubt on that fame, from which he had been debarred by lack of wealth, and wealth he determined to have as a means to the coveted end: and judging from his subsequent career, he determined, also, that when he should become rich, he would not deny to others what the rich had practically denied to him.

At the age of fifteen, he went to Enfield, Massachusetts, on the Swift River, and entered as a clerk, a country variety store, kept by Mr. Ezra Cary. Here were sold dry-goods, groceries, crockery ware, tin ware, and everything that people might want, for the village was not large enough for stores doing special kinds of trade.

Here he remained two years. He had a natural aptitude for the business, and he was faithful and trusty. His employer could leave him in charge for days, when he wished, and matters would go on and prosper. Young Morton found the two years were to him the same as two years of schooling. He brought not only what he had learned at home and in the country school into practical use, but he gained both training and knowledge. He became a ready calculator, and began also to learn the larger principles of trade, looking out for the interests of his employer in many ways. With Levi Morton the proprietor's business was as his own. He had come there to help, to clerk, to take oversight frequently, and he conscientiously strove to do his work well.

Besides this consideration, he had business habits that served him here in good need. True, no good habit can be so well formed but that it be improved. He might have learned merely to follow his business tastes by habit, but then he would have become a mere machine, and his tastes but part of the machine. The habit of always bringing original inventive business faculties to bear on one's business life makes the mechanical in one's life impossible; and, in his line, Levi Morton had inventive faculties. He had a fertility of resource that gave promise of his future success. He carried his home principles into everything he did; a stern integrity, a conscientiousness, a firm confidence in the machinery that produces results when set in motion by wisdom and prudence. This was his apparent coolness; but it was rather, in fact, the steady control of giant forces.

At the end of two years, he closed his work with Mr. Cary, and went into a store at Concord, New Hampshire, owned by Mr. W. W. Esterbrook. Here was a larger store, a larger trade, and here he received larger wages. The same fidelity that marked his course in Enfield, he manifested in Concord, and he also proved himself fully equal to his additional tasks.

The confidence his new employer had in him was soon to be shown in a marked manner. They had not been together many months, before Mr. Esterbrook sent him to establish a branch store in Hanover, New Hampshire, and conduct it himself. It was no ordinary good fortune, and no ordinary show of appreciation for a young man.

Hanover was on the Connecticut River, and was the seat of Dartmouth College. Its glory over ordinary villages, therefore, was no assumption; while its society, if not fastidious, was yet not satisfied with lack of culture and intelligence among those with whom it dealt, or whom it admitted to its circles. It is no small thing, therefore, to say that it opened its heart to the young merchant. Professors and students became his friends, and they, and the rest of the *élite* of Hanover, were glad to have his presence on occasions of intellectual or social assembling: for he had a natural grace and refinement that made him welcome in the homes of the rich, and made the poor his friends.

Thus young Morton found himself under the best influences that Dartmouth and Hanover could afford; for his associations were not of that class that detract from steadiness of life. He attended strictly to his business; he never lost sight of the fact that others' interests were bound up in his own; and, besides, he had no tastes for that companionship which did not in spirit harmonize with the seriousness of his aims in life. He sought rather the society of the cultivated, the thoughtful, and the conscientious. It can also be understood, from his birth and bringing-up, that he had a natural taste for that stern devotion that marked the lives of cultivated church-people in that day. Yet, withal, he was genial, companionable, and broad of mind and heart. He was not narrow nor bigoted in any sense.

In Hanover, Mr. Morton gained his first practical insight into the details of the commission business; and here he no doubt laid the foundations of his broad plans of life that brought him great returns of wealth. He dealt fairly and honestly. He managed the business with skill and enterprise. He attracted, by his gentlemanly manners and enterprising methods of conducting his store, the trade of professors, students, and all other classes. His goods were of the best quality. He also thoroughly satisfied those whose goods he was handling; and he won for himself a reputation for business integrity and capability that was to be of no little service to him in time to come. So he remained in Hanover, giving entire satisfaction to all with whom he dealt, until he was twenty-five.

Before this time, Mr. Morton had cast his first vote, in 1848. He had always had his convictions on the public questions of the day; and though he was so far removed from the great centres of conflict, yet he lived right in the midst of the people who had descended from those who had taken, at first, the deepest interest in American principles, and where that interest had never waned. He had always been a Whig, and his first vote was cast for Zachary Taylor.

He was among those that were always serious in political matters; and he never could understand how men, claiming to have the interest of the country at heart, could toy recklessly with the rights of the people. Hence he deplored the clinging to the Whig cause of politicians for personal or local interests, as had been the case since the days of Jackson. He believed the Whig cause would prosper better without them, in work and in numbers. There were many honest and true patriots in the United States whose minds were confused by these parasites. They knew the professions of the Whig party; but when these so-called friends manifested more trickery than principle, some of them having made speeches in behalf of better principles than they afterwards regarded while in office, these genuine patriots revolted from the idea of Whig purity. When there was evident conniving at corruption for the sake of gaining votes, these men could not believe in Whig sincerity. These things in that day, as in this, were called "politics," and condoned because they were "politics," and "politics" was right. But Mr. Morton did not believe in that kind of politics. He believed that manipulations might always be made on honest basis; and that a party with such principles as the Whig party professed, need not be ashamed of them anywhere, and that honest and open avowal of them, and open work for their success, would at last call the better elements of the government to rally around the Whig standard. He believed that people with American principles predominated in America. Believing as he did, he was of just the right material to put into the foundation of the new party that should afterwards rise, composed largely, perhaps almost altogether at first, of the very best of American patriots.

In 1849, there was another change in his personal affairs. He gave up the store at Hanover, and went to Boston to enter the large business house of Messrs. Beebe & Company, as clerk. So far, his march from boyhood was attended with success. Nor was his star destined to grow dim.

CHAPTER III.

BUSINESS AND FINANCIAL RECORD.

"BEEBE & COMPANY"—JOINED BY MR. MORGAN—MR. MORTON A RESIDENT PARTNER IN NEW YORK—DEATH OF HIS FATHER—"MORTON & GRINNELL"—FIRST MARRIAGE—A FINANCIAL FAILURE—A NEW FIRM—AN HONORABLE DEED—MR. BLISS ENTERS THE FIRM—"MORTON, ROSE & COMPANY," LONDON—DEATH OF HIS WIFE—YEARS OF BRAVERY UNDER AFFLICTION—ANOTHER HAPPY MARRIAGE—"HALIFAX AWARD"—STORY OF THE RESUMPTION OF SPECIE PAYMENT.

THE real business life of Levi P. Morton began in 1849, when he received an invitation to become clerk in the large dry-goods commission house of James M. Beebe & Company, Boston, which was, at that time, one of the largest and most reliable firms in New England.

He continued as clerk for the firm two years; and that he gave perfect satisfaction is witnessed by the confidence manifested in him in various ways, on the part of his employers, and especially by a promotion that came to him at the end of the two years.

On the 1st of January, 1851, Mr. Junius S. Morgan, who had been a member of the firm of Howe, Mather & Company, of Hartford, Connecticut, entered the firm of Beebe & Company, which then became Beebe, Morgan & Company.

About the same time, young Morton's first two years with the house ended, and he was now made a member of the firm.

One year after, in January, 1852, the firm opened a branch package house in New York City, and Mr. Morton was detailed as resident partner and manager.

It was in that year that his father, Daniel O. Morton, died in Bristol, New Hampshire, whither he had removed from Winchendon in 1842, and where he had done effective work as pastor of the Congregational Church. Thus passed away one of the strong pillars of the later Puritan faith: a defender of civil and religious liberty in its broadest, truest sense, and a conservator, in his life and teaching, of much that was good in past systems of social and religious doctrine.

Subsequently a memorial tablet was erected in the church at Bristol. It was of the finest, and most highly polished Italian marble. It was three feet four inches wide, by six feet high. On the top were molded scroll cornices and a Gothic cross. The whole was upheld by sculptured brackets. The following was the inscription: "In memory of the Rev. Daniel Oliver Morton, Pastor of the Congregational Churches in Shoreham and Springfield, Vermont, and Winchendon, Massachusetts, from 1812 to 1841, and of this church from June 8, 1842, to the day of his death, March 22, 1852. 'They that turn many to righteousness shall shine as the stars forever and ever.' Erected by his son, Levi Parsons Morton." The tablet stands to-day, one of the monuments to the devotion of the son to the memory of his father and his principles.

Mr. Morton served as New York partner of the Boston house until January 1, 1854. On that date both he and Mr. Morgan withdrew from the firm. Mr. Morgan became a partner in the American banking house of George Peabody & Company, London. When, in 1866, Mr. Peabody retired, the firm became J. S. Morgan & Company, and remains under that name. Mr. Morton, on the day of his withdrawing from the firm of Beebe, Morgan & Company, established the dry-goods commission house of Morton & Grinnell, on lower Broadway, New York, succeeding to the business of J. C. Bird & Company.

Here, as senior partner, Mr. Morton widened his sphere of business experience, and of knowledge of finance and men. He manifested the same tact and shrewdness that had hitherto characterized him; and the habits of faithfulness and watchfulness, acquired in caring for others' interests, now came to him as a reward in caring for his own.

Two years after entering into partnership with Mr. Grinnell, Mr. Morton was married. He was just thirty-two years old; but he had not before considered himself ready for the sacred alliance. He had now been but two years really independent in business. His mind had not, indeed, been so entirely engrossed with business that he was not before susceptible to the influences of love; but his thoughts had evidently formed an ideal home and companionship incompatible with his circumstances, while he felt himself in any wise dependent upon others in his business affairs. He now felt that the time of realization of a well-appointed home had come.

The young lady was Miss Lucy Kimball, daughter of Elijah H. Kimball, of Flatlands, Long Island. She belonged to one of the best families of Kings County. She was very beautiful, gifted, and accomplished. She was a leader in society. Withal, she was noble-minded, tender-hearted, and benevolent. Wherever there was suffering to be relieved, Lucy Kimball was found, if it was possible for her to be there. So true a woman was well fitted for the companionship of Levi P. Morton, who had set his heart on finding a wife for his ideal home and the sharing of his life. She became a faithful wife, and greatly assisted in making his life a still greater success.

Morton & Grinnell did a good business until 1861. In that trying year, with many other houses, they failed. Mr. Morton desired to pay every cent, but it was simply impossible, and a settlement had to be effected at fifty cents on the dollar. The settlement was open, and all that could be asked at that time.

Meanwhile, in 1859, his mother had died. The family had been broken up on the death of his father in 1852, and his mother had been dependent upon her children. She had received no little support from her honored and successful son, whose love for his parents, and whose liberality had been manifested in many ways. She had now been living in Philadelphia for sometime, and was there at the time of her death.

In this same year, also, his brother, Daniel O. Morton, of whom mention has been made, died in Toledo. He left a son and a daughter, now in some measure dependent upon their uncle, into whose family they were adopted. Mr. Morton provided for them as if they were his own children, securing for the daughter the best instruction, and placing the son in business as soon as it was possible for him to do so. He made him clerk in the firm of Morton & Grinnell until the failure. The daughter grew up one of the brightest ornaments of the social circles in which she moved, and one of the comforts of her uncle's home. She was subsequently married, at Newport, Rhode Island, to Ernest Chaplin, of England, whose brother was a member of Parliament.

After the failure, Mr. Morton, though not discouraged, was nominally out of business until 1863. In that year he established a banking-house in New York City, which was known as that of L. P. Morton & Company As was to be expected, in view of his experience and financial ability, he made money rapidly, and it was not long until he had retrieved all he had lost. He became prominent in the financial circles of New York City and the whole country. Large transactions, that foreshadowed those of greater fame and national good that came afterwards, brought him into notice as a financier. It is to be said for him that he never engaged in any transactions of a doubtful nature, or that brought suspicion upon his house. He was where he had every temptation to make himself rich faster and by doubtful methods; but he went straight on through lawful channels, and kept his opportunities always in view.

One day he issued invitations to the creditors of the late firm of Morton & Grinnell, to attend a banquet provided by him for them. They came, and when they sat down to dinner, each creditor found under his plate a check for his full claim, with interest, signed by Mr. Morton. It is needless to say that, while his character for strict honesty was well known to them, and while the act was one that might have been looked for from such a man as they knew him to be, they were greater friends to him than ever, from that time.

He was not legally bound to pay those claims. There had been no calls upon him to do so. Failure to pay, in such a case, was so common that men had ceased to look for it, and society had learned (to its own discredit) to still regard it as moral, merely because it was legal, and to consider men who refused to pay their debts when they became able to do so, as respectable. But Mr. Morton had no mere legal definition of morality, and would not screen himself with one. He had been brought up in a school of integrity, and had not forgotten his early lessons.

In January, 1869, Mr. Morton was joined by Mr. George Bliss, and the firm became Morton, Bliss & Company. It may be remarked that, in this case, as well as in others, Mr. Morton was both shrewd and fortunate in the choice of a partner. Mr. Bliss had been for many years engaged in the dry-goods trade. He was first in the firm of Phelps, Chittenden & Bliss, afterwards in that of Chittenden, Bliss & Company, then Phelps, Bliss & Company, and then George Bliss & Company. His capital share, when he entered into partnership with Mr. Morton, is said to have been $2,500,000.

The same year, Mr. Morton founded the banking house of Morton, Rose & Company, London. His principal partner was Sir John Rose, who, at one time, had been Finance Minister of Canada. The transactions of this house, in connection with the New York house, were large from the first, and it immediately won a wide reputation. Ernest Chaplin subsequently became a member of this firm.

About the year 1870, Mr. Morton bought the splendid "cottage" at Newport, known as "Fair Lawn." It was situated upon Bellevue Avenue, which, though not so attractive then with costly villas as now, was the most beautiful residence street in that beautiful resort. Here he hoped for the better health of his wife, but was doomed to a most sorrowful disappointment.

In 1871, while at Newport, his wife died. How deeply he felt the loss of the one dearest on earth to him, can only be understood by remembering how deep and strong ran the currents of his social and domestic nature, and his sensibilities.

He returned to New York, and after a time, continued in business at the bank. It was not necessary in order to keep alive his affection, that he should give way to grief at every return of the thought of the loved one gone. Lucy Morton had been a faithful Christian, full of good works; and her husband "sorrowed not as those who had no hope." It was but natural that he sought society and companionship; that his affections led him, whenever consistent, into the presence of his friends, and that these affections grew stronger as months went on.

Nor is it any wonder that this man of society and sense should have among his friends noble representatives of the fairer sex, and that his broad heart, never forgetting, but always fondly cherishing, the love of former years, found yet room for one who, in many ways, reminded him of one departed.

In Poughkeepsie lived the family of William I. Street, one of the famous and most respected families of the Hudson Valley. In that family was a daughter, accomplished, refined, versatile, of broad and noble thought and feeling, and full of tact and grace. She was very beautiful, and a leader in her circle. She was a blonde, with fascinating smile and features, and winning ways. She had gray-blue eyes, full of thought and of transfixing, but gentle, qualities. But, notwithstanding all her accomplishments, talents, and natural charms, she was tempted into no devoteeism of fashionable society, wherein the mind was lost in the study of the art of appearance, or into no girlish reliance upon a pretty face and pretty eyes and pretty ways, to give her a "place in society." She had no spirit that fawned at the feet of "society," praying for recognition, nor did she feel that her "recognition" already secured rested upon insecure favoritism on account of wealth, family prestige, or any other mere circumstance of life, so that she must be always watchful of these interests alone, lest she should lose her position. Nor did her reputation for accomplishments rest upon a diploma. She was not, in the popular sense, a "sweet-girl graduate," and had not come with a bound from the boarding-school hall into the arms of society, with an implied demand of favors. She did not belong to that class of society that honors for any mere circumstance, but she belonged to that class that delights in the companionship of culture, because it is cultivated itself, and is exclusive only in the sense of recognizing, through a feeling of kinship, those who are cultured, without taking the trouble or thought to exclude those who are not, as society, on the basis of merit and no barriers, adjusts itself. She could, therefore, appreciate merit in the lowest, and liked to have it near her; but she could appreciate those most, who had most merit. If she was invited by devotees of fashion to a banquet, she went, if the motive for the invitation she did not know to be dishonoring; and whatever was of merit in that company she thoroughly enjoyed, and whatever was not, she revolted from. Whatever refinement they had, she had, and more. She loved society and its banquets for the sake of the merit and kinship found in it, not because it was "society." Without knowing it, she was equal to every social task or emergency, and she never had a dream of remaining "out of society," or "in society," because she could not, or could, "appear well." There was no fear of blundering if she went too far, and so there was no need of that newspaper palliation, "she does not go much into society." And thus she found entrance through every door, not because the footman was convinced that she was one of the *élite*, but because she could lay her hand upon every latch, and open and enter and command glad welcome. It was genuine culture and refinement, downright ability and tact.

Miss Street was beyond twenty-five — mature in native powers, and in accomplishments of mind and heart. She met Mr. Morton at Poughkeepsie, and found in his great abilities and trained powers of mind, heart, and spirit, a kinship closer than she had ever found before. In 1873 they were married. She began to prove herself a help in life meet for such a man. She became the sunshine of his home, a faithful wife, affectionate and painstaking in ordering the home.

From that time Mr. Morton's life was even more of a financial success: for all the world knows the power of the social circle, even in trade; and none appreciates the importance of that element more than his wife appreciated it, as she strove to use every honest influence for his success. Mrs. Morton is the highest type of what an American lady and wife may become.

In 1876, Mr. Morton entered more actively into political life than he had ever done before. He had never, indeed, failed to have a keen interest in the affairs of his country, and his counsel and advice had been sought and given in the political concerns of the Republican party, especially of New York. The benefit of his counsel and labor was very great. His political life, as begun in the year mentioned, will be more fully given hereafter, but that year he rendered some business service to the country that deserves to be recorded.

This was in the matter of the "Halifax Award," which was the claim of Great Britain against the United States, and its acceptance — under protest — by our government, as a result of the treaty of Halifax on the fisheries question. The demands of England were not believed to be just; but to avoid quarreling, and perhaps something more serious, the United States decided to pay the claim, at the same time explaining through our envoy that it was done for peace and friendship, and not in the belief of its justice.

The following shows Mr. Morton's part in the transaction. It is a copy of the draft, and shows how large had become his business in that year. Mr. Morton hung the copy in his private office at No. 28 Nassau Street, New York, merely as a copy of a large draft.

LEGATION OF U. S., LONDON,
November 2, 1878.

Dollars 5,500,000.

Pay to the order of the most honorable, the Marquis of Salisbury, her Majesty's principal Secretary of State for Foreign Affairs, five millions, five hundred thousand dollars in gold coin, and charge the same to State Department special account.

JOHN WELSH,

Envoy Extraordinary and Minister Plenipotentiary for the United States to Great Britain.

To Messrs. MORTON, ROSE & CO.,

Bankers, Bartholomew Lane, London.

Endorsed across the face: £1,127,847, 4-9, accepted payable at the Bank of England, 25 November, 1878.

MORTON, ROSE & CO.

This is the draft to pay it:

LONDON, November 21, 1878.

Messrs. GLYNN, MILLS, CURRIE & CO.:

Pay to Halifax fishery award or bearer, one million, one hundred and twenty-seven thousand eight hundred and forty-seven pounds, 4-9.

MORTON, ROSE & CO.

Endorsed: Pay to the Government & Co. of the Bank of England.

SALISBURY, for the Government & Co.
of the Bank of England,
F. MAY, Chief Cashier.

When the story of the war and the decade and a half that followed is correctly written, it will be seen that there were men of great faith and patriotism who were not upon the bloody battle-fields. There were those in public life, and those in private life, who stood by the soldiers, and without whose powerful aid the war for the Union would have been a failure. Too much honor cannot, indeed, be given to the brave men who risked their lives facing the enemy's guns. But too much honor cannot be bestowed on those who, standing at the helm, kept the ship afloat and bearing between the breakers until the storm was over and the clear sea was reached: even though they stood where the waves of battle did not dash over them. Had the ship gone down, it would have carried them with it into the gulf of ruin — of conscription and death. For every one knows that there was no indication, in treatment of prisoners or in any other manner, that our enemies would have been so lenient with us, had they been the victors, as we have been with them. And had these men at the helm left their posts, as some did, they would have saved themselves from every danger. But Chase and Sherman, and such men as Mr. Morton, were not men to leave their posts.

Mr. Morton was not in a position, during the war, to render that assistance to our government which he was afterwards able to render. But, with the exception of the months preceding, and those immediately following the beginning of the war, those were not the dark financial times. Our darkest financial period was that which succeeded the panic of 1873. It was through that period that Mr. Morton assisted in piloting our ship through dangerous waters. The suspension of specie payment in 1862 was the indication of financial disaster, but the successful issue and putting on the market, in that year, of the United States notes, tided the government over that difficulty; however it portended future ruin in case the master hands should be taken away.

The Democrats, during the administrations immediately preceding the war, had systematically drained the National Treasury, so that the task of furnishing supplies to carry on the war was apparently hopeless. It became necessary, early in January, to issue some kind of paper money as the basis of the operations of the government. The debate on the legal-tender clause of the bill providing for this issue followed: the clause, through the efforts of Secretary Chase and Senator Sherman, was retained; the bill passed, February 25, 1862, authorizing the issue of $150,000,000 of notes not bearing interest, payable at the Treasury of the United States. There were other issues; and thus provision was made for carrying on the war.

But after the war, the questions of refunding the national debt and of resuming specie payment arose. The latter was not believed either possible or expedient by the majority of the members of Congress, or by the majority of the people of the United States. But there were men who saw that only in this way could the country be brought out of the danger of periodical financial disaster, and perhaps of ruin.

In 1874, a committee of nine, having John Sherman as chairman, was appointed by the Republican caucus in Congress, to "secure concurrence of action" on the part of Republican members. They agreed on a bill fixing the time for resumption January 1, 1879, and the bill was passed January 14, 1875. This but served to increase the panic in the country, and people believed that the hard times were caused by the measure. They were encouraged in that faith by political managers of other parties, and every possible effort was made to induce the relinquishing of the purpose of resumption.

But brave legislators and officers, like John Sherman, in constant counsel with brave business men, like Levi P. Morton, said that resumption would be successfully accomplished. In April, 1877, Secretary Sherman wrote to banking houses in New York City, and announced his purpose to sell bonds to secure coin with which to meet the redemptions required, provided the surplus revenue proved insufficient to enable him to redeem the notes as required by law. This but increased the storm of opposition. But they went on. In October of that year, during the special session of Congress, thirteen bills were introduced in one day, to repeal the resumption act. One such bill, in November, passed the House, but the House would not agree to the amendment subsequently made to it by the Senate.

On April 5, 1878, negotiations were begun in New York with certain bankers, for the sale of four-and-a-half per cent. bonds. Those bankers would not venture; but on that day a syndicate proposed to take $50,000,000 at 100 1-2. This syndicate was headed by Morton, Bliss & Company, and followed by Drexel, Morgan & Company, Baring Brothers & Company, J. S. Morgan & Company, N. M. Rothschild & Sons, and Jay Cooke, McCulloch & Company.

These firms oeing known, inspired confidence, and resumption was assured. The payment was promptly met. Treasurer Sherman reserved of the proceeds of the sales of four per cent. bonds now being made, an additional amount of $5,500,000 in gold coin, for the payment of that amount on account of the Halifax fisheries award.

It is enough to state that instructions were given to the

officers of the Treasury of the United States, to close up, in their accounts, all distinction between coin and currency, and after January to recognize that the government had resumed specie payment, and that no difference in values existed between the several kinds of money in circulation. On the 1st of January, so little coin was demanded in payment from the Treasury, and so much coin was brought in, that the government held more coin in the evening than in the morning.

Thus, by the assistance of financial friends of the country, we were able to see the dawn of an era of prosperity that four years of a political blundering policy has not been able to materially darken. It is thus illustrated how a man, apparently obscure, because he never thrust himself upon public attention, but went quietly about the duties of his life, became a potent influence in the life of every man in the nation.

MRS. LEVI PARSONS MORTON,

WIFE OF THE HON. L. P. MORTON.

CHAPTER IV.

CONGRESSIONAL EXPERIENCE.

A SURPRISE TO MR. MORTON — NOMINATED FOR CONGRESS — A REDUCTION OF DEMOCRATIC VOTES — NOMINATED AGAIN — AN OVERWHELMING MAJORITY — A PROMINENT POSITION IN CONGRESS — SOME BILLS HE INTRODUCED — SPEECH ON THE UNLIMITED SILVER COINAGE BILL — SPEECH ON THE BILL FOR EXCHANGE OF TRADE DOLLARS WITH LEGAL-TENDER DOLLARS — SPEECH ON APPROPRIATION FOR INTERNATIONAL FISHERY EXHIBITION — CHARACTERISTICS OF THE MAN IN HIS SPEECHES — A SOCIAL SUCCESS.

IN 1876, while the Tilden tide was rising in New York, Mr. Morton, living in practically a Democratic district, received quite a surprise. It was rather late in the season, and it was to be supposed that the man to be nominated for Congress would have had some intimation of the intention on the part of his friends. But without warning, he was nominated for Congress in the Eleventh District; and was expected to make a canvass for congressional honors. Moreover, Mr. Morton did not profess to be a speaker. He could talk at the fireside, or in the council room; and his counsel was always good, and when his suggestions were carried out, effective work was done. But he had had little experience in stump speaking.

Nevertheless, he would not disappoint his friends; and so he resolved to do what he could to stem the extraordinary Democratic tide. He made as thorough a canvass as was possible in the short time. His voice was heard, even from the stump, as well as on all private occasions, when consistent, in favor of the Republican party and principles. His influence was felt in the organization of the district and in the counsels of the party. The result was that he took 400 votes from the usual Democratic majority. It was really a victory, and was the beginning of greater success to come afterwards.

In 1878, Mr. Morton was appointed Honorary Commissioner to the Paris Exposition. There were some positions that he felt himself especially adapted for, and this was one of them, although it was but honorary, and did not call out his full talents which lay in that direction. That was reserved for the future. Yet to be, in any sense, a representative of America to France, requires more than a mathematical or systematic business talent. It requires an address and tact that are the result only of a geniality of spirit and broad personality. Frenchmen may have French ways of thinking and conform to French customs without these qualities, but Americans cannot do so without them.

In the fall of 1878, encouraged by what was really a success before, Mr. Morton consented to make the race again for Congress. Having now more time, and the cause, if possible, more than ever at heart, he made such a vigorous canvass that he received a larger majority than the number of all the votes of his opponent.

He moved to Washington, and took his seat March 18, 1879, in the Forty-sixth Congress. The houses were convened by President Hayes, "in anticipation of the day fixed by law for their next meeting," because the Forty-fifth Congress had adjourned "without making the usual and necessary appropriations for the legislative, executive and judicial expenses of the Government for the fiscal year ending June 30, 1880, and without making the usual and necessary appropriations for the support of the Army for the same fiscal year."

Mr. Morton immediately took a high position in the legislative counsels and work, and came to be relied on, especially in questions of finance. He introduced, during that term, several bills, some by special request. Among them were the following:

By request of the Chamber of Commerce of New York City, a bill for correction of certain errors, and amendment of customs-revenue laws.

By request of the American Geographical Society, a bill authorizing the Secretary of War to detail an officer of the Army to take command of the expedition fitted out by Messrs. Morrison and Brown, citizens of New York, to search for the records of Sir John Franklin's expedition, and to issue to such officer army equipments.

A bill to amend a certain section of an act approved June 20, 1878, entitled "An act making appropriations for sundry civil expenses of the Government for the fiscal year ending June 30, 1879, and for other purposes."

Mr. Morton, April 21, 1879, was appointed on the Committee on Foreign Affairs, and served acceptably and with distinction on that committee until his return home.

It will be remembered that his taking his place in Congress was but a few weeks after the resumption of specie payment, and that his part in that successful and triumphant measure was not unknown by his colleagues. To this fact may be attributed, in part, at least, the high esteem in which he was considered by them, and the confidence had in him especially on financial and foreign questions. To return, his successful canvass in the fall, for his seat, may have been due, largely, to his prominent and successful transactions in behalf of the government, that were at that time going on.

Mr. Morton reported, from the Committee on Foreign Affairs, and took great interest in, a bill relating to treaty negotiations with Russia, as to American Israelites holding land in Russia. A certain Israelite had established a large trade in sewing machines in Russia, had bought a large establishment for carrying on the manufacture and sale of the machines, and then found that he could get no title of his property. The bill was introduced with a view to remedy that evil. It was changed so as to include all American citizens, and was passed.

Mr. Morton took an active part against the bill introduced by Mr. Warner, of Ohio, providing for the unlimited coinage of silver. The following speech by him, will not only explain the bill itself, but show Mr. Morton's general position on the financial questions that agitated the country at that time, and his regard for the rights of the people as against great private interests and monopolies:

"Mr. Speaker: In behalf of the district I have the honor to represent on this floor, a district second to none in the United States in the magnitude of its business and property interests, I desire to protest against the passage of the bill now before the House, which provides for the unlimited and free coinage of silver and the unlimited issue of certificates against silver bullion.

"I believe, sir, and my constituents believe, that this bill means to-day the repudiation — pure and simple — of one-sixth part of all indebtedness, public and private. What the measure of repudiation in the future may prove to be, will be determined alone by the value of silver bullion.

"Are the interests of the people to be advanced by adding to the colossal wealth of the owners of silver mines, or discriminating in favor of this class of property owners? Will the dollar stamp of the United States upon eighty-four cents' worth of silver, belonging to private individuals, add to the wealth of the nation, or to the private individual, the owner of the bullion? Has the late coinage of silver in excess of the amount which has been used as a circulating medium, now stored in the vaults of the Treasury, added to the prosperity of the country? Every one will answer no!

"If this bill is to become a law, it is inevitable that the country will be drained, sooner or later, of its gold and coin bullion, and that silver will become the sole unit of value, and that, instead of a double standard, we shall have a single standard, and that of silver.

"If this bill is to become a law, the German Government and all who have silver bullion, the world over, will pour it into our mints to receive for every eighty-four cents a legal-tender silver dollar; they will make, by this simple process, nearly twenty per cent., and our own people, who will be obliged to receive the coins as legal-tenders, will be the losers.

"Coinage by the government is properly only an official attestation of the weight and fineness of the metal stamped or coined. A silver dollar thus attested to-day should contain

184.15 grains as the equivalent of a gold dollar. The present values of silver bullion, in London, is about fifty pence per ounce; until it is worth fifty-nine or sixty pence, the government should have the profit, if the fraud of stamping eighty-four cents as worth a hundred is to continue.

"If this bill is to become a law of the land, its title should be changed to read, 'An act for the relief of the owners of silver mines;' and an appropriation made for the purpose of erecting elevators and warehouses for the storage of silver coin and bullion. If the owners of silver bullion can have their property carried by the government, as this bill proposes, and can have certificates of its deposit made a legal-tender for all dues to the United States, including custom-house duties, why not clothe bonded-warehouse receipts and all other representatives of property with the same functions of money?

"My constituents are not the owners of silver mines, but they are largely interested in cotton, wheat, corn, flour, iron and copper. Why should not the government receive all these and other products of the earth on storage, issue certificates, and make them also a legal-tender? And if the supply of money should be still insufficient to satisfy the honorable gentleman from Ohio (Mr. Warner), receive also titles of real estate, issue money certificates, and so continue until every species of property becomes a part of the currency of the country? Then we can issue for general distribution, pledging whatever may remain of the faith and honor of the Nation, the billion of greenbacks asked for by the reverend and distinguished gentleman who occupies a seat on this floor (Rev. De La Matyr, of Indiana).

"No, Mr. Speaker, renewed and continued prosperity cannot be secured in this manner.

"The only safe way, in my opinion, is to stop the coinage of silver altogether, and to say to the leading commercial nations of the world, 'We will not attempt to help you out of your troubles until you agree with us to use silver as a measure of value. We are ready to enter into such a mutual compact with you as will have the effect of restoring silver to its old steadiness of value, so that it may again be a measure of other values.'

"Let us not attempt to force the issue of silver beyond the amount which can be used as a circulating medium, until European nations will join with us in making silver currency equivalent in value to gold. Let us rather maintain the honor and good faith of the nation at home and abroad; retain and maintain a gold standard, the commercial standard of value throughout the world, and, in my opinion, the day is not far distant when the city of New York will be the clearing-house for the commercial exchanges of the world."

Mr. Morton took part in the discussion of the bill "to prevent the exportation of diseased cattle, and the spread of contagious and infectious diseases among domestic animals." He submitted a letter from gentlemen in New York, setting forth the inefficiency of the laws on that subject then in force, and praying for a law that would protect honest men in exportations, and their honor as well as that of the country.

He also made a speech against the bill introduced by Mr. Fort, of Illinois, providing for the exchange of trade dollars for legal-tender dollars. The following is his speech upon that question:

"MR. SPEAKER: — A few weeks since, the honorable gentleman from Ohio introduced a bill for the relief of the owners of silver mines and silver bullion in the United States and Europe, and now the distinguished gentleman from Georgia (A. H. Stephens, who had reported back the bill from the Committee on Coinage, Weights and Measures) presents a bill for the relief of the subjects of the Emperor of China.

"In February, 1873, when the act was passed authorizing the coinage of the trade dollar, it was worth a fraction over $1.04 in gold. They were not coined as money, or for circulation at home, but for export, and as a measure of value in trade, as their title indicates. They were, however, made a legal-tender for $5.00 in any one payment: but the people of the Pacific States objected to their circulation, and on the 8th of May, 1876, the distinguished gentleman, now Speaker of the House, introduced a bill repealing the legal-tender quality of these coins.

"On the 10th of June, 1876, my distinguished colleague from New York (Mr. Cox) reported the measure, and it passed both Houses of Congress without an opposing vote or voice. All of these coins held at home were put in circulation months after they had, by the action of the present Speaker and the gentleman from New York, ceased to be a legal-tender for any amount.

"While I should favor an exchange of legal-tender silver for the trade dollar which speculators have palmed off upon our citizens, if that alone could be done, I am opposed to the passage of this bill, which discriminates against our people and in favor of the owners of silver in China, and for other reasons. The Director of the Mint, in his last annual report, estimated that not less than six millions of trade dollars, all of which were coined for exportation, were held in the United States, and about thirty millions in China, where they circulate as money, and are, I believe, a legal-tender at their bullion value. The trade dollar is worth to-day about ninety cents, which would make the value of the thirty millions held in China, worth $27,000,000. Now, if this bill becomes a law, we shall, so long as the government can maintain legal-tender silver dollars at par in gold, be paying to the holders of trade dollars in China $30,000,000 in gold for twenty-seven millions' worth of silver, or $3,000,000 more than we can buy the same quantity of silver for of our own citizens.

"The first silver bill which the honorable gentleman from Ohio presented, proposed a discrimination in favor of silver mine and bullion owners in the United States and Europe, of nearly twenty per cent., and now the gentleman from Georgia proposes a discrimination of eleven per cent. in favor of Chinese subjects. I shall be glad to know how the gentleman proposes to provide the thirty millions in gold necessary to carry out the provisions of this bill, if it becomes a law. The gentleman certainly cannot expect to exchange dollars of 412 1-2 grains with the trade dollars of 420 grains.

"Since the demonetization of silver in 1878, the government has coined 33,485,950 of the 'dollars of the fathers,' which it was claimed would be eagerly sought for, and how many of these dollars does the gentleman suppose was in circulation on the 1st of June? One dollar for every family or party of six in the United States, a total of 7,304,915 in a country with a population of 45,000,000, leaving 26,181,045 stored in the vaults of the Treasury, and carried by the government.

"At the end of the next fiscal year, without any new legislation, we shall have 59,485,950 silver dollars, and if the people have no more anxiety to secure them than heretofore, the government will then be warehousing and carrying about forty-seven millions.

"If the 36,000,000 of trade dollars are to be added, the appalling total on the 30th of June, 1880, will be over ninety-five millions.

"Do the gentlemen who favor this measure wish to donate $3,000,000 to the holders of trade dollars in China? Do they wish, in view of the sale for gold coins, since the demonetization of silver in 1873, of $1,299,000,000 of United States bonds, and the reduction since 1865 of nearly six hundred millions of principal and sixty-seven millions in the annual interest charge, to press the increased coinage of silver, and hazard the credit of the government by adding a sum to the amount of silver coin in the vaults of the Treasury, which may force the government to pay these bonds in depreciated silver, or coin of less value than that which the government demanded and received when the bonds were sold?

"Mr. Speaker, I think our only safe way is, instead of increasing the coinage of silver, to stop it altogether, and wait the result of negotiations with European nations, for which we have made an appropriation. Let us secure such joint action with other nations as will restore silver to its old steadiness of value, and thus provide a market throughout the world for our silver product. I am in favor of a bimetallic currency, whenever such joint action can be secured, and a dollar's worth of silver is coined in a silver dollar. The distinguished gentleman from Georgia, and those who act with him, on the contrary, aim to make this country a monometallic country; to drive all our gold to Europe, and to confine the silver market to the United States, thus limiting the demand, lowering the value of our silver product, and compelling us to be monometallists. We cannot maintain a double standard, except upon a basis of absolute equality, for the cheaper, poorer money will always drive the best out of circulation.

"The German Government has, within a few weeks, withdrawn its silver from the market; the question of the demonetization of silver in Germany and England has been under discussion, and now the bullion value of the standard dollar, which was recently at eighty-four cents, is about eighty-eight-and-a-half cents.

"We can, in my opinion, only maintain a double standard by joint action with European nations, and any attempt to do it single-handed, or to largely increase the coinage of silver legal-tender dollars, will, in my judgment, bring great disaster upon the business interests of the whole country.

"I hope the gentleman will be willing to withdraw the bill, or to defer its further consideration, until joint action with European nations can be secured."

On the 4th of February, 1880, during the second session of that Congress, Mr. Morton made a speech upon the bill favoring an appropriation of $20,000 for the representing of the United States in the International Fishery Exhibition, at Berlin. The question discussed was not one with which the people generally were acquainted; perhaps because politicians had not kept it before them. But it was one of much importance to the country, nevertheless, as will appear from the following outline of Mr. Morton's speech:

"At first glance," he said, "the proposition to expend money in an International Fishery Exhibition, at Berlin, is apt to be viewed with indifference. This indifference has existed for years, and was never more manifest than at this time.

"The production of fish is a source of national wealth. In the early history of the world, it was a preventative of famine and distress. Experience has shown that, while fish is a luxury of the rich, it is preëminently the poor man's food. This is understood thoroughly in countries where food-production and cheap living are carried to the greatest perfection. . .

"If properly developed, the price of fish would be so much lowered, that the man who could not buy would be rare indeed: and so little capital is needed for the business that there would be sufficient profit left to those who carry it on.

"One of these exhibitions was held in Norway, in 1865, at which the fish of all the great countries, and many of the lesser ones, were well represented; but our country sent only a few contributions. . . . . .

"The French Government has given so much material aid to this business of fish culture, that nearly all her waste waters have been turned into nests for the propogation of fish. .

"It is only necessary to call the attention of the public to this subject for it to appear that there is not a state which is not interested in the matter.

"Mr. Chairman, not many years ago the vast internal improvements of this country—the erection of mills, dams, and factories—threatened the extinction of the most valuable species of fish in our rivers. This calamity was prevented by the timely discovery of the art of propagating fish by artificial means; and at the same time the demand was greatly increased through the aid of railroads, which have made transportation in a brief time easy between remote points.

"In 1840–50, salmon cost twenty times the price it commanded when we ceased to be Colonies of Great Britain. The Connecticut River, which had been one of the most fertile fish streams in the world, became almost depleted. . .

"This result is due to a discovery made in Germany, and afterwards in France, that fish can be propogated to almost any extent by artificial means. This simple discovery has led to the creation of one of the most important industries of modern times. The nations of the world have derived incalculable benefit from this discovery, and we are now invited to join in an international comparison of the character of our fish and the methods of our fish culture. It is to this science to which I have referred, and which this resolution is designed to encourage and extend, that we owe the restocking of our waters—to this we owe the fact that millions of young shad were hatched at Holyoke, Massachusetts, and turned into the Connecticut River.

"In view of the possibilities of our shores, our measureless streams, and our inland seas, we should lead all the nations in the world in availing ourselves of every item of information on a subject of such importance to our people and their industries. The annual value of salmon alone, in Ireland, is now about $2,500,000, while in this country it averages from thirty to forty cents a pound. The oyster beds in Virginia alone, cover about 1,700,000 acres, containing 800,000,000 bushels. The following are a few figures, showing the comparative production and consumption of fish by the leading nations of the world:

	Annual Product.	Annual Consumption.
Norway. .	$13,600,000	$1,000,000
France.	12,807,000	9,845,786
United States.	8,898,000	8,777,000
Great Britain.	7,803,800	9,429,000
Russia, ...	5,745,000	8,659,000

"The United States exported, in 1874, about $2,200,000 worth.

"It appears from this statement that, in 1874, Norway and France, each smaller than some of our states, produced respectively one-third more fish than the United States. In 1862 the tonnage of American ships engaged in the sea fisheries amounted to 204,197; in 1874, it had fallen to 78,290 tons.

. . . .

"In the fish trade in 1865, Norway had a balance of trade in her favor of $12,588,975. Why was this? Because she resorted to fish production, as it is proposed the United States should do.

"In 1867, we imported about as much fish as we exported. If we devoted sufficient energy to the business, we could export one hundred times as much, and need import none at all.

"Fish culture is in its infancy. Its resources are immeasureable. It may approximate, and even rival, agriculture in importance. Its development will give employment to large numbers of men, and bring food within the means of the poor as well as the rich. The propriety and utility of international exhibitions, where the representatives of our nation can learn the nature of the products of others, as well as show its own in universal market, can no longer be questioned. . .

"The naturalization in our waters of European fish is a subject that should receive careful attention, and by a comparison of views in this body of scientific men much may be learned as to the nature and kinds of foreign fish which thrive in our waters. . . . .

"This international exhibition is conducted, directly under the patronage of the German Government, by the German Fisheries Association, a body consisting of prominent persons most eminent in fish culture and fisheries. Almost every nation in the world, having diplomatic relations with Germany, has accepted the invitation — exceptionally complete exhibitions being promised by China, Japan, and Siam. The United States alone has given no response, nor made arrangements to participate. As a matter of international comity, it would be eminently proper for the United States to take part."

It will be seen, from the extracts given of this speech, that Mr. Morton, while in Congress, took interest in other subjects besides those connected immediately with questions of finance. And it will be seen, not only from these extracts, but from the other speeches given, that he was always on that side which favored the interests of the people. No man was ever in a better position for influencing legislation in behalf of the moneyed classes alone, and hence in his own personal interest, than Mr. Morton. He had means at his hand, and could have been in league with rich lobbyists. But he was found always on the side of the people, and interested in legislation in their behalf.

Another fact appears from the speeches and extracts given. Mr. Morton was thoroughly informed on all the leading questions before Congress. He did not suffer himself to open his mouth nor to vote, unless he knew what he was doing. He had not only entered the Congress hall, a well-read, well-informed and broadly cultured man, but sought to more thoroughly inform himself upon those questions that came before him for his consciecytious consideration, in behalf of his constituents and of the people of the United States.

Mr. Morton's social career, while in Washington, was most brilliant. Of great social spirit and tact, he sought to surround himself with circumstances and influences of that nature. He realized also that a man may do more effective work, if his talents appear in their own peculiar setting. No man can work so well when his environments make it awkward for him, as when he lives in that atmosphere to which he has become accustomed.

Mr. Morton bought the house of Mr. Samuel Hooper, fitted it up elegantly but not gaudily — he and his wife were both of too pure taste to endure that which was merely for display in any of their surroundings — and here he entertained his friends in state, and Mrs. Morton reigned socially. The reputation of the latter for presiding at social entertainments and leading in the social circle, had preceded her to Washington, and her home became the centre of attraction for all who were so fortunate as to be included in the long list of her friends. She led in society at Washington, as well as she had led in society at New York, and her great social qualities, enabling her to be equal to every emergency, conduced no little to her husband's successful congressional career.

CHAPTER V.

MINISTER TO FRANCE.

THE CAMPAIGN OF 1880 — MR. MORTON DECLINES THE OFFER OF VICE-PRESIDENCY — DECLINES THE SECRETARYSHIP OF THE NAVY — ACCEPTS THE OFFER OF MINISTER TO FRANCE — WELL FITTED FOR THE POST — REMOVAL OF AMERICAN LEGATION OFFICE — A POLITICAL GATHERING PLACE — THE MORTON ENTERTAINMENTS IN FRANCE — MRS. MORTON'S SOCIAL TACT AND SKILL — THE DISABILITY REMOVED FROM AMERICAN CORPORATIONS — THE AMERICAN HOG — A SERIES OF IMPORTANT ACTS — TARIFF ON FRENCH ART — BIRTHPLACE OF LAFAYETTE — MINISTER MORTON'S SPEECH — PRESENTATION AND RECEPTION OF BARTHOLDI'S STATUE OF "LIBERTY ENLIGHTENING THE WORLD" — TWO SPEECHES.

ONE of the most brilliant periods of Mr. Morton's career was now at hand.

When the Republican Convention of 1880 had nominated James A. Garfield, of Ohio, for President of the United States, it then turned to New York to find a candidate for Vice-President. The Ohio delegation especially sought out Mr. Morton, and urged him to permit his name to be used for that nomination. He declined the honor, and the choice then fell on Chester A. Arthur.

During that campaign, which led to such successful issue, Mr. Morton, in his characteristic manner, gave the weight of his influence to the election of Garfield and Arthur. He did this by his frank social manner and skill, by speaking always, on public and private occasions, just when there was a demand for it, and stating clearly and urging his convictions, and casting his whole social, business, and publi: influence upon that side.

When the ticket was triumphant, President Garfield, in testimony of the confidence he had always had in Mr. Morton's abilities, offered him the port-folio of Secretary of the Navy. But Mr. Morton could not be persuaded to accept an office if he thought that other men might better fill it, and he therefore declined to take the offered position. But when the position of minister to France was proposed to him, he accepted it.

He was not unacquainted with the French capital, nor the important work at that time to be done there by the American minister, whomever he might be. He knew the tact and diplomacy then necessary to do what ought to be done. Yet he knew his own power among people preëminently social, and it is to his credit that he desired to lift the American standard higher, and to advance American commercial and social interests, in the sister republic, and also to promote the harmony and friendship of the two nations. Nor is it to his discredit that he deemed it desirable, with his family, to spend a time in France, as there was a culture to be given to his children by means of it, and there were benefits and pleasures to be derived from it by his wife and himself.

So, early in the summer of 1881, Mr. Morton and his family embarked for the gay French capital. Arriving there, he received a cordial welcome, both by French officials and the American colony. He at once proved his fitness for the high position, by his social and diplomatic tact. His advent into France was in the days of M. Gambetta, and he soon won that renowned President's friendship and esteem. This friendship continued until Gambetta's death, and was not only a source of pleasure to Mr. Morton, but was of great help to him as minister of the United States.

Again, Mr. Morton was already well and favorably known by the leading men of France. His vast commercial transactions alone would have been sufficient to bring this about. But he had also, in 1878, been Honorary Commissioner to the Paris Exposition. Also, his public services in the United States, not only in Congress, but in commercial services, had been matters of world-wide knowledge.

Add to these Mr. Morton's perfect manners, his suavity, his great financial ability, his diplomatic shrewdness and tact, his knowledge of men, and it is seen at once that no man could have been selected, of greater fitness for the French post. It will be seen, in the outcome, that President Garfield manifested great judgment in sending such a man, and if all the appointments of all the Presidents were as fitting as this one, the reform of the civil service would soon be accomplished.

Mr. Morton was able and faithful, and too conscientious, to use any office he might have for political influence. Moreover, it was characteristic of him that his office became such a part of his life that it assumed to him the interest of a social opportunity; and the more he so considered it, the more faithful he was in his office. Mr. Morton's duties as minister became his chief interest, and his first act on arriving, indicated his methods.

General Noyes, Mr. Morton's predecessor in office, though he received a salary of $17,000 per annum, kept the headquarters of the American Legation in dingy apartments in an unsavory locality. It was situated over a laundry and a grocery store on Rue de Chaillot. Among people like the French, this was not to be tolerated as respectable. It became a matter of ridicule and jest, and during all the time it was there, for that and other reasons, American affairs were not highly respected; and many laws and customs existed that worked decidedly to the disadvantage of the United States.

Mr. Morton determined at once on removing the Legation. He had no taste for a business whose environments were beneath its own dignity, and he had the pride of his own country too much at heart to allow, if possible to prevent it, even the shadow of excuse for its disparagement by the people of other nations. He felt himself under obligations to do all in his power to accomplish his mission in the best manner, and with most credit to the United States.

Fronting a park known as Place de la Biche, was a magnificent mansion, built seven years before by a prince. This was secured by Mr. Morton, and furnished in royal style; for the drawing-room he furnished with expensive furniture which had been ordered by a queen, but who was unable to pay for it. This was done largely at Mr. Morton's own expense. To this superb building was moved the office of the Legation. Thus, almost simultaneously with the presentation of his credentials as "Envoy Extraordinary and Minister Plenipotentiary of the United States in France," the American Legation assumed the attitude and proportions that accorded with the dignity and importance of the government it represented. It won a quick response from the French, and Mr. Morton commanded unbounded respect; and of these facts the French gave immediate evidence by changing the name of the park to that of Place des États Unis — a rich though merited compliment to Mr. Morton.

He began at once to exert a marked personal influence upon the French Government. The Legation headquarters became the gathering-place, not only of Americans, but of French officials and dignitaries. He thus brought together, in social relations, Royalists, Radicals, and Republicans, and the diplomatic corps; and he was thus enabled to smooth the way for his diplomatic success. Mr. Morton showed great tact by this arrangement. He knew that an envoy's success depended much, especially in France, upon personal friendship and social conduct. But he was not a hypocrite, and did not cultivate any friendship for policy; he was, rather, a friend by nature to people of refinement and culture, and had naturally a keen appreciation of art, artistic elegance, and all the accompaniments of the social life of the refined and cultivated. Yet, in the midst of his keen enjoyment of such a life, he not only did not forget, but kept as his chief aim, the mission on which he had come; and it was a marked evidence of his great tact that, in all his social intercourse, he met the French people as the minister of the United States, and not as a mere gentleman of elegance. His friendship for Gambetta was cordial and sincere; but that great man, by reason of no pompous flaunting of official emblem in his face on the part of Mr. Morton, was ever conscious that his own friendship was for the United States Minister to France.

In this spirit Mr. Morton began a series of entertainments,

given to the Americans in France, and to Frenchmen. These greatly increased his popularity. In these he was most ably, skillfully, and wisely assisted by his wife. Her matchless skill in entertaining has already been spoken of; and it was well, while in France, that she had this art. But she used it always as an American lady should; for she did not adopt manners nor customs, unless her independent taste and judgment pronounced them good. An instance of her American way of doing things, in spite of the contrast it made between herself and French ladies, may be related of their early days in that gay and exactingly polite country.

The people of Rouen invited the new minister and his wife to a *fête* of several days. The time was spent in entertainments, excursions, and in whatever their entertainers could devise for the honoring of their guests. One day there was an excursion upon the Seine to Yietat, made famous by the songs of Beranger. There was a party of twenty-five, not the least conspicuous of whom was the mayor of Rouen. A breakfast was served, and around it were gathered the twenty-five, representing vast wealth, and displaying all the ceremony that rural Rouen could display. The mayor sat next to Mrs. Morton. He desired to propose a toast to her. With great pomp, and an airy parade of words, he notified them that, whereas *Monsieur le Ministre* had been toasted nine times the day before, and had nine times responded, he must by this time be weary with speech-making. He (the mayor) considered that *Mme. Morton* should now be honored, and should have a greater part in the festivities. He then made a complimentary speech, and proposed her health.

Mrs. Morton here astonished the French people present, by an act that gave them to understand at once that she expected to totally ignore the social tyranny under which French women were compelled to live. She was not to be merely a pretty figure in society, and to receive compliments thrown at her in dumb silence and as a matter of course. She spoke out in fluent, idiomatic French, in a truly dignified and gracious and pleasant manner, but with thorough American courage and independence, and made a neat reply, complimenting the French, and Rouen in particular. Her womanliness was acknowledged at once, and cheer after cheer rang round the table in appreciation of that and the merit of her reply. It was a bold thing to do, but it was a triumph for her and her sex, even in France.

Under the social circumstances now fully inaugurated, Mr. Morton began to reap success as minister to France. When he made his advent in France, American corporations were laboring under the great disadvantage of being unable to collect any debt that was owing them anywhere in the French Republic, or from any French citizen there of whatever grade. Insurance companies, banks, even the Western Union Telegraph Company, were thus at the mercy of Frenchmen who refused to pay. It may be a matter of surprise to the un-informed, but there was only one country that was then under this disability, and that was the United States. In the *Journal Officiel*, August 9, 1882, was published the decree that relieved our corporations from this discrimination. The advantage that has accrued to these corporations on account of this relief is very great; and, taking all of them together, and their trade in France, an advantage scarcely to be estimated has been derived from it by the United States. The Equitable Life Assurance Society, the New York Life Insurance Company, the Singer Manufacturing Company, and, indeed, every company in America that does business in France will to-day testify to the great good that came to them by reason of emancipation from this disability. And let it be remembered that Mr. Morton was the sole influence in obtaining such a desirable result.

What was known as the "pork question" was also causing some trouble at the time Mr. Morton went to Paris. The French ports, as well as other ports, were closed against the American hog. This was due to a great European "scare," caused by an English consul in Philadelphia. He had heard through some source, reliable or unreliable, that some family here had been poisoned by trichinæ in pork they had eaten. He paraded the event before his own government, and the result was that the principal European governments prohibited the importation of American pork. Thus the "frightened" consul had succeeded in cutting off, almost entirely, the exportation of one of our chief staples.

Mr. Morton's predecessor had tried, by all means in his power, to have this restriction taken off, so far as France was concerned. He had procured expert testimony — the testimony of scientists well-known in France — to show that the American hog was not unfit for food, and that it was not infested with trichinæ. But his efforts had been unavailing; and it was nothing against General Noyes that they were, as will be hereafter shown. But it was much in favor of the personal influence of Mr. Morton that he succeeded in doing what General Noyes could not do. The decree revoking the prohibition of American pork was promulgated by the French Government in 1883, and was published in the *Journal Officiel* on November 27th, of that year.

Nevertheless, the decree did not immediately become a law. It was temporarily over-ruled by a vote of the legislature. This, however, but shows how great was Mr. Morton's influence with the government. The vote of the legislature indicated the strong popular feeling there against the article in question. Yet, in spite of this feeling, Mr. Morton was able to induce the government to issue such a decree.

Our envoy had much to do with bringing about the Monetary Conference that met in Paris in 1882, fourteen governments being represented; and he took an active part in the proceedings of the conference. He also bore an influential part in the discussions that finally brought about the treaty between the powers for the protection of the submarine cables; and represented the United States in the convention that was signed at Paris, March 14, 1884, by the plenipotentiaries of twenty-six governments, having the continued protection of the submarine cables as its object. On March 20, 1883, the conference for the protection of patents and trade-marks met in Paris; and Mr. Morton assisted greatly in the deliberations of that body, and in bringing about its important and beneficial results. Thus, whether it was to influence the French Government to recede from an attitude inimical to our interests, or to explain to our own government the wisdom of better policy toward France, or to bring about measures of importance in which many governments were interested, or to give his voice for harmonious relations of the United States with France, or for the interest of France in her policy toward other nations — as in the efficient part he bore in the negotiations of peace between France and China — Mr. Morton was always active in fulfilling his plenipotentiary duties.

Perhaps one of the most difficult tasks which Mr. Morton had to perform was to induce our own government to assume a different attitude toward the works of French artists. Had he been on our own shores, he could have protested more earnestly; but being a representative of our government, it was his duty not to disparage but to exalt his own country and all that pertained to it, if he could possibly do so, and not to criticise us before strangers. Again, while he was fully in sympathy with the principle of protection enunciated by the Republican party at home, and with the object to be obtained by that protection — the advancement of American wages, and the improvement of American handiwork — he observed that, in cases where skill might be acquired abroad to our own honor, and where competition of foreign workmanship was more in skill than price, and therefore beneficial, the very object might be reached by removing a tariff that protection reaches in most cases.

This was true in the case of French works of art. Paris was one of the greatest schools of art. Americans had there an equal advantage for becoming proficient with French citizens. Their works were admitted to exhibition on equal footing. Moreover, the removing of the tariff from works of art would allow here a competition in *production* and merit.

rather than in selling. The price of such works, at least among those who have the "artist's eye," depends almost altogether upon merit, and is not affected by production, especially as the demand must ever be greater than the supply. It was therefore no fawning at French feet that led Mr. Morton to endeavor to persuade our government to remove the almost prohibitive tariff from French works of art. It was an act wholly in harmony with his American spirit, and had in view the increased excellence of American production and price. His efforts in this direction were not entirely successful; but he did succeed in winning the attention and approval of President Arthur, who communicated his able dispatch to Congress.

In this connection, he was also instrumental in saving American artists from a French reprisal which, in view of our tariff upon their works, may have been considered just, though it would have wrought some harm to us. The French press and artists were loudly demanding this retaliation. But Mr. Morton was a lover of art and a friend to artists, and by his friendship and personal relations with them, and with the French Ministry prevented them from carrying out their design in this matter. He insisted before them, as before our government, that art can recognize no language, no national boundaries; and that artists speak to each other by their works, and are not bound by national ties or prejudices — they are a community by themselves. Nor was this high ground contrary to his duty in representing a distinct nation. To make the members of his nation, and those of the nation to which he was accredited, feel a common sympathy and common interests, was a large part of his mission. And to bind certain classes of the two nations into one class, if possible, was a step toward the accomplishment of his important duties.

Thus, in every respect our envoy to France sought to improve the relations between the two governments, and he made no endeavor that was not wholly, or in part, successful. While making no display of his wealth, being unostentatious and unassuming, as he had always been in his native country, he yet spared no pains or means to do his work well. He gave two receptions every year, and he succeeded by these in drawing around himself such men as became a great advantage to him as minister. His name was frequently in the French papers, and he was very popular. He upheld our Republic; he gave us such a dignity and prestige before the French Nation as we never before enjoyed. In 1882, he was president of the Monetary Conference that sat in Paris. He was well known as a financier long before he went to Paris. His transactions had been in London, Frankfort, Berlin, and Paris. He was, before all eyes, a man of integrity and solidity in money matters; and he could not, with any show of justice, be accused of making a display of his wealth, as if he had but yesterday fallen heir to it. His money had come to him by a long course of training and experience in business that had formed such habits as precluded the possibility of mere display. It was the personal popularity of the man, and the greatness of his character, as well as of his tact, that made him the very efficient minister that he proved himself.

On the 6th of September, 1883, the old town of Le Puy, on the upper Loire, unveiled the statue of Lafayette, whose name is more dear to the American heart than that of any other Frenchman. The town was decorated in gayest colors, the stars and stripes mingling everywhere with the tricolor. There were several arches of triumph, on the façade of the principal one of which, were two inscriptions — one that welcomed Waldeck-Rousseau, and the other as follows:

"AUX ÉTATS-UNIS.
"A LEVI P. MORTON, AMBASSADEUR."

At three o'clock the ceremony of unveiling took place, after which came the speeches. First, there were two local officials who spoke, and then Mr. Morton delivered the following address:

"Monsieur le Maire, Messieurs: I accepted as a privilege and a duty the invitation with which I was honored by the Department of the Haute Loire, and the town of Le Puy, to be present on this occasion, and to assist in the ceremonies connected with the inauguration of a statue of General Lafayette. I claim for my country, to whom he rendered such inestimable services, a full share in the inheritance of his fame, and I rejoice as its representative to unite on this occasion with the distinguished members of the government, and with the descendants and countrymen of Lafayette, in this tribute to his memory.

"I am happy to express to you the devoted and sympathetic interest of my government, and the grateful affection of the citizens of the United States for the illustrious patriot who, next to Washington, of all the heroes of the Revolution, awakens in American hearts the deepest sympathy and gratitude. And what is it that has won for him the honor, gratitude, and affection of my countrymen? I answer, the principles which directed his public life, the invaluable services which he rendered my country in the hour of her greatest trial. It was his love of liberty which led him, a youth of nineteen years, to embrace the cause of American independence, and inspired him to say, 'When I first heard the news of the struggle my heart leaped to your cause with enthusiastic sympathy.' And what is it that gives to Lafayette his spotless fame? I answer, his unfaltering devotion to constitutional freedom; for always — whether in the days of the Monarchy, the Empire, or the Republic — he was ever the consistent advocate of the supremacy of the law — ever demanding that liberty should be defined and protected by chartered rights. His love of liberty was a part of his very being — the inspiration of his life.

"This life-like statue — one of the triumphs of art — around which we are now assembled, will recall to generations yet unborn the great services which he rendered to the cause of constitutional liberty. More than a century has passed since Lafayette enlisted in the war of American independence, devoting to it his fortune, influence, and life. Would that he could this day rise from his grave and look upon the marvelous results of the work which he and his countrymen took so great a part in preparing. Would that he could hear the words of respect and gratitude which greet his memory to-day. Would that he could look out and see that the two countries which he loved and served so well were never more closely united in sympathy and good will than on this day, when the citizens of both are here engaged in inaugurating a statue to perpetuate his memory. Only a few weeks have passed since more than ten thousand people assembled at Burlington, in my native state, to inaugurate a statue of Lafayette, and re-lay the corner-stone of the University of the State of Vermont, which was originally laid by the illustrious general during his visit to the United States in 1825. Among those present were the governor of the state, all the living ex-governors, the president, faculty, and trustees of the university, battalions of United States troops, of the National Guard of the state, and of the Grand Army of the Republic. We have assembled to-day for a similar purpose, near the birthplace of Lafayette, and I esteem it a great privilege to stand in the presence of, and feel that I may claim, both for my country and personally, the friendship of the grandson — your distinguished Senator — M. Edmond de Lafayette, and other descendants of the great patriot and soldier. I will not attempt to even sketch the eventful life and distinguished services Lafayette rendered to his native land, or to the nation he sacrificed so much to serve: they form an important part of the history of France and of the United States during their struggle for independence. I may, however, repeat the prophetic words he uttered to a committee of the American Congress, appointed to present him, upon his return to France, with a letter addressed to the King, expressive of their high appreciation of the services he had rendered, when he said: 'May this immense Temple of Freedom ever stand, a lesson to oppressors, an example to the oppressed, a sanctuary for the rights of mankind! and may these happy United States attain that complete splendor and prosperity which will illustrate the blessings of their government, and for ages to come rejoice the departed souls of its founders.'

"The founders of this Temple of Freedom have long since seen the last of earth, but the temple they raised still stands in all its matchless proportions, a beacon light to the oppressed, a sanctuary for the rights of mankind, and we live to witness the realization of his prayer and prophetic words.

"General Lafayette made two visits to the United States, as the guest of the nation, after the War of Independence,—the first time during the life of Washington, his warm personal friend and companion in victory and defeat, and again in 1824. His reception by the government and the people was on both occasions a continual ovation from the time of his arrival to that of his departure. His name is a household word from the Atlantic to the Pacific, and will be for all time imperishably associated with that of Washington, the grandest character in American history. May the friendship formed, on the field and in the camp between Washington and Lafayette — typical representatives of the grand qualities of the French and American citizen-soldier — remain unbroken between the two great republics until the end of time."

M. Waldeck-Rousseau followed with a speech, of which the following were the important paragraphs:

"The Minister of the United States has just expressed for France sentiments of cordiality and friendship, which cannot go unanswered. I feel bound to thank him warmly for such sentiments, and to tell him, in the name of all republicans of this department here present, how happy we are, how much we are affected to see by the side of us, united in a like sentiment of veneration for that man of whom Senator Vissaguet has just spoken so eloquently, the accredited representative of that other great democracy, which is the American democracy, of that other great republic, which is the Republic of the United States, laborious as ours, pacific as ours, and convinced as we are that free people cannot buy that inestimable boon of peace except upon the double condition — to be firmly resolved never to undertake anything against others, but also never to permit others to undertake anything against them.

"The democracy of America is the true republicanism, and and we should esteem it a happy day for France when we arrive — as we believe we are now in the way of arriving — at the perfection of a republic such as Washington founded, with the aid of our own Lafayette. We seek no aggrandisement not founded upon the true development and just protection of our commercial interests, and these we hope to be always prepared to defend."

Mr. Morton afterwards, on September 12th, sent the following dispatch to the Secretary of State at Washington:

With true appreciation of what is due to America in the fame of Lafayette, the French authorities and the family of Lafayette expressed an earnest desire that the representative of the United States should be associated with the public tribute to his memory. In response to a most flattering invitation from the prefect of the department, the mayor of Le Puy, and Senator Edmond de Lafayette, the only one now bearing that illustrious name, I esteemed it a duty as well as a pleasure to attend the ceremonies connected with the unveiling of the statue, which were performed with fitting solemnity in presence of high functionaries of the French Government, of living representatives of the family of Lafayette, and of a large concourse of people, including quite a number of distinguished Americans.

I venture to send herewith extracts from newspapers . . . giving a full account of the speeches made at Le Puy, and of interesting incidents of the day.

You will notice with gratification, I am sure, that the whole proceedings evinced in the most flattering manner the existence of a strong and true feeling of good-will and amity between France and the United States. The French speakers were particularly emphatic in their expression of friendship for our country and government, and of admiration for our institutions. These sentiments were expressed not only by those who took part in the Le Puy proceedings: the unveiling of the statue was the occasion of a general expression of the warmest feeling of friendship for our government and people. Papers of all grades and political opinions have united in bestowing upon our country and political system the most flattering eulogies, and in rejoicing over the faithful and happy relations which have so long existed between the two nations.

. . . I am satisfied that in the opinion of the masses, as well as in the belief of the government, the United States is looked upon as the best and most reliable friend of France, the only one from whom she has nothing to fear, and perhaps also the only one in whose footsteps she is inclined to follow.

. . . .

I have, etc.,

LEVI P. MORTON.

To which the Secretary of State made reply as follows:

DEPARTMENT OF STATE,
WASHINGTON, October 1, 1883.

SIR,— Your dispatch No. 403, of the 12th instant, giving an account of the ceremonies which were observed on the occasion of the unveiling of the statue of Lafayette at Le Puy, on the 6th of the present month, has been read with great interest.

Your action in accepting the invitation to be present at the ceremonies as the representative of this country is heartily approved by the President, and he is gratified to learn that the event called forth so many warm expressions of the good-will of the people of France towards the government and citizens of the United States.

I am, etc.,

FREDK. T. FRELINGHUYSEN

On the 5th of July, 1884, a large number of French and Americans assembled at No. 25 Rue de Chazelles, to witness the presentation of Bartholdi's statue of "Liberty Enlightening the World" to the American representative, and the reception, on behalf of the United States, by Mr. Morton.

The following is the presentation speech by Count de Lesseps, President of the Union Franco-Américaine:

"France — monarchial, imperial, or republican — has been always the friend and ally of the United States. Our work to-day is not political; it is the work of a hundred thousand subscribers: 180 towns have participated in it; a large number of general councils, of boards of trade, and of various industrial societies. The thought which has inspired France upon such an occasion has been that of consecrating and cementing the friendship between the two countries that the vast ocean which rolls between cannot separate, because there exists between the two countries so strong a sympathy that when difficulties arise they are soon dissipated, so close is the sentiment between them.

"This is the result of the devoted enthusiasm, the intelligence, and the noblest sentiments which can inspire man. It is great in its conception, great in its execution, great in its proportions. Let us hope that it will add, by its moral value, to the memories and sympathies that it is intended to perpetuate. We now transfer to you, Mr. Minister, this great statue, and trust that it may forever stand the pledge of friendship between France and the great Republic of the United States."

After this speech, and the playing of the "Star Spangled Banner," Mr. Morton responded as follows:

"Mr. President and Gentlemen of the Committee: I am directed by the President of the United States to accept this colossal statue of 'Liberty Enlightening the World,' and to express the thanks of the government and people of the United States for the statue, as a work of art and as a monument of the abiding friendship of the people of France, and to assure the Committee of the Franco-American Union, the President of the Council, and the citizens of the French Republic, that the American people return most heartily the friendly sentiments which prompted this noble gift to America.

"It is proper that I should recall on this occasion the action of the government of the United States with regard to the statue of Liberty, the completion of which we witness to-day.

"When the American Congress was advised that the citizens of France proposed to erect on one of the islands in the harbor of New York, the colossal statue of 'Liberty Enlightening the World,' it authorized, by a unanimous vote, the President to accept the gift, and to set apart a suitable site for its erection.

"The President was also directed to cause the statue to be inaugurated, when completed, with such ceremonies as would serve to testify to the gratitude of the people of the United States for the monument so felicitously expressive of the sympathy of her sister Republic.

"The American Congress also ordered provision to be made for its future maintenance as a beacon, and for its preservation and permanent care as a monument of art, and of the continued good will of the great nation which aided her in her struggle for freedom.

"The President of the United States set apart Bedloes Island for the erection of the statue, and I have received a telegram from Messrs. Evarts and Spaulding, of the New York Committees, stating that the concrete base, fifty-two feet high, been completed, and the laying of the granite for the pedestal commenced.

"The thought which inspired M. Bartholdi, the eminent author of this triumph of art; the participation in this gift of Senators Oscar and Edmond de Lafayette, the Marquis de Rochambeau, and other descendants of the sons of France who fought by the side of Washington; the participation also of M. de Lesseps, the illustrious President of the Franco-American Union, of his distinguished predecessor, Senator Laboulaye, the French interpreter of the American Constitution; of Senator Henri Martin, the great historian, and their distinguished associates: the presence on this occasion of several members of the government, and the representative of the President of this great Republic; the proposal of the French Government, through the Minister of Marine, to transport this statue to New York in a government frigate, and the selection of the anniversary day of American Independence for this ceremony, will all only deepen the grateful appreciation with which your friendly gift will be received by the government and people of the United States.

"It was my good fortune, as the representative of my country, to drive the first rivet in this great statue, as it is now to accept it complete in all its grand proportions, on behalf of the President and people of the United States.

"The Committee of the Franco-American Union, of New York, which was organized to provide the foundations for the statue, will receive it, on its arrival, with the same feelings of gratitude and emotion which your friendly action has evoked in the heart of every American, and assume the agreeable task of its erection upon the pedestal on Bedloes Island.

"God grant that it may stand until the end of time, as an emblem of imperishable sympathy and affection between the Republics of France and the United States."

JAMES ABRAM GARFIELD,

THE FOURTH REPUBLICAN PRESIDENT OF THE UNITED STATES

Chapter VI.

BRILLIANT CLOSING OF MINISTRY TO FRANCE.

ELECTION OF 1884 — MR. MORTON PREPARES TO RESIGN — INAUGURATION OF ORIGINAL MODEL OF "LIBERTY ENLIGHTENING THE WORLD" — AN EARLY BANQUET — SCENE ON THE PLACE DES ÉTATS-UNIS — PRESENTATION SPEECH BY MR. MORTON — RECEPTION BY M. BRISSON — SPEECHES BY M. BOUÉ, M. DE LESSEPS, AND SENATOR LAFAYETTE — INVITATION TO A FAREWELL BANQUET — THE TOASTS — TESTIMONIES OF APPRECIATION FROM FRENCH AND AMERICANS — A RESPONSE BY MR. MORTON — REPORTS FROM PARIS AND LONDON PAPERS — A PERSONAL TESTIMONY BY PRESIDENT GRÉVY.

After the presidential election of 1884, Mr. Morton prepared to resign his commission in favor of whomever might be appointed by the Democratic administration. That choice was the Honorable Robert M. McLane, of Maryland, ex-governor of that State, who had also served the government in various other capacities.

But before closing the record of Mr. Morton's career in France, it will be due to him, as well as a pleasing task, to recount in some detail two important events which occurred near the close of his residence there, and which reflect much honor upon his whole course during the four years of his ministry.

On the 13th of May, 1885, occurred at Paris the inauguration of the original model of "Liberty Enlightening the World." A committee of Americans had caused it to be cast in bronze, and this was the day it was to be presented to France. It was not so large as the colossal statue then already on its way to New York Harbor, but it was considered the largest monumental figure in Paris. It was erected on the Place des États-Unis, just before the palatial official residence of the Minister of the United States.

On that morning, at Mr. Morton's invitation, the principal participants in the ceremony partook of such a breakfast as he had been noted for giving. There were present senators, deputies, artists, diplomatists, and journalists. President Grévy was represented by General Pittié. Others were M. Floquet, President of the Chamber of Deputies, M. Boué, President of the Municipal Council, M. de Lesseps, and M. Edmond de Lafayette, grandson of the great general of American fame. After breakfast, the company was joined by M. Henri Brisson, President of the Council of Ministers, who had been detained away until then. There were also present, at the breakfast and afterwards, many other eminent Frenchmen, as well as many noted Americans. In fact, the great drawing-room was filled with important personages. The spirit of the occasion was well indicated by Mme. Adam, the renowed editress of the *Nouvelle Revue*, who was present: "I put off my departure for the country until to-morrow, in order to participate in this international fraternization. I always wish to do what little I can to keep alive the old friendship which has united the two great republics for more than a century."

In harmony with this spirit the procession marched out of the drawing-room and on to the spacious park, to the strains of the "Star Spangled Banner" and "*Marseillaise*." There had gathered such a gay throng as Paris can furnish. French and American flags were fluttering everywhere, "while the light spring tints of the trees that bordered the square, and a soft May sun-light spreading over all, contrasted strongly with the dusky form of the towering statue."

Mr. Morton was to make the presentation speech, and when he rose before the vast assembly for the purpose, he was greeted with enthusiastic applause, which was repeated again and again as he proceeded. He spoke as follows:

"*Monsieur le Président du Conseil, Monsieur le Président de la Chambre des Députés, Monsieur le Président du Conseil Municipal:*

"GENTLEMEN, Upon the eve of my departure, I have one more mission to discharge, and that a very agreeable one. I desire to express to you the feelings entertained by my countrymen on this occasion. In a few days the colossal statue of 'Liberty Enlightening the World,' the generous gift of the French Nation to the United States, will leave the port of Rouen, on board the French Frigate *Isère*, and ere long it will be erected at the entrance of the harbor of New York, where it will stand forever in memory of the friendship which unites the two great sister Republics.

"An American committee in Paris has collected a fund for the casting in bronze of the model of this celebrated statue. It is eminently proper that this, the original work as it came from the hands of your distinguished artist, M. Bartholdi, should be preserved in imperishable form in the generous country which conceived the noble thought of a monument to commemorate the old Franco-American alliance.

"This bronze statue, offered to you by my compatriots, will remain a lasting souvenir of gratitude to France. It is fitting that it should be erected where the heart-beating of this great nation is felt so forcibly, and in a square to which you have so courteously given the name of my country.

"The city of Paris has most kindly seconded all efforts of the committee, and has graciously undertaken the erection of the monument. We tender the city authorities our most hearty thanks.

"In the name of my compatriots and the committee, I beg you to accept, for the French Nation, this token of our sympathy and friendship—sentiments which God grant may unite the two countries for centuries to come.

"In your persons, Mr. Chairman and Members of the Municipal Council of Paris, to whom we confide this gift, we salute the great capital which we admire and love, and to whose manners and usages we have become as accustomed as your own countrymen.

"May this statue of Liberty tend to perpetuate a friendship which the changing events of a hundred years have only served to strengthen.

"I desire, gentlemen, before closing, to avail myself of this occasion to express to the municipal authorities of Paris my high appreciation of the compliment which has been paid my country during my term of office, in giving to this square, in 1881, when the United States Legation was located here, the name of Place des États-Unis."

For this happy speech Mr. Morton immediately received the

warmest congratulations from the president of the council and other French officials, while the people applauded, as the French can when they are pleased. It would be unjust to refuse to make public, by giving M. Brisson's response, the esteem in which Mr. Morton was held by the highest of those officials, and by the French people, as well as the friendship he had, in fact, re-awakened and intensified in them for our country.

Said the president of the council:

"GENTLEMEN: I congratulate myself most heartily that circumstances have designated me to receive, in the name of the French Republic, both this magnificent gift of the American people, and especially the expression of friendly sentiments for our country, which you have just heard so eloquently expressed by Mr. Morton.

"Receive in return, Monsieur le Ministre, our thanks, both for yourself and the Americans for whom you have spoken. The history of our friendship is of long date. Before the exchange of these two monuments, one of which is to remain here, and the other so shortly to be transported to your shores, tokens of friendship between the two great Republics were not wanting, either upon this side of the Atlantic or the other. If our streets and public squares have American names, with you whole cities bear French names, not, as happens too frequently, in order to perpetuate the souvenir of bloody triumphs of one people over another, but, on the contrary, as an evidence of our secular friendship. Our friendship is like the 'Liberty' created by the genius of M. Bartholdi — it enlightens the world, but does not menace it. You celebrated not long ago your centenary; we are shortly to celebrate ours. May this ceremony of to-day serve as a bond of union between these two great jubilees.

"Who would be able to say to-day which of the two nations manifested itself to the world by this declaration? 'We hold these truths to be self-evident, that all men are created equal; that they are endowed by their Creator with certain inalienable rights: that among these are life, liberty, and the pursuit of happiness; that to secure these rights, governments are instituted among men, deriving their just powers from the consent of the governed.'

"It was your ancestors, gentlemen, who in 1776 gave utterance to these words, so humane and yet so bold. Happier than ourselves, established in a new land, surrounded with fewer enemies, it has perhaps cost you less trouble to realize the promises contained in these words. The only tragedy that has marked your history during a hundred years demonstrated, moreover, what a grand teacher liberty is in everything. Obliged to make and improvise war, you gave evidence of incomparable energy and resources. You conducted it upon a scale that surprised us. A single episode of this gigantic struggle — the campaign of Sherman — recalls, by its calculated temerity, the expedition of Hannibal. Ah! you have shown, gentlemen, what you are capable of doing; you can henceforth and forever return to works of peace.

"Peace, liberty, justice, friendship between nations — that is the work that we should, hand in hand, endeavor to accomplish.

"Why should there not be, Mr. Morton, associated with this *fête*, a sentiment of personal regret, which you will allow me to express? Guests, respected, appreciated, and loved by Parisian society, are about to leave us. And yet, welcome to the new envoy of the great American Republic. Let us hope, however, that Paris will exercise on you, Mr. and Mrs. Morton, its customary charm. It was said in antiquity, and is still said — you have heard it many times, M. de Lesseps — that whoever once tastes the water of the Nile wishes to drink it for the rest of his life. Paris flatters herself that she is capable of the same seduction — that she can inspire the same *nostalgia*. Mr. and Mrs. Morton, Parisian society will not, I am sure, lose you forever."

Responses were also made by M. Boué, M. de Lesseps, and Senator Lafayette. The neat impromptu by M. de Lesseps deserves a place here:

"As President of the Franco-American Committee, which has presented to the United States the Colossal Statue of Liberty, I thank Minister Morton and the American Committee for this beautiful gift to France and the city of Paris. This exchange of tokens of friendship is a fresh bond uniting the two grand Republics, and I am happy to state the fact in the presence of the noble heirs of the glorious names of Lafayette and Rochambeau."

During all this time, Mrs. Morton sat, with two or three of her daughters, on a seat near the front. After the speaking, she was approached first by M. Brisson, who assured her of his best wishes for her safe return to America, and then by a great number of the most eminent Frenchmen, who expressed themselves likewise. She was always ready to reply in neat and pointed phrases, expressing her regard for the French people and nation, and her gratitude for the great kindness that had been shown her.

The other event is explained by the following letter:

PARIS, April 23, 1885.

The Honorable L. P. Morton, Envoy Extraordinary and Minister Plenipotentiary of the United States in France.

DEAR SIR: We learn, with deep regret, that you are about to leave Paris. It is our wish, on the eve of your departure, to publicly express to you our appreciation of the invaluable services you have rendered to Americans in France.

During the four years that you have represented the United States in this capital, you have strengthened the bonds that unite the two Republics, and you have secured for our citizens in France advantages which they did not previously possess. Your home has been the centre of a most generous hospitality; to every work of charity you have been a devoted friend and supporter; you have extended to every citizen of our country, however humble, assistance and protection whenever needed, and in the long list of distinguished men who have filled the eminent position of American Minister in France, we feel there is not one who has been more faithful and devoted in maintaining national interests.

In recalling the honorable record of your services, we are united in a sentiment of cordial respect and gratitude for the past, and of earnest good wishes for the future. We beg, therefore, to invite you to a dinner, at such a time as may be most convenient to you, which will give us an opportunity of bidding you God speed, and of thanking you in person for the many kindnesses and services of which we have been the recipients during your term of office.

We beg to express to Mrs. Morton, through you, our cordial thanks for the most gracious welcome she has also extended to us, and our sincere appreciation of the qualities which have made her, in her sphere, what you have been in yours.

We are, dear sir,

Very faithfully yours, etc.

This letter was beautifully engrossed on parchment, and signed by sixty American gentlemen in Paris. Mr. Morton replied the next day, and after expressing his pleasure at the invitation, and the pleasure of Mrs. Morton, he said:

As the new American minister to France is expected to sail from New York on the 29th inst., it will be most agreeable to me, as I doubt not that it will be to you, to fix a date subsequent to his arrival. I therefore beg to suggest May 14th, when I shall be pleased to avail myself of your courteous invitation, and shall hope also to have the pleasure of presenting my successor, my late colleague in Congress and personal friend, the Hon. Robert M. McLane.

The farewell banquet was held at the Hôtel Continental, and was one of the most brilliant social events of the season. Not only Americans, but many of the most eminent Frenchmen were present. Mr. Morton's successor was also there, and the friendship shown to exist between the two was one of the most pleasant features of the evening. In all there were about two hundred gentlemen present, of the most distinguished Frenchmen and Americans, and others.

The arrangements for the banquet were most complete. Every expression of taste and art was brought into requisition to show the esteem in which the honored guest of the evening was held. The halls were ornamented with plants, and the band of the *Garde Républicaine*, under the leadership of M. Gustave Wettge, furnished the best and most artistic music for the occasion. The *ménu* was printed in Old English text, and announced the choicest that France might afford.

Mr. John Munroe was chairman of the committee of arrangements, and presided at the banquet table. He had Mr. Morton and Mr. McLane on his right.

"We have gathered together this evening," said Mr. Munroe, rising, "to do honor and to bid farewell to one who, during the past four years, has been a friend to all of us. The presence in our midst of so many distinguished members of the French Government, and others prominent in the spheres of art and science, is a brilliant testimony to the respect and affection in which Mr. Morton is held by all. Many other representative men would have been with us, to add still further lustre to the gathering, had it been possible for them to do so; and I shall, with your permission, read a few of the letters, expressing the high appreciation in which Mr. Morton is held by those to whose government he has been accredited."

He then read letters from M. Jules Ferry, M. de Freycinet, M. Henri Brisson, General Pittié, and others.

The toasts of the evening, some of which had now already been given, were as follows:

1. The President of the French Republic. Music: "The French National Air."

2. The President of the United States. Music: "The American National Air."

3. The Guest of the evening, the Hon. L. P. Morton. Remarks by Mr. John Munroe.

4. American Diplomacy. Remarks by Mr. Edmund Kelly. Reply by Mr. Morton. Music.

5. The Two Great Sister Republics. Remarks by M. Floquet. Music.

6. The Hereditary Friendship of France and the United States. Remarks by the Hon. Robert M. McLane, Minister of the United States.

7. The Development of Popular Education the True Basis of National Greatness. Remarks by M. René Goblet, Minister of Public Instruction. Music.

8. The Commercial Relations between France and the United States. Remarks by Consul-General Walker.

9. The Modern International Peacemaker — Arbitration. Remarks by General Keys, of the United States Army. Music.

10. Two glorious names always uppermost in the heart of every patriotic American — Washington and Lafayette. Remarks by the Marquis Edmund de Lafayette, and the Marquis de Rochambeau. Music.

It only remains to give briefly a few sketches, taken almost at random, from the many good things that were said on that brilliant evening.

Senator Lafayette, speaking of Mr. Morton, said: "During his mission in France, your worthy representative has shown himself to be the friend of our country, and he has known how to become acquainted with, to appreciate and admire our most eminent public men. . . . As for myself, I can never forget the marks of affection which Mr. Morton and his fellow-countrymen have always shown for the memory of Lafayette, the companion in arms and the friend of Washington; and we delight in the recollections of the old union between the two nations, and the glorious day of Yorktown, with which event the name of Rochambeau is also associated."

The Marquis de Rochambeau spoke as follows: "In less than four years Mr. and Mrs. Morton have won the approbation of everybody, and, I may say it without any fear of contradiction, none better than they have known how to keep alive the old friendship which unites France and America."

Said Mr. McLane: "I have accepted with great pleasure the invitation of your committee to unite with you in this banquet in honor of my predecessor. . . . Honest and efficient administration is consistent with party government, and, therefore, men of all parties can unite in rendering homage to faithful and capable public servants. It is in this spirit that we can all unite in cordial and generous courtesy to our guest, recognizing the fidelity and ability with which he has represented our country in France."

M. Floquet, President of the Chamber of Deputies, closed his remarks with the following: "Be pleased to convey to Mrs. Morton our respectful homage. Her exquisite qualities rendered her worthy to be at the head of that brilliant American colony, which constitutes one of the most graceful ornaments of our Parisian society. Her charms of manner and mind blended well with the courteous gravity of your temper and habits, and have made your house one of those in which hospitality was of the most amiable kind and eagerly sought after. Be sure that among us neither of you will be forgotten; and, when you are far away, preserve a little remembrance of us, and accept this evening our sad and cordial, and, if I may be allowed to say it, our fraternal, farewell."

Mr. Edmund Kelly, in his speech, gave a rapid and faithful sketch of Mr. Morton's diplomatic career in France. In closing the narrative, he said: "And then, too, not a single American enterprise, worthy of consideration, has been started in France during the last four years, but owes him a debt of gratitude. I see in this room living witnesses to the cordiality and effectiveness of his coöperation. For these last four years have been full of American achievement. A young engineer, of New York, has revolutionized the silk trade by an invention which, in delicacy of treatment, has not been surpassed by Edison, and, in fruitfulness of result, hardly equaled by Arkwright himself. Two of our fellow-citizens, during the hours they could spare from their already engrossing occupations, have out of their private means, added a couple of sub-marine cables to those that already united the shores of the two Republics. Another has built a veritable monument of gothic architecture in Paris, which will materially add to the beauty of what is already the most beautiful city in the world. Another of our countrymen (and this enterprise is, perhaps, of all the most stupendous in its presumptuousness, and the most amazing in its prosperity) has not only dared to undertake, but has actually succeeded in the publication of a daily newspaper in this country of France, to which he does not belong, and in the French language, which he hardly understands. It would be ungracious not to admit that the success of these men (especially in this last case) has been largely due to the intelligent assistance and welcome of the people among whom we live. Every one of them, however, has had his way made easy, and in some cases his success determined, by the puissant coöperation of our late minister."

In response, among other excellent things, Mr. Morton spoke the following:

"It has been my constant and earnest desire to discharge the duties of the position in a manner that would redound to the credit of the government and country I have had the honor to represent; and tend to cement and perpetuate the mutual affection and respect, which took their birth when France came to our aid during our struggle for independence. If my efforts have met with any measure of the success which your partiality awards to them, it is owing to the friendly consideration, in all official and personal relations, which I have received from the distinguished statesmen who preside over the destinies of our sister Republic, from all the officers of the government, and from the people of France, as well as from the encouragement and cordial support which I have received at your hands, representing as you do all the varied elements of American life in Paris. The intelligent and valuable services which have been rendered by the secretaries of Legation, Messrs. Brulatour and Vignaud, deserve special recognition, and will long be remembered by me with gratitude and pleasure. In all my official and personal relations with the President of the Republic, the distinguished gentlemen who have presided at the Quai d'Orsay, commencing with M. Barthélemy Saint-Hilaire, who was followed by that illustrious statesman and brilliant orator, Léon Gambetta, whose death was mourned by the friends of France throughout the world, and all the high functionaries of the government, I have found, not only the courteous attention to which the representative of a great nation is everywhere entitled, but a cordial sympathy for our country, an enlightened admiration for its institutions, and an earnest desire to contribute to a closer union between the two republics. . . . .

"We are honored also by the presence of my most distinguished successor, who has to-day assumed the duties of his office. Mr. McLane's eminent services in high official stations — in Congress, as commissioner to China, as minister of the United States to Mexico, and as governor of the State of Maryland — are an assurance that the duties of his new position will be discharged with conspicuous ability, and in a manner alike honorable to his country and himself. I could not ask more for my personal friend and late colleague in Congress than the friendly reception accorded to me by the government and people of France, and the hearty support which I have received from my countrymen."

The papers of Paris and London vied with each other in giving such accounts of this, and other banquets, as did honor to Mr. Morton. Speaking of the sentiments expressed on the occasions of the presentation of statue of Liberty and of the farewell banquet, the Paris *Temps* remarked: "They are so natural and unconventional, that they suggested other words than the common-place ones generally expressed on such occasions. In most of these utterances, there was a display of real feeling, a very rare thing in similar instances."

Said the London *Standard*: "Such a tribute of sympathy and good-will to a diplomatic agent on his retirement, as took place to-night at the Hôtel Continental, is without precedent in the French capital."

The London *Times*: "Mr. Morton, indeed, during his four years' residence in Paris, has shown great hospitality, and has realized the type of modern ambassadors, who succeed in inspiring affection for their own nation by manifesting affection for the nation to which they are accredited. Admirably seconded by Mrs. Morton, he has given the Legation an eminently social character, his brilliant receptions being attended not only by the numerous members of the American colony, but by French guests, who have found it a neutral ground such as is now rarely offered by French *salons*. This signal testimony of gratitude, on the part of the Americans, was therefore amply deserved, while it was equally just that Frenchmen should join in the expression of esteem inspired by Mr. Morton during his too brief stay."

The *Morning News*: "The honors paid to Mr. Morton yesterday were a fitting conclusion to perhaps the most successful reign ever enjoyed by an American Minister to France. It must not be supposed that the tribute offered to the departing minister last night was the consequence of a precedent. It was, in fact, a novelty. . . . Mr. Morton will carry with him to his American home the grateful remembrance of his fellow-citizens in France, and no future honors will be considered by them too lofty or too well-deserved."

In company with Mr. Brulatour, Mr. Morton presented himself, on the 14th of May, to M. Grévy, the President of the Republic, at the Elysée, to deliver his letters of recall.

In reply to Mr. Morton's words of appreciation of all the courtesies that had been extended to him, M. Grévy said:

"It is with lively regret that we witness your departure. We have always appreciated your high character and great courtesy. You have won the sympathy of all, and I only wish that the custom and tradition of the two countries permitted me to ask, as a favor, your retention in office.

"Mrs. Morton's departure will also be deeply regretted, as she has made herself universally popular by her perfect tact and amiability."

Soon after these events, Mr. Morton and his family sailed for home. He himself may not have felt fully satisfied with his work in France — as a faithful servant never feels that he has done all that he might have done — but he certainly did not feel that he could not congratulate himself on his success; nor could he have had any chidings of conscience on account of misspent time, or failure to do his duty. Nor was there a man in America, or in France, who knew anything about his career in the latter country, that could not heartily have said of his service, "Well done."

His popularity at home had not diminished, meanwhile. For no sooner was it there ascertained that there was to be a Democratic administration, and that Mr. Morton must return home, than his friends began to consider him as a candidate for nomination to the Senate of the United States. In January, 1885, while he was yet in France, his name was brought before the Republican caucus; and in spite of the fact that Mr. Evarts was also before the caucus, Mr. Morton showed great strength, the vote in the caucus being as follows: Evarts, 61; Morton, 28; and Depew, 3.

Two years afterwards, Mr. Morton's name was before the legislature for the same office. The result of the first ballot was, Morton, 33; Hiscock, 11: Miller, 43: and Smith M. Weed (Democrat), 61. Mr. Morton then withdrew in favor of Mr. Hiscock, and on the second ballot Mr. Hiscock received the entire Republican vote, and was elected.

Chapter VII.

HOME AND CHARITIES.

NO. 85 FIFTH AVENUE — "FAIR LAWN" — "ELLERSLIE" — DOMESTIC CHARACTER AND TASTES — FAITHFUL AND ACCOMPLISHED WIFE AND DAUGHTERS — A MAN OF BENEVOLENCE — "ONE-QUARTER OF THE CARGO OF THE CONSTELLATION" — DETERMINATION IF NOT ACCEPTED — $50,000 FOR RELIEF OF WORKINGMEN DURING ROCKAWAY BEACH IMPROVEMENT TROUBLES — TESTIMONY OF GRATEFUL EMPLOYÉS — A GIFT TO DARTMOUTH COLLEGE — OLEOMARGARINE LAWS — A RECORD WORTHY OF HONOR.

NOT the least brilliant and successful phase of Mr. Morton's life, has been his home-life. He has been one of the few rich men who have demonstrated that they deserve all their wealth by the use they make of it, as well as by their manner of obtaining it. The homes he has occupied have been true American homes, and not mansions for the display of wealth. He has bought, or built, fine houses, and furnished them as a man of taste and having a wife of taste and refinement, would naturally furnish them.

A detailed account of his private buying and selling is not necessary. From what has been written, no one would accuse him of a wrong transaction in the matter of a house-lot. His more public transactions were too large, and presented temptations and opportunities for underhanded dealing far too great, for him to have paused to bring the curses of a poor man or a common dealer upon him; and that his record in the smaller private matters is clean, is witnessed by the facts that it is clean in the other matters, and that there is no poor man or widow who has ever had dealings with him, who does not crown him with blessings.

Three large mansions have conserved the influences that Mr. Morton and his estimable wife have been able to gather under the sacred name of home. There are those with small means who have humbler cottages that inclose influences as pure and home-like, and as conducive to contentment and happiness; but it requires, therefore, a higher art to take more than is absolutely necessary for such a place, and weave it into the sacred fabric of a home, so that there shall be nothing surperfluous. In these mansions, this art has been displayed in its greatest perfection.

The first is a large, brown-stone house, on Fifth Avenue, New York. If it were standing alone, it would be considered magnificent in its outward appearance. But crowded among so many—and some of them much larger—monuments of architectural skill, it assumes modest proportions.

There is a wide hall running from the street doors to the dining-room at the rear. On the right wall hangs a large portrait of President Garfield. On the left is a large painting, by Constant, of an Eastern dwelling. The door on the right leads into the parlors; the door on the left, into the library. The stairway, also, leads up from the hall. The dining-room, at the end of the hall, is almost as wide as the house. The portraits that hang in the library, are those of Mr. Morton's father, the Rev. Daniel O. Morton; his uncle, Levi Parsons; Washington, Arthur, Lafayette, McMahon, Count de Rochambeau, and Gambetta. There is also a picture of the store of Mr. Esterbrook, in Concord, New Hampshire, where Mr. Morton went from Enfield to be a clerk. The last is a daguerreotype; the rest are all works of masters. The arrangement of these pictures betrays the same taste as their selection. Mr. Morton is a lover of art, and this fact is seen in all in the room. The books are the best and the rarest.

The "cottage" at Newport, Rhode Island, has been referred to. It was purchased about 1869 or 1870. It is of brick, painted a brown stone color. From the avenue, down to which the spacious grounds lead, "Fair Lawn" presents a cluster of gables and chimneys, so arranged as to give a most pleasing effect. Within, the appointments are not unlike those of No. 85 Fifth Avenue. But there are many houses on Bellevue Avenue more costly than this.

For several years Mr. Morton and his family made "Fair Lawn" their summer residence. But salt atmosphere was not always conducive to their health, and it became necessary to find a place farther inland for summer. For this purpose, a large tract of land was bought, just south of Rhinebeck, a village about ninety miles up the Hudson River, and three miles back from the river, on the west side.

Rhinebeck is one of the staid old towns of the Hudson valley. It is situated among the hills; and the quaint old houses, with those of more modern type, some of costly construction, together with the stately trees that arch the streets or half hide the cottages from view, make it very picturesque.

The site selected for the new house, which was to be known as "Ellerslie," was perhaps three miles south of the village. It overlooked the Hudson for miles up and down, and presented a view of the valleys and hills just across the river, and the Catskills a little to the north. The house was finished during the summer of 1888, and was constructed of brown-stone and tinted wood, the former reaching only to the second story. The floors are of polished oak. The dining-room is trimmed with black polished walnut. The oaken stairways lead from the halls to the second and third stories. Some of the rooms are decorated with rare and tinted wood, and there are mantels of Italian and Parian marble and onyx. The extensive grounds are inclosed by a stone wall. and the driveways are macadamized. There are nooks and groves, and lawns and fountains. The ample stables in the rear proclaim that the owner is a lover of horses.

There is nothing about all this that indicates an attempt at display, or, on the other hand, a close or selfish avoidance of expenditure. Everything witnesses to liberality and a love of the beautiful. The expenditure has all been cheerfully applied to some purpose, and every dollar adds its effect to the beauty or usefulness of the surroundings. Wherever there was a thing necessary for any part of the premises, it was purchased without any hesitancy; and there is evidence everywhere that the purchaser knew just what was wanted before the purchase was made.

The description of these houses has been given because they are all exponents of the domestic character and tastes of those by whom and for whom they exist. A cultivated family; a man of broad and liberal mind, and heart, and training, a wife of rare accomplishments and refinement, and daughters well-trained and of excellent and refined tastes. For there are five daughers, the eldest of whom was born in 1875.

These children have been brought up under most excellent care and instruction. The best of home teachers — governesses — have been employed, and nothing has been spared which will tend to place them among the noble women of the country — ornaments to, and useful members of, society.

But there are acts yet to be recorded that indicate, better than any direct words of praise, the character of Mr. Morton, and the kind of moral influences that pervade his home. His benevolence is a trait of his character, and is not manifested alone in great deeds that might honor him before men, nor alone in private deeds toward his own family or friends in a way that, after all, would be selfish.

In 1880 occurred the great famine in Ireland. There were thousands of sufferers, sick and dying of starvation, and little relief afforded by England. Our Congress placed at the disposal of any benevolent-hearted Americans who might be willing to contribute to the relief of the sufferers, the large ship *Constellation*, for the transportation of what might be donated. Some time went on, and no one seemed to realize the importance of contributing. After some weeks the following letter was printed in the New York *Herald:*

> You are authorized to announce that a gentleman known to *you*, who declines to have his name made public, offers to pay for one-quarter of the cargo of the *Constellation*, if other parties will make up the balance.

It was not long until this notice served as a spur to others, and the proprietor of the *Herald* and Mr. W. R. Grace, each contributed a fourth, and the remaining fourth was made up by a number of other gentlemen. So the *Constellation* sailed with her full cargo, and carried relief to the famishing of Ireland.

The author of the letter and the contributor of the first

quarter was Mr. Morton. It was his intention, if the offer was not accepted, to furnish the cargo himself. He was not one of those men who offer to do great things, in case some other impossible or wholly improbable thing occurs.

During the same year occurred what was known as the Rockaway Beach Improvement troubles. An enormous hotel was begun at Rockaway Beach, and five hundred workmen were employed. The great scheme failed, and the workmen were not only thrown out of employment, but their wages, which had been kept back, they now found impossible to obtain. They were poor, and they needed bread for their wives and children. Certificates of indebtedness were issued to them, but nobody would pay cash for the worthless paper, or give food for it.

It was at this moment that Mr. Morton came forward, and joining with the firm of Drexel, Morgan & Company, the two firms contributed $50,000 each, paying the full amount of the certificates, and refusing to accept any discount.

Nor did Mr. Morton wait until late in life, when he had amassed his fortune, before he manifested the charitable and benevolent characteristics. When the firm of Morton & Grinnell failed in 1861, the senior partner assumed the whole indebtedness, refusing to allow Mr. Grinnell to bear any part of it. And it has already been related how, after going into business again and becoming able to pay the full amount, he did so by checks to which his own name alone was signed.

Sometime since, a gentleman strolling along Bellevue Avenue, in Newport, came to "Fair Lawn," and seeing the gate open, and the gardener trimming some shrubbery near at hand, he went in. He was invited by the gardener to the latter's cozy cottage that stood not far from the large "cottage" known as "Fair Lawn."

"Does Mr. Morton come here in summer now?" asked the stranger.

"No. He has not been here for two or three years."

"Would you be glad to see him?"

"Indeed, I would."

"Was he kind?"

"He was. He was not too big to come out now and then, and talk friendly to me. He treated all the servants on the place kindly."

"Why, only think!" spoke up the gardener's wife enthusiastically, "when he and Mrs. Morton came to Newport, two or three years ago, just before they started on a trip to Europe, they stopped here a whole week. And they came over here to this little house every morning and ate with us. They would sit down to our table, just like any common folks; and they would enjoy being with us — but not near as much as we did to have them come! Why, sometimes Mrs. Morton would come over and talk awhile before meal time, and sometimes she would take hold and help me; or she would show me how to do this or that. Oh, she's a lady that *is* a lady, I tell you!"

There could be given no better proof of the thorough Americanism of Mr. and Mrs. Morton than this. They had no aristocratic rules that kept them aloof from others of real worth. Believing that the merit of character alone should entitle one to recognition and association, they dared show it in their actions.

Some years ago, Mr. Morton presented a park to the city of

Newport, which, though now unimproved, will one day be one of the attractions of the city. It is situated in the angle between Brenton Street and Coggeshall Avenue.

In 1885, he bought a house and lot at Hanover, New Hampshire, for which he paid the sum of $7,500. He then presented the property to Dartmouth College. The gift was to enable the college to erect an art gallery and museum.

It can thus be seen that Levi P. Morton's sympathies are with the people, poor or rich, whose cause is just. He makes no class distinctions; though, no doubt, from his own early experience of poverty, at Shoreham, Springfield, and Winchendon, and the inconvenience, denial of opportunities, and even suffering, to his father's family, consequent upon that poverty, his inclinations are toward the defense of the poor. He has always been quick to relieve suffering of any kind. He has been as quick to appreciate a cause of justice, and place himself upon that side. In Congress, he was always found upon the side where he believed the interests of the people to be. Out of Congress, he watched with interest the legislative acts of the country and his own state, and was always ready to do what he could to induce legislation in behalf or the interests of the people. He watched with jealous and anxious eye those interests especially on which the welfare and happiness of all classes were based — business interests.

A gentleman and a Christian, a business man and a statesman,— in the broad, true sense of each of those terms,— Mr. Morton is preëminently a representative of the highest type of American men. His history and character, domestic, social, business, and public, are such as to challenge the patriotic pride of every true citizen of our Republic.

PART III.

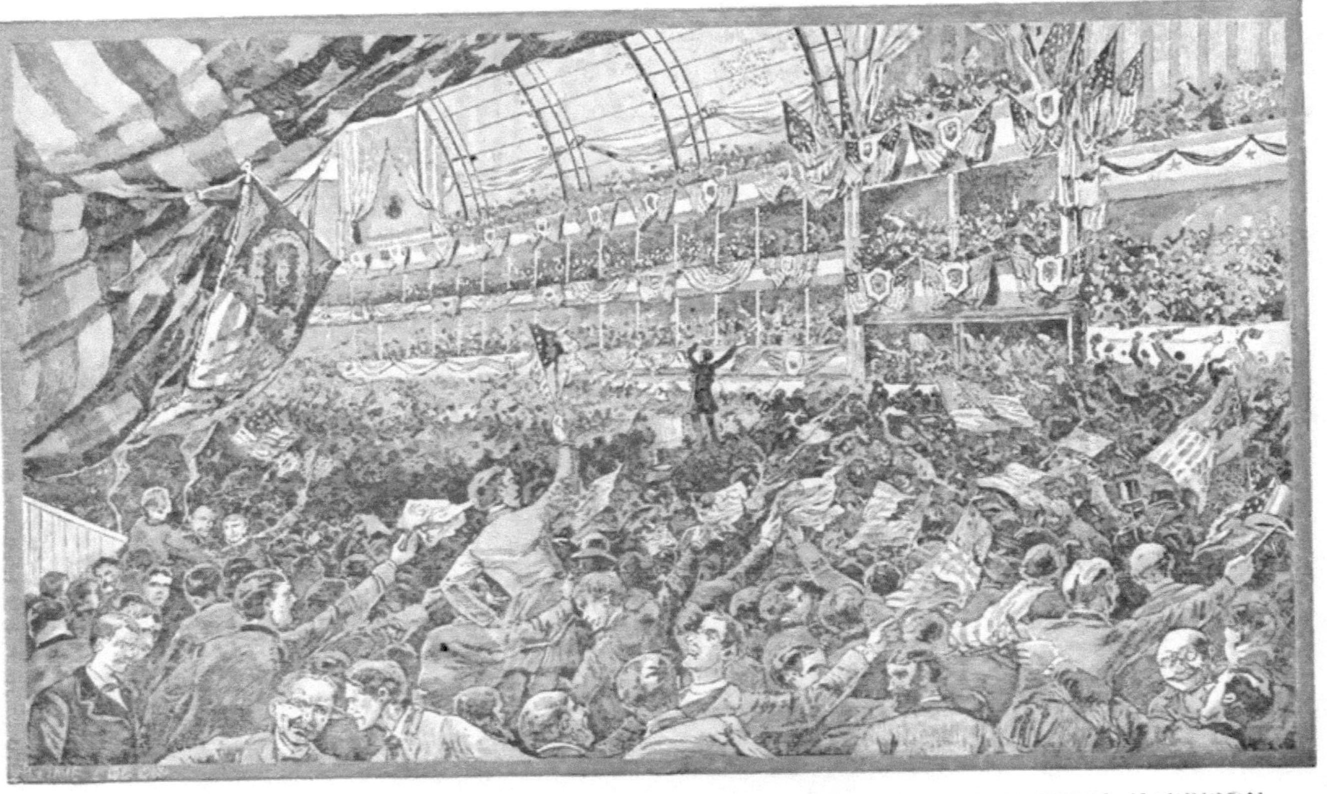

SCENE IN THE REPUBLICAN CONVENTION ON THE NOMINATION OF GENERAL HARRISON.

PART THIRD.

THE REPUBLICAN PARTY—ITS RECORD AND ITS PRESENT POSITION.

CHAPTER I.

ITS GLORIOUS ACHIEVEMENTS.

REPEAL OF THE MISSOURI COMPROMISE—POLITICAL BREAK-UP—FORMATION OF THE REPUBLICAN PARTY—ELECTION OF 1856—FREEDOM OR SLAVERY IN THE TERRITORIES—LINCOLN AND DOUGLAS DEBATE—ELECTION OF ABRAHAM LINCOLN—SECESSION—WAR FOR THE UNION—UNPATRIOTIC ATTITUDE OF THE DEMOCRATIC PARTY—THE REPUBLICAN PARTY THE DEFENDER OF NATIONALITY—EMANCIPATION—ENFRANCHISEMENT OF THE COLORED RACE.

IN 1852, Franklin Pierce, of New Hampshire, was elected President by the Democratic party, receiving the electoral votes of twenty-seven states. Four States only, Massachusetts and Vermont in the North, and Kentucky and Tennessee in the South, cast their votes for General Scott, the Whig candidate.

The Democratic platform, upon which Mr. Pierce was chosen, was framed in entire subserviency to the interests and the wishes of the Southern slave-holders. The Democratic Convention resolved that "all efforts of the Abolitionists or others to induce Congress to interfere with questions of slavery, or to take incipient steps in relation thereto, are calculated to lead to the most alarming and dangerous consequences." The compromise measures by which the extension of slavery into free territory had been restricted were approved: but so also was the fugitive slave law by which Congress had enacted that a man or woman or child, possibly free-born, might be consigned to life-long slavery by the judgment of a United States commissioner, without having a trial by jury to decide the rightfulness of a claim to freedom. The Democratic platform further declared that "the Democratic party will resist all attempts at renewing, in Congress or out of it, the agitation of the slavery question, under whatever shape or color the attempts may be made." The Democratic Convention adopted this pro-slavery platform with entire unanimity and unrestrained enthusiasm. The Whig Convention of 1852 was divided on the slavery question.

After long discussion and against strenuous protest, the Whigs agreed upon a platform no less in the interest of slavery than that of the Democrats.

The resolutions declared that the compromise measures, including the fugitive slave law "are received and acquiesced in by the Whig party of the United States as a settlement in principle and in substance of the dangerous and exciting questions which they embrace."

The public sentiment of 1852 was strongly opposed to any further agitation of the slavery question, and the North acquiesced in unrighteous and cruel laws, violative of the primal rights of man, for the sake of peace and commercial interests.

And Pierce proved the stronger candidate, because the Democratic party was united in upholding the settlement of the slavery controversy that had been so solemnly made, while among the Northern Whigs were multitudes who could not, in good conscience, give their consent to the fugitive-slave law. Divided and disheartened, the Whigs were beaten in many states where they had been in the ascendant, but the Democratic majority in the popular vote was not so great as in the vote in the electoral colleges.

Pierce received a total of 1,601,274 votes, Scott, 1,386,580, and Hale, the candidate of the Free Soilers, 155,825. The absolute majority for Pierce was but 58,896.

In his first message, sent to Congress in December, 1853, President Pierce declared that when "the grave shall have closed over all who are now endeavoring to meet the obligations of duty, the year 1850 will be recurred to as a period of anxious apprehension." He declared of the Compromise of 1850 that "it had given renewed vigor to our institutions, and restored a sense of repose and security to the public mind," and pledged that this "repose" should suffer no shock if he "had the power to avert it."

That very winter Stephen A. Douglas, Democratic Senator from Illinois, reported to the Senate a bill to organize Kansas and Nebraska as territories, and in one section of the bill the Missouri Compromise of 1820 was declared to be inoperative and void. By the famous Missouri Compromise a vast territory westward and northwestward of Missouri and Iowa, stretching from the north line of Arkansas to the British border, twelve and a half degrees of latitude, and westward to

Utah and Oregon, was solemnly dedicated to freedom. The proposition of Senator Douglas now was that the solemn guaranty of the men of 1820 — South and North joining in the compact that the territory north of 36° 30′ should be free soil — should be repealed, and the way left open for the extension of the slave system of the South over all that magnificent domain. Douglas was an ambitious candidate for the Presidency, and sought by this act of subserviency to Southern demands to secure the solid support of the South. In his heart he did not desire the spread of slavery, and he doubtless believed as well as hoped that slavery would gain the form, and freedom the substance, in the conflict for the control of this imperial domain, which his proposition invited. He trusted that settlers from the free states would outnumber those from slave states, and that the institutions of the new territories would be moulded by the forces of freedom.

Meanwhile he expected to be rewarded with the presidential office for his service to the South in leading in an effort to repeal the covenant by which the South, in an earlier and more honorable day, had excluded her peculiar institution from that then unpeopled and almost unknown region.

The excitement throughout the North that this proposition to repeal the Compromise called forth was unequaled hitherto in our political history. The North was ablaze with indignation, and protest was thundered in the ears of Congress. The Democratic party in Congress followed the lead of Douglas; with some honorable exceptions, the Southern Whigs united with the Southern Democrats, and on the 30th of May, 1854, the Compromise was repealed, and the door was opened for the advance of slavery over the plains of the Northwest. Pierce, the Democratic President who had pledged himself not to permit the violation of the compacts which had secured political repose, perfidiously signed the bill repealing the first of the two compromises which were the bases of repose.

The repeal of the Missouri Compromise was quickly followed by the breaking up of old political organizations. The Whig party perished in an hour. The Southern Whigs were left to drift, some at once and some more slowly, into the ranks of the Pro-Slavery Democracy. The great mass of the Northern Whigs, with tens of thousands of freedom-loving Northern Democrats, coalesced as Republicans, animated by the purpose of opposing the aggressions of the slave power and preserving forever free the soil not yet devoted to the slave system. Such was the origin of the Republican party, in the year 1854. Before the end of that year a large majority of the people of the Northern States were united as Republicans under the banner on which was inscribed "Free Soil, Free Speech, and Free Men"; and a majority of the people of the South was ranged under the flag of the Democratic party as the upholders of slavery, not only in the states where it already existed, but as an institution to be extended as far as circumstances would permit it to be carried. From 1854 to 1860 a continuous struggle was waged in Congress, in the Supreme Court, at the polls in every Northern state, on the plains of Kansas and Nebraska, over the question whether slavery should be permitted or prohibited in the territories. The new Republican party took the field in the presidential election of 1856 with General John C. Frémont, of California, as its standard bearer. Douglas failed of his reward. Neither President Pierce nor Senator Douglas were considered available by the Southern Democrats, who, under the rule of the Democratic National conventions that two-thirds of all the delegates must concur in a nomination, always dominated in the conventions of the party. Both Pierce and Douglas struggled desperately for the Democratic nomination for President in 1856, but both were set aside in favor of James Buchanan, of Pennsylvania. Buchanan had never given a vote offensive to the South on the slavery question, but his absence from the country as minister to England had saved him from the obloquy which attached to Pierce and Douglas, the responsible authors of the repeal of the Compromise.

In the election every Southern state voted for Buchanan, except Maryland which voted for Fillmore the candidate of the ephemeral "American" organization.

Buchanan carried in the North his own state of Pennsylvania, and the states of New Jersey, Indiana, Illinois, and California.

Eleven Northern States voted for Frémont.

The popular vote was: for Buchanan, 1,838,169; Frémont, 1,341,264; Fillmore, 874,534.

Although defeated, the moral victory was with the Republicans. They had in their first national struggle obtained the votes of a large majority of the people of the free states.

From the beginning to the end of President Buchanan's term the struggle between freedom and slavery for the control of the territories continued. There was bloodshed in Kansas, hot and angry debates in Congress. Threats to dissolve the

Union were frequently made by representatives of the South.

During Mr. Buchanan's administration there took place on the hustings in Illinois the famous joint debate between Abraham Lincoln, the champion of the Republicans, and Senator Douglas, the advocate of the doctrine of non-interference by Congress with the question of slavery in the territories. In his opening speech Mr. Lincoln uttered these memorable words: "I believe this government cannot endure permanently half slave, half free. I do not expect the Union to be dissolved; I do not expect the house to fall; but I do expect it will cease to be divided. It will become all one thing or all the other. Either the opponents of slavery will arrest the further spread of it, and place it where the public mind shall rest in the belief that it is in the course of ultimate extinction, or its advocates will push it forward till it shall become alike lawful in all the states, old as well as new, north as well as south."

Lincoln advocated a positive prohibition of slavery in the territories by the general government. Douglas argued in favor of submitting the question of slavery to the people of the territory itself. The South was not satisfied with the position of Mr. Douglas. The contention of the Southern Democrats was that where the Constitution went slavery might go, and that no power existed either in Congress or the people of any territory by which slavery could be excluded. Buchanan threw all the influence of the administration against Douglas in his contest for the Senate with Lincoln (the debate occurred in a senatorial canvass), and gave countenance to the *ultra* demands of the slave power.

The unwillingness of Douglas to take the position that the people of a territory had no right to banish slavery from their borders, secured him a reëlection to the Senate from the people of Illinois, but it fatally damaged his prospects for the presidency by alienating the Southern democracy which would be satisfied with nothing short of absolute subserviency to the interests of slavery extension. In 1860 Mr. Lincoln was nominated for President by the Republican Convention on a platform of opposition to slavery extension. The Democratic Convention split in twain after a prolonged and bitter controversy at Charleston, S. C. The Southern wing of the party nominated John. C. Breckinridge, of Kentucky, and the Northern wing Stephen A. Douglas. The Republicans marched to an easy and certain triumph. Lincoln carried every free state with the exception of New Jersey which divided her electoral votes, Lincoln obtaining four. Breckinridge carried every slave state save four—Virginia, Kentucky, and Maryland voting for John Bell, Conservative Unionist; and Missouri for Douglas.

The Southern leaders who were bent on secession from the Union had wrecked the fortunes of the Democratic party, and the subserviency of that party to the slave power while not satisfying the demands of that arrogant political class, had forfeited forever the confidence of the masses of the people in the Northen States. At no presidential election since 1856 has the Democratic party carried more than four of the old free states, and its pluralities in the four states it has twice carried have in the aggregate been less than the Republican plurality during all that period in either of several Northern States.

"The long political struggle was over. A more serious one was about to begin. For the first time in the history of the government, the South was defeated in a presidential election where an issue affecting the slavery question was involved. There had been grave conflicts before, sometimes followed by compromise, oftener by victory for the South. But the election of 1860 was the culmination of a contest which was inherent in the structure of the government; which was foreshadowed by the Louisiana question of 1812; which became active and angry over the admission of Missouri; which was revived by the annexation of Texas, and still further inflamed by the Mexican War; which was partially allayed by the compromises of 1850; which was precipitated for final settlement by the repeal of the Missouri Compromise, by the consequent struggle for mastery, in Kansas, and by the aggressive intervention of the Supreme Court in the case of Dred Scott. These are the events which led, often slowly, but always with directness, to the political revolution of 1860. The contest was inevitable, and the men whose influence developed and encouraged it may charitably be regardad as the blind agents of fate. But if personal responsibility for prematurely forcing the conflict belongs to any body of men, it attaches to those who, in 1854, broke down the adjustments of 1820 and of 1850. If the compromises of those years could not be maintained, the North believed that all compromise was impossible; and they prepared for the struggle which this fact foreshadowed. They had come to believe that the house divided against itself could not stand; that the Republic half slave, half free, could not endure. They accepted as their leader the man who proclaimed these truths. The peaceful revolution was complete when Abraham Lincoln was chosen President of the United States."

The election of Mr. Lincoln was made the pretext for the secession of eleven of the Democratic slave states from the Union. Then ensued the war for the Union. Upon this unhappy period the people do not care to dwell except when on proper occasion they recall the valor and the devotion of the soldiers of the Republic, and remember to discharge the debt of honor the Nation owes to its patriotic defenders. In examining or discussing the record of political parties since the old-fashioned Democracy went to pieces on the rock of slavery in 1854, it is, however, only historic justice that the position of the Democratic and Republican parties during the war should be presented and contrasted.

President Lincoln, as a war measure, issued an Emancipation Proclamation on the first day of January, 1863, declaring free all slaves within certain designated territory. This great act, one of the most illustrious in all history, was condemned by the leading Democrats of the North as unconstitutional.

The next year, 1864, the Democratic presidential convention adopted as the first resolution of its platform the following:

"That this convention does *explicitly declare*, as the sense of the American people, that *after four years of failure to restore the Union by the experiment of war*, during which, under the pretense of a military necessity of war power higher than the Constitution, the Constitution itself has been disregarded in every part, and public liberty and private right alike trodden down, and the material prosperity of the country essentially impaired, justice, humanity, liberty, and the public welfare demand that *immediate efforts be made for a cessation of hostilities*, with a view to the ultimate convention of the states, or other peaceable means to the end that at the earliest practicable moment peace may be restored on the basis of the Federal Union of the states."

In strong contrast to this weak, cowardly, and unpatriotic declaration, were the first and second resolutions of the National Union Republican Convention which nominated Mr. Lincoln for reëlection the same year:

"That it is the highest duty of every American citizen to maintain against all their enemies the integrity of the Union and the paramount authority of the Constitution and laws of the United States; and that, laying aside all differences of political opinions, we pledge ourselves as Union men, animated by a common sentiment, and aiming at a common object, to do everything in our power to aid the Government in quelling by force of arms the rebellion now raging against its authority and in bringing to the punishment due to their crimes the rebels and traitors arrayed against it. That we approve the determination of the Government of the United States not to compromise with rebels or to offer them any terms of peace, except such as may be based upon an unconditional surrender of their hostility, and a return to their just allegiance to the Constitution and laws of the United States; and that we call upon the Government to maintain this position and to prosecute the war with the utmost possible vigor to the complete suppression of the rebellion, in full reliance upon the self-sacrificing patriotism, the heroic valor, and the undying devotion of the American people to the country and its free institutions."

The verdict of the loyal people of the country was overwhelmingly in favor of the administration of Mr. Lincoln, and the Democratic platform of 1864 fell under a weight of popular odium. Any young American may be proud to range himself as a member of the great historic party, whose record during the war is of courage and fidelity to the Union and to liberty, and which sustained Abraham Lincoln in his masterly struggle for the integrity of the government. No young American can join with pride a political party whose representatives were so recreant to high principle and patriotic duty as those of the Democratic party in the hour of the Nation's severest trial.

Just before the close of the war the thirteenth amendment of the Constitution of the United States, abolishing slavery throughout the Nation, was proposed by Congress for the ratification of the states. January 31, 1865, the vote was taken in the House of Representatives. All the Republicans voted in favor of the amendment. Just eleven Democrats were prepared, in that hour of approaching triumph for the Union cause, to vote in favor of abolishing slavery. Fifty-six Democrats, more than five times the number voting for freedom, voted no on the proposition to submit to the states the abolition amendment. The amendment had previously passed the Senate with six votes, all Democratic, against it.

After the war the Republican party reconstructed the Union upon the basis of general amnesty and manhood suffrage. The Republican statesmen, after long deliberation, decided, and decided wisely as history will recognize, that it was not practicable or just to restore civil government in the seceding states without giving to the colored race exact civil and political equality with the white race. The Democratic party offered the most bitter opposition to every measure designed to secure equality before the law to the colored race. Not a single Democratic vote was given in either house of Congress in favor of the submission to the states of the fifteenth amendment of the Constitution, and that amendment received scarcely a Democratic vote in the state legislatures throughout the Union.

Later on we shall consider the present relations of the colored race to our politics in connection with the subject of free and fair elections in certain states; but we turn now to the subject which is uppermost in the public mind.

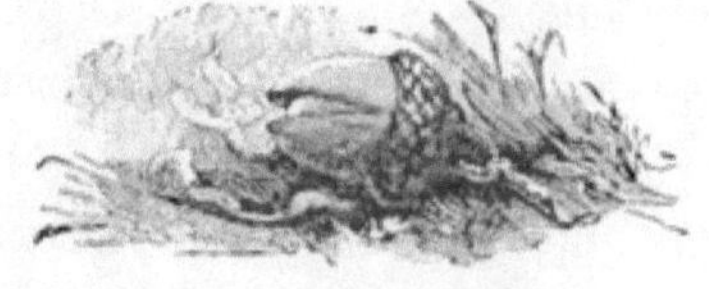

CHAPTER II.

THE TARIFF.

REVIEW OF THE TARIFF CONTROVERSY — THE QUESTION STATED BY MR. BLAINE — INJURIOUS EFFECTS OF TARIFF REDUCTIONS — TARIFF OF 1857 — PROTECTION AND FREE TRADE AS A POLITICAL ISSUE IN THE UNITED STATES — TARIFF OF 1883 — PRESIDENT CLEVELAND'S MESSAGE — THE RAW MATERIALS QUESTION — THE DOCTRINE OF PROTECTION.

By common consent the presidential election of 1888 involves a decision of the issue of whether the duties levied by the general government upon imports from foreign countries shall be imposed for the purpose of fostering American industries and protecting them against the competition in the markets of the United States of the products of foreign countries where the cost of production is less than in America. A succinct presentment of the tariff issue cannot be so easily and effectively made as by copious extracts from the discussion of it by Mr. Blaine, recognized by his political opponents as one of the ablest defenders of the protective system. Accordingly such quotation will be made:

"The slavery question was not the only one which developed into a chronic controversy between certain elements of Northern opinion and certain elements of Southern opinion. A review of the sectional struggle would be incomplete if it did not embrace a narrative of those differences on the tariff which at times led to serious disturbance, and, on one memorable occasion, to an actual threat of resistance to the authority of the government. The division upon the tariff was never so accurately defined by geographical lines as was the division upon slavery; but the aggressive elements on each side of both questions finally coalesced in the same states, North and South. Massachusetts and South Carolina marched in the van-guard of both controversies; and the states which respectively followed on the tariff issue were, in large part, the same which followed on the slavery question, on both sides of Mason and Dixon's line.

"Anti-slavery zeal and a tariff for protection went hand in hand in New England, while pro-slavery principles became nearly identical with free-trade in the cotton states. If the rule had its exception, it was in localities where the strong pressure of special interest was operating, as in the case of the sugar-planter of Louisiana, who was willing to concede generous protection to the cotton spinner of Lowell if he could thereby secure an equally strong protection, in his own field of enterprise against the pressing competition of the island of Cuba. The general rule, after years of experimental legislation, resolved itself into protection in the one section and free trade in the other. And this was not an unnatural division. Zeal against slavery was necessarily accompanied by an appreciation of the dignity of free labor; and free labor was more generously remunerated under the stimulus of protective laws. The same considerations produced a directly opposite conclusion in the South, where those interested in slave labor could not afford to build up a class of free laborers with high wages and independent opinions.

"In the beginning of the controversy it was expected that the manufacture of cotton would grow up side by side with its production, and that thus the community which produced the fibre would share in the profit of the fabric. During this period the representatives from the cotton states favored high duties; but as time wore on, and it became evident that slave-labor was not adapted to the factory, and that it was undesirable if not impossible to introduce free white labor with remunerative wages side by side with unpaid slave labor, the leading minds of the South turned against the manufacturing interest.

"The tariff question has in fact been more frequently debated than any other issue since the foundation of the Federal Government. The present generation is more familiar with questions relating to slavery, to war, to reconstruction; but as these disappear by permanent adjustment, the tariff returns, and is eagerly seized upon by both sides of the controversy. More than any other issue, it represents the enduring and persistent line of division between the two parties which in a generic sense have always existed in the United States: the party of strict construction and the party of liberal construction; the party of states rights and the party of national supremacy; the party of stinted revenue and restricted expenditure and the party of generous income with its wise application to public improvement.

"Public attention may be temporarily engrossed by some exigent subject of controversy, but the tariff alone steadily and presistently recurs for agitation, and for what is called settlement. Thus far in our history, settlement has only been the basis of new agitation, and each successive agitation leads again to new settlement."

Alexander Hamilton, Secretary of the Treasury under General Washington's administration, submitted his celebrated report on manufactures to the House of Representatives in answer to its request of December, 1790. This report sustained and elaborated in a masterly manner never since surpassed, the argument in favor of a protective tariff.

"Mr. Hamilton sustained the plan of encouraging home manufactures by protective duties, even to the point in some instances of making those 'duties equivalent to prohibition.' He did not contemplate a prohibitive duty as the means of encouraging a manufacture not already domesticated, but declared it 'only fit to be employed when a manufacture has made such a progress, and is in so many hands, as to insure a due competition and an adequate supply on reasonable terms.' This argument did not seem to follow the beaten path which leads to the protection of 'infant manufactures,' but rather aimed to secure the home market for the strong and well developed enterprises."

From the organization of the government in 1789, to the time when the Republican party obtained control of national affairs, the tariff policy of Congress was vacillating and unsettled. Several times by unwise reductions of the tariff, always under the lead or the compulsion of the Democratic party, severe injury was inflicted upon the prosperity of the people. In 1857, in the closing session of Mr. Pierce's administration, Congress enacted what has since been known as the tariff of 1857.

"By this law the duties were placed lower than they had been at any time since the War of 1812. The act was well received by the people, and was, indeed, concurred in by a considerable proportion of the Republican party."

It is instructive to note that the seductive appeals to New England men made by the free traders in 1857 on the subject of free raw materials had far greater influence upon those to whom they were addressed than similar appeals to-day have upon the puplic opinion of New England. A majority of New England representatives voted for the low tariff of 1857.

"It was an extraordinary political combination that brought the Senators from Massachusetts and the Senators from South Carolina, the Representatives of New England, and the Representatives from the cotton states to support the same tariff bill — a combination which had not before occurred since the administration of Monroe. The singular coalition portended one of two results: either an entire and permanent acquiescence in the rule of free-trade, or an entire abrogation of that system, and the revival with renewed strength of the doctrine of protection. Which it should be was determined by the unfolding of events not then foreseen, and the force of which it required years to measure.

"The one excuse given for urging the passage of the act of 1857 was that under the tariff of 1846 the revenues had become excessive and the income of the government must be reduced. But it was soon found to be a most expensive mode of reaching that end. The first and most important result flowing from the new act was a large increase of importations, and a very heavy drain in consequence upon the reserved specie of the country, to pay the balance which the reduced shipments of agricultural products failed to meet. In the autumn of 1857, half a year after the passage of the tariff act, a disastrous financial panic swept over the country, prostrating for the time all departments of business in about the same degree. The agricultural, commercial, and manufacturing interests were alike and equally involved. The distress for a time was severe and wide-spread. The stagnation which ensued was discouraging and long continued, making the years from 1857 to 1860 extremely dull and dispiriting in business circles throughout the Union. The country was not exhausted and depleted as it was after the panic of 1837, but the business community had no courage, energy was paralyzed, and new enterprises were at a stand still. It soon became evident that this conditions of affairs would carry the tariff question once more into the political arena as an active issue between parties." . . . "The convention which nominated Mr. Lincoln met when the feeling against free trade was growing, and in many states already deep-rooted. A majority of those who composed that convention had inherited their political creed from the Whig party, and were profound believers in the protective teachings of Mr. Clay. But a strong minority came from the radical school of Democrats, and, in joining the Republican party on the anti-slavery issue, had retained their ancient creed on financial and industrial questions. Care was for that reason necessary in the introduction of new issues and the imposition of new tests of party fellowship. The convention therefore avoided the use of the word 'protection,' and was contented with the moderate declaration that 'sound policy requires such an adjustment of imposts as will encourage the development of the industrial interests of the whole country.' A more emphatic declaration might have provoked resistance from a minority of the convention, and the friends of protection acted wisely in accepting what was offered with unanimity, rather than continue the struggle for a stronger creed which would have been morally weakened by party division. They saw also that the mere form of expression was not important so long as the convention was unanimous on what theologians term the 'substance of doctrine.' It was noted that the vast crowd which attended the convention cheered the tariff resolution as lustily as that which opposed the spread of slavery into free territory. From that hour the Republican party gravitated steadily and rapidly into the position of avowed advocacy of the doctrine of protection."

Mr. Blaine in closing the tariff chapter contained in Vol. I of *Twenty Years of Congress* uses the following language:

"In the foregoing summary of legislation upon the tariff, the terms free trade and protection are used in their ordinary acceptation in this country;—not as accurately defining the difference in revenue theories, but as indicating the rival policies which have so long divided political parties. Strictly speaking, there has never been a proposition by any party in the United States for the adoption of free trade. To be entirely free, trade must encounter no obstruction in the way of tax, either upon export or import. In that sense no nation has ever enjoyed free trade. As contradistinguished from the theory of protection, England has realized freedom of trade by taxing only that class of imports which meet no competition in home production, thus excluding all pretense of favor or advantage to any of her domestic industries. England came to this policy after having clogged and embarrassed trade for a long period by the most unreasonable and tyrannical restrictions ruthlessly enforced, without regard to the interests or even the rights of others. She had more than four hundred acts of Parliament regulating the tax on imports, under the old designations of 'tonnage and poundage,' adjusted, as the phrase indicates, to heavy and light commodities. Beyond these, she had a cumbersome system of laws regulating and in many cases prohibiting the exportation of articles which might teach to other nations the skill by which she had herself so marvelously prospered.

"When by long experiment and persistent effort England had carried her fabrics to perfection; when by the large accumulation of wealth and the force of reserved capital she could command facilities which poorer nations could not rival; when by the talent of her inventors, developed under the stimulus of large reward, she had surpassed all other countries in the magnitude and effectiveness of her machinery, she proclaimed free trade, and persuasively urged it upon all lands with which she had commercial intercourse. Maintaining the most arbitrary and most complicated system of protection so long as her statesmen considered that policy advantageous, she resorted to free-trade, only when she felt able to invade domestic markets of other countries and undersell the fabrics produced by struggling artisans who were sustained by weaker capital and by less advanced skill. So long as there was danger that her own marts might be invaded, and the products of her looms and forges undersold at home, she rigidly excluded the competing fabric and held her own market for her own wares.

"The essential question which has grown up between political parties in the United States respecting our foreign trade is whether a duty should be laid upon any import for the direct object of protecting and encouraging the manufacture of the same article at home. The party opposed to this theory does not advocate the admission of the article free, but insists upon such rate of duty as will produce the largest revenue and at the same time afford what is termed 'incidental protection.' The advocates of actual free trade according to the policy of England — taxing only those articles which are not produced at home — are few in number, and are principally confined to *doctrinaires*. The instincts of the masses of both parties are against them. But the nominal free trader finds it very difficult to unite the largest revenue from any article with 'incidental protection' to the competing product at home. If the duty be so arranged as to produce the greatest amount of revenue, it must be placed at that point where the foreign article is able to undersell the domestic article and thus command the market to the exclusion of competition. This result goes beyond what the so-called American free trader intends in practice, but not beyond what he implies in theory.

"The American protectionist does not seek to evade the legitimate results of his theory. He starts with the proposition that whatever is manufactured at home gives work and wages to our own people, and that if the duty is even put so high as to prohibit the import of the foreign article, the competition of home producers will, according the doctrine of Mr. Hamilton, rapidly reduce the price to the consumer. He gives numerous illustrations of articles which, under the influence of home competition, have fallen in price below the point at which the foreign article was furnished when there was no protection. The free trader replies that the fall in price has been still greater in the foreign market, and the protectionist rejoins that the reduction was made to compete with the American product, and that the former price would probably have been maintained so long as the importer had the monopoly of our market. Thus our protective tariff reduced the price in both countries. This has notably been the result with respect to steel rails, the production of which in America has reached a magnitude surpassing that of England. Meanwhile rails have largely fallen in price to the consumer. The home manufacture has disbursed countless millions of money among American laborers, and has added largely to our industrial independence and to the wealth of the country. While many fabrics have fallen to as low a price in the United States as elsewhere, it is not to be denied that articles of clothing and household use, metals and machinery, are, on an average, higher than in Europe. The difference is due in large degree to the wages paid to labor, and thus the question of reducing the tariff carries with it the very serious problem of a reduction in the pay of the artisan and the operative. This involves so many grave considerations that no party is prepared to advocate it openly. Free traders do not, and apparently dare not, face the plain truth — which is that the lowest priced fabric means the lowest priced labor.

"On this point protectionists are more frank than their

opponents; they realize that it constitutes indeed the most impregnable defense of their school. Free traders have at times attempted to deny the truth of the statement: but every impartial investigation thus far has conclusively proved that labor is better paid, and the average condition of the laboring man more comfortable in the United States than in any European country.

"An adjustment of the protective duty to the point which represents the average difference between wages of labor in Europe and in America, will, in the judgment of protectionists, always prove impracticable. The difference cannot be regulated by a scale of averages, because it is constantly subject to arbitrary changes. If the duty be adjusted on that basis for any given date, a reduction of wages would at once be enforced abroad, and the American manufacturer would in consequence be driven to the desperate choice of surrendering the home market or reducing the pay of workmen. The theory of protection is not answered; nor can its realization be attained by any such device. Protection in the perfection of its design, as described by Mr. Hamilton, does not invite competition from abroad, but is based on the controlling principle that competition at home will always prevent monopoly on the part of the capitalist, assure good wages to the laborer, and defend the consumer against the evils of extortion.

"The assailants of protection apparently overlook the fact that excessive production is due, both in England and in America, to causes beyond the operation of duties either high or low. No cause is more potent than the prodigious capacity of machinery set in motion by the agency of steam. It is asserted by an intelligent economist that, if performed by hand, the work done by machinery in Great Britain would require 700-000,000 of men, — a far larger number of adults than inhabit the globe. It is not strange that, with this vast enginery, the power to produce has a constant tendency to outrun the power to consume. Protectionists find in this a conclusive argument against surrendering the domestic market of the United States to the control of the British capitalists, whose power of production has no apparent limit. When the harmonious adjustment of international trade shall ultimately be established by 'the parliament of man' in 'the federation of the world,' the power of production and the power of consumption will properly balance each other; but in traversing the long road and enduring the painful process by which that end shall be reached, the protectionist claims that his theory of revenue preserves the newer nations from being devoured by the older, and offers to human labor a shield against the exactions of capital."

The tariff question has been slowly returning to its old prominence in political discussion ever since the war closed in 1865. There have been several complete or partial revisions of the tariff since the war. We are not under the war tariff now. In 1882 a tariff commission appointed by President Arthur, in accordance with an act of Congress, made an exhaustive inquiry into the relation of the industries of the country to the tariff, and in 1883, following the report of the tariff commission, a general revision of the tariff was made by which the duties upon nearly all the imports were considerably reduced. The wisdom of this reduction was disputed by the strong protectionists in Congress, and the result has justified their opposition. Excessive importations have affected unfavorably certain industries and the revenue of the government has correspondingly increased. Mr. Blaine well knowing that the tariff would inevitably come before the country during the administration of the government from 1885 to 1889, when the nominee of the Republican party for President in 1884, both by his letter of acceptance and afterwards in public addresses, discussed the tariff question in the frankest manner, presenting honestly and clearly the doctrine of protection to American industry, in which he and his party believed. Grover Cleveland, on the other hand, in his letter of acceptance made no reference whatever to the tariff, and he implied by the words, "It should be remembered that the office of President is essentially executive in its nature," that he should have no personal policy on the subject.

Had he avowed in the campaign the opinions he has since declared, had it been understood by all that the leading feature of his administration would be the enforcement, by the influence and patronage of the presidential office, upon the Democratic party of the policy of a tariff for revenue only, with merely incidental protection, and that in a small degree — Mr. Cleveland would have been overwhelmingly defeated. From the beginning of the present administration efforts have been making with the approval and under the lead of the President to bring about a general reduction of the tariff. Unmindful of the rebuke administered by the people in the congressional elections of 1886, when the Democratic majority in the House of Representatives was so nearly wiped out, and Morrison and other free traders defeated, Mr. Cleveland in his message to

Congress in December, 1887, startled the Nation and attracted the attention of Europe by a vigorous attack upon the protective system. Ambitious for a reëlection to the presidency, Mr. Cleveland deliberately determined to force upon the Democratic party its ancient creed upon the tariff. It was, indeed, impossible to avoid meeting this issue. Mr. Blaine, in the campaign for Governor Beaver's election in Pennsylvania in 1886, pointed out that as it would be some years before the government would have the option of making further payments upon the public debt, there would soon be a dangerous accumulation of surplus money in the national treasury, that reduction of revenue would be absolutely necessary, and that we should be brought face to face with the sharpest tariff crisis in our history. Another general reduction of the tariff upon protected articles, if such reduction were only moderate, would doubtless have the effect of so stimulating importations as to still further increase the surplus. President Cleveland in his message thus speaks of the surplus and its dangers: "The public treasury, which should only exist as a conduit, conveying the people's tribute to its legitimate objects of expenditure, becomes a hoarding place for money needlessly withdrawn from trade and the people's use, thus crippling our national energies, suspending our country's development, preventing investment in productive enterprises, threatening financial disturbance, and inviting schemes of public plunder."

The President anticipated that by the 30th of June, 1888, the accumulation of surplus in the Treasury would reach $140,000,000. This surplus would not have been so alarmingly great had Mr. Cleveland and the Democratic party in

Congress been willing to consent that certain just and judicious expenditures should have been made — for pensions for needy soldiers of the Republic; for public buildings in many towns where they are needed; for coast fortifications, and for the education of the children in the Southern States. Condemning all proposals for the expenditure of the surplus the President proceeded to discuss the means by which the public revenues could be reduced.

The internal revenue taxes levied upon the comsumption of tobacco and spirituous and malt liquors, he considered to be not burdensome to the people. The President then proceeded to recommend that reduction in revenue be accomplished by reducing the duties levied upon imported articles, including especially those coming into direct competition with the products of our own labor. We quote from the message:

"But our present tariff laws — the vicious, inequitable, and illogical source of unnecessary taxation — ought to be at once revised and amended. These laws, as their primary and plain effect, raise the price to consumers of all articles imported and subject to duty, *by precisely the sum paid for such duties.*

"Thus the amount of the duty measures the tax paid by those who purchase for use these imported articles. Many of these things, however, are raised or manufactured in our own country, and the duties now levied upon foreign goods and products are called protection to these home manufactures, because they render it possible for those of our people who are manufacturers, to make these taxed articles, and sell them for a price equal to that demanded for the imported goods that have paid customs duty. So it happens that while comparatively a few use the imported articles, millions of our people, who never use and never saw any of these foreign products, purchase and use things of the same kind made in this country, and pay therefore nearly or quite the same enhanced price which the duty adds to the imported articles. Those who buy imports pay the duty charged thereon into the public Treasury, but the great majority of our citizens who buy domestic articles of the same class, pay a sum at least approximately equal to this duty to the home manufacturer."

The message contains many such paragraphs as that quoted, the intention evidently being to represent the protective system in an odious light, and convince the people that it is a burden. Mr. Cleveland indeed disclaims being a free trader, but his message is filled from beginning to end with the stock arguments of the free traders, the fallacy of which the common sense of the people easily detects. The gross blunder into which Mr. Cleveland falls when he says that the price of an article of domestic production is enhanced by precisely the same amount as the duty levied upon the same article when imported, exposes him to the ridicule of all intelligent persons.

Mr. Cleveland holds up before the protected industries the threat that if they do not now consent to a reduction of protective duties they will in the end fare worse. His language of warning is: "Opportunity for safe, careful, and deliberate reform is now offered, and none of us should be unmindful of a time when an aroused and irritated people, heedless of those who have resisted timely and reasonable relief, may insist upon a radical and sweeping rectification of their wrongs."

Mr. Cleveland especially recommended the "radical reduction of the duties imposed upon raw material used in manufactures, or its free importation." Especially he suggested the removal of the duty upon wool.

The only "aroused and irritated people" heard from since the message are the people of the wool manufacturing state of Rhode Island, and the people of the wool growing state of Oregon, condemning by Republican majorities the tariff proposals of the President.

The position of the Republicans on the raw material question is well stated in a speech by Congressman McKinley, of Ohio, in the House of Representatives, April 30, 1884:

"Free raw material has nothing to commend it to legislative favor which is not common to every other American product. The same necessity for protection, within reasonable limits, applies to what are commonly called raw materials as to the finished or more advanced manufactures. There is no such thing as raw materials distinguished from other products of labor. Labor enters into all productions, the commonest as well as the highest forms. The ore costs something to mine it; the coal, to take it from the ground; the stone, to quarry it; much labor enters into the production of wool; leather costs something to tan; and to the extent that labor enters into their preparation, what are usually termed raw materials should have ratable protection with the completed product. Pig-iron is the raw material for bar-iron, and yet no one has been heard to advocate free pig-iron. Cloth is the raw material for the tailor, the finest steel is the crude material of the watchmaker, and so on interminably. There can be no just line drawn, and no reason exists for such a discrimination. When the country is ready for free trade let us have it in all things without exception or restriction."

Considering that the wool growing states have much more political power in the Union than the wool manufacturing states, the proposal to abolish all protection on wool while retaining protection, although insufficient, on cloth, is a most extraordinary one. Free wool means free cloth, and either or both mean the prostration of the American people.

The claim of the Democratic party is that the agricultural sections of the country are oppressed by the tariff, and that the American farmer can rely upon a foreign market for his food products. This claim is answered by Mr. McKinley in the speech already quoted from:

"It has always seemed to me that it was infinitely better that the farmer should have a market at home, a market at his very door, than to be compelled to seek a market in distant countries and among distant populations. As long as there is a demand at home it is a self-evident proposition that it is better than to seek consumers abroad, and that the home demand is safer, more reliable, and more profitable than any foreign market can possibly be. American buyers are the best in the world." He did not tell the committee what is the fact, that *ninety* per cent. of the food products of the United States is consumed at home, and that only about ten per cent. has to find a market abroad.

It is not competition with Europe only which tariff reduction invites, but in the near future with India and China. A prominent American in a public speech in the year 1885 declared:

"India and China are learning more than the lessons of war from Europe. They are learning the uses of machinery; both have coal and iron; both can produce wool and cotton, and India grows wheat. China has just now contracted with an American firm to work its coal mines—rich, but undeveloped. India already has ten thousand miles of railway, with cotton factories and iron mills. India with 250,000,000 and China with 400,000,000 of population, with their workers often living on a shilling a day or less, and with their cheap labor, will become not only competitors of England but all other nations. It would be poor statesmanship if, by a blind adherence to a phantom policy, American labor should ever, for any reason, be brought into competition with that of India and China. Foreign markets may afford temporary relief for commercial depression and low wages, but they cannot settle the principle upon which wealth may be better distributed and wages kept above the cost of living. It will not do to depend upon any external agency. The disease is within; the fault grows out of the existing industrial system."

The Republican protectionists maintain these propositions:

1. Diversity in national industry is essential to the development of a high civilization.

2. Local centres, which manufactures widely spread build up, are essential to the prosperity and the happiness of the people.

3. The power of association is developed among men by diversity of industry and local centres, and this power is what gives to man command over the forces of nature.

4. Domestic manufactures cheapen prices. "Dear bought and far fetched," is an old and true maxim.

5. The home market is the best market. Under the present tariff we do not control entirely our home market, we ought to obtain control of that before thinking of the conquest of foreign markets.

6. The reduction of the tariff means a reduction of wages of American workmen greater than any possible increase in the purchasing power of their wages; and a fall in prices in this country resulting from tariff and wage reduction, means the ruin of the debtor class of the country.

7. The tariff should be revised by those who understand and believe in the protective system.

CHAPTER III.

THE MILLS BILL, AND THE SURPLUS AND WHISKEY TAX QUESTIONS.

ASCENDANCY OF THE FREE TRADE DEMOCRATS — THE MILLS BILL — ITS PASSAGE IN THE HOUSE OF REPRESENTATIVES — THE WOOL QUESTION — THREATENED PROSTRATION OF INDUSTRIES — UNWISE POLICY OF THE COTTON INTEREST — MINNESOTA AND THE TARIFF — THE MILLS BILL NOT A MEASURE FOR THE REDUCTION OF THE SURPLUS — SUGAR TARIFF — TRUSTS — THE REPUBLICAN PLAN FOR REDUCING THE SURPLUS — THE WHISKEY TAX.

FROM the day of Grover Cleveland's election, the influence in the Democratic party of Mr. Randall and other Democratic protectionists has been waning, and the ascendancy of Mr. Carlisle, Mr. Morrison, and other free traders has been growing. Speaker Carlisle organized the Ways and Means Committee of the first Congress in Mr. Cleveland's administration in the interest of free trade, and Mr. Morrison, the chairman, pushed to a vote a bill making a horizontal reduction of twenty per centum in most of the tariff schedules. The Congressional elections of 1886 showed some reaction against the Democratic party, and Mr. Morrison himself was defeated for reëlection on the tariff issue. But the Ways and Means Committee of the second Congress of this administration which met in December, 1887, was organized by Mr. Carlisle, reelected speaker, in the same interest, and Roger Q. Mills, of Texas, a radical free trader, was made chairman. The absolute control of the committee was given to the cotton planting interest. The committee proceeded in the preparation of a tariff bill in the most arbitrary and unprecedented manner. Mr. McKinley, in presenting the minority report of the committee to the House, says:

"If any consultations were held the minority was excluded. Thus originating, after three months of the session had gone, it was submitted to the committee. Since, there has been no consideration of it. Every effort upon the part of the minority to obtain from the majority the facts and information upon which they constructed the bill proved unavailing.

"The industries of the country, located in every section of the Union, representing vast interests closely related to the prosperity of the country, touching practically every home and fireside in the land, and which were to be affected by the bill, were denied a hearing."

The majority of the committee reported a bill reducing the duties upon nearly all classes of manufactures, and placing upon the free list wool, salt, lumber, and certain other products of the country, commonly called by Free Traders "raw materials." The greatest tariff debate in our history has been had in the House upon this bill. Some amendments were made by the Democrats increasing the duties fixed by the bill in cases where Democratic influences were brought to bear in favor of protected industries located in states whose vote in the presidential election was doubtful. Finally, on July 21, 1888, the Mills Tariff Bill passed the House by a majority of thirteen votes. Only two Representatives, elected as Republicans, voted for the bill — Mr. Fitch, of New York, who has already entered the Democratic party, and the Honorable Knute Nelson, of Minnesota.

Four Democrats only voted against the bill, but Samuel J. Randall would have voted against it had he not been prevented by illness from being present in the House. The corner-stone of the bill is free wool. The opponents of the protective system, despairing of successful direct attack upon the protective system as a whole, have undertaken to turn the flank of the tariff by assailing the protection long afforded to sheep husbandry. The wool growers, although numbering more than one million voters, are not as a class possessed of the wealth or influence of manufacturers, and are mainly located in Republican states. The design of the Democrats is to secure by the offer of free wool, the support of the manufacturing states of New York, New Jersey, Connecticut, Rhode Island, Massachusetts, and New Hampshire, and having thus planted the seeds of discord between the East and the West, to afterwards, with the aid of the West, accomplish the destruction of the protective system. Indeed, the free-listing of wool involves the abandonment of the principle of protection.

Since Mr. Cleveland and his party have chosen to wage the battle on wool, let us examine somewhat the subject of the wool tariff.

1. The present tariff divides wool into three classes: clothing wools, combing wools, and carpet wools. Upon clothing and combing wools a duty is levied; if the value at the place

whence exported to the United States shall be 30 cents or less per pound, of 10 cents per pound; if such value shall exceed 30 cents per pound, the duty is 12 cents per pound. Upon carpet wools is levied a duty of 2 1-2 or 5 cents per pound, according to the value. The duties on all classes of wool were considerably reduced in 1883, when the tariff was last revised, greatly to the dissatisfaction of the wool growers, who have ever since striven to secure a restoration of the former rates of duty. A large reduction in the number of sheep and the wool clip has resulted from the reduction in the wool tariff, showing how vain is the hope that with wool on the free list wool growing could survive in the United States. The present tariff imposes a specific duty upon woolen manufactures of from 10 to 35 cents per pound, and in addition thereto an ad valorem duty of either 35 or 40 per centum, varying with the kind and value of the goods. The duties upon woolen manufactures were slightly reduced by the revision of 1883. Increased importation of woolens has resulted. The importations of wool in 1882 were 63,016,769 pounds; in 1887, 114,404,174 pounds. The duty collected in 1882 was $3,854,653.18; that in 1887, $5,899,816.63.

2. The Mills Bill abolishes all specific duties (the only duties that cannot be evaded by under-valuations) on woolens and fixes a duty of forty per cent. ad valorem. This is on most classes and on the largest quantity an increase of five per cent. upon the present ad valorem duty, which is in most cases thirty-five per cent. When the specific and ad valorem duties upon wool and woolens were established by the tariff of 1867, after full consultation and agreement between the wool growers

and the manufacturers, and again when these duties were readjusted in 1883, it was upon the distinctly avowed plan that the specific duties on woolens were intended as compensatory merely to the manufacturer for the duty levied on foreign wools, and the specific rates were nicely adjusted to this end. while the ad valorem duty of thirty-five per cent. (in a few cases forty per cent.) was intended as favoring or strictly protective to the manufacturer. So that the Mills Bill by increasing the ad valorem duty from thirty-five to forty per cent., professes to give an additional favor to the manufacturer, the duties on wool and specific duties on cloth being abolished together. It is openly claimed by the organs of the free-wool manufacturers that the Mills Bill is in their favor.

3. It is claimed by the Democrats and by the free-wool New England manufacturers that the effect of free wool will be to cheapen woolens to the consumer, to maintain wages of workers in woolen mills while increasing their purchasing power, and that no harm will result to the American wool grower.

4. It is claimed by the tariff reducers that trusts or combinations of manufacturers are formed for the purpose of extorting from the people monopoly prices. and that these trusts are protected in their extortion because so largely given a monopoly of the home market by the tariff, that the only way to get fair prices is to admit foreign competition more freely. It is hard to see, if this claim be true, how prices are to be reduced to consumers of woolens, for the claim is that the protection of manufacturers of woolens has been fully preserved. and even increased by the Mills Bill. Whether the price of wool fell or

not, the manufacturers could still take advantage of the tariff of forty per cent. and plunder the consumers by combination. However, the wool growers are distinctly and loudly told by the Democrats and free-wool manufacturers that the price of wool will not fall, that the protective duties have already lowered the price of wool, and that by permitting the free importation of foreign wools of the finest grade needed to mix with American wools, manufacturing will be so stimulated as to create a better and more remunerative market for American wool. If this claim is true, the fact, in connection with the forty per cent. duty, will certainly prevent the cost of production of all woolens, except, possibly, a few classes of the finest and highest-priced goods worn by the rich, from being lessened.

So the Mills Bill, according to the theory of its friends, will not give to the wage-earners and the farmers the promised boon of cheaper clothing.

5. The real effect of free-listing wool upon the wool growers, will be to destroy as if by magic the business of wool growing in the United States. Under the present reduced tariff, the number of our sheep fell off from 50,620,626 in 1884, to 44,759,344 in 1887, with a corresponding reduction in the wool clip from 308,000,000 pounds in 1884, to 265,000,000 in 1887, a shrinkage of 43,000,000 pounds, while importations increased.

6. The first effect of free wool upon the price of wool will be to reduce it considerably in price but not to the level of present European prices, for increased importations into this country will somewhat raise the price of wool in European

markets. The increase of price of wool in Europe by slightly raising the cost of European manufacture will assist the American manufacturer in maintaining prices. There is good reason to believe that free wool manufacturers believe their profits will be increased.

The secondary effect of free wool upon the price of wool will be to place American manufacturers at the mercy of European combinations controlling the Australian and South American wool clip, and to increase the price in a very few years to a figure above that paid at present. As soon as the American Congress abandons the wool-growing interest, which should be cherished as the apple of our eye, European policy grasping for our market will be devoted to cornering against us the wool grown under the flags of our rivals, and compelling us to import our wool in the form of cloth, thus giving the profit of the fabric to Europe. The money that woolen manufacturers in the United States make, because of free wool, they must make quickly, for the foreign monopolist will avenge the wrongs of the American wool grower. We already produce the greater part of the clothing wool consumed by our people, and with adequate protection to wool and woolens can easily produce all that is now or ever can be consumed; and our American wools are as durable as any in the world and among the finest.

7. Free wool will soon be followed by a sharp reduction of the duty upon foreign woolens. The Western farmers sacrificed in the matter of their wool upon the altar of selfishness, and experiencing no reduction in the price of woolens, will swiftly unite with the deadly foes of American manufactures,

the Democratic cotton planters of the South, and strike a fatal blow at the woolen industry of New England and the East, and the striking of this blow would not be long delayed. Mr. Mills, in his report to the House, says of his bill:

"The bill herewith reported to the House is not offered as a perfect bill. Many articles are left subject to duty which might well be transferred to the free list. Many articles are left subject to rates of duty which might well be lessened."

The country has fair warning from our Bourbon masters that the Mills Bill is only the entering wedge of free trade. The object of the Southern tariff reducers in touching the tariff is to obtain for the South cheaper clothing and supplies. They do not expect the free listing of wool to reduce the price of cloth, but they do expect to strip the manufacturer of his political defenses, so that he can shortly be immolated on the altar of sacrifice he has helped to build.

8. The final result of free wool will be, unless a political revolution not so easily accomplished takes place, that wool growing and wool manufacturing will become lost arts in the United States.

9. If the Mills Bill contained no other changes than those in the wool and woolen duties, a few woolen manufacturers might, perhaps, rapidly amass fortunes, and their operatives might for a very few years maintain their present wages, although all attempts to increase wages or to shorten hours, would be defeated in advance; but the bill aims deadly blows at flax and hemp, earthenware, glass, plate-glass, metal, steel, steel rail, and other industries. Hundreds of now flour-

ishing industries would be undermined, and an atmosphere of gloom and despondency would spread over the land. Wages would be generally reduced, and in the "sorrowful degradation of labor would be planted the seeds of public danger." A general fall in prices is the end sought by the tariff reducers; if their end was realized, debts would not shrink with the price of property, and the mortgaged farms and homesteads of the Nation would be sold under the hammer of the sheriff to the money-holders of America and Europe.

And as the prostration of business would be general, the woolen industries would share in the general depression, and free-wool manufacturers would drink with the rest the waters of affliction.

10. To New England the consequences of her folly if she listens to the siren song of the tempter would be sad indeed. In the constellation of the Union these "once jubilant stars of the morning would be silent and dim." Our Bourbon masters of the South, skilled in the cunning of the politician, tireless in the pursuit of the ends they seek, are now seeking with fair sounding words and beguiling measures to separate the Eastern Republicans from the Western Republicans in sympathy and in interest. It will be an evil hour for labor in the North when it consents to accept either political economy, politics, or social or industrial ideas from the Bourbon Democrats of Texas, Arkansas, or Mississippi.

It will bear reiteration that the Nation is now witnessing a renewal of the old fight of the cotton planter in alliance with the foreign importing interest to impose by successive steps the policy of free trade upon the Republic. The logic of the situation is plain. Ninety per cent. and more of all the products of the agriculture of the United States finds a market at home; less than 10 per cent. is exported; but of our cotton crop almost two-thirds is exported, so that the cotton planter to-day, as of old, is tempted to say that in the markets of Europe his cotton is king. If Speaker Carlisle is to be believed, the cotton planter holds the home market, present or prospective, in small esteem. This is the whole secret of the movement for free trade in the United States. If it were not for the cotton interest, the advocacy of tariff reduction would be confined to a few theorists having small acquaintance with the real facts, and whose influence would count for nothing.

The true policy for the South is to develop her mines of iron and coal and other natural resources, to foster sheep raising, to build towns, educate her children, protect the colored race in their rights, and accept with enthusiasm the principles of Republicanism.

The Democratic party, on the tariff, as on questions of human rights, is the representative of Southern sectionalism and of a reactionary policy unfavorable to the moral and material well being of the continent.

11. The only real Republican vote in the House for the Mills Bill was that of Knute Nelson, of Minnesota. Mr. Nelson is a Norwegian by birth and a sterling representative of the Scandinavian settlers of the Northwest. The Scandinavians, conspicuous ever for their intelligence and loyalty to human freedom, constitute very largely the Republican party

of Minnesota. Faithful to established connections, loving liberty and education, they are Republicans by conviction.

Mr. Nelson himself, although differing somewhat from his party associates on the tariff, indignantly spurns the suggestion that he could go over to the Democratic party because of a difference of opinion on an economic issue. He believes that the farmers of his state are unfavorably affected by high duties.

He, and such as he, deserve high praise for recognizing that above all questions of tariff or finance are the supreme issues of liberty, education, and progress. It is natural that the idea should suggest itself to the mind of a citizen of Minnesota, because that State has been largely dependent upon the hard-wheat crop, which commands a ready sale in England, and is less susceptible to the competition of Indian or Russian wheat, because the best in the world. But fuller consideration of the question will incline Minnesota strongly to the side of the protective system.

The price of even Minnesota wheat would be lowered in European markets, did not the home market absorb so large a proportion of the crop. And the European market for American wheat will take less rather than more in the future. The true market for the Minnesota and Dakota of the future is at their very doors. Montana, not a wheat region, is destined to a mining and manufacturing future, and will call for wheat. In Mr. Nelson's own district the new-found wealth of iron ore, the best in the world for steel, will bring home to the people a realization of the benefits of a diversified industry. The increasing butter product of Minnesota has no market except in the United States. Southwestern Minnesota is the natural home of the sheep, whose hoof is shod with gold. Even in the production of sugar, Minnesota has a future. And, besides all this, her interests are in many ways so bound up in the prosperity of her fellow-countrymen that Minnesota will in the end be as soundly protective as Wisconsin, Kansas, or California.

12. As a measure for the reduction of the surplus the Mills Bill is a failure. The duties on braid, plaits, laces, and trimmings were reduced by the act of 1883 from thirty to twenty per cent. ad valorem, and the sum paid in duties in 1887 was $114,482.76 more than in 1883. The reduction on tin plate, under the act of 1883, was one-tenth of a cent per pound, while the duty collected in 1887 was $715,468.57 greater than in 1883. Bronze — in powder — was reduced by the law of 1883 from twenty to fifteen per cent., yet the sum received by the government for duty in 1887 was $14,000 more than was received from the same source in 1883. The duty on writing paper was reduced from thirty-five to twenty-five per cent. ad valorem. The receipts in 1883 under the higher duty were $19,406.87; under the reduced duty in 1887 the receipts were $242,216.27, showing an excess of duties of $222,000 in 1887 over 1883. And, as before shown, the same result has been attained in wool and woolens.

Mr. Cleveland warns the country that the continuance of the surplus will bring a commercial crisis. He is right, but his policy of tariff reduction will increase the surplus and precipitate the disaster.

13. The way to reduce the surplus is to abolish the internal tax on tobacco, and revise the tariff by imposing such

higher rates of duties upon imports coming into competition with articles produced in this country, in proper cases, as to check such imports and diminish the receipts at the custom house, while reducing duties upon articles, other than luxuries, not produced in the country.

Such is the Republican plan.

In dealing with sugar a difference of opinion has always existed among protectionists. Some Republicans favor removing in whole, or in part, the duty upon sugar, on the ground that only about one-tenth of the domestic demand is supplied by American producers. The abolition of the tobacco tax and a protectionist revision of the tariff upon other articles, will so reduce the revenues as to render it necessary to retain for revenue purposes, at least half the sugar duties.

The Mills bill, in accordance with the declared opinion of Mr. Mills that "upon correct principles of taxation there should be a higher duty upon sugar than upon any other article in the dutiable list," fixes a high, although somewhat reduced, duty upon sugar. There is nothing surer than the rapid increase of sugar production in the United States, and it ought to be fostered by protective duties.

If combinations of domestic producers oppress consumers. relief can easily be secured, either by authorizing the President in his discretion to temporarily free-list sugar, or by more direct legislative remedies. The same remark applies to all combinations or trusts. The advantages of combinations are within our reach, without our being compelled to suffer their evils.

The Surplus and Whiskey Tax Questions.

The Republican platform of 1888 has the following plank:

"The Republican party would effect all needed reduction of the national revenue by repealing the taxes upon tobacco, which are an annoyance and burden to agriculture, and the tax upon spirits used in the arts and for mechanical purposes, and by such revision of the tariff laws as will tend to check imports of such articles as are produced by our people, the production of which gives employment to our labor, and release from import duties those articles of foreign production (except luxuries) the like of which cannot be produced at home. If there shall still remain a larger revenue than is requisite for the wants of the government, we favor the entire repeal of internal taxes rather than the surrender of any part of our protective system, at the joint behests of the whiskey trusts and the agents of foreign manufacturers."

Taken in connection with the explicit declarations in favor of the protective system and against free wool, the declaration here quoted is the strongest and soundest protection platform ever adopted by a national convention of any political party. The firm adhesion of the Nation to the principles of the Chicago platform would give us a basis for a national prosperity grander than any yet attained.

The Republican party is practically united in support of the foregoing declaration, except that as to the concluding sentence, which implies the possible repeal of the whiskey tax, some apparent divergence of opinion exists; but this divergence is more apparent than real. The platform does not declare for the abolition of the whiskey tax; it only declares that if, after repealing the tobacco tax and revising the tariff in a judicious manner, a surplus income should remain, all internal taxation should be abolished rather than any part of the protective system be sacrificed. That is to say the Republican party prefers to tax imports from foreign countries rather than the productions or business of our own country. As an economic doctrine this is sound, and no intelligent protectionist will dissent from the proposition. At the same time it ought to be well understood that no necessity for considering the question of the repeal of the whiskey tax can arise during the next administration.

The repeal of the tobacco tax and the revision of the tariff in accordance with the principle of protection will effect a sufficient reduction in the revenues of the government. At a more distant day the question of whether the whiskey tax is to be permanently retained or abolished will come up for discussion. When it does, Congress may have to choose between the proposition of Mr. Blaine, that the tax on whiskey be retained as long as there is any whiskey to tax, and the proceeds of the tax be turned over to the state governments to assist in defraying their expenses, and the abolition of the tax altogether. The public mind is not at present fully prepared for the decision of this eventual question; nor is it necessary that it should be considered at all in deciding the paramount tariff issue now to be met. The Republican party in Congress has given no support to the repeal of the whiskey tax, and the general drift of sentiment among the leaders of the party has been all along averse to such repeal. There is a moral side to be considered in connection with the whiskey tax. The Prohibition party is, however, in no position to attack the Republican party as a free whiskey party, for the Prohibition platform upon which Clinton B. Fisk was nominated, declares "For the immediate abolition of the Internal Revenue System, whereby our National Government is deriving support from our greatest national vice."

If the party which founds itself upon the single idea of National prohibition demands the immediate abolition of the whiskey tax, and claims to be thereby promoting the true interests of temperance, judicious and candid temperance men will think twice before they too hastily condemn the Republican party because of the declaration on that subject made at Chicago. The framers of the Republican resolution evidently had in mind and gave some weight to the theory advanced by temperance men that a tax on the manufacture of liquors tends to protect and foster the liquor traffic, when they alluded to the desire of the "whiskey trusts" that the tax be maintained.

But the opinion of Mr. Blaine and most other sagacious men is that the abolition of the tax would lead to the increase of distillation and the increase of consumption.

The moral and financial questions connected with the whiskey tax will come up hereafter for deliberate examination. No issue is now presented on that subject, and voters will wisely direct their votes to the issue now to be decided between protection and free trade.

General Harrison expresses the practical truth about this matter when he says in his letter of acceptance that the question of the whiskey tax is too remote for present consideration.

CHESTER ALLAN ARTHUR,

THE FIFTH REPUBLICAN PRESIDENT OF THE UNITED STATES.

CHAPTER IV.

THE LABOR QUESTION.

LABOR QUESTION RELATED TO POLITICS — SPEECH OF S. B. ELKINS — THE REPUBLICAN PARTY THE LABOR PARTY OF THE COUNTRY — THE HOMESTEAD ACT — PROTECTION — FAIR ELECTIONS AND NATIONAL AID TO EDUCATION ESSENTIAL LABOR MEASURES.

ALTHOUGH it is generally felt that a labor party, so called, representing exclusively the interests of wage earners, has no field of usefulness in the United States, it is nevertheless recognized by all thoughtful persons that the labor question, or the relations of labor to capital has come to be a subject of deep concern with vast numbers of people. With the development of republican institutions the aspiration for approximate social equality has become a master passion dominating the age. It ought not to be an unregulated nor a wholly selfish passion, and in America it will not be. The labor movement is essentially a generous one and attracts the sympathy of all generous men, who, deploring the mistakes, follies. and excesses which may temporarily and in certain instances attend it, hope and confidently believe that its general course will be constructive rather than destructive. The social and labor questions are inevitably in the field of politics. The policy, the tendency of the Republican and Democratic parties have a direct relation to labor questions.

An address delivered by Hon. Stephen B. Elkins one of the

most prominent Republicans of the country, at Columbia. Missouri, June 3, 1885, on the labor question, contains many passages which ought to be reproduced in connection with a discussion of the great industrial issues which are pending in the election of 1888:

"The world was never so rich in accumulated wealth, comforts of civilization, culture, intelligence, and charity. The average condition of the people is better than in any former period. Civilization has reached a higher point and light is breaking all around the globe. . . . The material progress made during the nineteenth century, especially in the last fifty years, surpasses that of all other periods of history. In Europe and the United States wealth has increased since 1850 three times faster than population. Machinery has multiplied until its productive power in the United States and England alone is equal to the power of a thousand million men. Huxley says the 7,500,000 workers in England can produce as much in six months as would have required, one hundred years ago, the entire working force of the world one year to equal. In the United States wealth has increased from 1850 to 1884 forty-two thousand two hundred and forty millions of dollars. According to Mulhall, since 1830 Great Britain has almost trebled her wealth; France has quadrupled hers, and the United States has multiplied in wealth six fold, and at present we are growing nearly four millions richer at sunset than sunrise each day. *It is estimated that it requires less than one-half of the manual labor that was required in 1865 to produce an equal amount of subsistence.* During this period great progress has been made in political and intellectual development. The schools, colleges, asylums, hospitals, churches, and benevolent institutions found everywhere are the monuments of increasing charity and philanthropy. The nineteenth century will be set down in the world's history as the century of material progress. May we not believe that it will furnish the foundation for a moral progress not less wonderful in the twentieth century, in the shadow of whose portals we now stand, in which the moral forces will grow and be strengthened, and man will be made gentler, wiser and purer, so that in the stately procession of centuries the twentieth will take its place as the century of moral progress. The signs point in this direction and encourage this belief.

"In this great march of progress the United States takes the lead. In this rich world this nation stands the richest. The valuation of property in 1884 was $51,670,000,000 in round numbers; that of Great Britain, mother and rival, being more than six thousand millions less. Gladstone, in his article on 'Kin Beyond the Sea,' declared 'that the census of 1880 would exhibit the American Republic as certainly the wealthiest of all nations,' and he did not err. . . . While we recount with pride and pleasure the progress made by the nations of Europe, and particularly by the United States, we cannot forget that an undertone of discontent reaches us, which gives us pause. In the very nations where this advance has been so great, there is wide-spread depression in trade and commerce, and dissatisfaction among the people. While making all these splendid triumphs and material progress in works of charity and benevolence, conditions necessary to the highest social progress have been neglected. In Europe this discontent is due to two causes. One, the unfinished struggle on the part of the people for political freedom. . . . These nations have also to deal with another cause — the industrial question, involving the relations between labor and capital, employer and employed, the rate of wages, and the proper distribution of wealth, which is the recurring question of all civilization, the problem of all the ages. . . . The settlement of one of these problems has made this nation great and its people happy. . . . Having secured a government by the people and for the people, which has stood the test of foreign and civil war, shown its ability in dealing with the most complicated questions, and is about completing the first century of its existence, the nation now has to deal with the industrial problem. The great increase in population, large immigration from Europe — amounting in four years to over twenty-four hundred thousand people — overcrowding of cities, rapid absorption of public lands, consideration of wealth, importation of contract labor, and other causes, are reproducing in New England, and in many of the Middle and Western States, many of the economic and social conditions of Europe. In the midst of great wealth, with powers of production unsurpassed, with material success unparalleled, there is, nevertheless, depression in trade and commerce.

"In this land of plenty, there is, in places, the beginning of want; 350,000 workers are without employment, upon whose labor more than a million women and children depend for food, shelter, and clothing. How many are working on half-time, fighting hunger, and in this way supporting their own existence and the existence of those dependent upon them, cannot be estimated. Many who have employment are forced, by competition, to accept a rate of wages that yields a bare subsistence. . . . In the cities workers are forced into packed and crowded tenement houses, where foul air breeds disease and certain death. The tenement house population of New York City, amounting to 500,000, live in 20,000 houses. . . . These evils have grown with our growth. They are largely the outcome here, as in Europe, of the existing industrial system. It would be folly to condemn, as a whole, a system which, with all its faults, has merits, and has brought us thus far on our onward march. But in a century the United States will have a population of two hundred millions. It behooves us, therefore, to seriously consider whether we should take the risk of going on under a system that permits such evils as now exist, and encourages industrial war between employer and employed. . . . The question is both industrial and social, and concerns, not the capitalist nor the wage receiver exclusively, nor the one more than the other, but the whole body of society and the state itself. No question more serious or of graver moment ever came before the American people, and upon its right settlement may not only depend the future of society, but ultimately the fate of the great Republic. . . . In this great Republic; in its fresh morning life, before wrong, error, and injustice have had time to crystallize; with no inherited disposition to classes or caste; with all power in a people advancing in intelligence; with sixty centuries of recorded example and experience behind us; the underbrush of the tyrannies, errors, and prejudices of centuries cut away; the situation clearly in view, and the question pressing for solution, this would seem the time to begin and our country the place to solve the problem of ages. *To prevent industrial war, to regulate the forces of competition, to secure to labor a larger share of the products it helps to create, shorter hours for work, longer hours for leisure and improvement, and to lessen the cares and distresses of poverty, is an ambition worthy of American manhood.* If we shrink from the duty so plainly laid upon us, or fail in the great undertaking, hope will be well-nigh extinguished.

"Struggling humanity awaits the action of the great Republic, to see if, after giving man government on a Christian basis, it will give him industry on a Christian basis, and thus take the next great step in civilization. Sparse population in most of the states; the general diffusion of property, real and personal; the accumulation of savings; the restraint of passions; the slumber of pride and envy, and the comparative freedom from want, are all guarantees of peace and order for the present, and permit us to hope that danger is remote, and that no revolution threatens the form and substance of society and government. We can, therefore, calmly approach the consideration of the question, gather information, study causes, avoid the errors of other ages, and seriously consider in a spirit of fairness, relying upon no fancied advantage or security, what as individuals and as a nation we ought to do. Let us feel that we are on the threshold of a revolution, having for its end and aim the bettering of the condition of our fellow-man, to be wrought out through peaceable methods, with sublime thoughts 'that pierce the night like stars,' and noble ideas and deeds for weapons. . . . In the United States it is true that wages have advanced during the last twenty-five years. But the wants to be satisfied, in order to support life on the same relative plane as before, have also increased. And this is right; it would be a violence to human nature if it were not so. As the world grows in power of production, man ought to grow in taste and needs. His desire for a larger and higher state of existence does grow, and ought to grow as fast as the means of satisfying that desire. *Hence, at all times the true question is, not whether workers receive more than before, but whether they produce more and get a larger proportion of what is produced than before.* . . . . . .

"It is plain that some adjustment must be reached by which the war now raging between employer and employed in the industrial world must come to an end, and be superseded by a system that will unite the interests of the employer and those of the employed. . . . .

"Nature has made provision for all her sons. *The industrial system which does not permit the worthy to get enough is at fault.* One of the greatest statesmen and orators of our times has said '*wages are unjustly reduced when an industrious man is not able by his earnings to live in comfort, educate his children, and lay by a sufficient amount for the necessities of age.*' [Mr. Blaine.]"

Mr. Elkins proceeds to express his dissent from the "*laissez faire*" doctrine, to advocate national aid to education, restriction in the amount, and reform in the methods of local taxation "which falls heaviest on the worker, and often robs him of the ability to save from his earnings."

"Legal restraints are needed against the holding of lands

for speculative purposes, depending upon increased population and settlement to make them valuable." "All public lands suitable for agriculture should be reserved as homes for the people, and hereafter sold only to American citizens, or those who in good faith declare their intention of becoming actual settlers. Grants of land not earned should be forfeited to the government." "There should be a better supervision of state and inter-state commerce, wiser supervision of banks, trust companies, and life insurance companies, and adequate measures for the establishment of popular savings banks in all parts of the country. Protection of American industry and American labor should be more wisely fostered and more efficient. Pauper immigration and importation of contract labor should be more effectively prevented. Laws should be passed to restrict child labor, to provide for the health of those employed in factories.

"Over capitalization of corporations, watering of stocks, the people should take care to check by stringent legislation."

Mr. Elkins proceeds in the same address to advocate:

1. Arbitration and conciliation,
2. Coöperation, and
3. Profit sharing.

We have quoted thus at length from this eloquent and thoughtful address of Mr. Elkins because, first, of its intrinsic merits, and second, because it is the utterance of a representative Republican.

The Democratic politicians have artfully endeavored to create an impression that the Republican party has not been as friendly to the interests of the poorer citizens as the Democratic. A more monstrous perversion of the truth could not be made. The truth is that the Democratic party cannot point to a single achievement, during the last fifty years, of that party in the interest of labor. The Democratic party has ever been the party of mere negation, the party of obstruction, the do-nothing party. The Republican party has been the great labor party of the country. The homestead policy, the preservation of the Western territories as free soil, the restoration of the protective system, the abolition of slavery, the enfranchisement of the colored race, were all Republican measures, all great labor measures, and were all bitterly resisted by the Democrats. The Homestead Act was carried through Congress by the Republicans with little help from Democrats in the year 1860 when the presidential election was pending. The bill was vetoed by President Buchanan, the last Democratic President elected before Mr. Cleveland, on the ground that it was unconstitutional, unjust to the old states, and because it was a measure which "will go far to demoralize the people." The bill failed to pass the Senate over the veto of Buchanan, the Democrats voting eighteen against the bill and nine in favor. The Republican platform in 1860 contained a strong declaration in favor of free homesteads, and the poor man's homestead triumphed in Republican success. In 1862 a homestead bill, granting 160 acres to every actual settler on the public lands, twenty-one years or more of age, who is or has declared his intention to become a citizen, was enacted. The vote in the Senate on the bill was yeas 33, nays 7. Of the yeas, 30 were Republicans and 3 Democrats; of the nays, 6 were Democrats and 1 Republican. In the House the vote stood yeas 114, nays 18. Of the yeas, 92 were Republicans and 22 Democrats; of the nays, 15 were Democrats and 3 were Republicans.

Abraham Lincoln signed the Homestead Act.

The Republican party is now striving to bring about three things that are in the interest of labor in every part of the United States. One of these things is the maintenance and the perfection of the system of protection to American labor by the tariff on foreign imports.

This is indispensable to the progress of labor in this country. No intelligent protectionist claims that the higher wages in this country than in Europe or China are due *entirely* to the tariff protection, nor that protection is all that labor needs. But every intelligent man knows that without protection wages and the standard of living would fall; and that if into our own field of labor, of study, and of experiment in the solution of labor and social questions, the American mechanic and laborer permits to come the competition of the industries of foreign countries, over whose policy and whose customs we have no control and no influence save that which is indirect, the end of progress and hope for labor and social reform in America will have been reached.

Stripped of all disguise, Mr. Cleveland's reëlection will be a decision in favor of giving up the control of the markets of the United States to those who can come and take them. Such a verdict the intelligent workingmen of the United States will never render.

Labor has a great stake in the restoration of the colored race to political activity, in the restoration of that race to a large measure of political power. If that race, destined to be multiplied to many millions, shall sink down into insignificance and ignoble content with poor and lowly conditions, a ball and chain will be thereby hung about the limbs of labor in the North. No party demanding to be led in the path of popular progress, no party mindful of justice to the poor and to labor, is possible in such states as South Carolina and Mississippi except a party founded in large part upon the basis of the colored vote. If the negro fails to regain the ballot, his wages will remain very low, and his practical slavery will constantly depress the condition of labor in the North.

The position of the Republican party upon the subject of national aid to education gives the Republicans title to every labor vote in America.

CHAPTER V.

FREE AND FAIR ELECTIONS.

THE SUPPRESION OF SUFFRAGE IN THE SOUTH — GROVER CLEVELAND NOT FAIRLY ELECTED — MR. BAYARD'S PROPHECY — IMPARTIAL TESTIMONY AS TO DEMOCRATIC FRAUD — THE SILENT SOUTH — REPUBLICANS PLEDGED TO RESTORE THE BALLOT TO THE COLORED RACE — MR. BLAINE'S AUGUSTA SPEECH — A FREE BALLOT THE GROUND OF REPUBLICAN UNITY — THE SOUTH DAKOTA QUESTION.

THE Republican Platform adopted at Chicago, in June, 1888, contains this declaration:

"We reaffirm our unswerving devotion to the National Constitution, and to the indisoluble union of the states; to the autonomy reserved to the states under the Constitution; to the personal rights and liberties of citizens in all the states and territories in the Union, and especially to the supreme and sovereign right of every lawful citizen, rich or poor, native or foreign born, white or black, to cast one free ballot in public elections, and to have that ballot duly counted. We hold the free and honest popular ballot, and the just and equal representation of all the people to be the foundation of our republican government, and demand effective legislation to secure the integrity and purity of elections, which are the fountains of all public authority. We charge that the present administration and the Democratic majority in Congress, owe their existence to the suppression of the ballot by a criminal nullification of the Constitution and Laws of the United States."

Every intelligent man in the country knows, or may know, that Grover Cleveland would not now be the President of the United States, if a fair election could have been had in the States of South Carolina, Mississippi, Louisiana, Florida, Arkansas, and Alabama. These six states cast forty-seven electoral votes for President. In a fair election they are all Republican. Especially certain for the Republicans are South Carolina, Mississippi, Louisiana, and Florida. These last four states cast thirty electoral votes. Any three of these four states would have elected James G. Blaine. The leaders of the Democratic party have, ever since the war, been planning for the restoration of their power by the thrusting out of the negro as a factor in determining political results. In the Forty-second Congress, Senator Bayard attached his name to a minority report of a committee which had investigated Southern elections, in which these words occur:

"But whenever the Republican party shall go down, as go down it will at some time not long in the future, that will be the end of the political power of the negro among white men on this continent."

The resistance of the Southern Democrats to the constitutional rights of the colored race has been continued so long and so successfully, that a large part of the Northern people have become wearied with the subject, and are inclined either to doubt whether the Republican allegation that suffrage has been suppressed in Southern States is true, or to a belief that nothing can be done by political action to remedy the wrongs complained of.

It is not the part of honor or of wisdom for the people to grow careless as to whether the colored race is stripped of the rights which the Nation conferred.

The Republican party has resolutely refused to become blind or indifferent to this long continued stifling of the popular will by Democratic fraud and violence, and not only protests against the wrong, but expresses its purpose of correcting these evils as soon as it recovers power.

A vast amount of proof of Democratic crime in elections in the South has been accumulated and brought to the attention of the people through Congressional investigations, but we have thought it well to adduce here some evidence of a convincing and conclusive character. In 1879 there was published in New York a book entitled *White and Black; the Outcome of a Visit to the United States.* The author was Sir George Campbell, a Scottish member of the British Parliament, a gentleman of intelligence and character who had occupied a responsible post in the administration of the government of India. Mr. Campbell made an extensive tour throughout the South in the year 1878, and was an attentive observer of the condition of the colored race in the states he visited. He was present in South Carolina at the time of the Congressional election in 1878, when the famous tissue ballot frauds were perpetrated, and his testimony is of great value because it is that of an intelligent witness, entirely disinterested and impartial, who had full opportunity to learn the truth of the case. It will be remembered that the Republican party was first overthrown in South Carolina in 1876 through the agency of the rifle clubs organized by the Democractic party.

Actual violence carried to the extreme of murder having accomplished a political revolution in 1876, it was now resolved by the Democrats, in 1878, to complete this ascendancy by equally criminal but less brutal methods. Fraud took the place of force.

Mr. Campbell thus narrates what he witnessed in South Carolina in 1878:

"To return to the history of South Carolina. After the withdrawal of the United States troops the carpet-baggers were entirely routed and put to flight, and Wade Hampton assumed the undisputed government. He has certainly had much success. His party claims (I believe with justice) that he has done much to restore the finances, promote education, and protect blacks and whites in the exercise of peaceful callings. As regards political matters, his policy amounts, I think, to this — it is in effect said to the blacks: 'If you will accept the present *régime*, follow us, and vote Democratic, we will receive you, cherish you, and give you a reasonable share of representation, local office, etc.; but there shall be nothing for those who persist in voting Republican.' Some of them accept these terms, but to vote Democratic is the one thing which the great majority will not do. They may be on excellent terms with white men with whom they have relations, will follow them and be guided by them in everything else, but they have sufficient independence to hold out on that point of voting, even when they have lost their white leaders and are quite left to themselves. They know that they owe their freedom to the Republicans, and it is to them a sort of religion to vote Republican. In South Carolina that is the view of the great body of the blacks, as the Democrats fully admit. Stories are told of personal dependents of the present governor who owe everything to him, and would do anything else in the world for him, but who will yet openly vote against him. Such, then, was the state of things when the elections of November, 1878, came on. It seemed to be well known beforehand that the Democrats were determined to win everything in the South.

"It was said to be a necessity finally to emancipate *all* the states from the scandal of black and carpet-bag rule, and so far one could not but sympathize with the feeling; but so much had already been achieved, and there was not the least risk of a reaction. On the contrary, the power of the native whites was thoroughly reëstablished. In South Carolina Wade Hampton's reëlection was not opposed, and there was no question whatever that by moderate means the Democrats could retain a very decided majority in the state legislature. But they were not content with this; they aimed at an absolute possession of everything, leaving no representation to their opponents at all, and especially at a 'Solid South' in the United States Congress. 'They are determined to win,' I was told. 'They will get the votes by fair means if they can, and if not, I am sorry to say, they will steal 'em.' And that is just what was done in South Carolina. . . . There is a remarkable frankness and openness in speaking of the way in which things were managed, and I believe I violate no confidences, because there was no whispering or confidence about it. There was not a very great amount of violence or intimidation. Some

Republican meetings were violently interfered with before the election, and on the day of the election there was at some places a certain amount of galloping about, firing guns, and such-like demonstration by men in red shirts; but any intimidation used was rather moral than physical. In all districts where the parties in any degree approach equality, perhaps there would be no very strong grounds for disputing the victory of the Democrats. It is in the lower districts, where the Republicans are admittedly in an immense majority, that great Democratic majorities were obtained by the simple process of what is called 'stuffing the ballot-boxes.' For this purpose the Democrats used ballot-papers of the thinnest possible tissue paper, such that a number of them can be packed inside of one larger paper and shaken out as they are dropped into the box. These papers were freely handed about; they were shown to me, and I brought away specimens of them.

"I never heard a suggestion that these extraordinary little gossamer-web things were designed for any other purpose than fraud. Of course, the result of such a system was that there were many more ballot-papers in the box than voters. At one place in the Charleston district, where not above one thousand persons voted, there were found, I believe, three thousand five hundred papers in the box.

"In such a case, the practice (whether justified by law or not, I know not,) is that the election managers blindfold a man, who draws out and destroys the number of papers in excess of the voters. Of course, he takes care to draw out the thick papers of the opposite party, and to leave in the thin papers of his own party; and so when the process is completed the Democrats are found to be in a great majority, and the return is so made by the returning board. There are some other grounds of complaint. In some of the black districts the number of polling-places has been so reduced that it is impossible for all who wish to poll to do so in the time allowed. At one or two places the ballot-boxes were stolen and carried off. At one place of which I have personal knowledge, the appointed election managers simply kept out of the way, and had no poll at all. Hundreds of blacks who came to vote were told that they must go elsewhere, when it was too late to do so.

"In short, I have no hesitation in saying, as matter within my own knowledge, that, if these elections had taken place in England, there were irregularities which must have vitiated them before an election judge a hundred times over."

"The result of these elections was that, except in the single county of Beaufort, not one Republican or Independent was returned to the state legislature; nor, I believe, was a single office-bearer of those persuasions elected. The dominant party took everything, and the Republican members of Congress were all ejected. South Carolina returns a solid Democratic representation to the next Congress."

Having thus obtained full control of affairs by crimes of force and fraud, the South Carolina Democrats desired to perpetuate their power without the necessity of resorting at each recurring election to the same methods.

Accordingly, in 1882 the Democratic legislature enacted a new law regulating the registration of voters and the conduct of elections. The provisions of this law are ingeniously contrived to accomplish the disfranchisement of voters. One extraordinary requirement is that each voter shall present at the polls where he offers to vote, a certificate of registration, which he receives when he registers. As a result of the violence and fraud employed in the past to carry elections, and finally of the outrageous election legislation, the vote of the people in South Carolina has been almost entirely suppressed.

Very similar results have been effected by similar causes in other Southern States.

The following tables show to what extent the suppression of suffrage has proceeded in South Carolina, Mississippi, and Georgia. Comparison is made between the vote in years when suffrage was free and the Congressional election of 1886, under a Democratic President when the nullification of the constitution had been accomplished:

SOUTH CAROLINA.

VOTE IN CONG. DISTRICTS, 1886.				VOTE IN CONG. DISTRICTS, 1870.		
DIST.	REP.	DEM.	TOTAL VOTE.	REP.	DEM.	TOTAL VOTE.
1	No opp.	3,315	3,317	20,221	11,628	31,849
2	"	5,212	5,235	15,700	16,686	32,386
3	"	4,402	4,409	20,564	13,997	34,561
4	"	4,470	4,470	16,746	13,442	30,188
5	"	4,696	4,701	....	....	....
6	"	4,411	4,469	...	...	....
7	5,961	6,493	12,476	....	....	....

Total Vote, 1886, . . .	39,077	VOTERS, 1880.	
Total Vote, 1884, . . .	90,689	White, . . .	86,900
Total Vote, 1882, . . .	121,399	Colored, . . .	118,889

MISSISSIPPI.

	VOTE IN CONG. DISTRICTS, 1886.			VOTE IN CONG. DISTRICTS, 1872.		
DIST.	REP.	DEM.	TOTAL VOTE.	REP.	DEM.	TOTAL VOTE.
1	No. opp.	3 140	3,167	4,954	9,670	14,624
2	4,417	6,837	11,254	14,831	8,216	23 047
3	2,382	4,518	6,900	15,047	6,410	21,457
4	No. opp.	2,064	3,086	15,795	6,879	22,674
5	"	4 289	4,316	14,817	8,073	22,990
6	3,825	8,284	12,117	15,161	8,509	23,610
7	No. opp.	4,508	4,514	....	..	...

GEORGIA.

VOTERS, 1880.

White, ...	177,967
Colored, ...	143,471
Total, ...	321,438
Total vote in Congressional Districts, 1886,	27,520

Ten members of Congress were chosen by 27,520 votes, more than that number being usually required to choose a single congressman in the North.

It has been said that as the Republican party during its continuance in power failed to protect the colored voters of the South in the exercise of their rights, there is no reason to believe that a restoration of Republican rule would correct these evils, and it is further alleged that there is under our system of government no remedy for such wrongs. To these objections there is an easy answer. The Republicans lost control of the House of Representatives in 1874, and have but once since elected a majority of the house; and that once was in 1880, when General Garfield was elected President, whose unhappy death and the resulting political disturbances prevented the accomplishment of Republican policy, until in 1882 the Democrats again carried the House. The Democrats have been able to hold the Republicans in check on all questions, by means of the representation at Washington secured by the criminal methods of the Southern Democracy.

With the return of the Republicans to power in both Houses of Congress and in the Presidency, the restoration of fair elections in the South will not be found difficult. Members of Congress elected by fraud will then be unseated, and laws adequate to protect the purity of the ballot can then be passed and enforced. Little, however, of coercion will be needed. The moral effect of a popular condemnation of Democratic election crimes will be sufficient to break up the political solidity of the South, already beginning to dissolve.

A leading Ohio editor states the issue for 1888 in these words:

"The question whether we shall have a government of nullifiers, is that upon which we, the people of the United States who ordained and established the Constitution, shall enter judgment in the election of 1888."

When the result of the presidential election of 1884 was fully known, Mr. Blaine in his famous Augusta speech thus spoke of the suppression of suffrage in the South, which at last had given to the Democratic party the Presidency:

"This subject is of deep interest to the laboring men of the North. With the Southern Democracy triumphant in the states and in the Nation, the negro will be compelled to work for just such wages as the whites may decree; wages which will amount, as did the supplies of the slave, to a bare subsistence, equated in cash perhaps at thirty-five cents per day, if averaged over the entire South. The white laborer in the North will soon feel the destructive effect of this upon his own wages. The Republican party has clearly seen from the earliest days of reconstruction that wages in the South must be raised to a just recompense of the laborer, or wages in the North ruinously lowered, and it has steadily worked for the former result. The reverse influence will now be set in motion, and that condition of affairs reproduced which years ago Mr. Lincoln warned the free laboring men of the North will prove hostile to their independence, and will inevitably lead to a ruinous reduction of wages."

When Mr. Bayard, speaking the sentiment of the Democratic leaders, declares that the political power of the negro on this continent has come to an end, the Republican party takes issue; and standing upon the Constitution of the Republic, upon the law of the land, upon the immortal declaration that all men are created equal, upon the rights of human nature, it flings back to the Southern Democracy the disloyal sentiment, and declares that the political power of no American citizen, and of no class of American citizens shall come to an end in this free republic.

The Republicans welcome the issue. Strong as they are on the tariff, deserving as they are of the confidence of the business interests, stronger they are by far when they proclaim that the fraudulent rule of a usurping class shall come to an end, and that the fountain of political power shall flow pure and free.

Republicans not entirely in accord with the party policy o

the tariff will be united in favor of the restoration of Republican rule on the paramount issue of a free ballot.

THE EXCLUSION OF SOUTH DAKOTA.

Not only has the Democratic party seized control of the government by the fraudulent suppression of the suffrage of the colored race in the Southern States, but it has now for years refused to admit South Dakota to the Union, although the people have formed a state constitution and urgently demanded admission. A great wrong has been done to the people of South Dakota, and the disfranchisement of 400,000 people is a great wrong to the whole Union. No state admitted since the organization of the government has been so well prepared for admission as South Dakota. The Republicans of the Senate have twice passed a bill to admit the new state, but the Democratic House refuses to act on the measure. South Dakota is denied admission, because she will be a Republican State. Union veterans from older Western States constitute an important part of the population of the new state, while the foreign immigrants are chiefly Swedes, Norwegians, and Germans, whose political affiliation is with the Republicans. A Democratic Senator objected in debate in the Senate to the admission of South Dakota because there were so many foreigners in the State. General Harrison while in the Senate was the especial champion of the rights of South Dakota to statehood.

The triumph of the Republican party will be followed by the admission of South Dakota and other Northwestern States, thus strengthening in the Union the forces of education, of popular progress, and true national development.

CHAPTER VI.

PENSIONS.

DEPENDENT PENSION BILL OF 1887 — VETO OF PRESIDENT CLEVELAND — DEPENDENT PENSION BILL OF 1888 — MR. CLEVELAND AND THE DEMOCRATS UNWILLING TO DO JUSTICE TO THE SOLDIERS OF THE UNION — WASHINGTON AND CLEVELAND IN CONTRAST — VETOES OF SPECIAL PENSION BILLS.

A CLEARLY defined issue has arisen between President Cleveland, supported by the Democrats in Congress, on the one side, and the Republicans in Congress on the other.

January 27, 1887, a bill passed the Senate, in concurrence with the House of Representatives, entitled a "Bill for the relief of dependent parents and honorably discharged soldiers and sailors, who are now disabled and dependent upon their own labors for support."

This bill provided, first: "That in considering the pension claims of dependent parents, the fact and cause of death, and the fact that the soldier left no widow or minor children, having been shown as required by law, it shall be necessary only to show by competent and sufficient evidence that such parent, or parents, are without other present means of support than their own manual labor, or the contributions of others not legally bound for their support;" and second, "that all persons who served three months or more in the military or naval service of the United States in any war in which the United States has been engaged, and who have been honorably discharged therefrom, and who are now, or who may hereafter be suffering from mental or physical disability, not the result of their vicious habits or gross carelessness, which incapacitates them for the performance of labor in such a degree as to render them unable to earn a support, and who are dependent upon their daily labor for support, shall, upon making due proof of the fact according to such rules and regulations as the Secretary of the Interior may provide in pursuance of this act, be placed on the list of invalid pensioners of the United States, and be entitled to receive, for such total inability to procure their subsistence by daily labor, twelve dollars per month."

This bill was passed to meet the cases of parents who were not actually dependent upon their sons for support at the time the sons enlisted, but who have since been deprived of other means of support than their own labor. All such parents are now aged persons, and very many are in extreme poverty, who would be dependent upon their sons who gave their lives to the country, if such sons were now living.

The other and more numerous class of cases which this bill was passed to relieve, is that of soldiers and sailors who are without property and so disabled or infirm that they cannot earn their subsistence by labor, but who are unable to prove that their present disability is the result of injury received, or disease contracted in the service. The relief extended to this class of soldiers and sailors by the bill, proceeds upon the ground that the nature of the service was such that constitutions were impaired and premature disability caused in numerous cases where the same cannot be directly traced by evidence, as now required by law. It is also maintained by the Republicans in Congress that aside from the presumption that present disability is really due in many cases to the effects of the service, a further reward is due to the soldiers who saved the Nation, and that the Nation is bound in gratitude and honor to provide for all its defenders, when through advancing years and natural decay they become unable to support themselves. The passage of this bill was demanded by the general voice of the veterans of the War of the Rebellion. President Cleveland vetoed this bill on February 11, 1887.

The President argued in his veto message that the bill was substantially a service pension bill, and suggested that our soldiery, "in their pay and bounty, received such compensation for military service as has never been received by soldiers before, since mankind first went to war." He also advised Congress to "meditate somewhat" upon the probable cost, and expressed the opinion that it would prevent a reduction of the tariff which he claimed the people demanded.

The Committee on Invalid Pensions of the House of Representatives to whom was referred the President's veto message, unanimously recommended that the bill be passed, notwithstanding the objections of the President: and a large majority of the House voted to pass the bill over the veto, but as most of the Southern Democrats, including many who served in the rebel army, voted to sustain the veto, the bill failed to receive the required two-thirds vote.

The Republicans voted to pass the bill over the veto.

At the first session of the Fiftieth Congress, which opened on the first Monday in December, 1887, the Republican Senate passed another bill, granting pensions to ex-soldiers and sailors who are incapacitated for the performance of manual labor, and providing for pensions to dependent relatives of deceased soldiers and sailors. The bill was essentially like the one vetoed, except that the incapacity for manual labor was required to be "total." The rate of pension to a disabled soldier or sailor was $12 per month, as in the vetoed bill. This bill came down from the Senate to the House March 10, 1888, and on the 14th of April, 1888, was reported to the House by the Committee on Invalid Pensions with certain amendments, which the Democratic majority of the committee had agreed to. The principal of these amendments was one changing the rate of pensions from $12 per month to one cent per month for each day's service in the military or naval service of the United States. Another amendment gives every soldier and sailor who has attained the age of sixty-two years a pension at the rate aforesaid. This last pension has not been asked for by the Grand Army of the Republic, which has petitioned for the pensioning of those incapacitated for labor, and the Republican minority of the committee dissent from this mere service pension as compromising the interests of the disabled and suffering veterans. The Republican minority also dissent strongly from the proposal of the Democrats, to pay a less pension than $12 per month to any disabled soldier or sailor. Under the Democratic amendment a soldier who had served three months would get ninety cents a month; if six months, $1.80; if nine months, $2.70; if twelve months, $3.60; if twenty-four months, $7.20; if three years, $10.80.

Such a provision would be inadequate and contemptible,

but it is the offering of the Democrats of the House committee to the disabled soldiers of the Republic.

The Republican minority say in their report:

"It is variously estimated that there are in almshouses from ten to twenty thousand of the men who patriotically responded to the call of the government, and bravely fought for the preservation of the Union. Had it not been for these men and others like them, the Union would have been destroyed and the government overthrown. That a single one of these men should be the object of public charity, unless perchance the destitution which has overtaken him is the result of his own misconduct, is a reproach and shame to this great government, the treasury of which is groaning under a rapidly accumulating surplus."

Unless President Cleveland is defeated for reëlection, and the Republicans restored to power in Congress, there is small hope that justice will be done to the soldiers of the Union.

An instructive contrast is presented by the attitude of General Washington and that of Mr. Cleveland. A committee of our army in 1778 called upon Washington and made known their demands and sufferings. In his address to them he replied:

"It is not indeed consistent with reason or justice to expect that one set of men should make a sacrifice of property, domestic ease, and happiness, encounter the rigors of the field, the perils and vicissitudes of war, to obtain those blessings which every citizen will enjoy in common with them without some adequate compensation. It must also be a comfortless reflection to any man that after he may have contributed to securing the rights of his country, at the risk of life and the ruin of his fortune, there would be no provision made to prevent himself and family from sinking into indigence and wretchedness." —*Journal of Congress*, volume IV., page 211.

President Cleveland has also vetoed a very large number of special pension bills, passed by Congress for the relief of disabled soldiers or their needy dependents. These vetoes in nearly every instance have been based upon frivolous and heartless reasons, and have aroused throughout the country the intense indignation of all well-informed and right-minded persons. Attempt has been made to claim for the President special credit for courage and a disposition to protect the treasury against reckless pension legislation by Congress. The record will not sustain this theory. Wherever the merits of these pension bills and the cruel vetoes have been discussed, the sober judgment of the people condemns the course of the President.

It is a petty and unprecedented use of the veto power, to nullify the act of Congress in granting a pension to a needy soldier or his dependents. These pensions are never granted without careful consideration, by the committees of Congress, of sworn evidence in support of the claim, and the bill in each case originates with a representative of the people, who has the best opportunity for knowing what the real merits of the case are.

Mr. Cleveland's vetoes have been based upon a hasty and unadvised reading of the evidence, and the vetoes themselves exhibit a narrow and ungenerous spirit. Mr. Cleveland was not a soldier, nor were his sympathies with the great cause for which the soldiers fought.

CHAPTER VII.

CIVIL SERVICE REFORM.

THE PRESIDENT'S PROMISES.

A DELUSION AND A SHAM UNDER PRESIDENT CLEVELAND'S ADMINISTRATION — THE PRESIDENT'S PROMISES — THE PRESIDENT'S PERFORMANCE.

BOTH the Republican and Democratic platforms of 1884 recognized the growing demand among the people for civil service reform.

The Democratic declaration was:

"We favor honest civil service reform."

The Republican declaration was much more explicit, and was in these words:

"Reform of the civil service, auspiciously begun under Republican administration, should be completed by the further extension of the reform system, already established by law, to all the grades of the service to which it is applicable. The spirit and purpose of the reform should be observed in all executive appointments, and all laws at variance with the objects of existing reform legislation should be repealed to the end that the dangers to free institutions which lurk in the power of official patronage may be wisely and effectively avoided."

An especial effort was made by Mr. Cleveland, when a candidate for the Presidency, to secure the support of the ardent friends of civil service reform. His letter of acceptance contained these words :

"When we consider the patronage of this great office, the allurements of power, the temptation to retain public places once gained, and, more than all, the availability a party finds in an incumbent when a horde of office-holders with a zeal born of benefits received, and fostered by the hope of favors yet to come, stand ready to aid with money and trained political service, we recognize in the eligibility of the President for reëlection a most serious danger to that calm, deliberate, and intelligent political action which must characterize a government by the people.

. . . .

"The people pay the wages of the public employés, and they are entitled to the fair and honest work which the money thus paid should command. It is the duty of those intrusted with the management of these affairs to see that such public service is forthcoming. The selection and retention of subordinates in government employment should depend upon their ascertained fitness and the value of their work, and they should be neither expected nor allowed to do questionable party service. The interests of the people will be better protected; the estimate of public labor and duty will be immensely improved; public employment will be open to all who can demonstrate their fitness to enter it. The unseemly scramble for place under the government, with the consequent importunity which embitters official life, will cease, and the public departments will not be filled with those who conceive it to be their first duty to aid the party to which they owe their places, instead of rendering patient and honest return to the people."

Subsequent to the election, and before his inauguration, on December 25, 1884, Mr. Cleveland, in a letter to Mr. George William Curtis, used the following language to assure him of his good intentions respecting the civil service.

His letter was called forth by a letter of Mr. Curtis' inquiring as to the policy the President-elect intended to pursue in the matter of removals from office.

"I am not unmindful of the fact to which you refer, that many of our citizens fear that the recent party change in the national Executive may demonstrate that the abuses which have grown up in the civil service are ineradicable. I know that they are deeply rooted, and that the spoils system has been supposed to be intimately related to success in the maintenance of party organization. and I am not sure that all those who profess to be the friends of this reform will stand firmly among its advocates when they find it obstructing their way to patronage and place. But fully appreciating the trust committed to my charge, no such consideration shall cause a relaxation on my part of an earnest effort to enforce this law.

"If I were addressing none but party friends. I should deem it entirely proper to remind them that, though the coming administration is to be Democratic, a due regard for the people's interest does not permit faithful party work to be always rewarded by appointment to office; and to say to them that while Democrats may expect all proper consideration, selections for office, not embraced within the civil-service rules, will be based upon sufficient inquiry as to fitness, instituted by those charged with that duty, rather than upon persistent importunity or self-solicited recommendations on behalf of candidates for appointment."

In his inaugural address delivered March 4, 1885, the President makes the following declarations of his views as to reform:

"The people demand reform in the administration of the government and the application of business principles to public affairs. As a means to this end, civil-service reform should be in good faith indorsed. Our citizens have the right to protection from the incompetency of public employés who hold their places solely as the reward of partisan service, and from the corrupting influence of those who promise, and the vicious methods of those who expect, such rewards; and those who worthily seek employment have the right to insist that merit and competency shall be recognized instead of party subserviency or the surrender of honest political belief."

The President's first annual message to Congress, of December 8, 1885, further discussed the subject as follows:

"I am inclined to think that there is no sentiment more general in the minds of the people of our country than a conviction of the correctness of the principle upon which the law enforcing civil service reform is based.

"Experience in its administration will probably suggest amendment of the methods of its execution, but I venture to hope that we shall never again be remitted to the system which distributes public positions purely as rewards for partisan service. Doubts may well be entertained whether our government could survive the strain of a continuation of this system, which upon every change of administration inspires an immense army of claimants for office to lay siege to the patronage of the government, engrossing the time of public officers with their importunities, spreading abroad the contagion of their disappointment, and filling the air with the tumult of their discontent.

"The allurements of an immense number of offices and places exhibited to the voters of the land, and the promise of their bestowal in recognition of partisan activity, debauch the suffrage and rob political action of its thoughtful and deliberative character. The evil would increase with the multiplication of offices consequent upon our extension, and the mania for office-holding, growing from its indulgence, would pervade our population so generally that patriotic purpose, the support of principle, the desire for the public good, and solicitude for the nation's welfare would be nearly banished from the activity of our party contests and cause them to degenerate into ignoble, selfish, and disgraceful struggles for the possession of office and public place.

"Civil-service reform enforced by law came none too soon to check the progress of demoralization.

"One of its effects, not enough regarded, is the freedom it brings to the political action of those conservative and sober men who, in fear of the confusion and risk attending an arbitrary and sudden change in all the public offices with a change of party rule, cast their ballots against such a change."

The President's Performance.

Senator Hale, of Maine, in a speech delivered in the Senate, January 11, 1888, presented the following table, which he declared "was carefully made up to June 11, 1887, from figures furnished by the departments." It shows that at that time the President had nearly effected a "clean sweep" of the offices:

OFFICES.	Places filled by Cleveland.	Whole number of places.
Presidential postmasters, (estimated)	2,000	2 359
Fourth-class, (estimated)	40,000	52,609
Foreign ministers	32	33
Secretaries of Legation	16	21
Consuls	138	219
Collectors of customs	100	111
Surveyors of customs	33	33
Naval officers of customs	6	6
Appraisers, all grades	34	36
Superintendents of mints and assayers	11	13
Assistant treasurers at sub-treasuries	9	9
Collectors of internal revenue	84	85
Inspectors of steam vessels	8	11
District attorneys	65	70
Marshals	64	70
Territorial judges	22	30
Territorial governors	9	9
Pension agents	16	18
Surveyors-general	16	16
Local land officers	190	224
Indian inspectors and special agents	9	10
Indian agents	51	59
Special agents, General Land Office	79	83
Total	42,992	56,134

And ever since June, 1887, Mr. Cleveland has been steadily appointing Democrats to fill places in the civil service still held by Republicans, so that when nominated for reëlection at St. Louis, very few Republicans remained in office.

From Senator Hale's speech we extract the following passages, still further illustrating the infidelity of Mr. Cleveland to the pledges which he gave as candidate and as President:

"The difference between word and deed is clearly shown in the case of Secretary Lamar, who took occasion in April last to commend John C. Calhoun for his opposition to the spoils system, and to congratulate himself upon belonging to an Administration that was engaged in carrying out the policy that Calhoun advocated.

"The stern facts are that in the service over which Mr. Lamar has presided every territorial governor has been removed; sixteen out of eighteen pension agents; every single surveyor-general; four-fifths of the local land officers; nine-tenths of the inspectors and special agents of the Indian service; fifty-one out of fifty-nine Indian agents; seventy-nine out of eighty-three special agents of the General Land Office, and more than two-thirds of the special examiners of the Pension Office. But Secretary Lamar to-day stands on record as against the spoils system and takes high rank as a reformer.

"If I were not consuming too much time, Mr. President, I could select from the figures which are before me other departments of the government, not covered by the table which I have presented, showing this conquering march of the Democratic party in pursuit of the offices.

"In all the departments in Washington are found able and honest men, who have given their lives to the service of the government. They have begun as clerks in the lower grades and have been steadily promoted until they have at last reached the highest places to which they may reasonably aspire. They were found, when the reform Democratic administration came into power, as chief clerks and chiefs of divisions. They made the eyes and ears of the departments, and, one would suppose, should be considered as almost indispensable. In the Treasury Department there are seventy-nine chief clerks and chiefs of divisions, and up to June, 1887, sixty-six of these seventy-nine had been changed. In not more than a half a dozen cases the person appointed was a promoted clerk. The introduction into this force was almost entirely from the outside. Every deputy auditor, deputy comptroller, and deputy commissioner of internal revenue has been changed. In many cases chiefs of divisions have been reduced in grade, and new men, from the outside world, of the Democratic party, have been appointed. In more than one case the head of a division has been reduced to a lower clerkship and the Democratic politician has been appointed in his place, and the old incumbent, in his reduced grade and at his reduced pay, is performing all his old work, and the new incumbent does practically nothing. But this is civil service reform.

"Let us now, Mr. President, turn to the other side of this subject of reform in the civil service, that which relates to the offensive participation of office-holders in politics. That this should not be permitted in any well-regulated civil service goes without saying. The President saw this clearly, and his utterances in relation to it are as clear and distinct as they were upon appointments and removals.

"I have already quoted from his letter of acceptance, in which he deprecated the existence of 'a horde of office-holders, with a zeal born of benefit received, and fostered by the hope of favors yet to come, who stand ready to aid with money and trained political services' the party to which they belong. And we have seen further his declarations, after assuming his high office, of the things which he believed to constitute a true civil service reform, namely:

"The separation of the offices from politics, the non-participation of office-holders in elections and conventions.

"During the first year of the President's administration, and as the time approached for the campaign which preceded the State and Congressional elections in 1886, it was discovered that things were going on in the Democratic party very much after its old fashion. The men in office were 'manipulating conventions,' 'fixing nominations,' and taking upon themselves the conduct of the campaign generally. So apparent was this in Maryland, in Indiana, in Kentucky, in New York, in Pennsylvania, and in other contested states, that a voice of complaint was heard, not from the Democrats, who desired this condition of things, nor from the Republicans, who expected it, but from the 'Independents,' who had contributed to the President's election, and who now were fain to admit that matters were not going to suit them.

"The President was ready, as usual, with letters of assurances, and with proclamations tending to appease the discontent of his 'Independent' allies.

"The statute which I have recited in the resolution upon which I am speaking is definitive and explicit in its terms, and its passage by a Republican Congress, and approval by a Republican President, as I have said, was followed by a complete change in the organization of the party, all men holding Federal office disappearing from its committees and staff of political workers.

"On the fourteenth day of July, 1886, the President issued his famous order from the Executive Mansion in Washington, 'To the heads of the departments in the service of the general government.' As this whole proclamation has been read from the desk of the Secretary, I will not here take up the time of the Senate by repeating it. In it the President declares that his purpose is 'to warn all subordinates in the several departments and all office-holders under the general government, against the use of their official positions in attempts to control political movements in their localities.' In it he declares that 'office-holders are the agents of the people — not their masters.' In it he warns Federal officials against 'offending, by a display of obtrusive partisanship, their neighbors who have relations with them as public officials.' In it he declares that 'they have no right as office-holders to dictate the political action of their party associates.' In it he declares that the duty of the office-holder to his party is 'not increased to pernicious activity by office-holding.'

"These plain declarations of the President form a policy under which, if properly followed, the civil service of the country would indeed be divorced from politics. The Independents felt this and, taking new courage from the President's declarations, and forgetting how far the performance had fallen short of his promises in appointments and removals, still clung, in many cases, to the Democratic organization.

"The Civil Service Commissioners, or at least two of them, interpreted the statute in accordance with the President's instruction, and this added weight to the executive direction. But the leaders and the masses of the Democratic party felt by this time that they clearly understood the situation, and at this point begins to be clearly marked the change of tone among these leaders in their comments upon the President. They realized fully that in view of coming elections the party must ride two horses; that the President was to steadily maintain in all his public declarations the cause of civil-service reform, with the view of retaining the support of the Independents; but that, as in the case of appointments and removals, no real obstruction was to be placed in the way of any and every office-holder participating, whenever he chose, in caucuses and conventions and in the elections which followed.

"In the Indiana election, in November, 1886, the participation of Federal office-holders in the primaries, and subsequently in the election, raised a scandal of which papers in that State, at the time and afterwards, were full. In the closely-contested districts these men left their business and their homes, and devoted themselves to securing the nomination and election of the members to whom they had owed their appointments. In the Matson district, in the Holman district, and especially in the Fort Wayne district, the intrusion of Federal office-holders into every stage of the canvass previous to the nominating conventions and elections was so offensive that honest people revolted and defeated the Democratic candidate. Whoever will read the testimony offered in the Lowry-White contested-election case will find ample proof of this statement.

"When 1887 came round the President's declarations and proclamations were treated as waste-paper, and the President himself seems by this time to have fallen into such harmony with the spirit of his party that he not only acquiesced in this wholesale disregard of his previously expressed sentiments and directions, but himself joined in the movement. His most intimate friends, both in and out of office, took charge of the conduct of conventions and elections in the year which was considered as having so close a bearing in its results upon the great coming battle of 1888.

"At the Saratoga meeting of the Democratic state committee of New York, when the preliminaries of what then looked like the dawning contest between the national administration and the state administration were to be settled, Deputy Collector John A. Mason and Second Auditor William F. Creed, of the New York Custom-house, were most prominent and active.

"At the Pennsylvania State convention more than forty of the Federal officials of that State appeared to marshal the forces of the administration. The names of some of these have been furnished me as taken from a Democratic newspaper: E. J. Bigler, collector of internal revenue; D. O. Barr, surveyor of the port of Pittsburgh; McVey and Ryan, special treasury agents; Fletcher, chief clerk in a bureau of the Navy Department; Glozier, hull inspector; Guss, oleomargarine inspector; Chester, Warren, and Bancroft, from the

Philadelphia mint, and many others. In Baltimore the naval officer, the appointment clerk, Higgins, and Indian Inspector Thomas, Customs Agent Mahon, Postmaster Brown and his assistant, United States marshal and deputies, deputy collector of internal revenue, and a host of clerks, inspectors, and janitors monopolized the direction of the entire campaign.

"I might go on and give like instances in other states, but I leave that to be more fully brought out by the committee which I hope will take this matter in charge.

"Mr. Hawley. — May I make an inquiry?

"Mr. Hale. — Certainly.

"Mr. Hawley. — Is the Senator certain that these men have not been indignantly and virtuously removed?

"Mr. Hale. — Not only have I yet to learn of a removal for such action, but I have yet to learn of any censure being visited upon one of these men. I do not know of a case where the President has put his strong hand upon these men and made it seen that he meant to perform what he had promised. In fact, so gross was the violation of every principle of reform and of the President's directions and pledges that even the *Evening Post* declared that 'this playing fast and loose with orders and promises, which the President is now permitting among those around him, will be used in the campaign with terrible effect.' But the President has not hesitated to deal deadly blows at reform with his own hand. A remarkable manifestation of the desire of the people for a practical reform in the selection of important officers was shown in the city of New York previous to the last election. Public suspicion had for a long time rested upon officials in the municipal government, and had at last demanded and secured an investigation, which disclosed the most corrupt and shocking practices on the part of municipal officials, implicating them and well-known parties outside in extensive schemes involving corruption and bribery.

"Public indignation, expressed through almost the entire press of New York, was aroused, the intervention of the courts was sought, and from time to time trials of the accused had proceeded in some cases to conviction of the criminals. The work was by no means completed, and as the time for the election of a district attorney who should represent the State and the public in the conduct of these trials came near, a pronounced and general movement grew up in favor of the selection of Mr. Delancy Nicoll, an able and brilliant young Democratic lawyer, who had found thrown upon him, as an assistant in the district attorney's office, the burden of largely managing and conducting the hitherto successful prosecution of these cases.

"Nobody claimed that the movement for Mr. Nicoll had its origin in any party preference. It came from the people, and the demand was taken up by the newspapers. With few exceptions the Republican, Democratic, and Independent press demanded the nomination and election of Mr. Nicoll in the interest of reform and good government. He was nominated by different independent organizations, indorsed by all of the civil-service-reform associations and newspapers, and, although a Democrat, accepted generally by the Republicans.

"Here was a plain, spontaneous, earnest, honest movement on the part of the people in the direction of reform. It would seem to have been political wit on the part of the Democratic managers in New York City to have accepted this movement and to have joined in the election of a man who had always been a Democrat, but whose character and services were so high that good men demanded generally that he should be retained in the public service. But, as I have said, long before this the Democratic leaders had found that in the practical management of politics they were in the saddle, and the nominating conventions of the two branches of the New York Democracy joined in rejecting Mr. Nicoll and in setting up as his opponent an old-fashioned, worn, bruised, and battered New York City politician, whose personal character was not high, and who had been a crony of and a beneficiary at the hands of Tweed in the worst days of New York City's corruptions.

"The business men of New York, the Independents, the Reformers, and Republicans generally accepted the issue, and a contest almost unequaled in intensity and bitterness ensued. Here, Senators, was the opportunity for the President not only to say but to do something for reform. If, in accordance with his declarations in favor of non-interference of Federal office-holders in elections, he had, including himself as the head of all Federal official life, determined to keep aloof from the contest, he still might in many ways have breathed expressions giving aid and comfort to the men in New York City who were fighting against thieves and robbers and bribe-takers and bribe-givers in the interest of good government. All of the so-called reform element in New York City that had hitherto adhered to the President looked to him for some such expression. How bitterly were they disappointed! The President was now completely in the hands of the party-leaders in New York, whose stern rule had always been to support regular nominations, and to shoot down bolters and deserters.

"While the contest was at its thickest, and men everywhere throughout the country turned their eyes expectantly upon the result, and when the battle had become one of national importance, and when the issues were, seemingly, well nigh evenly balanced, a great Tammany Hall ratification meeting was held in the interest of Mr. Fellows, the Tammany Hall and county Democratic candidate for district attorney in opposition to Mr. Nicoll. I have before me a full report of the proceedings of this meeting and of the parties who participated therein. Their names have not been found upon the lists of any civil-service-reform association heretofore made known to the public. General John Cochrane called the meeting to order. Congressman S. S. Cox presided. State Senator Raines, of Monroe, was followed by the candidate, Colonel Fellows, and Honorable Charles A. Dana, editor of the *Sun*. Speeches were also made by George Blair and Congressman William McAdoo, of New Jersey. The following letter was read:

"It will be impossible for me to comply with your courteous invitation to meet with those who propose to ratify to-morrow evening the nomination of the united Democracy. With a hearty wish that every candidate on your excellent ticket may be triumphantly elected,

"I am yours very truly,

"GROVER CLEVELAND.

"Of this attitude of the President Mr. Carl Schurz said, only a few days later:

"'What malignant enemy of President Cleveland was it that induced Mr. Cooper to extort from him that most unfortunate letter, intermeddling in New York City politics on the side of the typical "dead-beat"'?

. . . .

"'I shall say nothing in extenuation of the fact that the President permitted himself to be so misused. But certain it is that the bitterest enemies of the President and of the Democratic party could not have dealt them a more vicious blow. For more than thirty years I have been an attentive observer of political events, and never, never have I witnessed more wanton recklessness of party leaders, sacrificing the interests and good name of a great municipality, the character of a national administration, as well as the interests of their party and cause, to their blundering folly or small selfishness.'

"Mr. Schurz, and Mr. Curtis, and Mr. Dorman B. Eaton, and the select body of Independents, who are ranked with them in sentiment upon this subject do not enjoy this. Not one of these men who possesses ordinary discernment can fail to see that the whole course of this administration on this subject has been a delusion and a sham. With them the searching question that each man must put to himself will now be, 'How long shall I be constrained to minister to and uphold this delusion, this sham?'

"The President himself, who, I am bound to believe, is not

a born hypocrite, does not enjoy this condition. His only satisfaction must be that he is getting more clearly in line with his party and its leaders and the sentiments of its masses, and that in the time to come he will be called on to make no more professions."

No administration in the history of the government has been more distinctly a "spoils" administration than that of Grover Cleveland.

The statesmen of the Republican party recognize the need of removing as far as possible the evils of patronage, and the Chicago Convention renewed Republican pledges of fidelity to the cause of reform in explicit terms.

CHAPTER VIII.

THE FISHERIES QUESTION.

THE HONOR OF THE REPUBLIC INVOLVED IN THE PROTECTION OF THE RIGHTS OF ITS CITIZENS — NATIONAL VALUE OF THE FISHING INTEREST — TREATY OF 1818 — CANADA COVETS OUR MARKET — CANADIAN OUTRAGES — TREATY OF 1854 — TREATY OF WASHINGTON — THE FISHERIES AWARD — MORE OUTRAGES — THE DISGRACEFUL SURRENDER OF CLEVELAND AND BAYARD TO ENGLAND.

THE Republican National Convention at Chicago declared in its platform:

"We arraign the present Democratic administration for its weak and unpatriotic treatment of the fisheries question, and its pusillanimous surrender of the essential privileges to which our fishing vessels are entitled in Canadian ports under the treaty of 1818, the reciprocal maritime legislation of 1830, and the comity of nations, and which Canadian fishing vessels receive in the ports of the United States. We condemn the policy of the present administration and the Democratic majority in Congress toward our fisheries as unfriendly and conspicuously unpatriotic, and as tending to destroy a valuable national industry and an indispensable resource of defence against a foreign enemy."

The fisheries question is perhaps but little understood, except by the hardy fishermen of New England whose interests are directly involved. But the honor of the Republic is involved when the rights of any of its citizens are in peril or in dispute; and the preservation of our fishing interests is vitally connected with the defense of the country in time ot war. Senator Frye, of Maine, declares:

"If we have another war, it will be on the ocean. Who will man our ships? Eighty-five per cent. of the sailors on ships in the foreign trade are foreigners, owing the Republic no allegiance, willing to render her no service. These fishermen are eighty per cent. American citizens, sixty-five per cent. American birth; inured to hardship, constantly exposed to the perils of the sea, brave, skillful, patriotic, they would respond to a man to the bugle-call of the country. Why should not the Republic stand by them when they are in peril, when they are suffering wrong at the hands of a foreign power?"

England spares no effort, counts no cost, when the liberty or the rights of her subjects are in danger, but her military and naval power is instantly put forth to its utmost to protect the humblest man who may rightfully claim the protection of her flag. If an American administration has been neglectful of the honor of our flag and the rights of our citizens, it is cause for the popular condemnation of that administration. What is the fisheries question? It concerns the right of fishermen of the United States to fish in the waters of the ocean, and near the shore of the northeastern part of the Dominion of Canada, and the right of American fishermen to resort for shelter, to repair damages, to purchase wood and take water, nd for other commercial privileges, to the bays, harbors, and ports of Canada. The New England colonies, under the flag of England, wrested from France the possession of the Canadian provinces, and our people before the Revolution had equal rights and equal enjoyment with Canadians in the fisheries along the shores of the maritime provinces; and after the Revolution we continued in the enjoyment of the fisheries in the Northeastern waters down to 1818. In 1818 a treaty was made between the United States and England, which somewhat restricted our fishery rights.

Article I. of the treaty of 1818 contained this provision:

> "And the United States hereby renounce forever any liberty heretofore enjoyed or claimed by the inhabitants thereof, to take, dry, or cure fish on or within three marine miles of any of the coasts, bays, creeks, or harbors of His Britannic Majesty's dominions in America, not included within the above mentioned limits."

And there was a proviso that our fishermen might enter these bays, etc., for shelter or to repair damages, to purchase wood and take water, but for no other purpose whatever.

It has ever been a source of regret in the United States that our government consented to any restriction of our right in these fisheries, which were acquired by the blood of our fathers. We should at least be disposed on every occasion to insist upon a liberal construction of the treaty of 1818, and especially should we resist any attempt by means of forced and unreasonable interpretations to deprive us of any of the rights preserved to us by the terms of the treaty.

As time wore on and the market of the United States became valuable, Canada desired above all things to enter our market, and in order to drive us to admit her into our market, she permitted her people to commit many outrages upon our fishermen. "She drove our vessels to sea in storms, when they had sought shelter, seized and searched them on the high seas, even; placed armed men on board, practically making captives of their captains and crews in their own vessels, the American flag flying over them; tried them in the colonial courts on the testimony of colonial witnesses, and confiscated one after another; and this went on until, indeed, the perils of the sea on these Grand Banks were no greater than the dangers of the law on the shore."

Presidents Van Buren and Pierce sent fleets to protect our fishermen, but as soon as our war vessels were withdrawn the outrages were resumed. Finally England sent a fleet, and extorted from a Democratic administration in 1854 a treaty known as the Reciprocity Treaty, under which we were permitted to fish within these Northeastern waters, Canadian fishermen in our waters, and free entry to our market for Canadian fish was granted. Canada had obtained all she wanted. At the end of twelve years the United States abrogated the treaty of 1854, the sentiment in this country being strongly against the treaty. Canada then imposed heavy taxes upon our vessels, for the privilege of fishing in her waters.

In 1871 the treaty of Washington was made between England and the United States. This treaty, made primarily for the purpose of settling the "*Alabama* Claims," included, also, the question of the fisheries. The Canadians were committing outrages again. The treaty provided for the free entry of fish into our market, and gave to us the privilege of the Canadian fisheries, and an arbitration was provided to determine whether any sum of money should be paid by the United States for the enjoyment of the fisheries during the term of twelve years fixed by the treaty, in addition to the consideration given in admitting Canadian fish to our market free of duty. England over-reached us in the selection of the umpire, and secured a prejudiced tribunal, and an award of $5,500,000 was made against the United States. The award was grossly unfair, the fact being that the duties remitted amounted to more than the value of the fisheries. We paid the award, but not without plain speaking in Congress.

James G. Blaine, then in the Senate, exposed on the floor of the Senate the chicane by which we had been beaten in the arbitration. As soon as the terms of the treaty permitted, the United States abrogated it, and on July 1, 1885, we again had no treaty for the fisheries, except that of 1818.

Republican statesmen maintain that the honorable and prudent course for us to have then adopted was to negotiate no more treaties, unless one to abrogate the treaty of 1818, but to stand upon our rights under the treaty of 1818, and to maintain those rights with all the power of the Republic, insisting at the same time that general commercial privileges, including the right to purchase supplies at any time and to tranship cargoes in Canadian ports should be granted to our fishermen: and that if such privileges were denied us, we should retaliate by denying similar privileges to Canadian vessels of all sorts in our ports, which privileges we have always held ourselves bound to grant by the comity of nations.

But President Cleveland, at the solicitation of the British Minister, sent a message to Congress recommending that it provide for a commission to settle the fishery rights. The Senate passed a resolution declaring that such a commission ought not to be provided for by Congress.

The suggestion of the President was an extraordinary one, in view of the fact that the treaty-making power is vested in the President and Senate alone.

The Canadians now recommenced their outrages upon our fishermen.

Senator Frye, in a speech before the Senate on the 29th of May, 1888, thus describes some of these outrages:

"Now, in this open session, addressing the people as well as the Senate, I feel it necessary to reproduce a few of the outrages committed by Canada on our fishermen. I am not certain that if Senators on this side of the Chamber listen to the recitals once more they will feel conscience-stricken and vote to reject the treaty. They would have done it then. Now, see what Canada was doing to us in 1886. In the month of July, as the American schooners *Shiloh* and *Julia Ellen* were entering the harbor of Liverpool, Nova Scotia, the Canadian cruiser *Terror*. Captain Quigley, fired a gun across her bows, to hasten their coming to, and placed an armed guard on board each vessel, which remained there until the vessels left the harbor; and that was when they were more than four miles from the shore, and under no pretense whatever of fishing. Seventy-five years ago, if that had not been apologized for, there would have been a declaration of war.

"More than four miles from shore an armed guard put on board, our captain and our sailors made prisoners of war on an American vessel with the American flag at the masthead.

"The schooner *Rattler*, of Boston, fully laden and on the voyage home, sought shelter from stress of weather in Shelburne Harbor, Nova Scotia, was compelled to report at the custom house and have a guard of armed men kept on board, there being no suspicion that she was intending to fish within the three-mile shore-line. Sixty million people, a great, magnificent Republic, and a little country of 5,000,000 people putting an armed guard on board under the American flag without any suspicion of any violation of the law!

"In August the *Mollie Adams*, of Gloucester, on the homeward voyage, full laden with fish from the fishing banks, was compelled to put into Port Mulgrave for water, and duly made report and entry at the custom house. The water tank had bursted on the voyage by reason of heavy weather. The captain asked leave to purchase two or three barrels to hold a supply of water for the crew on their homeward voyage of about three hundred miles. The application was refused and his vessel threatened with seizure if barrels were purchased. In consequence the vessel was compelled to put to sea with an insufficient supply of water, and in trying to make some other port to obtain a supply, encountered a severe gale, which swept away a deck-load of fish and destroyed two seine boats.

"Is any comment necessary? If that vessel under the same circumstances had penetrated any part of the waters of the Fiji Islands, would they have refused her a tank of water?

"Again, in July the schooner *A. R. Crittenden*, of Gloucester, on the homeward voyage from the open-sea fishing-ground, while passing through the Strait of Canso, stopped at Steep Creek for water. The customs officer at that place boarded the vessel and notified the captain that if he took in water his vessel would be seized. He was compelled to sail without obtaining the needed supply, and to put his crew on short allowance during the homeward voyage, notwithstanding the treaty of 1818 gave him a clear right to take water, and notwithstanding the dear Lord has given us all the right to take water — 'a cup of cold water.' Driven to sea because the poor fellow wanted water!

"In October the collector at Shelburne, Nova Scotia, refused to allow Captain Rose, of the steamer *Laura Sayward*, to buy sufficient food for himself and crew to take them home, and retained his papers unnecessarily, thus compelling him to put to sea with an inadequate supply of provisions. The crew was put on half rations. Why, you may go to one of the islands off the coast of China and say to those half-civilized people, 'I am out of food, give me something to appease my hunger,' and you would not expect to find men barbarous enough there, or anywhere else in the wide world, to refuse. Yet these men were compelled to put to sea on short allowance.

"In October Captain Tupper, of the schooner *Jennie Seaverns*, of Gloucester, was prevented by Captain Quigley, of the Canadian cutter *Terror*, from landing to visit his relatives in Liverpool, Nova Scotia. His relatives were forbidden to go on board his vessel by Captain Quigley, and an armed guard was placed on board to insure that he should not see his relatives, nor they him, making him practically a prisoner on his own vessel with the American flag floating at its masthead. No charge that he was fishing, no charge that he was violating the law.

"Now take the *Novelty*. She is a fishing steamer I should say of about two-hundred tons burden. She had been out to the Banks fishing. She came into Canadian waters, not to fish there. Her coal fell short; she went in to purchase; the officer refused to allow her to do so: the captain appealed to the terms of the treaty; the reply was, 'the treaty said "wood," not "coal."' And they would not let him have any coal. He appealed to the authorities in Ottawa, to whom a right of appeal is reserved in this wonderful treaty now under consideration, and the authorities at Ottawa replied that the treaty said 'wood,' and 'you cannot have coal.' They threatened seizure, and the captain went home, giving up his trip entirely. Wood, not coal! There was not a vessel sailed the sea in 1818 that did not use wood, and hardly a vessel sails to-day that does. Fishermen do not use wood: they all use coal; and yet because the treaty of 1818 said 'wood' they could not buy any other kind of fuel; and in this treaty which the President has sent here to the Senate, and heralded as generous and equitable, our commissioners have left 'wood' to stand, and to-day, notwithstanding everybody uses coal, no one can get any in the Dominion of Canada for his fishing vessel. They might have obtained that concession for fuel, one would have supposed.

"Take the case of the *Caroline Vought*. She was a fishing schooner from Boothbay, Maine. In August, being on mackerel grounds, short of water, she ran into the port of Paspebiac, New Brunswick. A government steamer or cruiser was there. Captain Reid, ordered on board, stated his necessities, was directed to leave at once on penalty of seizure. Fortunately a storm came on and he caught sufficient rain-water to save his crew from death. He carried the American flag.

"Now, take another case, and this is a very remarkable one, that of the *Mollie Adams*, commanded by Captain Solomon Jacobs. When off Mal Peque, Prince Edward's Island, in a heavy blow she fell in with the Canadian schooner *Neskelita* in distress. The *Mollie Adams* had her full load of fish. She stopped as humanity demanded; she rescued seventeen men from the British schooner, took them on board, placed what material on the schooner that she could save for them, what clothing they could, and sailed for a Canadian port. She was three days about this humane work, feeding seventeen men, British, besides her own. Captain Jacobs then ran into the harbor of Mal Peque. The captain of the Canadian cruiser *Critic*, which was lying there, boarded the *Adams*, and was informed of the facts of the wreck and the condition of the crew. He refused to lend any assistance whatever.

"Captain Jacobs asked permission to land some of the wrecked material he had on board, but was refused by the captain of the cruiser, who told him if he did so he would seize him. None of the people on the shore would take the wrecked crew. They were still on Captain Jacobs' hands. Captain Jacobs finally took from his own pocket sixty dollars and gave it to the crew to get home with.

"But there is a bar in Mal Peque where a vessel drawing over fourteen feet of water cannot pass. Captain Jacob's vessel drew fourteen feet, and he was compelled to lay there some eight or ten days, until a tide would come that should be sufficient to float his vessel over. The result was that when the opportunity came for Captain Jacobs to sail, he had not a pound of flour on his vessel. These British sailors had eaten it all up. He put into Port Medway, and asked permission of the collector to purchase half a barrel of flour, or enough provisions to take his vessel and crew home. This was absolutely refused, and the collector threatened to seize his vessel if he purchased anything whatever. Captain Jacobs left without obtaining anything, went home a distance of 300 miles, on short rations, and the last day he had not a single thing on his vessel for his crew to eat.

"In the nineteenth century, nineteen hundred years, almost, after our dear Lord was born, by a country that claims to be civilized and Christianized, this terrible act of inhumanity was committed, and committed for but a single purpose, to get our markets and free fish; and the Senator from Alabama may wish to give it to them under stress like that.

"One more case. I am not citing these cases because I think the Senators on the other side have never heard of them. I am citing them because I wish the American people to weigh your treaty with the threats and the outrageous acts which produced it. Take the *Marion Grimes*. In October the American vessel *Marion Grimes*, of Gloucester, Massachusetts, Captain Landry, put into Port Shelburne in a terrible gale, anchored in the outer port; anchored in the first place she had safety in, six or eight miles from the custom-house port, without the slightest intention of going into that. She laid there nearly the whole night. The storm abated. She hoisted her sails and started out for sea, when Captain Quigley of the cruiser *Terror*, fired a shot across her bows, brought her to, went on board, took possession of her, and told her that she must go to port, make entry, and report. He took her six miles out of her way, when she had not been within three miles of the shore, and Captain Quigley knew that she was in there to escape the storm, and for no other purpose whatever. He told them that if she did not go in and report and enter, she would be fined four hundred dollars. She was fined four hundred dollars as it was, and the money was deposited to pay the fine.

"Mr. Payne.—It was remitted afterwards by the court in Canada.

"Mr. Frye.—I doubt it. I do not know.

"Mr. Gray.—Yes, it was.

"Mr. Payne.—Most of them have been remitted.

"Mr. Frye.—No, sir; most of them have not been remitted.

"Mr. Payne.—I hope the Senator will be fair when he states these cases. He omits to state that the several acts were not committed by the direct authority of the Government of Canada, and that when they were brought before the Council of Canada, in every instance, they were either apologized for or remitted, so that the government was not responsible for any act of outrage, except under the general custom laws.

"Mr. Frye.—There is not a case that I have here that the Government of Canada is not responsible for, and there is only one that she has ever apologized for.

"Mr. Payne.—We shall see.

"Mr. Frye.—We shall see about it. I know the facts about as well as the Senator from Ohio. I am pretty familiar with them.

"The *Marion Grimes* was fined four hundred dollars. This fine was imposed by the urgency of Captain Quigley, of the *Terror*, and Captain Landry was informed that he would be detained at the port of Shelburne until a deposit to meet it was made.

"While the vessel was in the custody of Captain Quigley, Captain Landry hoisted the American flag, hoisted it on an American vessel,—on his own—as he had a right to do, and Captain Quigley ordered this American citizen to haul it down.

"Mr. Payne.—Please follow it up.

"Mr. Frye.—Do not interrupt me now. I decline to be interrupted.

Mr. Payne.—That is not fair.

Mr. Frye.—Captain Quigley ordered the American flag hauled down, and it was hauled down. Then, shortly afterwards, when Captain Landry was ready to sail, he hoisted the American flag once more on that American ship, as he had a right to do, and Captain Quigley came on board and with an oath took the halyards in his own hand, hauled down your flag, and you to-day, sir, are apologizing for him in the United States Senate.

Mr. Payne.—That is not true.

Mr. Frye.—The Senator wants me to say that an apology was made for that. A weak apology, readily accepted by a weak Administration, was made, but Captain Quigley kept his office as captain of the ship. He sailed afterwards through those waters and seized vessels as he met them bearing the American flag. Seventy-five years ago, if Captain Quigley had not been been immediately displaced by his government, there would have been a declaration of war. We made the the declaration of war in 1812 for no offense that was any greater than that. They seized our vessels, I admit; they searched them and took our sailors; but they seized this vessel without right of law, and they tore down with their own hands the emblem of the sovereignty of a republic of sixty million people."

Congress passed a law authorizing the President to retaliate by forbidding Canadian vessels to come into our ports, and if necessary, by terminating all commercial relations with Canada. Instead of employing the powers given him by Congress, or in any way protecting the rights of our fishermen, President Cleveland appointed plenipotentiaries to negotiate another treaty upon the fisheries. These representatives of the United States met the representatives of England and proceeded to agree to a treaty which completely surrenders the rights and interests of our fishermen.

Senator Frye denounced this treaty in the Senate as "the most disgraceful, humiliating, and cowardly surrender the American Republic has ever been called upon to submit to, not excepting the treaty of 1818." This treaty deals first with the question of defining the right of our fishermen to fish in the waters along the Canadian coast, under the treaty of 1818. The treaty of 1818 preserves to us the right to fish, but not "within three marine miles of any of the coasts, bays," etc.

The English have in the past advanced a theory that the three miles was to be measured from "headland to headland" of the bays. But England never strenuously insisted upon this theory, and the United States always refused to tolerate any such construction. But strangely enough, this treaty which Mr. Bayard entered into and Mr. Cleveland sent to the Senate provides that the three marine miles mentioned in article I. of the convention of October 20, 1818, shall be measured seaward from low-water mark; but at every bay, creek, or harbor, not otherwise specially provided for in this treaty, such three marine miles shall be measured seaward from a straight line drawn across the bay, creek, or harbor, in the part nearest the entrance at the first point where the width does not exceed ten marine miles.

The treaty further provides that if the market of the United States is thrown open to Canadian fish duty free, commercial privileges shall be granted to our fishermen in Canadian ports. The treaty simply enlarges the danger of our fishermen being subjected to seizure and confiscation unless all that is asked for by Canada, namely, the market of the United States, be conceded. England and Canada virtually dictated terms to the Cleveland administration.

After a long and acrimonious discussion, the Senate, in August of the present year, rejected the treaty. The Republicans voted unanimously against it, while the Democrats voted as solidly in its favor.

The whole tone of the Democratic debate and of the voice of the Democratic press was to the effect that the Nation ought not to permit itself to be embroiled for the sake of the interests of a few fishermen in New England.

But no sooner was the treaty rejected than President Cleveland gave evidence that he recognized the weakness of his position and the discredit which was likely to attach to his administration.

He immediately sent to Congress a special message in which he seemingly sought to "out-Herod Herod" in the vigor with which he denounced the Canadian outrages. Professing, however, to consider that he ought to have from Congress more definite instructions as to what particular measure of retaliation to adopt, he recommended that authority be given to retaliate by stopping the transport in bond over the railroads of the United States of merchandise in transit to Canada from Europe. This method of retaliation, while calculated to inflict injury upon Canada, is one sure, also, to severely damage our own railroad interests.

Congress had already pointed out the true method of retaliation, namely: the denial of commercial privileges to Canadian vessels in our ports. Such moderate application of the principles of retributive justice, together with the vigorous presentment of our claims for damages would probably be sufficient to secure from the British Government reparation for the past and security for the future.

The bellicose message of President Cleveland appears, even to many of the supporters of the President, as designed merely as a move on the chess board of politics; and is one of the most extraordinary acts of an administration destined to take rank as one of the least honorable or successful in the history of the government.

CHAPTER IX.

THE TEMPERANCE QUESTION.

ONE GREAT ISSUE AT A TIME — PROHIBITION NOT THE ISSUE — THE REPUBLICAN PARTY THE TRUE REFORM PARTY — THE DEMOCRATIC PARTY HOSTILE TO TEMPERANCE MEASURES — THE PROHIBITION PARTY A HINDRANCE TO REFORM.

WHEN the authority of the constitution shall have been vindicated, and the suppression of suffrage ended in the southern section of the Republic: when the industrial future of the Nation shall have been settled upon the sure foundation of the protective system in its complete development, the American people will enter upon an epoch when the public problems considered will be chiefly social in their character. Among the social questions already long pondered and made the subject of legislation, but still unsettled, is the question how most wisely to deal with the traffic in intoxicating liquors. This question is coming into larger prominence. The impetuous zeal of earnest men and women deeply interested in the temperance question has sought to thrust it forward as a political issue, prematurely, and so as to put in peril the dearest rights of man and the most important of material interests. Appeal ought to be made to the patriotism and the foresight of these citizens, whose public spirit and whose devotion to duty no one can question, to forbear hurrying forward this new political issue until the public mind, released from prior occupation, turns instinctively and naturally to the discussion and settlement of this leading social question. A great party, embodying the majority of the progressive forces of the Nation, and charged with the duty of leading in the advance movement, cannot permit itself to be diverted from great tasks first undertaken and not yet discharged — the army which comprises at once the forces of both conservatism and of reform should not divide to its death. A little later and nothing will remain for discussion in the forum of politics save social questions, and the temperance question will be well to the front A century crowded with material progress draws to its close. The twentieth century — promising to be one of moral grandeur hitherto unequaled — is soon to open. It may safely be predicted that before that century opens this long-vexed problem of how best to regulate and restrain the sale of intoxicating liquors will have been finally solved by the American people and solved in such manner that there will be a great decrease in the consumption of intoxicating liquors by our people, with a corresponding diminution of the evils and burdens of intemperance. The evils and burdens resulting from the general use and abuse of intoxicating liquors are in truth enormous. If the expenditure for alcoholic drinks in the United States amounts, as has been estimated, to more than nine hundred millions of dollars annually — a sum greater than that of the combined annual earnings of all the railroads in the country — the burdens directly and indirectly resulting must be very great. Now it cannot be too strongly emphasized that the too general and excessive use of intoxicating liquors can most effectually and satisfactorily be done away with through the moral elevation of the masses, to be chiefly accomplished by the regenerating and strengthening influences of religion and education. The church and school and home are now, as in the early days, the props of the Nation's power. Everything, too, that gives heart and hope and prosperity to labor will powerfully aid in stimulating the manlier virtues into life and strength. There has of late been too great a reliance upon law and too little upon educational and religious work. Saying this and emphasizing it, we ought not to understate the importance of a sound legal method for dealing with the common sale of intoxicating liquors. This is properly a political question, as well as a moral one. In our time most moral questions are political ones. The state should have a fixed policy on this subject, and that policy should strongly favor the interests of the home rather than those of the saloon. Public sentiment is deeply moved on this question. In the face of the adoption of constitutional prohibition in Maine by an enormous popular majority after trial of statutory prohibition for a generation; the adoption of the same policy in Kansas and in Iowa by popular majorities; the three-fifths vote in Rhode Island for the prohibitory amendment of the constitution, and the adoption of a prohibition constitution by the coming new State of South Dakota, it is impossible to deny the great strength of the movement for constitutional prohibition; and in the states of Michigan, Ohio, Oregon, and Tennessee, prohibition, although defeated, was supported at the polls by a minority so strong numerically, and embodying so large a proportion of the property and intelligence of those states, as to give signal proof of the coming power of the temperance sentiment of the Nation.

In Ohio, however, this sentiment has since the defeat of constitutional prohibition, found legislative expression in a system of taxation and regulation which seems to be the best presently attainable system for that state. Illinois, Nebraska, Missouri, Wisconsin, Minnesota, Pennsylvania, and New Jersey have passed high license laws which contain many restrictive provisions calculated to lessen the number of saloons and bring this dangerous business under control. The Republican party in all these states has adopted the policy of favoring the home against the saloon, and has sought to enact as strong temperance measures as there was reason to believe public sentiment would sustain. In doing so it has bravely run the risk of defeat at the hands of the liquor interest. It has not been behind public sentiment, but somewhat in advance, or, to speak more correctly, it has enacted temperance measures which public sentiment sustains, but which endanger Republican ascendency because Temperance Democrats continue voting with their party, while some Republicans are alienated. It is to temperance legislation rather than to free trade that Republican loss in Minnesota and Michigan is to be ascribed. In Ohio moderate temperance legislation for a season threw the Republicans out of power, but the tide turned soon in their favor and brought them back into control more firmly resolved than ever to persist in a temperance policy. The best hope for temperance legislation in the future is that Temperance Democrats will finally come to the Republicans and join them in maintaining such a policy as befits a Christian American commonwealth.

The Democratic party in every state in the North has constantly opposed every measure looking either to the submission of constitutional amendments or the enactment of temperance legislation. A national prohibition party is a worse than useless organization of forces that are needed where they would be most effectual. Whether a uniform policy in all the states to be imposed by national authority is essential to the success of the movement against the saloon, is a question which only a small portion of the people are ready even to consider. An amendment of the constitution is required before national prohibition can be enacted.

Such an amendment can only be submitted by the concurrence of two-thirds of each house of Congress, and can only be ratified by the consent of three-fourths of the states.

National prohibition or restraint of the liquor traffic, except through taxation, involves a more radical application of national ideas than any yet made in the legislation of the Republic.

Without entering, prematurely, upon a discussion of the wisdom of the policy of national prohibition, this is to be said: that advocates of that policy ought to see the necessity of aiding by their votes the restoration of the power and prestige of the great historic party which is the exponent of the national idea, to the final ascendency of which they must look for the fulfillment of their hopes. The National Prohibition party has succeeded already in putting the national government under the control of the extreme advocates of state rights, and unless better counsels prevail, may be destined to give perpetual control to the reactionary party which is hostile to all legislation in restraint of the liquor traffic. The particular amendment of the national constitution sought by the Prohibition party is not the measure most easy of attainment. A more practical proposition would be one that merely proposed extending the jurisdiction of Congress to the subject of the liquor traffic, thus placing that subject on the same footing as bankruptcy and the conduct of congressional elections. Under such an amended constitution Congress would be free to deal with this question when and in such manner as public opinion, finally crystallizing, might dictate. The demand now urged that the states put prohibition in the fundamental law of the Republic, is impractical in the last degree. In the course of the famous debate between Abraham Lincoln and Stephen A. Douglas in 1858, Mr. Douglas deprecated "uniformity in all things local and domestic, by the authority of the federal government," saying: "But when you attain that uniformity you will have converted these sovereign, independent states into one consolidated empire with the uniformity of despotism reigning triumphant throughout the length and breadth of the land."

Mr. Lincoln in reply said: "I do not believe in the right of Illinois to interfere with the cranberry laws of Indiana, the oyster laws of Virginia, or the liquor laws of Maine." So that the opinion of the sagacious Lincoln — Whig, Republican, and Nationalist as he was — at that time concurred with that of the greatest and most patriotic leader of the Democratic party since Andrew Jackson, that any attempt, by means of national authority, by one state to dictate the liquor laws of another is alien to the spirit of our government. Mr. Lincoln held views almost as conservative upon the question of slavery, but he lived to proclaim emancipation. Since 1858 the Republican party has advanced very far in its appreciation of the demands of our national life, and when the reactionary tide which has rolled in recedes, new applications of the national idea will be made. Whether the liquor traffic will be brought within the field of national politics, and whether, if it is, the public mind will advance to the radical plan of prohibition, the future will unfold. But the Prohibition Republicans, once as radical as any in their devotion to the equal suffrage of the colored race, should realize that until the authority of the Nation has proved itself equal to the duty of protecting the freedom of elections against open violence, it is unwise to urge the undertaking of the task of enforcing a prohibitory liquor law upon unwilling states.

In the course of his debate with Douglas, Mr. Lincoln enunciated and emphasized one idea which should take possession of the people on the temperance issue. Denying that he was an abolitionist, Mr. Lincoln said: "I think the opponents of slavery will resist the further spread of it and place it where the public mind shall rest with the belief that it is in course of ultimate extinction."

The extreme abolitionists of that day were not satisfied with the position of Mr. Lincoln or the Republican party on the slavery question, and with scorn and bitterness refused their coöperation to the Republican organization. But the good sense of practical men recognized in the Republican party an agency that was sure to place slavery in a position where it would be in course of ultimate extinction. The extreme abolitionists of 1856 and 1860 find their parallel to-day in the Prohibitionists.

The third-party Prohibitionists are to-day doing greater injury to the cause of temperance than to the liquor traffic.

They insist that the prohibition issue shall have immediate consideration to the exclusion of the tariff question. This demand is impracticable, and cannot be heeded. The tariff question comes before the people inevitably for settlement. If there had been no St. John vote in New York in 1884, Mr. Blaine would have been elected, the tariff revised in accordance with the protective principle, the interests of education in the South provided for, and by 1888 the temperance question would have been a leading issue in politics. A vote for the Prohibition ticket in 1888 is a vote to delay the real consideration of the temperance question.

Instead of the feeble Abolition party (which, by diverting Whig votes from Clay to Birney in 1844, gave the country to the Democrats,) waxing stronger until it finally ascended to power, the truth of history is that the Abolition organization died out and its unconstitutional and impracticable propositions were abandoned, while it was reserved for the Republican party rising up, not to abolish, but to restrict the spread of slavery, to give universal freedom to the Nation.

The Prohibition party of St. John and of Fisk is analagous to the Abolition party of Birney, while the Republican party is tending rapidly in the same path of practical reform on the liquor question that brought it into power on the slavery issue.

CHAPTER X.

THE REPUBLICAN PLATFORM FOR 1888.

THE Republicans of the United States, assembled by their delegates in National Convention, pause on the threshold of their proceedings to honor the memory of their first great leader, the immortal champion of liberty and the rights of the people — Abraham Lincoln; and to cover also with wreaths of imperishable remembrance and gratitude the heroic names of our late leaders who have more recently been called away from our councils — Grant, Garfield, Arthur, Logan, Conkling. May their memories be faithfully cherished!

We also recall with our greetings, and with prayer for his recovery, the name of one of our living heroes, whose memory will be treasured in the history both of Republicans and of the Republic — the name of that noble soldier and favorite child of victory, Philip H. Sheridan.

In the spirit of those great leaders, and of our own devotion to human liberty, and with that hostility to all forms of despotism and oppression which is the fundamental idea of the Republican Party, we send fraternal congratulation to our fellow-Americans of Brazil upon their great act of emancipation, which completes the abolition of slavery throughout the two American continents.

We earnestly hope that we may soon congratulate our fellow-citizens of Irish birth upon the peaceful recovery of Home Rule for Ireland.

We reaffirm our unswerving devotion to the National Constitution, and the indissoluble union of the States; to the autonomy reserved to the States under the Constitution; to the personal rights and liberties of citizens in all the states and territories in the Union, and especially to the supreme and sovereign right of every lawful citizen, rich or poor, native or foreign born, white or black, to cast one free ballot in public elections, and to have that ballot duly counted. We hold the free and honest popular ballot, and the just and equal representation of all the people, to be the foundation of our republican government, and demand effective legislation to secure the integrity and purity of elections, which are the fountains of public authority. We charge that the present Administration and the Democratic majority in Congress owe their existence to the suppression of the ballot by a criminal nullification of the Constitution and laws of the United States.

We are uncompromisingly in favor of the American system of protection; we protest against its destruction as proposed by the President and his party. They serve the interests of Europe; we will support the interests of America. We accept the issue, and confidently appeal to the people for their judgment. The protective system must be maintained. Its abandonment has always been followed by general disaster to all interests, except those of the usurer and the sheriff. We denounce the Mills Bill as destructive to the general business, the labor and the farming interests of the country, and we heartily indorse the consistent and patriotic action of the Republican representatives in Congress in opposing its passage.

We condemn the proposition of the Democratic party to place wool on the free list, and we insist that the duties thereon shall be adjusted and maintained so as to furnish full and adequate protection to that industry throughout the United States.

The Republican party would effect all needed reduction of the national revenue, by repealing the taxes upon tobacco, which are an annoyance and burden to agriculture, and the tax upon spirits used in the arts and for mechanical purposes; and by such revision of the tariff laws as will tend to check imports of such articles as are produced by our people, the production of which gives employment to our labor, and release from import duties those articles of foreign production (except luxuries), the like of which cannot be produced at home. If there shall still remain a larger revenue than is requisite for the wants of the government, we favor the entire repeal of internal taxes rather than the surrender of any part of our protective system at the joint behests of the whiskey trusts and the agents of foreign manufacturers.

We declare our hostility to the introduction into this country of foreign contract labor and of Chinese labor, alien to our civilization and Constitution, and we demand the rigid enforcement of the existing laws against it, and favor such immediate legislation as will exclude such labor from our shores.

We declare our opposition to all combinations of capital organized in trusts or otherwise to control arbitrarily the condition of trade among our citizens, and we recommend to Congress and the state legislatures in their respective jurisdictions, such legislation as will prevent the execution of all schemes to oppress the people by undue charges on their supplies, or by unjust rates for the transportation of their products to market. We approve the legislation by Congress to prevent alike unjust burdens and unfair discriminations between the states.

We reaffirm the policy of appropriating the public lands of the United States to be homesteads for American citizens and settlers — not aliens — which the Republican party established in 1862, against the persistent opposition of the Democrats in Congress, and which has brought our great western domain into such magnificent development. The restoration of unearned railroad land grants to the public domain for the use of settlers, which was begun under the administration of President Arthur, should be continued. We deny that the Democratic party has ever restored one acre to the people, but declare that by the joint action of Republicans and Democrats in Congress, about 50,000,000 of acres of unearned lands originally granted for the construction of railroads have been restored to the public domain, in pursuance of the conditions inserted by the Republican party in the original grants. We charge the Democratic administration with failure to execute the laws securing to settlers titles to their homesteads, and with using appropriations made for that purpose to harass innocent settlers with spies and prosecutions under the false pretense of exposing frauds and vindicating the law.

The government by Congress of the territories is based upon necessity, only to the end that they may become states in the Union; therefore, whenever the conditions of population, material resources, public intelligence and morality are such as to insure a stable local government therein, the people of such territories should be permitted as a right inherent in them to form for themselves constitutions and state governments and be admitted into the Union. Pending the preparation for statehood, all officers thereof should be selected from the *bona fide* residents and citizens of the territory wherein they are to serve. South Dakota should of right be immediately admitted as a state in the Union, under the constitution framed and adopted by her people, and we heartily indorse the act of the Republican Senate in twice passing bills for her admission. The refusal of the Democratic House of Representatives, for partisan purposes, to favorably consider these bills, is a willful violation of the sacred American principle of local self government, and merits the condemnation of all just men. The pending bills in the Senate to enable the people of Washington, North Dakota, and Montana Territories to form constitutions and establish state governments should be passed without unnecessary delay. The Republican party pledges itself to do all in its power to facilitate the admission of the Territories of New Mexico, Wyoming, Idaho, and Arizona to the enjoyment of self government as states, such of them as are now qualified, as soon as possible, and the others as soon as they may become so.

The political power of the Mormon Church in the territories, as exercised in the past, is a menace to free institutions, a danger no longer to be suffered. Therefore we pledge the Republican party to appropriate legislation asserting the sovereignty of the Nation in all territories where the same is questioned, and in furtherance of that end, to place upon the statute books legislation stringent enough to divorce the political from the ecclesiastical power, and thus stamp out the attendant wickedness of polygamy.

The Republican party is in favor of the use of both gold and silver as money, and condemns the policy of the Democratic administration in its efforts so demonetize silver.

We demand the reduction of letter postage to one cent per ounce.

In a republic like ours, where the citizen is the sovereign, and the official the servant; where no power is exercised except by the will of the people, it is important that the sovereign — the people — should possess intelligence. The free school is the promoter of that intelligence, which is to preserve us as a free nation; therefore the state or nation, or both combined, should support free institutions of learning, sufficient to afford every child growing in the land the opportunity of a good common-school education.

The first concern of all good government is the virtue and sobriety of the people, and the purity of the home. The Republican party cordially sympathizes with all wise and well-directed efforts for the promotion of temperance and morality.

We earnestly recommend that prompt action be taken by Congress on the enactment of such legislation as will best secure the rehabilitation of our American merchant marine, and we protest against the passage by Congress of a free-ship bill, as calculated to work injustice to labor by lessening the wages of those engaged in preparing materials, as well as those directly employed in our ship-yards. We demand appropriations for the early rebuilding of our navy; for the construction of coast fortifications and modern ordnance, and other approved modern means of defense for the protection of our defenseless harbors and cities: for the payment of just pensions to our soldiers; for necessary works of national importance in the improvement of harbors, and the channels of internal, coastwise, and foreign commerce; for the encouragement of the shipping interests of the Atlantic, Gulf, and Pacific States, as well as for the payment of the maturing public debt. This policy will give employment to our labor, activity to our various industries, increase the security of our country, promote trade, open new and direct markets for our produce, and cheapen the cost of transportation. We affirm this to be far better for our country than the Democratic policy of loaning the Government's money, without interest, to "pet banks."

The conduct of foreign affairs by the present Administration has been distinguished by its inefficiency and cowardice. Having withdrawn from the Senate all pending treaties effected by the Republican administrations for the removal of foreign burdens and restrictions upon our commerce, and for its extension into better markets, it has neither effected nor proposed any others in their stead. Professing adherence to the Monroe doctrine, it has seen, with idle complacency, the extension of foreign influence in Central America, and of foreign trade everywhere among our neighbors. It has refused to charter, sanction, or encourage any American organization for constructing the Nicaragua Canal, a work of vital importance to the maintenance of the Monroe doctrine, and of our national influence in Central and South America, and necessary for the development of trade with our Pacific territory, with South America, and with the islands and further coasts of the Pacific Ocean.

We arraign the present Democratic Administration for its weak and unpatriotic treatment of the fisheries question, and its pusillanimous surrender of the essential privileges to which our fishing-vessels are entitled in Canadian ports under the treaty of 1818, the reciprocal maritime legislation of 1830, and the comity of nations, and which Canadian fishing-vessels receive in the ports of the United States. We condemn the policy of the present Administration and the Democratic majority in Congress toward our fisheries as unfriendly and conspicuously unpatriotic, and as tending to destroy a valuable industry, and an indispensable source of defense against a foreign enemy.

The name of American applies alike to all citizens of the Republic, and imposes upon all alike the same obligation of obedience to the laws. At the same time that citizenship is and must be the panoply and safeguard of him who wears it, and protect him, whether high or low, rich or poor, in all his civil rights, it should and must afford him protection at home, and follow and protect him abroad, in whatever land he may be on a lawful errand.

The men who abandoned the Republican party in 1884 and continue to adhere to the Democratic party, have deserted not only the cause of honest government, of sound finance, of freedom or purity of the ballot, but especially have deserted the cause of reform in the civil service. We will not fail to keep our pledges because they have broken theirs, or because their candidate has broken his. We therefore repeat our declaration of 1884, to wit: "The reform of the civil service auspiciously begun under the Republican administration should be completed by the further extension of the reform system already established by law, to all the grades of the service to which it is applicable. The spirit and purpose of the reform should be observed in all executive appointments and all laws at variance with the object of existing reform legislation should be repealed, to the end that the dangers to free institutions which lurk in the power of official patronage may be wisely and effectively avoided."

The gratitude of the nation to the defenders of the Union cannot be measured by laws. The legislation of Congress should conform to the pledges made by a loyal people, and be so enlarged and extended as to provide against the possibility that any man who honorably wore the Federal uniform shall become an inmate of an almshouse or dependent upon private charity. In the presence of an overflowing treasury it would be a public scandal to do less for those whose valorous service preserved the government. We denounce the hostile spirit shown by President Cleveland in his numerous vetoes of measures for pension relief, and the action of the Democratic representatives in refusing even a consideration of general pension legislation.

In support of the principles herewith enunciated we invite the coöperation of patriotic men of all parties, and especially of all workingmen, whose prosperity is seriously threatened by the free trade policy of the present administration.

Chapter XI.

GENERAL HARRISON'S LETTER OF ACCEPTANCE.

INDIANAPOLIS, IND., September 11, 1888.

To the Hon. M. M. Estee and Others, Committee:

GENTLEMEN: When your committee visited me on the Fourth of July last and presented the official announcement of my nomination for the Presidency of the United States by the Republican Convention, I promised as soon as practicable to communicate to you a more formal acceptance of the nomination. Since that time the work of receiving and addressing almost daily large delegations of my fellow-citizens has not only occupied all of my time, but has in some measure rendered it unnecessary for me to use this letter as a medium of communicating to the public my views upon the questions involved in the campaign. I appreciate very highly the confidence and respect manifested by the convention, and accept the nomination with a feeling of gratitude and a full sense of the responsibilities which accompany it.

It is a matter of congratulation that the declarations of the Chicago Convention upon the questions that now attract the attention of our people are so clear and emphatic. There is further cause of congratulation in the fact that the convention utterances of the Democratic party, if in any degree uncertain or contradictory, can now be judged and interpreted by Executive acts and messages, and by definite propositions in legislation. This is especially true of what is popularly known as the tariff question. The issue cannot now be obscure. It is not a contest between schedules, but between wide apart principles. The foreign competitors of our market have, with quick instinct, seen how one issue of this contest may bring them advantage, and our own people are not so dull as to miss or neglect the grave interests that are involved in them. The assault upon our protective system is open and defiant. Protection is assailed as unconstitutional in law, or as vicious in principle, and those who hold such views sincerely cannot stop short of an absolute elimination from our tariff laws of the principle of protection.

The Mills Bill a Step Toward Free Trade.

The Mills Bill is only a step, but it is toward an object that the leaders of the Democratic thought and legislation have clearly in mind.

The important question is not so much the length of the step, as the direction of it. Judged by the Executive message of December last, by the Mills Bill, by the debates in Congress, and by the St. Louis platform, the Democratic party will, if supported by the country, place the tariff laws upon a purely revenue basis. This is practical free trade — free trade in the English sense. The legend upon the banner may not be "free trade"; it may be the more obscure motto "tariff reform," but neither the banner nor the inscription is conclusive, or, indeed, very important. The assault itself is the important fact.

Those who teach that the import duty upon foreign goods sold in our market is paid by the consumer, and that the price of the domestic competing article is enhanced to the amount of the duty on the imported article; that every million of dollars collected for customs duties represents many millions more which do not reach the Treasury, but are paid by our citizens as the increased cost of domestic productions resulting from the tariff laws — may not intend to discredit in the minds of others our system of levying duties on competing foreign products, but it is clearly already discredited in their own. We cannot doubt, without impugning their integrity, that if free to act upon their convictions they would so revise our laws as to lay the burden of the customs revenue upon articles that are not produced in this country, and to place upon the free list all competing foreign products.

I do not stop to refute this theory as to the effect of our tariff duties. Those who advance it are students of maxims and not of the markets. They may be safely allowed to call their project "tariff reform" if the peocle understand that in the end the argument compels free trade in all competing products. This end may not be reached abruptly, and its approach may be accompanied with some expressions of sympathy for our protected industries and our working people, but it will certainly come, if these early steps do not arouse the people to effective resistance.

The Republican party holds that a protective tariff is constitutional, wholesome and necessary. We do not offer a fixed schedule, but a principle. We will revise the schedule, modify rates, but always with an intelligent prevision as to the effect upon domestic production and the wages of our working people. We believe it to be one of the worthy objects of tariff legislation to preserve the American market for American producers, and to maintain the American scale of wages, by adequate discriminating duties upon foreign competing products. The effect of lower rates and larger importations upon the public revenue is contingent and doubtful, but not so the effect upon American production and American wages.

Less Work and Lower Wages Inevitable.

Less work and lower wages must be accepted as the inevitable result of the increased offering of foreign goods in our market. By way of recompense for this reduction in his wages, and the loss of the American market, it is suggested that the diminished wages of the workingman will have an undiminished purchasing power, and that he will be able to make up for the loss of the home market by an enlarged foreign market. Our workingmen have the settlement of the question in their own hands. They now obtain higher wages and live more comfortably than those of any other country. They will make choice between the substantial advantages they have in hand and the deceptive promises and forecasts of those theorizing reformers. They will decide for themselves and for the country whether the protective system shall be continued or destroyed.

The fact of a treasury surplus, the amount of which is variously stated, has directed public attention to a consideration of the methods by which the national income may best be reduced to the level of a wise and necessary expenditure. This condition has been seized upon by those who are hostile to protective custom duties as an advantageous base of attack upon our tariff laws. They have magnified and nursed the surplus, which they affect to deprecate, seemingly for the purpose of exaggerating the evil in order to reconcile the people to the extreme remedy they propose. A proper reduction of the revenue does not necessitate and should not suggest the abandonment or impairment of the protective system. The methods suggested by our convention will not need to be exhausted in order to effect the necessary reduction. We are not likely to be called upon, I think, to make a present choice between the surrender of our protective system and the entire repeal of the internal taxes. Such a contingency, in view of the present relation of expenditure to revenue, is remote. The inspection and regulation of the manufacture and sale of oleomargarine is important, and the revenue derived from it is not so great that the repeal of the law need enter into any plan of revenue reduction. The surplus now in the treasury should be used in the purchase of bonds. The law authorizes this use of it, and if not needed for current or deficiency appropriations, the people, and not the banks in which it has been deposited, should have the advantage of its use by stopping interest upon the public debt. At least, those who needlessly hoard it should not be allowed to use the fear of a monetary stringency, thus produced, to coerce public sentiment upon other questions.

The Importation of Contract Labor.

Closely connected with the subject of the tariff is that of the importation of foreign laborers under contracts of service to be performed here. The law now in force prohibiting such contracts received my cordial support in the Senate, and such amendments as may be found necessary effectively to deliver our workingmen and women from this most inequitable form of competition will have my sincere advocacy. Legislation prohibiting the importation of laborers under contracts to serve here will, however, afford very inadequate relief to our working people if the system of protective duties is broken down. If the products of American shops must compete in the American market, without favoring duties, with the products of cheap foreign labor, the effect will be different, if at all, only in degree, whether the cheap laborer is across the street or over the sea. Such competition will soon reduce wages here to the level of those abroad, and when that condition is reached we will not need any laws forbidding the importation of laborers under contract—they will have no inducement to come, and the employer no inducement to send for them.

In the earlier years of our history, public agencies to promote immigration were common. The pioneer wanted a neighbor with more friendly instincts than the Indian. Labor was scarce and fully employed. But the day of the immigration bureau has gone by. While our doors will continue to be open to proper immigration, we do not need to issue special invitations to the inhabitants of other countries to come to our shores or to share our citizenship. Indeed, the necessity of some inspection and limitation is obvious. We should resolutely refuse to permit foreign governments to send their paupers and criminals to our ports.

We are also clearly under a duty to defend our civilization by excluding alien races whose ultimate assimilation with our people is neither possible nor desirable. The family has been the nucleus of our best immigration, and the home the most potent assimilating force in our civilization. The objections to Chinese immigration are distinctive and conclusive, and are now so generally accepted as such that the question has passed entirely beyond the stage of argument. The laws relating to this subject would, if I should be charged with their enforcement, be faithfully executed. Such amendments or further legislation as may be necessary and proper to prevent evasion of the laws and to stop further Chinese immigration would also meet my approval. The expression of the convention upon this subject is in entire harmony with my views.

Plain Words about Election Frauds.

Our civil compact is a government by majorities; and the law loses its sanction and the magistrate our respect, when this compact is broken. The evil results of election frauds do not expend themselves upon the voters who are robbed of their rightful influence in public affairs. The individual, or community, or party, that practices or connives at election frauds has suffered irreparable injury, and will sooner or later realize that to exchange the American system of majority rule for minority control is not only unlawful and unpatriotic, but very unsafe for those who promote it. The disfranchisement of a single legal elector by fraud or intimidation, is a crime too grave to be regarded lightly. The right of every qualified elector to cast one free ballot and to have it honestly counted must not be questioned. Every constitutional power should be used to make this right secure, and punish frauds upon the ballot.

Our colored people do not ask special legislation in their interest, but only to be made secure in the common rights of American citizenship. They will, however, naturally mistrust the sincerity of those party leaders who appeal to their race for support only in those localities where the suffrage is free and election results doubtful, and compass their disfranchisement where their votes would be controlling and their choice cannot be coerced.

The Nation, not less than the states, is dependent for prosperity and security upon the intelligence and morality of the people. This common interest very early suggested national aid in the establishment and endowment of schools and colleges in the new states. There is, I believe, a present exigency that calls for still more liberal and direct appropriations in aid of common school education in the states.

The territorial form of government is a temporary expedient, not a permanent civil condition. It is adapted to the exigency that suggested it, but becomes inadequate, and even oppressive, when applied to fixed and populous communities. Several territories are well able to bear the burdens and discharge the duties of free commonwealths in the American Union. To exclude them is to deny the just rights of their people, and may well excite their indignant protest. No question of the political preference of the people of a territory should close against them the hospitable door which has opened to two-thirds of the existing states. But admission should be resolutely refused to any territory, a majority of whose people cherish institutions that are repugnant to our civilization or inconsistent with a republican form of government.

Against all Arbitrary Combinations.

The declaration of the convention against "all combinations of capital, organized in trusts or otherwise, to control arbitrarily the condition of trade among our citizens," is in harmony with the views entertained and publicly expressed by me long before the assembling of the convention. Ordinarily, capital shares the losses of idleness with labor, but under the operation of the trust, in some of its forms, the wage-worker alone suffers loss, while idle capital receives its dividends from a trust fund. Producers who refuse to join the combination are destroyed, and competition as an element of prices is eliminated. It cannot be doubted that the legislative authority should and will find a method of dealing fairly and effectively with these and other abuses connected with this subject.

It can hardly be necessary for me to say that I am heartily in sympathy with the declaration of the convention upon the subject of pensions to our soldiers and sailors. What they gave and what they suffered, I had some opportunity to observe, and in a small measure to experience. They gave ungrudgingly; it was not a trade, but an offering. The measure was heaped up, running over. What they achieved, only a distant generation can adequately tell. Without attempting to discuss particular propositions, I may add that measures in behalf of the surviving veterans of the war, and of the families of their dead comrades, should be conceived and executed in a spirit of justice and of the most grateful liberality, and that, in the competition for civil appointment, honorable military service should have appropriate recognition.

The law regulating appointments to the classified civil-service received my support in the Senate, in the belief that it opened the way to a much-needed reform. I still think so, and therefore, cordially approve the clear and forcible expression of the convention upon this subject. The law should have the aid of a friendly interpretation, and be faithfully and vigorously enforced. All appointments under it should be absolutely free from partisan considerations and influence. Some extensions of the classified list are practicable and desirable, and further legislation extending the reform to other branches of the service, to which it is applicable, would receive my approval. In appointments to every grade and department, fitness, and not party service, should be the essential and discriminating test, and fidelity and efficiency the only sure tenure of office. Only the interests of the public service should suggest removals from office. I know the practical difficulties attending the attempt to apply the spirit of the civil-service rules to all appointments and removals. It will, however, be my sincere purpose, if elected, to advance the reform.

I notice with pleasure that the convention did not omit to express its solicitude for the promotion of virtue and temperance among our people. The Republican party has always been friendly to every thing that tended to make the home life of our people free, pure, and prosperous, and will in the future be true to its history in this respect.

A Dignified and Firm Foreign Policy.

Our relations with foreign powers should be characterized by friendliness and respect. The right of our people and of our ships to hospitable treatment should be insisted upon with dignity and firmness. Our Nation is too great, both in material strength and in moral power, to indulge in bluster or to be suspected of timorousness. Vacillation and inconsistency are as incompatible with successful diplomacy as they are with the national dignity. We should especially cultivate and extend our diplomatic and commercial relations with the Central and South American States. Our fisheries should be fostered and protected. The hardships and risks that are the necessary incidents of the business should not be increased by an inhospitable exclusion from the near-lying ports. The resources of a firm, dignified, and consistent diplomacy are undoubtedly equal to the prompt and peaceful solution of the difficulties that now exist. Our neighbors will surely not expect in our port a commercial hospitality they deny to us in theirs.

I cannot extend this letter by a special reference to other subjects upon which the convention gave an expression. In respect to them, as well as to those I have noticed, I am in entire agreement with the declarations of the convention. The resolutions relating to the coinage, to the rebuilding of the navy, to coast defenses, and to public lands, express conclusions to all of which I gave my support in the Senate.

Inviting a calm and thoughtful consideration of these public questions, we submit them to the people. Their intelligent patriotism and the good Providence that made and has kept us a Nation, will lead them to wise and safe conclusions.

Very respectfully,

Your obedient servant,

BENJAMIN HARRISON.

The Popular Vote for President in 1884.

	Cleveland. (Dem.)	Blaine. (Rep.)	St. John. (Prohib.)	Butler. (Gr.)	Cleveland's Plurality.	Blaine's Plurality.	Electoral Vote. Cleveland	Electoral Vote. Blaine.
Alabama	92,973	59,144	610	762	33,829	......	10	....
Arkansas	72,927	50,895	......	1,847	22,032	......	7	....
California	89,288	102,416	2,920	2,017	......	13,128	....	8
Colorado	27,603	36,166	762	1,961	......	8,563	....	3
Connecticut	67,182	65,898	2,494	1,685	1,284	......	6	....
Delaware	16,976	13,053	64	10	3,923	......	3	....
Florida	31,769	28,031	72	......	3,738	......	4	....
‡Georgia	94,653	47,692	168	135	46,961	......	12	....
Illinois	312,584	337,411	12,005	10,849	......	24,827	....	22
Indiana	244,992	238,480	3,028	8,293	6,512	......	15	....
Iowa	*177,316	197,089	1,472	......	......	19,773	....	13
Kansas	90,132	154,406	4,954	16,341	......	64,274	....	9
Kentucky	152,961	118,122	3,139	1,693	34,839	......	13	....
Louisiana	62,546	46,347	338	120	16,199	......	8	....
Maine	51,656	71,716	2,143	3,994	......	20,060	....	6
Maryland	96,866	85,748	2,827	578	11,118	......	8	....
Massachusetts	122,352	146,724	9,925	24,382	......	24,372	....	14
Michigan	*189,361	192,669	18,403	753	......	3,308	....	13
Minnesota	70,065	111,685	4,684	3,583	......	41,620	....	7
Mississippi	76,510	43,509	......	......	33,001	......	9	....
Missouri	235,988	†202,929	2,153	......	33,059	......	16	....
Nebraska	*54,391	76,903	2,899	......	......	22,512	....	5
Nevada	5,578	7,193	......	26	......	1,615	....	3
New Hampshire	39,187	43,250	1,571	552	......	4,063	....	4
New Jersey	127,778	123,366	6,153	3,456	4,412	......	9	....
New York	563,048	562,001	25,001	17,002	1,047	......	36	....
North Carolina	142,952	125,068	454	......	17,884	......	11	....
Ohio	368,286	400,082	11,269	5,179	......	31,796	....	23
Oregon	24,604	26,860	492	726	......	2,256	....	3
Pennsylvania	392,785	473,804	15,737	17,002	......	81,019	....	30
Rhode Island	12,391	19,030	928	422	......	6,639	....	4
South Carolina	69,764	21,733	......	......	48,031	......	9	....
Tennessee	133,270	124,090	1,151	957	9,180	......	12	....
§Texas	223,679	91,701	3,508	3,321	131,978	......	13	....
Vermont	17,331	39,514	1,752	785	......	22,183	....	4
Virginia	145,497	139,356	138	......	6,141	......	12	....
West Virginia	67,317	†63,096	939	805	4,221	......	6	....
Wisconsin	146,459	161,157	7,656	4,598	......	14,698	....	11
Total	4,911,017	4,848,334	151,809	133,825	469,389	406,706	219	182
Cleveland's plurality	62,683							
Per cent	48.87	48.25	1.51	1.33				

The total popular vote for President in 1884 was 10,067,610; the total electoral vote was 401.

www.ingramcontent.com/pod-product-compliance
Lightning Source LLC
Chambersburg PA
CBHW052335110726
47901CB00005B/1234